THE
BONE FLOWER
GODDESS

BOOK THREE OF THE BONE FLOWER TRILOGY

THE
BONE FLOWER
GODDESS

BOOK THREE OF THE BONE FLOWER TRILOGY

TL MORGANFIELD

FSB

THE BONE FLOWER GODDESS
BOOK THREE OF THE BONE FLOWER TRILOGY

Published by Feathered Serpent Books
Thornton, Colorado

Printed in the USA

ISBN 978-0-9909207-5-5

For Dad and Jeri

The Basin of Mexico
10th Century CE

Tollan

Tultepec

Teotihuacan

Acolman

Lake
Meztliapan

Chapultepec

Culhuacan

Chimalhuacan

Xochimilco

Xico

Chalco

Xochicalco

PART ONE
THE YEAR THREE REED

CHAPTER ONE

I didn't see the giant hole in the ground until just before I fell into it. I tried to stop my sprint, but my worn sandals slipped in the damp grass and I went over head-first, arms flailing, tumbling like a rubber ball falling back to earth after having been kicked by the gods. My stomach dropped for only a breath before I hit the water.

Instinct made me gasp for air after the impact, but when water gushed into my lungs, those same instincts brought visceral panic. But after a few desperate gasps, my rationality set in: I didn't need to breathe. I wasn't human, so I couldn't drown or bleed to death anymore. I didn't even need to breathe at all. But thirty-five years of conditioning was hard even for a reborn goddess to overcome.

I swam to the edge of the pool and pulled myself out onto the sandy bank, my dress clinging to me. Shouts echoed above and I looked up to see a handful of warriors peering down from the lip of the cenote I'd fallen into. A big man wearing a leather and bone headdress pushed his way through the others and grimaced down at me. "Why do you run?" he called, indignant. "Have I not been kind to you?"

I tried to answer, but the water in my lungs rendered me silent. I coughed it up then called back, "It's for your own good." My voice sounded raw.

He scrunched his nose. "Ungrateful! I give you food, I give you a bed, I give you protection, and this is how you repay me?"

He *had* given me all of that, in exchange for sharing my body with him, but if he knew that was the true food he gave me, I doubted he'd be so eager to have me back.

Human men have no sense of self-preservation, my desire whispered in my head. *All they care about is the pleasure of the moment.*

I'd spent much of my adult life teaching myself to ignore that other voice, fearing her power and actions when I let her have her say; I still thought daily about that fateful night when I'd nearly killed Citlallotoc because I hadn't been strong enough to hold her back. She scared me, but there were precious few others to talk to anymore now that I tried to avoid humans while I searched for more of my own kind.

Yet sometimes circumstances drove me back to them. I limited my feeding habits to no more than twice with any single person, for any more than that had horrific consequences. But often the men were reluctant to let me go, which is why I'd snuck away from this one's camp in the middle of the night. It didn't surprise me that he'd tracked me down—he wasn't the first—but I'd hoped he wouldn't make me expend magic to escape. The more magic I used, the more I had to feed. It was a vicious circle I was incapable of escaping.

I scraped the wet hair back from my face. "This is the only time I'm going to tell you to go back home and forget about me."

The man scowled. "Bring the ropes!" he barked at the men next to him, but then he shouted down at me, "No one makes a fool of me, woman!" The men unrolled a maguey rope over the cenote's grassy lip and he grabbed onto it, preparing to rappel down after me.

I looked for a way out, but the walls angled over the jade-colored water. There was a tunnel though, directly across the water from me. I looked up to see the man shimmying down the rope, clenching his obsidian blade between his teeth. *It's now or use magic.* I dove back into the water.

I wasn't a strong swimmer—I'd had little reason to be, either as a priestess or the Queen of Tollan, since I rarely left the sanctuary of the city—but without the threat of drowning, I didn't worry. I stayed submerged; if the man wanted me, he would have to work for it.

But when something brushed against me, I stopped mid-stroke. The water was startlingly clear with sunbeams stabbing through from the surface, but I could make out little beyond the cloud of my own dark hair floating around me. Something crashed into the water to my left though, followed by a watery surge of sound pounding against my eardrums. *Is that screaming?* I turned and pushed my hair out of the way.

The man was in the water now, tangling with a monstrous beast. Red bubbles gushed as the creature flashed its claws back and forth. I froze, but when I saw the grasping hand on the end of the creature's tail, I made for the shore as fast as I could, my heart thudding. *He's found me again!* I expected the slimy grip of a clawed hand on my ankle at any moment.

I pulled myself ashore and pushed my tangled hair away from my eyes, desperate to know if the creature had followed me. I was alone on the bank, with the tunnel entrance still on the opposite side of the cavern; I'd gotten turned around in my panic.

And now the water lay eerily still. Above me, the men peered down in absolute silence, waiting for their leader to resurface.

Eventually he did, bobbing like a gassy corpse. All of his fingers were gone, chewed off at the knuckles and floating as flotsam in the ripples around him. He stared up into the sky with empty eye sockets as a cloud of red bled through the water from his body. Something large circled the grisly display, its sleek, furry back cresting the water like a serpent.

My heart still didn't slow. I'd take being pursued by humans over who was waiting for me in that water. I hadn't seen Black Otter—my former husband—since the night he'd forced me to kill him after he'd confessed to murdering my son in some disgusting plan to win me back. Drowning him had given me a moment's satisfaction, until I realized that it had been my own divine nature that had poisoned his mind.

Yet even then death couldn't stop his obsession; moments after I'd killed him, he'd risen from the dead as a monster under the thrall of the river goddess Jade Skirt. He'd sold away everything human in himself in hopes of possessing me again.

I glanced again at the tunnel. It seemed even further away now.

Black Otter ceased his circling and came towards me, swimming fast.

I gathered my magic in my hands, my whole body vibrating with anticipation and fear.

The water rose up and a huge otter-like creature leaped out, dagger-shaped fangs flashing, claws outspread. "Mine!"

I released, hitting him squarely in the chest with my magic, and he flew backwards into the water again, sending the waves washing up over my feet. The sandy mud sucked at my sandals as I made my way along the narrow bank, glancing over my shoulder as I went. Black Otter still thrashed around, disoriented by my octli magic.

But when I reached the tunnel, the muddy ground gave way under my left foot, sending me sliding down into the water. I scrambled and clawed my way back ashore and into the opening of the tunnel just as Black Otter popped up right where I'd fallen in. I scurried deeper into the dark, expecting him to lunge after me.

But he remained submerged to his waist, gripping the muddy bank with his clawed fingers. He bared his teeth, droplets of water dangling from his whiskers, his ink-black eyes vacant. "Mine!"

"Leave me alone!"

He bristled and growled. "Mine!" But when I didn't respond, he set into a keening cry that sounded terrifyingly like a baby calling for its mother.

My son had never cried as an infant—no doubt a side effect of being divine like me—but still the taunting sound set my heart racing with fury. I ripped off a muddy sandal and pelted him in the nose with it.

He scratched at his face, startled, but then he roared and lunged out of the water at me. I shuffled backwards on all fours.

Yet he stopped short. The hand on his long, sleek tail gripped onto the bank; my only saving grace, that he couldn't completely separate himself from water. "Mine!"

I threw my other sandal at him, setting him into a pawing frenzy, but then I pressed further into the tunnel, leaving him shrieking and crying.

Eventually the light faded, giving way to complete darkness. My skin gave off a soft orange glow; not real light, just my divine essence, and when I tripped over a rock, I crawled instead, to make sure I didn't walk off a cliff. I couldn't even see the ground under my glowing hands. I followed the trickle of water in the distance, hoping that would lead to another cenote. It might mean facing off against Black Otter again, but what else could I do?

A dim glow grew in the distance and I picked up the pace, eager to be free of the darkness. The light grew brighter, but not as much as I would expect for a cenote. And it had a strange blue hue more akin to moonlight. Surely I hadn't been underground so long that night had fallen?

The tunnel opened onto a cavernous room lit by blue-flame torches mounted along the shimmering walls. A trail of black water wound among the stalagmites, leading to a cliff. I eyed the water as I walked by, keeping at a distance.

I wondered why I didn't hear the sounds of a waterfall, but my arrival at the edge answered that. The water became a fat rope that snaked along the edge of a set of stone stairs that descended into the bowels of the earth to a landing. The right side of the staircase opened onto a sheer drop, and when I peered over the edge, darkness shrouded the bottom. Halfway down the stairs stood a gate.

My stomach constricted. *This all seems familiar.*

Hissing brought me whirling around. Black Otter slunk out of the water nearest the stairs, fangs bared. "Mine!" He lunged at me.

I stepped to the left, narrowly avoiding being knocked over the edge. He caught my arm with his claws though, shredding my dress sleeve and laying open the flesh beneath. I collided with the wall but then fell, and the world became a jumble of sound, light, and pain as I rolled head over feet. It didn't stop even when I did.

I blinked, dazed. The stairs now rose ahead of me, and Black Otter clung to the edge of the cliff above, his tail-hand thrashing around, trying to get extra purchase.

I looked behind me; the gate had stopped me from rolling all the way down the steps to the landing below. I sat on the cliff-side though, and with an endless drop just a breath away, I scrambled and pressed up against the wall, clutching my knees to my chest, my heart hammering. Glowing gold stardust spewed from multiple cuts on my body.

Black Otter finally clawed his way up onto the ledge then limped out of sight. The sound of splashing echoed through the cavern, but then he reappeared, glaring down at me from the top step. "Mine!" He started down the stairs, the hand on his tail dragging along the rope of water pouring down the corner of the stairs.

I looked behind me again, through the white bars of the gate. The stairs continued at least another hundred steps before leveling off onto the platform. Black Otter was nearly upon me, fangs bared, his inky black eyes flashing....

There's only one place left to run. I pushed the gate open and crawled through.

But when I slammed it shut behind me, Black Otter skidded to a stop, confused. He pressed closer, nostrils flaring as he sniffed. He also peered over the cliff edge. "Mine!" His cry echoed into the nothingness. He turned his glare upon the gate and after a tense silence, he pounded his paws on the stone steps. "Mine! Mine! Mine! Mine!"

I watched, as confused as he, but then I realized, *He can't see me anymore.* I turned my attention to the gate between us.

Arm and leg bones bundled together with sinew formed the bars, and numerous skulls crowned the top—bears, jaguars, deer, rabbits, rodents, even some birds. They stared down at me with empty eye sockets, grinning at a private joke. *I've seen this before*—

Suddenly the gate swung open again.

I pushed back on it, fearing this would break whatever fragile magic kept me hidden from Black Otter, but no matter how hard I pushed, the gate wouldn't be denied. I fled down the steps, expecting to hear claws scraping the stone as he scrambled after me.

But instead his voice grew fainter. I paused to glance back.

He paced and prowled on the other side of the open gate, but now a man walked down the stairs with a small brown dog leading the way. I stepped aside for them—they passed me without so much as a glance— then watched them descend to the platform. The man followed the dog to the left and disappeared. After a quick check that the gate had closed, I continued down the stairs.

A corbelled arch formed a doorway in the wall along the side of the landing, opening into another cavern. The trickle of water wound over the threshold to a broad black river bordering the cavern's right side. A small house of stone and bones sat opposite it, shrouded by a skeletal tree where orbs of blue light bobbed among its branches like monstrous fireflies. One of them broke from the others and floated towards the man and the dog standing next to the river.

It circled them a few times then spiraled down and was absorbed into the dog's body. The dog in turn doubled in size, and when it looked up at the man, its once black eyes glowed with the orb's light. *For your sacrifice, I shall lead you through Lord Death's trials,* a voice whispered in the air. *Come, so you may find your eternal rest.* It turned to the river and waded in, the man following.

Ayya! This is the underworld! I backed away from the doorway, overcome

16

by nightmarish memories. I *had* been here before, after Quetzalcoatl betrayed me to the Earth Monster. I'd stood on the banks of this very river, the wounds from my grandmother's murderous claws still fresh on my body, but they weren't the cause of the pain in my heart. Even now Quetzalcoatl's last words continued to haunt me: *Death is your true gift, my love.*

I must get out of here! I rushed back to the stairs.

But when I tried to take the first step up, I bounced back like a rubber ball hitting a wall. I landed on my rump and blinked in surprise. I tried again, but still failed to pass beyond the landing, as if an invisible force blocked my way. Further up, Black Otter had finally given up, but I waited until he disappeared from sight before launching myself at the stairs, firing magic ahead of me.

But the barrier tossed me back even harder. I skidded all the way across the platform and over the edge, but I caught myself on the lip. I hung, my legs dangling heavy and arm muscles shaking, before managing to pull myself back up, legs scrambling against the rock face. Back on solid ground, I curled up into a ball against the wall, far from the edge. "I can't face the trials of the underworld again! I can't! I can't!"

Get a hold of yourself, the desire growled.

"I can't do it again!"

More people—both men and women—walked by with their guide dogs, completely oblivious to me huddled on the floor.

Do they look terrified? the desire scolded. *Do you see any of them blubbering like a mewling child?*

"They don't know what awaits them," I fired back.

And you do, which means you have an advantage they don't. You're a goddess, for pity's sake! Act like one!

She successfully shamed me, but it still took at least two dozen more calming breaths to get me to my feet again, and even then I lurked in the doorway, rubbing my arms for comfort. *Perhaps Xolotl can raise the barrier, so I can go back.* Determined, I headed for the dilapidated house.

I pulled aside the tattered cloth curtain covering the house's doorway. The inside was empty, and judging from the thick layer of dust everywhere, no one had been there for many bundles of years. I let the curtain drop along with my stomach. *What now?*

Last time, Xolotl had been waiting to guide me through the trials that all the dead had to conquer to reach Mictlan. There had been no orbs, but there also hadn't been a steady stream of dead coming from the platform; there had been far fewer people in the world back then. I looked up at the bobbing orbs. "I need to speak with Xolotl."

But they continued floating serenely, new ones emerging from the dead tree's spindly branches as others left to join with the dogs—the sacrifices to Xolotl that humans buried with their dead. If they had any awareness that I was there, they didn't show it.

"Nantli?" a small voice squeaked from behind the house.

My heart stopped. *I know that voice.* I stepped toward the edge of the house.

At the back corner, a small boy of no more than seven peered back at me. He wore a tattered rabbit costume with lacquered maize leaves for ears, and though the eyes gazing back at me were as dead as any I'd ever seen, joy brought my heart jumping back to life. "Yamehecatl?"

CHAPTER TWO

Yamehecatl's chalk-pale cheeks turned up in a broad smile, showing off his missing front teeth, and he raced to me, his arms spread wide. "It is you, Nantli!"

He knocked me over backwards when he leaped into my own outspread arms but I didn't care. I never really thought I'd ever get to hold my son again. I clutched him, tears drenching my cheeks. He felt so very cold in my arms, but I didn't dare let go of him.

"I told Xolotl you would come for me, but he didn't believe me! I knew you and Tatli would come eventually!" He leaned to look around me. "Where's Tatli?"

I shook my head. "It's just me, my darling."

"Oh?" The confusion in his eyes broke my heart. "You're not dead, are you?"

I smiled, tears clouding my vision. "No. I'm quite alive, my darling breeze."

Yamehecatl embraced me again.

"I haven't the words to tell you how happy I am to hold you again, but why haven't you started on the trials yet?"

He dried his own cold tears away. "Xolotl was here for a little while and tried to get me to swim the river, but I wasn't going anywhere without you, Nantli. Eventually he just left. There were times when I started doubting—when the voice in my head said you and Tatli were never coming for me, but I knew better."

Guilt bubbled up inside me; I'd been looking for other gods, not my son; I was only here now by accident.

But really, what did it matter? "Well, I'm here now."

"And I finally get to leave this place." He pulled at my arm, eager to go.

I looked over my shoulder at the doorway I'd come through. "We can't go back that way."

"No, that way's blocked," he acknowledged. "Xolotl said you can only go one direction on the road into Mictlan." He looked too before admitting, "And I already tried, just to see if he was telling the truth."

"Which means we have to cross the river."

Yamehecatl shook his head, alarmed. "Xolotl warned me not to try it without him or I'll get pulled under and never surface. I saw some people try it and it happened just as he said it would."

"Where is Xolotl anyway? He's supposed to be leading you through these trials—"

"He stayed with me for a long time, but then one day he wasn't here anymore and I haven't seen him since."

"After we paid him with a dog? Ayya! He's going to get an earful when I see him again." I glared at the river, wondering what to do next.

A woman came through the archway, accompanied by a dog. One of the orbs broke off from the others circling the spindly tree and made for the river, where the woman and the dog waited. It joined with the dog then the two waded out into the river. *Maybe the orbs are Xolotl's nahuals.* I hurried to the river bank. "Xolotl! I need to speak with you!"

But the dog ignored me, as did the woman. I shouted a few more times and even waved my hands around when the dog reached the opposite shore, but still no response.

"Xolotl told me that the dead can't see each other," Yamehecatl said. "At least not the mortal dead."

I turned to him, about to ask how he could see her, but then the truth hit me. "How long have you known that you're not mortal?"

He flashed his gap-tooth smile. "Night Wind told me, a few weeks before I died, but he made me promise not to say anything to anyone about it, especially to you."

"Why not me?"

"Because you're a priestess, and you would say I was being blasphemous."

I knelt and held him by both hands. "I wouldn't ever call you blasphemous, my darling. I love you too much to do that."

"I know. But Nantli, why didn't you tell me?"

"I didn't know. If I had...I definitely wouldn't keep that secret from you. It's too important. If Night Wind hadn't told you the truth, you would have died a mortal and there would be no chance for you to come back to life again."

His face lit up. "I can live again?"

I nodded. "And you will, I promise. We just need to find a way out of here." I returned to studying the river and wondering how I might get one of Xolotl's nahuals to help us when I had no dog to entice it.

"Nantli?"

"Yes, my darling breeze?" But when he started crying, I pulled him into my arms to comfort him. "What's wrong?"

"I'm sorry."

"For what?"

"For not telling you that I knew...about you."

I frowned, confused. "What do you mean?"

"I knew you were a goddess and I didn't say anything."

"You knew? But what...how...how did you know?"

Yamehecatl wiped his nose with his wrist. "I figured it out. I mean, it wasn't difficult, really. You can use magic, and we both remember everything, so what else could it be? I told Night Wind and he said you were but that I couldn't say anything to you about it."

"Why not?"

"He said if I did, you would get hurt, and that if I loved you, I would keep my mouth shut about it. I'm sorry, Nantli."

As he broke into still more tears, I hugged him tight. He felt so cold, but the anger boiling inside me would surely warm his dead flesh. "There is nothing to forgive, dear. Night Wind is a callous liar who just wants to hurt us. I know this may be difficult to hear, but he isn't your friend."

"What do you mean?"

"Night Wind is really the Smoking Mirror, and as a god of lies, you can't trust anything he says." *Though if not for him, you wouldn't know your true identity, would you?*

"But why would Smoking Mirror want to hurt us, Nantli? What did we do to him?"

I sighed. "You, my darling, did absolutely nothing. Smoking Mirror just hates Quetzalcoatl, and since you're Quetzalcoatl's son...."

"He hates me too." Yamehecatl frowned.

"I'm sorry. None of this is your fault."

"But why does he hate you?"

"Because I kept him from taking over the valley, and I killed his chosen high priest."

"Then it's true what everyone says? That you unleashed Quetzalcoatl on the false king?"

I nodded. "I let the Feathered Serpent take control of my body so we could battle Smoking Mirror, who was trying to kill your Tatli, and that's...how you came to be."

"Wow!" He gazed at me with wide, wondering eyes. "You're a really powerful goddess, Nantli!"

I laughed. "Not really, dear, but thank you."

He shook his head. "I bet Xolotl left because he knew you were coming and he wouldn't be able to stop you from saving me! He was scared!"

"I doubt that."

I took another look at the river. Mortals couldn't walk the road into Mictlan alone, but perhaps a goddess could?

But when I started towards the water, Yamehecatl grabbed onto my wrist. "Where are you going?"

"I must test a theory." When he didn't let go, I gently pried his fingers from my arm then knelt in front of him again. "There is only one way out of the underworld, and it's over that river and through the other trials. I think I can be Xolotl for you, but I must test my hunch before letting you try to cross. I thought I lost you forever once already; I won't risk it again."

Yamehecatl pursed his lips but nodded. "Xolotl did say that anyone living must walk the road too, but if they take too long, they will be dead when they reach Mictlan."

"Then time is urgent." I rose but made sure he was calm before heading for the river again. At the bank I paused, breathed deeply, then stepped into the water.

Icy cold drilled into my feet, bringing with it needles of fear. I continued on, one slow step at a time, until the water reached my waist. My heart hammered as I waited for my nightmarish memories to come to fruition.

I jolted when boney fingers closed around my ankle and began pulling. Instinct told me to kick and flee—and I almost did—but then I remembered what Xolotl had told me so many bundles of years ago: *One must overcome the fear of the unknown to cross the river. To not do so is to drown in fear.* I squeezed my eyes shut and strove for calm, and soon the tugging and clawing ceased.

I waded back to shore, my heart light with excitement.

Yamehecatl rushed to the river bank. "Is it safe, Nantli?"

"Perfectly, my dear." I held my hand out.

"But Xolotl said those without a guide get lost forever."

"Xolotl isn't the only one who knows the way. This isn't my first time in the underworld, remember?"

Yamehecatl thought on that then he smiled brightly. "Oh, because the Earth Monster—" He didn't go on though, looking acutely distressed.

"She killed me," I finished for him. "So yes, I've walked the road before, and I know what to expect. Don't worry, we'll get to Mictlan together."

He smiled as he took my hand. "I love you, Nantli."

I bent to kiss his cold forehead. "And I missed you so very much, my darling."

He wiped it away with the back of his hand, just as he used to when he was still alive. "We just have to swim the river?"

"This is just the first trial. There will be eight more after that."

"I'm not a strong swimmer, Nantli." He eyed the water with trepidation.

"You will ride on my back. I need you to remember one thing though."

"What's that?"

"No matter what you feel, none of it is real and it can't hurt you. Understand?"

He nodded, but fear still shone in his eyes.

I gave his hand a squeeze. "It will be all right."

He climbed onto my back when I knelt on the bank to let him up. "Arms around my neck." I supported his legs with my arms as I waded out into the river, walking slow and methodical as not to let the fast-moving water knock me over. Yamehecatl squealed when the water reached his feet—"So cold!"—then I eased down into the current and swam out into the middle of the river, paddling hard.

Yamehecatl did all right for the first minute—shivering but not complaining—but suddenly he buried his face in the back of my head. "Something's touching me, Nantli! Something's touching my leg!"

"Just remember...it's not real," I panted between waves hitting my mouth. "It can't...hurt you...unless you...let it." Bony fingers brushed against my legs and feet, but I focused on keeping the fear at bay.

"It's not real. It's not real," he sputtered into my wet hair, his grip so tight he would have strangled me if I were still mortal. He repeated it over and over, like a prayer, but his shivering grew worse. "They're trying to pull me down, Nantli! Sing me a song! Please!"

The only ones I could think of were praises for Quetzalcoatl, and he was the last god I wished to say anything nice about, but with Yamehecatl shaking violently, now wasn't the time for the anger. Singing songs about the Feathered Serpent always put him at ease.

With the water slapping into my mouth and his strangling grip around my neck, I had to sputter and gasp the words out. But it started working right away. His grip loosened and his breathing slowed, and soon he joined in. For a moment, even I forgot we were fording the black river instead of sitting in my bed in Tollan, singing together as we so often had. I hadn't felt so happy in over a year now and I desperately wanted to hold onto that.

Soon I felt mud under my feet again and once I was able to stand upright, Yamehecatl jumped down and ran ashore, ecstatic. "We made it! We made it, Nantli!"

I trudged ashore, surprisingly tired. I hadn't felt fatigued since rediscovering my divinity—it seemed gods required no rest—but now my muscles protested just as they used to after a brisk walk up and down the temple steps in Tollan. *An ominous portent?* I wondered, but I shook it off. The sooner we moved on, the sooner we'd be done.

¤

An archway in the wall led into a short tunnel that opened into another vast cavern, but when we stopped at the entrance, all of Yamehecatl's excitement fled. Obsidian arrow and spear heads rained from the darkened cavern ceiling. He tightened his grip on my hand. "How do we get past this?"

"We have to run."

"But it's so far!"

"There's no way around it. You have to run, and not stop. It only gets worse if you stop. Just remember that the arrows can't kill you; you're already dead, after all."

"But what about you? You're not."

The sound of shattering obsidian made my stomach clench, but the longer we waited, the harder the downpour became.

But then I remembered how the blades had bounced off of Xolotl when he'd led me through the cavern, as if he had an invisible shield protecting him—his magic, undoubtedly. Maybe my own would do the same for me?

I reached out into the open, but within a couple breaths, an arrowhead sliced deep into the muscle of my forearm. I yanked my arm to my chest with a yelp, holding the wound with my other hand as golden star dust bled through my fingers. So much for my magic protecting me.

I clenched my teeth and pulled the blade out. "Don't worry about me." I tried to sound unconcerned despite the dread growing in the pit of my stomach.

"But I *am* worried about you, Nantli," he insisted. He thought a moment then asked, "Do you remember how Tatli always told this part of the story, of Quetzalcoatl's journey into the underworld?"

I nodded. "The Feathered Serpent carried Xolotl on his shoulders, to cloak himself from the blades."

"I could do that for you." When I opened my mouth to tell him "absolutely not!" he pointed out, "Like you said, I'm already dead, so it can't kill me."

"It still hurts like nothing you've ever known," I warned. "We'll just run—"

"But what if it kills you?"

And if that happens, who's going to guide him to Mictlan. I wasn't sure how matters worked when one died on the road; would I have to start the journey all over again, and would Xolotl take mercy on me and guide me despite the lack of a sacrifice? *He skipped out on guiding Yamehecatl. That's a far cry from mercy.*

"Please, Nantli. I want to help you," Yamehecatl said, holding my hand between both of his. "I know I'm just a little boy, but I can be brave, because I love you and you're my nantli. If Tatli were here, he would do this for you, but since he's not...." He looked ready to cry.

That was enough to set my own tears threatening. "No, he's not, and I know you're brave, my darling. I just can't stand the thought of you hurt—"

"And Tatli always says there's nothing more honorable than making sacrifices for the ones we love." He squeezed my hand, suddenly seeming so much older than his mere seven years. "You made many for me, so please let me make this one for you."

I wiped away the tears that had broken free and I went to my knees and pulled him into a fierce hug. "You are the bravest boy I've ever known, Yamehecatl."

"I learned it from you, Nantli," he whispered back.

After a brief discussion on how to proceed, we decided I'd get the best cover by putting him upon my shoulders; that would expose the least amount of both of our bodies to the arrow-storm. He was quite heavy and I had to lever myself up using the wall for support, but soon I stood facing the cavern with Yamehecatl hunched over upon my shoulders. The storm had grown nastier, with twice as many obsidian blades raining down as before. Memories of the pain made me hesitate, but if we remained here much longer, the storm might become impassable. "Ready?" I asked Yamehecatl.

"Ready!" he called.

With a deep breath, I dove out into the cavern.

I didn't make it any further than a single step before Yamehecatl squealed in pain, and for half a breath, I stopped, overcome by the need to make sure he was all right, but then my good sense won out. Stopping would only bring him more pain. I gripped his legs tightly with both hands and ran.

Yamehecatl's awkward hunch over the top of me had me leaning forward more than I would have liked, so I felt off balance and on the verge of crashing over every step I took. My world became the sound of his cries—each one more agonized than the last—and blurs of black and grey streaking all around me. I wasn't even sure if I was going in the right direction but I kept moving, even when a blade got past Yamehecatl and caught my calf in stride. I hardly noticed the pain though; I was a blubbering mess, thinking of my son taking the brunt of the attack.

When I finally reached the next archway, I couldn't get to my knees fast enough. Yamehecatl clung to me with a petrified grip and it took a full minute of coaxing to get him to finally let go and slide down my back. I wept when I saw the mess of arrow and spearheads all over his back and arms; I'd told him to shield his head, and he looked like a porcupine on his upper body.

"You were so very brave, my love," I whispered, tears flooding down my cheeks as I carefully worked the blades from his body. He shuddered each time, but he made no noise as I worked. Like a drained corpse, he didn't bleed from his wounds, but the blades left his rabbit suit in tatters. When I pulled the last one from him, I drew him onto my lap and held him close, stroking his head while I rocked him.

We sat that way a very long time before Yamehecatl came back to himself. "We made it through all right?" he asked, his voice still distant, but I was glad he'd finally spoken again.

"We did," I whispered.

"You didn't take the blade out of your leg."

I'd been so wrapped up in caring for him that I hadn't even noticed my own wound. It didn't throb as I would expect, but it burned when I yanked it out. Shimmering gold dust oozed out thick, like sap, and the wound showed no signs of sealing on its own, as it normally would, so I tore off the hem of my dress and tied it around it. "Don't worry about me, my dear. I'll be all right. How are you feeling?"

He shrugged. "It doesn't hurt much anymore."

"You're so brave, my love," I whispered, returning to stroking his head. He sighed and snuggled against my breast, holding me tight.

We sat like that for a long time, but I didn't have forever to wait. I made sure Yamehecatl was physically ready to go though before insisting we move onto the next cavern. My own wounded leg had grown stiff and I had to hobble around before being able to put weight on it.

"I told him he was wrong about you," Yamehecatl said as he took my hand when I held it out to him.

"Who?"

"The voice in my head. He always said you didn't love me."

My stomach clenched. "I love you more than anything, Yamehecatl."

"I know you do, Nantli. He always said mean things, like that you wanted me to stay a baby forever, and that's why you kept calling me Yamehecatl instead of Ehecacone."

"I'm sorry. It's just, for so long you were Yamehecatl to me...but I understand. I will make sure to always call you Ehecacone for now on."

He smiled brightly. "Thank you, Nantli."

"What else does he say?"

"Just nonsense, really. He claims you wanted to get rid of me before I was even born."

My son had never brought this subject up when he was in a rational state of mind; the accusation always came when the drunkenness had taken over, when he became someone so completely unlike the sweet little boy I knew, and for a very long time, I'd dreaded having to answer that. And though it really wasn't a question this time, I couldn't baldly lie to him. It was time we had the discussion.

I took both of his hands in mine and knelt in front of him. "I don't ever want to keep the truth from you, no matter how much it pains me...but...it's true that I thought of ending my pregnancy."

He furrowed his brow. "What do you mean?"

I took a deep breath. "For a few weeks, when I first learned that I was going to be a mother, I didn't want to be one, and I was planning to take some medicine that would make it so I wouldn't be."

He stared at me, devastated, and it took all my willpower to not turn away in shame. "But why?"

"I was very scared," I admitted, my voice catching as the tears came on. "I knew you were the god's son, and...." I paused to collect myself then went on, "You know how your Tatli is the god's son too? Well, my mother—your grandmother—she died giving birth to him because, while it's already dangerous business giving birth to a normal mortal child, it's especially dangerous for a mortal woman to give birth to the child of a god. I was at your grandmother's side when she gave birth to your Tatli, and...and I saw what it did to her. It's one of the worst memories of my life. And I was afraid that I too would die if I carried you to birth."

"But you're not mortal, Nantli," Ehecacone pointed out.

"But I didn't know that back then; that's something I only found out recently. At the time, I very much thought I would die."

"And so you really planned to get rid of me?"

I pursed my lips, trying not to burst into guilty tears as I admitted, "I did."

He looked uncertain and didn't respond right away, but eventually he said, "But you didn't do it." When I shook my head, he asked, "Why not?"

"Because I finally started listening to my heart," I said. "And she loves you so much she would risk everything for you. I've never once regretted my decision to keep you, not even when Black Otter took you from me."

"Black Otter?" he asked, confused.

I wiped away tears and nodded. "I would have given my life to stop him, and I wouldn't have thought twice about it."

Ehecacone sniffled, trying to hold back his own tears. "I'm so sorry, Nantli...all those things I used to say when the other voice took over...."

I pulled him into a tight hug and whispered, "You have nothing to be sorry about, my dear sweet breeze. I'm the one who should being saying sorry to you. Can you ever forgive me?"

His tears wetted my shoulder. "Can you forgive me for ever saying that you hated me?"

"Of course, my love. It's all right."

He kissed my cheek then pulled away to wipe his runny nose with his wrist. "I would do anything for you too, Nantli."

Looking at the plethora of holes in his rabbit suit left by the obsidian blades, my heart swelled painfully with pride and thankfulness. "I know you would, dear."

CHAPTER THREE

Based on my own memories, I estimated it would take us only a handful of hours to finish the journey, but for the first time in my life, my perfect memory proved imperfect.

After the cavern of arrowheads, the tunnel opened into a gorge surrounded by steep, jagged rock walls. The temperature plummeted and as we hiked further in, snow began drifting down from above. We followed a winding creek, trying to avoid crossing it and possibly wetting our feet, especially as the storm picked up and the wind began howling through the canyon, but the longer we walked, the narrower the gorge became until we had no choice but to walk in the middle of the creek. My feet went numb long before the water finally froze hard enough for us to walk on without falling through. All the while we clutched each other for warmth; futile since Ehecacone's dead body gave off only more cold.

"How much further, Nantli?" he asked as we shuffled through the frozen wasteland.

"Not far now," I told him, though I didn't entirely trust my memory anymore in that regard.

And I felt as if I were growing weaker the further along I went. My feet were numb and my legs felt heavy, each step more difficult than the one before. The wind cut like knives across my exposed skin, and not even shivering did much to help it. The monotony of the swirling whiteness lulled my brain and increasingly I thought of curling up in the snow and just going to sleep. I hadn't slept in over six months, not since that fateful night when Smoking Mirror changed the entire course of my life. There'd been a few times when I'd wished I still didn't know the truth—that I wished I was back in Tollan with Little Reed, celebrating the birth of the next heir to the throne. I wished I didn't know the child was actually Citlallotoc's because Little Reed was so wrapped up in the poison I cast over all mortals that he couldn't bring himself to bed another woman. I wished I didn't know that that same poison had driven Black Otter to murder my son. As an immortal that never slept anymore, I never got any peace from the questions and regrets that constantly plagued me since that night.

I flinched when someone suddenly shook my shoulder, and to my confusion, I realized I was lying on the ground. Ehecacone gazed down at me with wide, concerned eyes. "What happened?" I asked, sitting up, disoriented.

"You were walking and all of a sudden you just fell over, like you passed out," he sputtered, shivering in his thin rabbit suit. "Are you all right?"

I looked around, still confused and trying to get my bearings. "Yes, I'm fine. I'm just...feeling tired." And what did that mean for me?

"Maybe you should rest for a while," he suggested.

But I shook my head. "It's much too cold here, and there's no shelter. We must press on." I stumbled to my feet with his help and we continued on into the blinding storm. I felt more alert now, but the cold started really sinking its teeth into me. I worried for my numb toes directly exposed to the snow, but I had nothing to protect them with; I'd lost my shoes to Black Otter, and because it was summer up in the living world, I was dressed in nothing more than a thin dress. What I wouldn't do right now for a fur-lined cloak, or some leathers to cover my feet!

Soon the exhaustion hit hard and my mind started drifting again in the maddening whiteness. Back to that final time I'd spoken with Quetzalcoatl in the Divine Dream, how he'd lied so shamelessly, how he tried to convince me to give him the chance to fill my head with more lies to cover for his treachery, lies such as that he loved me and hadn't meant to hurt me. *Death is your real gift*, he'd told me so long ago, and even now I could still hear his laughter in my head.

"Are we almost there, Nantli?" Ehecacone asked, clutching my hand tightly with his own ice-cold one.

"I don't know," I admitted. I hoped so, for I wasn't sure how much more of this cold and swirling snow and memories of betrayal I could handle. "Will you sing me a song, my sweet breeze, to help us pass the time?"

"Of course, Nantli." He then set into one of the prayer songs we always sang.

"Not one about Quetzalcoatl!" I snapped, the fury overcoming me. It came on like a brush fire and my skin seemed to burn. "Never sing of that deceitful snake again!"

Ehecacone stared up at me with scared eyes, and he started pulling his hand from mine, but I tightened my grip.

"I'm sorry. I didn't mean to snap at you, my dear," I said.

He gave me a wary look before finally letting me pull him along.

I don't know how much longer we walked, but eventually I saw the faint outline of a tunnel in the side of a mountain right ahead of us. Ehecacone hooted when he too saw it, and he pulled me along faster. We stumbled over the icy rocks, the wind tearing at us, and it still followed us when we ran into the tunnel, out of the elements. I hobbled along, trying to remember what came next, but my mind was crying for sleep. The wind only followed us so far, and I noticed a marked temperature increase the further in we went.

"You should rest for a while, Nantli," Ehecacone suggested. I couldn't see him in the dark, but he pulled on my arm, motioning me to sit down. I followed his instructions without argument and leaned against the tunnel wall, thankful to be off my feet. He climbed onto my lap and I held him close, not minding how chilly he was, for the air had grown quite hot by now. I rested my head on his, holding my breath against the musty smell of decay seeping off of him; instead, I tried to remember how he used to smell when he was alive; like papayas and fresh flowers, and love....

"Nantli?" Ehecacone's words seemed to come from a dream, but I realized I was awake again, my body aching and my toes burning badly. I tried to move them but the effort only sent shocks of pain through my feet.

I gritted my teeth then asked, "Yes, my dear?"

"You've stopped glowing."

I looked down at my hands to find them completely lost in the darkness. Did this mean I was turning mortal? I had started sleeping again, and I feared my toes were deeply frostbitten. At the very least, my magic was so low I couldn't heal myself anymore. Xolotl's warnings about taking too long to walk the road repeated in my head, but it still wasn't enough to convince my muscles to wake up.

Ehecacone snuggled against my chest. "Why can't we sing about Quetzalcoatl anymore?"

I stroked his head in the dark. "You can sing about the Feathered Serpent if you like. I had no right to tell you that, and I'm sorry."

He remained quiet before tentatively asking, "But you don't want to sing about him anymore?"

I didn't want to talk about this; I'd spent his whole life teaching him to love and honor the Feathered Serpent—to honor his father—but in my exhaustion, I'd opened the door to the conversation. I sighed. "No, I don't."

"Why not?"

My voice broke as I replied, "Because he's not who I thought he was."

"What do you mean?"

"You remember the story I told you, about Quetzalcoatl and

Mayahuel?"

"Of course."

"Well...it's all true, and you were right about Quetzalcoatl; he wasn't very heroic at all. In fact, he was treacherous; he lured me down from Heaven, claimed he loved me, but when the Earth Monster came, he abandoned me and let her tear me apart. He didn't even try to help me." I hadn't wanted to cry, but the tears had their own ideas. "He told me my real gift to humanity wasn't love; he intended me to die all along so humanity could have the maguey, to make octli and commune with the rest of the gods."

"Oh Nantli!" Ehecacone whispered, reaching up to wipe my tears away with his cold fingers.

"I never should have listened to him...never should have left the garden...." But as I hugged my son tighter, I had to admit, "Though then again, he gave me you, so I can't say it was all terrible and horrible." Though given that Quetzalcoatl never said a word to me about our son nor showed any evidence he cared that Ehecacone had died, I had to believe that our son hadn't been part of his grand scheme against me, but a happy accident. The only one I could really claim, since Little Reed was just as much a source of torment for me as one of happiness.

"I will never sing about him again either," Ehecacone said, anger in his voice.

"He has much to answer for," I whispered, wiping away my own tears. "But I won't tell you that you must shun your father—"

"No one is allowed to hurt you, Mother. No one."

"No," I agreed.

"You were right. Tatli is my father, and nobody else matters."

I choked on more tears as I said, "And I know for a fact that you were as important to Topiltzin as any child he might have put in my belly himself, had circumstances been different."

"When we get out of here, can we go back to Tollan and see Father?" Ehecacone asked as he helped me to my feet. "I want to tell him that I love him."

I gritted my teeth against the sharp pain in my toes. "He already knows you love him, but yes, absolutely. We'll go back and see him. But now, let's get going or we'll never get to see anyone again."

¤

Once we reached the light streaming in from the other end of the tunnel, I saw that my toes had blistered and turned black. Every step was like walking on obsidian shards. I focused on meditation techniques I'd learned in the priesthood to keep my mind off the pain, but with minimal success.

The next cavern consisted of a bridge over a deep chasm, and flaming flags dangled from poles along the edges. Ehecacone started walking out, seemingly unconcerned, but I pulled him back. "We're going to have to run," I warned him. "I want you to go on ahead without me, because I'm hobbled and I'll just slow you down. Wait for me at the other end, all right?"

"But what about you?" he asked.

"There's nothing you can do to help me on this one. I just have to face the fire and make it to the other side. If for some reason, I don't make it...remember you're brave, and you can go on without me. You have to. For me. Understand?"

The boy who stood before me looked only seven summers old physically, but something had changed in his eyes since we'd started this journey together. He looked back at me with the gaze of someone older, someone wiser. "All right."

I hugged him firmly then pointed to the bridge. "Go as fast as you can, and try to stay to the middle. The flames have to reach far to get you there, so they are thinner and do less damage to your body."

He nodded then walked to the head of the bridge. He paused to give me an encouraging smile, then he sprinted, keeping to the middle as I'd told him.

As soon as he stepped out onto the bridge, the flaming flags sprung to life, snapping out at him. But to my astonishment, when he reached the first flame, he took to all fours and instead of running through it, he leaped over it. After that first one, he skittered under the next and dodged the third. He traversed the obstacle course of flaming flags with the skill of a crafty old rabbit outrunning ocelots and sneaking past hunters' traps—an image only reinforced by his ratty rabbit suit. I held my breath as he skipped past the last two flaming flags then slid to a stop on the other side of the bridge. He looked back at me and leaped into the air, pumping his fist. "Did you see me, Mother? Not a single scratch!"

"You were amazing, my darling!" I called back, my heart overcome with pride and joy. "I knew you could do it!"

"Now it's your turn," he called back.

But when I took my first limping step forward, I knew I would have a much harder time of it. I stopped at the mouth of the bridge, breathing deeply to calm my frayed nerves.

"You can do it!" Ehecacone hollered to me.

I nodded then started across.

The flaming flags sprang to life again and whipped out at me. I took it slowly, thinking maybe I could maneuver my way past them as they snapped back and forth, but I was too slow; the one to my right kissed my cheek with its blistering tongue, making me step closer to the left side where the other one lashed me across the back. Panicked, I ran, screaming each time the flames sliced into my skin. I wasn't even sure which direction I was going anymore; I just ran, pain surrounding me from every direction. I vaguely felt one of my frostbitten toes snap off in my scramble, but I kept going, stumbling forward like a drunk. I heard Ehecacone yelling, but I couldn't find him. I plunged through another set of flaming flags, and I felt myself falling, but I blacked out before the crash.

¤

I woke up sprawled out, my entire body stiff and crusty and oozing. I tried to move, but the shocks of fresh pain rendered me paralyzed. I panted, the air hot and dry in my lungs, and my tongue felt like a piece of dried leather in my mouth. "Ehecacone?" I croaked, making myself turn my head to search for him.

He sat just inside the mouth of the tunnel, staring at me with sunken, haunted eyes, as if he couldn't believe what he was seeing. He soon shook it off and rushed over to me though, tears streaming down his face. "I thought for sure you'd died," he whispered, hovering over me, the uncertainty and fear plain in his eyes.

I'm not going to survive this ordeal, I suddenly thought, but before the fatalism could fully seep in, the voice of my desire—so absent until now—suddenly spoke up. *Stop giving up. If you give up, Quetzalcoatl wins. And who's going to guide Ehecacone? You told him to go on without you, but he's shown he hasn't the fortitude to do so. Xolotl isn't going to help him, and Quetzalcoatl doesn't give a damn about him. So stop laying here and get up already.*

As much as I despised that voice, sometimes I was grateful that it knew exactly what to say to shame me into action. I fought past the shocks of pain to make myself sit up, and Ehecacone rushed to help me, being careful not to touch my burns. *This must be how Citlallotoc felt after the surgeon cauterized his arm,* I thought, struggling to my feet. I glanced down to see I'd lost not just one toe on my blackened feet, but three. If I made it through this, I wondered if they would be permanently gone, like the fingers I cut off when I was mortal.

Not if, the desire scolded me. *When.*

"We should get moving again," I said, and together Ehecacone and I limped down the hallway to the next trial.

But there I stopped again, my heart sinking. The next cavern was small, no more than twenty paces across, but between us and the next tunnel were the jagged walls of two mountains smashing against each other every few breaths. My earlier doubts now turned to certainty: I was going to die.

Ehecacone looked expectantly up at me. "How do we get through this one?"

I motioned him to follow me and I went to the far left side of the tunnel, just outside the reach of the clashing mountains. "See that?" I pointed to a small alcove cut out from the side of the right-hand mountain just before the two came crashing together again.

He nodded.

"There are three of those along the way; two on that side, one on the opposite. To make it to the other side, you have to make it to each before the mountains come together and crush you."

"What happens if we don't make it in time?"

"You'll get mangled, and it will make the remaining trials more difficult for you, but otherwise you'll be all right."

"But what about you?"

I took a deep breath. "Ehecacone. I can't go on."

"Then I'm not either!"

"You can't stay here because of me—"

"But if you stay here, you'll run out of time—"

"It doesn't matter, my dear breeze—"

"But you promised to guide me to Mictlan! You told me good people don't break their promises; you don't break promises, Mother!"

I gritted my teeth. Such arguing used to annoy me when he was still alive, but now it just made me ashamed. "All right," I choked, terrified and trying to hold back tears. "But we must go separately because I'll just slow you down and you'll get injured."

"And you promise you will come right after me?"

"I promise."

He nodded then turned back towards the walls. He flinched when they crashed together, sending shards of rock and clouds of dust flying into the air. While he crouched, timing the number of breaths between each collision, I massaged my leg muscles and stretched, making sure I was as loose and ready to move as possible. "Two long breaths once they stop moving," he murmured as he stood again.

"I'd go as soon as they separate enough for you fit between them," I suggested. "The first one is pretty close, but the other two are further apart. You shouldn't have much trouble, since you're small, but make sure you can see where the next one is before attempting to go to it."

Ehecacone nodded and set himself up at the edge of the walls, pointed towards the first alcove. I leaned over him, making some last moment timings of my own, then said, "Go!"

He sprinted at full speed between the parting walls and made it to the first alcove even before the walls stopped moving. He looked ahead for the next, but I shouted, "Stay there until after they crash together!" At the last moment, he pulled back inside, avoiding being crushed as the walls slammed together, raining dirt and stone into the air. I held my breath as I waited for the walls to part so I could see him again.

I breathed in agonized relief when I saw my son tucked in the alcove, unharmed. "Let it go again, then go when they start parting again!"

The walls crashed again but this time when they parted, the alcove was empty.

"I made it!" Ehecacone called from beyond my sight.

I lined myself up, my heart thudding. I let the walls crash together again then I made a dash for the alcove.

I felt as if I were moving in slow motion, every muscle protesting and my burnt skin screaming, but I made it to the alcove a hair before the walls slammed in around me. The crash was deafening and I clamped my eyes shut against the storm of dust spinning around me. When the walls parted, I turned around and rubbed the dust from my eyes, searching for Ehecacone in the next niche.

But he wasn't there. "Are you all right?" I called, but before anyone could answer, the walls smashed together again. I pressed myself hard against the walls of the alcove, cringing away from the dust and rock showering over me.

But when the walls parted again, he called back to me. "I'm fine. I'm in the third alcove!"

"I'm heading to the second one soon," I called back. "Don't wait for me!"

The walls clashed again and this time I made myself keep my eyes open, so I could see the next alcove as soon as possible, and when I spotted it, I dashed again, my heart pounding. I didn't even notice my protesting muscles this time. The second niche scooped me up as the walls jerked together, encasing me in darkness and dust. As the walls slid back, I retreated with the niche and pinned myself against the back, my heart pounding so hard it hurt. I checked the next niche to see Ehecacone still there—making sure I made it to mine—but the next time I looked, he was gone. It looked so far away and this time I hesitated to go until the walls came together and parted another four times.

I made it, but just barely. The walls caught the tail of my dress and ground it together hard, pulling me against the joint between the walls and the alcove. I tore my dress up the front trying to pull away, then I fell forward when the walls finally parted. I had to scramble to my feet to avoid being brained when they came crashing back again. When I glanced ahead, in the direction out of the walls, I briefly spotted Ehecacone waiting for me, peering back anxiously. The gap was even longer than the last. There was no way I was going to make it.

I couldn't wait here forever, but I didn't want Ehecacone to see the walls crush me either. "I want you to keep your back turned," I called to him.

But he shook his head vehemently. "You're going to make it, Mother." He had that same wild look in his eyes as he used to get when the drunkenness took over. "You're going to make it." He held his hands out to me.

I waited another three crashes, working up the courage to make that last dash, then as soon as the walls started creaking apart, I started squeezing my way out. I tried to banish all thoughts of what it must feel like to be full-body crushed but it kept creeping in as I ran, blood thudding in my ears. I felt as if I was moving in slow motion, but I kept my gaze focused on the absolute certainty on my son's face directly ahead of me.

The walls crashed behind me, and for a breath I stopped short, something holding me back, but then a sickening ripping sound brought me tumbling to the ground. I didn't feel any pain, but then I was so numb and dizzy I probably wouldn't have felt it if the walls had crushed me to a pulp. I just hoped the damage wasn't so bad I couldn't go on. I took a few deep breaths then turned over.

But to my surprise, my dress lay in tatters on the ground and I was naked save for my cotton undergarment. The ripping had been my dress coming apart when the walls caught it again and I'd literally fallen out of it. I laid back and laughed, my whole body shaking.

Ehecacone gathered up the remains of my dress and knelt next to me. "I knew you would make it," he said, his voice startlingly calm. "It takes more than mountains to kill you, Mother."

CHAPTER FOUR

Making it unscathed through the clashing mountains gave me the boost of confidence I needed to believe I wasn't destined to die again. From there, we came to another river, this one guarded by giant serpents, but they proved little challenge; they swam near us when we tried to cross, but they always turned away when they came close. *That's because like you, they are earth monsters,* Xolotl had told me long ago. *And despite what your grandmother did to you, most earth monsters feel a kinship with each other.* One of them did take a snap at Ehecacone, but when I punched it in the nose, it snorted and retreated.

When we climbed back ashore and I wrung out the remains of my dress before tying it back around myself, Ehecacone glared into the water. "You'd think they could at least respect the fact that I'm a fellow snake," he grumbled.

I chuckled. "While Quetzalcoatl is your father, you're not very much like him, my dear." Remembering how like a rabbit he'd looked when dodging the flaming flags, it was obvious he took more after me; I was the one whose nahuals were rabbits, and who had been born into the mortal world on the day Tochtli.

"Good," he grumbled as we turned away from the river and stood facing the next challenge.

We didn't have to pass through any more tunnels, for we'd reached the lowest—and largest—cavern of the underworld, and just beyond this mountain lay the plains of Mictlan, where Lord Death ruled.

We both scrutinized the path winding up the mountain in front of us. The whole side was made of countless obsidian blades, jutting in all directions, leaving only a very narrow foot path that had to be taken single file, placing one foot in front of the other. It was impossible to make it to the top without cutting oneself on the blades, but one could at least mitigate the damage.

"When we get out of here, I'm going to make Quetzalcoatl answer for what he did to you," Ehecacone said, holding my hand as we started up the path.

"Don't even think about rushing off to confront him," I said. "He's a very powerful god, and you...well, we don't even know what your real powers are yet. And I won't have you sacrificing yourself in the name of revenge."

"He can't just get away with this though, Mother!"

"He won't. I promise. But in the meantime, patience, my dear."

The going was long and at times difficult, especially when the path narrowed so much that one couldn't even place one foot in front of the other without blades slicing into our ankles and feet. Ehecacone seemed unaffected by the wounds, but my own feet had become a bloody mess—my golden stardust had not only thickened to bloodlike consistency, but it had turned red as well. I stopped halfway up and tore up more of my dress, to tie around my feet for protection. Two more of my toes came off as I wrapped, and I suspected I would lose at least a couple more before this was all over.

It took several more hours, but eventually we reached the summit. From there the plain of Mictlan spread out below us, obscured by a mask of fog. "I thought we were almost there!" Ehecacone exclaimed, frustration coloring his voice.

"There are only two more trials left, and the next one is probably the easiest of them all. We just need to descend the mountain."

"Over more obsidian blades?"

"No, it's all dirt on this side."

"Then let's go!" He made to start down, but I caught his arm.

"I know it looks innocent, but you must go carefully, and slowly."

"Why?"

"Because one false step and you tumble to the bottom, and it's a long way down."

Ehecacone contemplated the slope then took my hand. "We'll go slowly then."

That worked for a while. The slope was steep; at every step it felt as though my body were becoming heavier and heavier, and sharp pains radiated up through my shins. The more exhausted I became, the harder it was to focus on my steps and my speed, and several times I nearly went down, taking Ehecacone with me. Eventually I let go of him, if only because it was just a matter of time before my attention wandered enough that I would pitch over.

And no sooner had I done so than the ground shifted under me like water and I went down, rump-first. I tried to grab onto a nearby rock, but my fingers slipped over it as if it were slick with ice and I rolled down the hill. Ehecacone's scream was drowned in the noisy avalanche of dirt and debris, and the crash of trees snapping.

I suddenly stopped, sprawled out on dry, dusty ground, my teeth tingling in my head. I closed my eyes, a burning pain radiating up my right leg. When I dared look down, no bones jutted out, but my leg was bent at an unnatural angle.

Ehecacone shouted that he was coming to help me but it still took a while for him to navigate his way down. "Are you all right?" he panted, dropping to his knees next to me.

"I'm pretty sure my leg's broken." I tried to sit up but the pain shooting up my leg made me dizzy. I lay down again, trying to keep my wits as Ehecacone looked down on me with growing panic. I set a supportive hand on his arm. "Don't worry, we'll get through the last trial; I promise."

"But can you even walk?"

Gritting my teeth, I rolled over onto my belly then dragged myself to a nearby spindly, dead tree anchored into the hard, cracked earth. I wailed and wept as I pulled myself up, and though I was dizzy and sweating profusely, eventually I got up onto my good leg. I hugged onto the tree, drawing in deep, calming breaths. When I opened my eyes, Ehecacone stood next to me, his dirty face even paler than normal. "It will be very slow going, but we'll make it," I said, my voice thick with pain. "I'll need to lean on you though, all right?"

"What if I'm not strong enough?"

"You're strong enough. Trust in yourself."

Ehecacone nodded then looked into the fog stretching across the plain. "Is it far?"

"Under normal circumstances, not really; with my leg as it is, it will take a while."

In fact, it took longer than crossing the gorge in the snow. Even without putting any weight on my bad leg, every movement brought a cry of pain to my lips; at first I tried biting them back, but it felt better to let them go. Still, after a while, my head swam too much for the pain to register except on the periphery of my attention.

The fog swallowed us as soon as we started across the plain and we couldn't see much beyond a dozen paces around us. When we first headed into the fog, there was silence, save for our shuffling feet and my agonized cries, but as we went further in, a buzzing began to fill the air, and it grew in intensity with each passing moment; the volume didn't increase, but the sheer number of sounds did, like bees coming together at a hive. I didn't remember hearing this the last time I'd been here.

Ehecacone looked around anxiously. "What is that sound, Mother?"

"I don't know." My own anxiety began building.

Suddenly a man appeared from the fog, dressed like a warrior. Both Ehecacone and I stopped, startled. He stood facing to the side away from us, staring blankly at the ground, but when I called out to him, he looked up and the buzzing intensified. He gazed at us with haunted eyes, and when he turned towards us, I saw he bled from a gaping gash just below his ribcage on the right side. I immediately recognized it as a sacrificial wound. He said nothing and soon went back to staring at the ground, and as we pressed on, more like him appeared from the fog, all with that same hopeless look about them and a hole in their chests where someone had torn their hearts out.

Ehecacone gripped my hand even tighter, his breath growing rapidly. "Who are all these people, Mother?"

"I don't know." We'd seen hundreds so far, mostly clustered in small groups at the edge of our field of view, so there were likely thousands more out in the fog, unseen. They all watched us pass with forlorn gazes, and I choked a bit when I thought I spotted Ozomatli among them, dressed in his black high priest robes, the front untied and hanging open to show off his wounded chest. I looked away, overwrought with guilt, but when I looked back, the fog had consumed him again.

But when I saw my father standing ahead of us, by himself, my heart flopped. He didn't wear his royal regalia; instead he wore only a tattered night xicolli ripped open in the front, and his gruesome, ruined chest peered out at me, a grisly reminder of what I'd found when I came to his room that night that seemed so very long ago now.

I didn't realize I'd picked up my limping pace until I was within a few steps of him. "Tatli!" I cried, flinging my arms around him and hugging him tight. His jagged rib bones stuck me in the chest but I was just grateful to finally hold him again. In my memories, he had been a giant, and now that I held him again as a fully grown woman, he seemed larger than ever; I couldn't even reach all the way around him.

He didn't hug me back though. He stared down at me with a hollowness, so I gave up hugging him and instead held his face between my hands and looked up at him. His cheeks were so cold. "It's me, Father. Quetzalpetlatl."

There was still no recognition in his distant eyes; he looked confused and irritated. Disappointment punched me in the chest, and I let my hands drop back to my sides.

Ehecacone edged closer to me. "That's your father, Mother?"

I nodded, the tears coming fast. "My mortal father...your grandfather."

He eyed the gaping hole in Mixcoatl's chest. "What happened to him?"

"My uncle sacrificed him...." I looked around at the other men gathered around—I hadn't seen a single woman among them this entire time—and the truth of what I saw hit me. "These are all the Smoking Mirror's sacrifices!"

"Very good, Mayahuel!" a screechy voice spoke up behind us and I nearly fell over in fright.

But when we turned to find the skeletal figure dressed in a robe of brown and gray owl feathers looming over us, we both shrieked and went over backwards in a heap.

The creature chuckled, his transparent skin stretching thin over his skull. He wore a necklace of extruded eyeballs, but his own orbital sockets contained glowing blue orbs similar to those that swam around the tree outside Xolotl's house. Insects writhed up from beneath his bone-feet jutting out from under the hem of his robe, scattering in all directions.

Once I overcame my revulsion at the sight, my memory provided a name for the face. "Lord Death."

He bowed slightly, acknowledging my greeting.

A one-eyed, hunched-shouldered man lurked behind his robe, crouched close to the ground. "Xolotl," I said, my pulse rising again, this time in anger.

Ehecacone eyed both gods and clung to my arm like a monkey as I struggled back to my feet.

"My, you're looking quite the shambles, my dear," Lord Death said. "I confess myself surprised you would come back here again so soon, but I'm impressed that you took the difficult path."

"It wasn't by choice," I said. "I had no desire to ever come here again."

Xolotl shuffled out from behind him. "You should move beyond the sacrificial stone soon, My Lady, otherwise you'll die—"

"And I told you not to talk!" Lord Death made to slap Xolotl across the head with the back of his bone-hand, but Xolotl cowered and clamped both hands over his mouth. Appeased, Lord Death turned back to me and put his creepy smile back on. "He's of course right. Your time is nearly up."

I sneered at him. "And I'm sure that just slipped your mind until Xolotl mentioned it."

He kept smiling but now stepped aside, his arm held up to point the way for me. "Do hurry, my dear."

With a final glare, I shuffled forward again, Ehecacone still clinging to me. We soon exited the fog bank, coming out next to a large stone table.

The surface was slick with blood and a flint knife sat ready. I paused to look at it before Xolotl came up next to me and took my hand with his and led me on further.

Once we passed the table, I felt magic bubble up inside me, starting down in my toes. Such a sweet relief! As I'd hoped, my body started healing itself—my missing toes re-grew, my broken leg mended, and my burns disappeared. Magic pulsed in my fingertips; not strong, but enough to make the desire purr.

But Ehecacone's grip on my hand suddenly broke, making me stumble. I turned back to see him lying face-down on the ground, his body completely still, eyes staring blankly into the dust.

"Ehecacone!" I rushed to pick him up, but as soon as I touched him, flaming pain raged through my hands and arms. I tried to hold onto him through it, but soon the skin of my hands started blistering and the flesh swelled, threatening to burst. I had to let him go.

As soon as I did, my hands returned to normal and the pain disappeared, leaving me breathing heavily but unscathed.

"We mustn't touch what isn't ours anymore," Lord Death said with a gruesome grin.

The rage rose like a jaguar inside me and I flung myself at him. "Give me back my son!"

But Xolotl stepped between us, keeping me from colliding with Lord Death. I still flailed, swinging my fists at the grinning skeleton, but he held me back firmly.

"I'm tempted to tell him to let you go, Mayahuel," Lord Death said. "It would be amusing to see the look on your face when you realize that to touch the lord of death is to know death itself."

As his words sunk in, I stopped struggling against Xolotl and finally stepped away, pacing and feeling foolish for what I'd nearly done to myself. "I want my son back," I panted.

"Then you and I have business to discuss, don't we?"

Finally catching my breath and reclaiming my calm, I answered, "Indeed we do."

Lord Death motioned to Ehecacone. "Xolotl, gather him up and bring him along." He then started down the dusty path through the field of reeds leading to his palace of black glass in the distance. "Come along, my little thorny one," he told me.

I gritted my teeth at the name, but I followed behind Xolotl as he lugged Ehecacone upon his shoulder like a sack of masa, following his master's bony footsteps.

◻

Even though I'd spent eons in Mictlan, I'd never been inside Lord Death's palace. I wondered what new terrors awaited me in there. He led the way down a dusty stone path lined with gnarled, white leafless trees, with me and Xolotl following a few steps behind.

I stared at Xolotl's twisted back with contempt. "I can't believe Topiltzin and I wasted a perfectly good dog on you, you wretch," I hissed. "I should have known you'd take our sacrifice and then abandon my son to walk the road on his own."

Xolotl eyed me over his shoulder, looking as if he wanted to say something, but he didn't.

"And still nothing to say for yourself. How unsurprising, the one who once touted Quetzalcoatl's goodness turns out to be as two-faced as he is."

Xolotl flinched, but Lord Death broke into muted laughter. "There is a reason the humans fear both snakes and dogs: both are evil and strike without warning."

The palace's walls were made of bones pressed between thin sheets of obsidian, and the front doors resembled the gate on the stairs, except these were crowned with human skulls. I stared up at them as I passed through, unnerved that their empty gazes followed me.

The inside wasn't much better; skeletons of large predatory animals decorated the long main hallway, each articulated by way of Lord Death's glowing blue magic. I stared up at the huge lizard-creature with dagger-like fangs that formed the archway for the great hall—obviously the bones of an earth monster—and wondered if I was related to it in some way. Perhaps the mother or father missing from my recollections?

Xolotl loped ahead of his master and held open the great hall's large owl-feathered curtain with his free hand, my son still dangling over his gnarled shoulder. I stepped inside after Lord Death, but stopped to gawk at the floor-to-ceiling pane of obsidian glass forming the back wall, providing a dark view of the Black Lake and the foggy plain beyond.

A throne of bones plated in light green jade sat alone upon the dais before the window, and Lord Death alighted upon it with the grace of a bird of prey. He smoothed the owl-feather gown over his knobby knees. Where his feet touched the ground, insects burst from the stone floor, as if fleeing a coming flood. He reclined to the left side, resting his elbow against the only armrest—there wasn't one on the throne's right side.

I looked for somewhere to sit too, but apparently Lord Death didn't entertain guests. Xolotl propped Ehecacone against the obsidian pane then returned to the dais's step and sat there. I could have followed his example, but the thought of sitting so close to either of them gave me chills.

"So, my little thorny goddess, what brings you back home again?" Lord Death asked.

"This isn't my home," I snapped.

Lord Death chuckled. "And yet you've come back—"

"I didn't realize I was entering the underworld when I went past the gate."

"Then there are still holes in your memory? Understandable; you were dead a very long time. Regardless, Xolotl and I welcome you back."

"I don't intend to stay."

"Then we shall start by discussing the toll you intend to pay to leave again." Lord Death stared at me expectantly.

"Toll?"

"Everyone pays to pass through Mictlan, my dear. The dead must pay with their hearts, so it's only fair that the living offer me something too, am I right?"

I chewed my lip before saying, "I have nothing to give you."

He grinned wide, his blue glowing eyes intensifying. "If you were anyone else, Mayahuel, I would scold you for claiming you have nothing to barter with, for all gods have very high currency. But when you've been a goddess for so little time, I must excuse your ignorance of our ways. Come look." He rose and went to the pane overlooking the Black Lake. Once I joined him, he pointed out. "Your payment, my dear, resides out there."

I followed his gesture, beyond the Black Lake to the plain covered in fog. "I don't see anything."

"Why your sacrifices, of course."

"I don't have any sacrifices—"

"Oh, but there will be. Unless you're planning on dying again soon." He arched his hairless eyebrow ridge at me.

"Of course not."

"The longer you're alive, the more sacrifices you will accumulate, and they will all come here to linger in the mist, crowding the plain of Mictlan with their vacant stares and incessant buzzing." He grated his teeth but then put on a smile again. "I do not mind storing your sacrifices for you...for a price."

"But people only make offerings of octli and maguey spines to honor me."

"For now. But times change. Not all that long ago, Smoking Mirror settled for burnt tobacco, but now look at his collection of souls—"

"I'm nothing like Smoking Mirror," I shot back. "I'm happy with what the people give me."

"They all say that. But gods cannot live on devotion alone, not even the Feathered Serpent. Why else offer blood at all?"

I narrowed my eyes at him. "What exactly do you want from me?"

"You haven't a heaven to send your sacrifices to, so I hold them for you, and all I ask is a modest fee for my generosity."

I crossed my arms. "And what would that fee be, exactly?"

He stood taller, a broad smile on his face. "A portion of the magic you siphon off from your human sacrifices, of course."

That sounded reasonable. "How much do you want?"

"For every twenty sacrifices you accumulate, fourteen of those go directly to me."

"Fourteen?" I wanted to laugh, but given the meaningful look Xolotl gave me, I decided this was merely the opening offer. After scrutinizing Lord Death's robes a long moment, I countered, "One of twenty."

Now he laughed. "You insult me, child, but again, I will excuse your ignorance—for now. Twelve out of twenty."

"Three."

"Twelve."

"Eight."

"Twelve," he repeated, his smile stretching thinner with amusement.

"Ten?" I offered.

He raised his pale lips with derision. "Fourteen of twenty, Mayahuel. Or remain here forever."

I glared out at the Black Lake. I doubted he'd demanded such insulting terms of Smoking Mirror.

"Well?" Lord Death asked.

I turned the glare upon him. "Let me think about it."

He bowed his head. "Take your time." He looked highly pleased with himself. He shooed Xolotl out of his way as he stepped down off the dais.

It's ridiculous that he should get more magic from our sacrifices than we do! the desire hissed. *If only we didn't have to store them down here....*

"What must I do to get a heaven of my own, so you don't have to store sacrifices for me?"

He laughed. "You will never get a heaven of your own, my dear. Smoking Mirror has countless sacrifices and yet even he has yet to earn his own heaven. And as you've pointed out already, you don't even have any yet."

"So one gets their own heaven for their sacrifices by having enough people sacrificed to them?"

"Yes. And as you no doubt saw while venturing through the fog, that number can be uncountable." Lord Death crossed his arms. "I'm growing impatient, Mayahuel."

His demands weren't fair, but what choice did I have? I couldn't stay in the underworld for eternity. I may have descended from earth monsters, but I didn't share their love of the darkness. I craved the warmth of the sunlight, and if I had to agree to such an uneven split to get that back....

Maybe, but if we're not careful, we'll bargain away everything we have before we can negotiate for our son. My gaze fell to Ehecacone sitting slumped against the glass, oblivious. *Let me make a counter proposal while we still can.* "Fourteen out of twenty, but you also raise my son from the dead and he comes back to earth with me."

Lord Death shook his head, chuckling. "You ask so much but offer so little. No, the son of the Feathered Serpent is much more valuable than that."

"Then take fifteen out of twenty of my sacrifices."

"Not even all of your sacrifices will buy his life, Mayahuel, so don't waste your breath. He is valuable enough as he is right now."

I clenched my fists. "Name your price then."

With a grotesque grin, he answered, "Nothing short of giving me the Feathered Serpent himself would make me release your son."

"Then you shall have the Feathered Serpent," the desire growled for me.

My heart thudded. *Revenge won't bring Ehecacone back—*

Of course it will, you idiot, the desire snapped. *You heard Lord Death. And turning Quetzalcoatl over to him is no more than the snake deserves after what he's done to us.*

Lord Death stared back at me, intense. "Do not fool with me, Mayahuel."

I stood taller. "If I bring you Quetzalcoatl, will you give me back my son, alive and well?"

"And how exactly would you do that? The Feathered Serpent is the most powerful god in Omeyocan, and you...you're little more than a wisp of magic in the wind."

"That's for me to worry about, not you. If I fail, you're out nothing, right?"

Lord Death pondered before conceding, "That much is true."

"Ehecacone isn't the one you want sitting on the banks of the Black Lake; he's not the one who embarrassed you, who tricked you into surrendering what was rightfully yours." I pointed to the missing armrest on his throne, the bone the Feathered Serpent had taken to restore humanity long ago.

Lord Death hissed through his teeth. "Indeed not."

"You will finally have your revenge, and all it will cost you is a fledgling god."

The grin returned and Lord Death rubbed his bone-hands together. "I have waited so long for this...."

"Then we have a deal?" I held my hand out to him.

He looked at it with an amused smile. "I don't think you want to do that, my dear. To touch death is to know death, remember?"

I withdrew, embarrassed by my mistake, but pressed on. "Well?"

"Bring me Quetzalcoatl and I will return your son to you. Those are the terms."

"And you open the way out of here, so I can fetch your prize," I added.

"Done." He looked around, seemingly lost in his own scheming, and as an afterthought, he added, "Xolotl will escort you out."

I took one last look at Ehecacone, feeling resolute. *I will see you again very soon, my little Warm Breeze.* I then followed Xolotl—now in dog form—out of the great hall.

But when we reached the front doorway, Lord Death materialized, blocking my way. "You're right that I lose nothing by accepting this deal," he said, "but should you fail to deliver as promised, remember that I have your son and I can raise him from the dead at any time, for any reason—including making him pay for your failures. Don't fail me, Mayahuel."

The desire bristled, but I kept a calm demeanor. "I won't fail you, My Lord."

"And don't take forever," he warned. "I'm not a patient god."

"Neither am I." I then followed Xolotl out the doorway.

CHAPTER FIVE

Xolotl kept up his silence as we climbed the steep stone stairs out of the underworld; he didn't even look back when I asked him if he knew where I could find Mextli, since I hadn't found any sign nor heard any whisper of the war god since our last meeting in Teotihuacan. Mextli had offered me his assistance back then and now I needed that help more than ever.

Seeing the sun again brought such joy I nearly cried. "It feels like years since I've stood in sunlight," I said as I stopped in a beam shooting down from the opening of the cenote. It wasn't the same one I'd entered the underworld from; here the air was dry and hot, and the pool of water was shallow and brackish. I couldn't see any trees or bushes around the lip of the cenote, and there wasn't a cloud to be seen.

Xolotl said nothing, just vanished. For a moment I thought he'd left me, but then I saw him at the lip of the cenote, peering back down at me over the edge.

"How do you do that?" I called up to him. "Be here one breath and suddenly up there the next?"

Xolotl merely snorted.

I looked around until I found a place to climb out, but even then it took me a long time to finally pull myself up over the lip of the cenote.

The bare ground was blistering under my hands and the sun shone blindingly down on me, so I had to shield my eyes when I looked around. A vast desert stretched around us for as far as I could see in any direction. "Why did you bring me here?" When he just stared at me, a frown on his ugly, mangled dog face, I sneered back at him. "Fine. I don't need your help anymore, so along with you."

He sighed and turned to leave, but then he stopped. He turned back into his deformed human body and knelt to scribble something in the dirt. I watched him, but the symbols he drew made no sense to me. He looked up at me and pointed at them, an eager expression in his black eyes. When I shook my head, he pointed to my eyes and then back at the writing, more vehemently this time.

"If you want to say something to me, just say it!" I cried, annoyed.

He opened his mouth as if to speak, but then grimaced, as if suddenly gripped with pain. He swallowed then pointed to the drawings once more, a sad expression on his face. When I shook my head, exasperated, he turned back into the black dog and jogged away. He jumped down into the cenote, but I heard no splash, and when I went to look inside, he was gone.

I returned to the writing in the sand and stood staring at it, growing increasingly vexed.

But the longer I stared at it, the more meaning crept into my brain. First one word, then another, as if I were reading a language I had known as a young child but forgot from lack of use. Eventually the meaning came to me.

Mind whom you put your trust and faith in.

"I've learned that the hard way," I muttered, sweeping the words away with my bare foot, disgusted. "I don't need reminders."

◻

Unsure what else to do, I sought shelter from the sun by heading for a large rock formation to the north. A single spindly mesquite tree grew in the shade, but there wasn't much else to be found once I got there. I sat down to survey the desert and decide what to do next. There had to be some way I could find Mextli.

At first glance, the land seemed dead, but the wildlife slowly made its presence known. Fluffy white clouds trooped across the sky, providing a good canvas for the hawks, buzzards, and eagles soaring overhead. A multitude of biting flies buzzed around me, though they quickly dropped to the ground in death throes after sampling my golden blood. A brown lizard watched me from the side of the rock formation, his black eyes shimmering like obsidian in the sunlight, and a tan rattlesnake slithered out of the shade to bask in the sunlight. All harsh creatures for a harsh environment. I couldn't imagine any humans surviving out here. I sat watching the animals and insects go about their routines for an hour or more, until suddenly I heard scraping behind me.

I looked over my shoulder to see a group of men standing at the corner of the rock formation. They wore little clothing; mostly deer skin breeches that went to their knees, though some also had vests, but they all wore gnarled leather sandals. They'd smeared mud over all their exposed skin— to protect their skin from the blistering sun?—and a few wore headdresses of hawk or eagle feathers fanned over their foreheads, to shield their eyes from the harsh light. Every man carried a weapon —flint-headed spears and knives, thick wooden clubs, and the occasional bow.

I didn't move as they scrutinized me, but when I heard more noise, I turned to see more of them in front of me, surrounding me. In response, a surge of desire slithered through me. *Lucky us! We need something to replenish our magic.*

The lead man—who had painted the left side of his mud-covered face blue—spoke to the man next to him, and that man in turn motioned to the others, who then pressed slowly in towards me, weapons held loose but ready. I held my hands up, signaling my surrender.

They took me around to the other side of the rocks where still more people stood—twenty-three in all: three guards and twenty men bound together by a long length of leather rope tied around their necks. Many of the wounded had been carefully patched up, but they all looked upon me with dead eyes. The guards however regarded me with expressions of dreamy longing, but they soon broke it off when the leader barked and cuffed each. They hurried for an extra length of rope from a deerskin bag one of them held.

"You needn't tie me up," I tried to assure the leader. "I'll come willingly."

He seemed to understand me, for he held his hand up to the man with the rope, but when he spoke to me next, I had no idea what he said. The language wasn't like the dialects spoken back in the valley, or even Tollan. "I'm sorry, but I don't understand," I told him and he looked at me in puzzlement. He spoke again, slower this time, but still I couldn't make much of it, so I held my hands up and shook my head.

He took the rope but instead of tying it around my neck—like the others—he tied it loosely around my waist. He looked up at me expectantly and I nodded my agreement. Whatever would make him comfortable. Hopefully we could develop enough trust that by the time night fell, he wouldn't feel the need to bind me when he brought me to his bed, making my escape easier once I'd replenished my magic from him.

But to my surprise, we walked no more than an hour before I spotted a large encampment on the horizon. The warriors hooted and smiled, and they prodded the group of prisoners to go faster. The leader kept hold of my rope the whole time, remaining silent and stoic as an example to his men, though when women came running from the tents to greet us, he finally cracked a smile and embraced a woman who ran to him. She looked a few years younger than me, and was round with child. Three small children rushed to greet him too, the eldest no more than six or seven, and the youngest—the only boy—no more than a year old, judging from how tightly he held his sisters' hands as they helped him. The woman gave me a cursory glance but then returned her smiling attention to the man—*Her husband,* I concluded. He handed my rope off to one of the other men then hefted his son up onto his shoulders and took his wife by the hand. He walked the rest of the way into camp with his family.

The sight left me feeling melancholy; not all that long ago, that had been me and Little Reed and Ehecacone. *But it will be again, soon,* I reassured myself. *Or at the very least you'll have your son back.*

More women and children hurried from the tents to see their husbands and fathers. I garnered just as much attention as the warriors paraded us through the encampment to the central area where several shamans awaited us.

Their faces were painted black with gold stripes across their cheeks. The hairs on my nape stood up. *Priests of Smoking Mirror?*

They looked us over one by one, nodding at each prisoner in turn, but when they came to me, they conferred in whispers until the head priest nodded. They hurried me from the line as a third priest started flicking his blood-soaked fingers at each man in a purifying ceremony. A woman handed out bits of plant for them to eat.

A tall, pointy-nosed man dressed in bones and a feathered headdress came from across camp to examine the line of prisoners. *Not the chief, but maybe his son,* I concluded, given his youthful arrogance and the guards hovering nearby. His gaze clouded when he saw me, then he turned to talk to the priests. Much discussion ensued, but when he pointed at me, the priests' words turned heated. The man grew increasingly agitated, but when the head priest pointed to another tent not far beyond us—sitting in front of a sacrificial stone—the young man frowned and snapped something, but turned and walked away. The priests grinned at each other but then wrenched me over to the tent overlooking the altar.

I'd hoped they would leave me there alone, so I might sneak off, but one of them remained, holding my rope while the other returned to the line of sacrifices.

A crowd began gathering in the center of the encampment and the priests took to chanting and laying out baskets and flint blades. They waited until the first man in the prisoner line started swaying on his feet, then the head priest made a speech in front of the crowd. The men and women listened with rapt attention; even the children stood silent and reverent. I listened carefully too, but I couldn't make anything out of it.

When the head priest gave the signal, his assistants cut the first prisoner loose from the ropes and dragged him towards the sacrificial stone. He didn't fight; he stared around with wide, awestruck eyes, drooling from the side of his mouth. He didn't resist when they laid him over the stone, his chest puffed out, and he didn't scream when the head priest cut him open and pulled his heart out with the quickness of a seasoned professional; he just slowly drifted away as the other priests hoisted his body off the stone. They tossed it aside, where a small group of women relieved it of the head and slashed the wrists before stringing the body up by the ankles from a tree growing behind the tent. There they collected the blood in a large clay jar; a curiously bulky item for a nomadic people to keep. Before that first one was even fully hung, the priests had hustled the second man to the stone and the head priest extracted his heart too. With this efficiency, they would make it through all the prisoners in less than an hour.

I managed to observe the first full process without losing my composure, but with sickening heat rising up inside me at the sight of so much gore, I took to staring at the side of the tent I stood next to. My heart thudded painfully loud in my ears as memories of my human father swept upon me. I only looked up again when the flap on the tent swished open to my left.

Given the priests' decorations, I'd expected they were Smoking Mirror worshippers, but instead a giant of a man came out. He wore only a loincloth, showing off the fact that the entire left side of his body was painted blue, and when he stood straight, he towered over everyone. I couldn't fathom how he'd ever fit into that tiny tent, but like myself he glowed, with a soft turquoise color. *Mextli!* It seemed Xolotl had been listening after all.

The people chanted but lay prostrate upon the ground, trembling in terror as he settled onto the mat in front of his tent and pulled one of the dripping baskets of hearts over in front of him. The head priest approached, prostrating himself, but then hurried forward when Mextli motioned him to stand up straight. The priest whispered to him, pointing at me, but Mextli thundered, "War prizes go out after I've eaten my fill." He then started shoveling handfuls of hearts from the basket into his broad mouth.

I moved towards him, but the priest holding my rope pulled me back. I yanked in response, but my strength wasn't a match, so I shouted, "Mextli!"

PART TWO:
THE YEAR EIGHT FLINT

Chapter Six

"Mextli!" I cried as the priest nearly yanked me off my feet. "It's me! Mayahuel!"

But Mextli was so engrossed in the hearts that he either ignored me or didn't hear me. Given his insistence that I had a friend in him, I chose to believe it was the latter, and so pulled what magic I could muster to my hands and unleashed it on the priest.

The attack took the priest by surprise and he went over with a yelp. This drew the attention of the warriors guarding the sacrifices and they rushed towards me, but I sent them tumbling with another shot of magic. It only disoriented them though—I'd have to dig very deep into my magic stores to incapacitate them, and I didn't dare let myself become completely helpless. Instead I took off running, heading for Mextli.

The head priest stopped with the bloody blade poised above his head when he saw me. He shouted, and the other two priests dropped the dead body they'd been carrying then moved to cut me off. I ran into them full-speed and we went down in a heap right in front of Mextli, tipping over the baskets of hearts. I rolled over and landed right in Mextli's lap.

But he dumped me unceremoniously on the ground when he rose to his feet, roaring in displeasure. Wetness soaked through my tattered dress where I landed and an unpleasant liquid squish accompanied it when I moved to sit up. Mextli grabbed me one-handed, his giant fingers encircling both my neck and right shoulder as he hauled me up, a wild, alien look churning in his wide eyes. He flexed his free hand and a flint blade materialized in it.

"Mextli! It's me! Mayahuel!" I gasped. "Surely you remember me?"

He glared at me with hard, implacable eyes, but slowly the expression softened into recognition. "Mayahuel?" Embarrassment lit his fleshy cheek as he lowered me gently to the ground. "It is you!"

I finally breathed again, but when I looked down to see I'd reduced most of the hearts to a juicy, dirt-coated pulp, I cringed. "Forgive me...about your meal."

He looked down at the mess under my feet and frowned, annoyed, but when he looked up at me again, he looked contrite. "Never mind that; the humans will bring me more. Forgive me for not recognizing you and...manhandling you so."

"No harm done." Though the memory of that focused anger and dispassion troubled me. As did the words Xolotl had written in the dust only a few hours ago.

The priests had scrambled away when Mextli lunged to his feet, but now all three crawled back, crying and scraping at his feet. He waved them away, disgusted. "Never mind the mess. Bring me what's left and next time you will make up for the loss."

They bowed deeply as they backed away, groveling. The rest of the crowd stood in terrified silence, so Mextli whispered, "Let us talk where we have no audience." And he ducked inside the tiny tent, leaving the flap swaying in the hot evening air.

I glanced back at the watching crowd, not entirely trusting the priests or soldiers to not come at me again, but everyone just stared, so I too ducked inside the tent.

I expected to run into Mextli immediately upon entry, but to my amazement, I now stood in the entrance of a great hall similar to the one in any palace. An icpalli throne made of rushes and eagle feathers sat at one end, though it was massive compared to my throne back in Tollan. It creaked and strained under Mextli's weight as he sat down. "Please, come sit." He picked up two clay cups and dipped them into a large vat sitting next to the throne.

When I came forward and accepted a cup, I found it was filled with blood. So this was what the women were doing out there with the remains of the sacrifices. My heart rebelled at the thought of drinking it, but I was so low on magic.... *Forgive me,* I thought and drained the cup in one mighty swig. I wasn't even sure who I was begging forgiveness from, but it felt like the right thing to do.

Euphoria filled my veins as the magic surged, and I swallowed down a second cup after Mextli refilled it for me. "Thank you," I whispered, feeling half-drunk from the pulsing magic beneath my skin. Not as powerful as the aftermath of taking a man to bed, but good enough for now. I settled down on the floor next to the throne, unsure if I could keep my feet much longer.

"My pleasure." Mextli drained his own cup then set it aside. "You looked as if you needed it."

I gazed around the room, taking in the murals of bloody battle decorating the walls, and the sunlight leaking in through the exposed windows. "What is this place?"

"My house, of course."

"But the tent...it's so small!"

"Makes it very easy for the humans to transport it when they move, as they often do."

"But how...can it be so big inside?"

Mextli chuckled. "We are gods, Mayahuel; what do such human concepts mean to us? We can exist inside a grain of sand if we wish, or within one of the countless grains within that single grain." He shook his head. "The Feathered Serpent truly taught you nothing, did he?"

Mention of Quetzalcoatl made me surly, and again reminded me of why I was here. "Indeed not."

Mextli nodded. "I'm glad you sought me out, though I'd hoped you would do so much sooner than this."

"I found you as soon as I could. It's only been a few months."

"Have you become so lost you cannot keep track of time anymore? It's been five years, Mayahuel."

"Five years!" But then, I had been in Mictlan a long time, and it was said that time didn't move in the same way there as it did on the mortal plane.

I wasn't sure I wanted to tell him yet about my trip into Mictlan or my deal with Lord Death—especially in light of Xolotl's warning—so I opted for, "I guess I have been quite lost since that night in Teotihuacan, and you didn't tell me where to find you."

"I didn't," he conceded. "I just assumed...well, I assumed wrong, and I apologize."

Someone cleared their throat and I looked towards the entrance to see the high priest on his knees, bent in supplication over a basket of hearts.

The other two priests carried the large jar of blood upon their shoulders, but they kept their eyes downcast. A pool of crimson gathered on the floor under the basket. The head priest said something and bowed deeply.

Mextli rose, looking deadly serious. "Bring your offerings forward then."

The three men hurried to deposit the blood jar next to the one already there and they placed the basket of hearts at Mextli's feet. They slashed their palms with their flint knives and babbled reverently in their foreign tongue as they squeezed their wounded hands over the hearts, continuing the litany until Mextli interrupted them, irritated. "Yes yes, and keep the darkness from overcoming the day. I accept your offering and promise to rise again tomorrow in the east, and see the Mexica forward on their journey to greatness."

The priests muttered in gratitude and backed slowly down the hall and out the tent flap on the other side of the arched stone doorway.

Mextli sat and pulled the basket between his feet. He started to take a bite out of one of the hearts but then he held it out to me. "Hungry?" The look on his face reminded me of a petulant child who'd been told he must share his toys.

The blood oozed off the organ, painting Mextli's bare hand red, making my heart race. Panicked heat rose in my gut. I'd only ever held an actual human heart twice in my short life—first my father's when my uncle had cut it from him, and then that poor man Black Otter murdered on the pretense of summoning Smoking Mirror. I had no desire to ever hold another. "Thank you, but no." I didn't catch the grimace in time though.

He chuckled like a coyote, that sharp, cruel look in his eyes again. "We all have our particular appetites. Tell me what yours is and I'll order the priests to bring it for you right away, and we can share our first meal in friendship." He popped the heart into his mouth as if it were a small nut.

What a ridiculous scene that would be—Mextli chewing hearts on his throne while I ravaged someone on the floor in front of him—yet the desire purred like an interested jaguar. "Blood is all I need," I assured him with a feigned smile.

"Nonsense! I pride myself on being a good host, so come, tell me what I can get for you."

"Truly, the blood is enough."

"Enough? Of course it's enough, when there's nothing else available.

No one lives on blood alone, Mayahuel; that would be like...like the humans eating nothing but cactus—it keeps them alive during famine, but they don't ignore all the other things they can eat—things that make them healthier and stronger—"

"Blood is just fine!" My cheeks lit with heat; I hadn't intended to yell.

Mextli scrutinized me then said, "Those humans you lived with...they made you ashamed about how you feed, didn't they? Probably told you it was evil. You don't have to be embarrassed anymore, Mayahuel. You're among your own kind now." When I didn't answer, he sighed but asked, "Would you like more blood then?"

I handed my cup to him and when he returned it refilled, I stared into it instead of drinking. "Forgive my snappishness. These last five years have been difficult...and trying. I thought I would never find you."

"Forgive my not telling you where I would be. I just assumed you'd know how to find me."

"I'm afraid my knowledge of everyday living as a goddess is poor at best."

"Then our first order of business shall be to fix that. What kinds of things can you do already?" When I hesitated, he added, "So I know where to focus our efforts."

When I still resisted answering, the desire growled, *If we aren't going to accept his help, why in Mictlan did we seek him out at all?*

"Well, I can't do much; there's the maguey plants, as you know—I can make them do things for me, like attack enemies with their roots and spines. I can also talk to rabbits."

"Your nahual, maybe?"

"I think so, but I haven't worked as much with them as with the maguey."

"But that's not your most potent magic. I saw what you did on that temple top in Chimalhuacan."

I'd rendered half the city intoxicated with a good stiff push of magic, and even poisoned King Toxtli when he stabbed me. "It is very powerful magic, but I don't have control over it." An understatement, considering I'd nearly killed Little Reed with it.

Mextli waved me off. "Our most powerful magic always takes the longest to properly cultivate. What else?"

I shrugged. "That's it."

"What about using the teoyoh?" When I squinted at him, not understanding, he went on, "Moving from place to place with magic?" When I shook my head, he looked taken aback. "How do you travel around?"

"I walk, of course."

"Walk!" Mextli leaned forward, muttering under his breath.

"I don't mind walking," I assured him. "I had to do it all the time when I was a human being—"

"You're not a human being, Mayahuel; you're a goddess, and a goddess who can't use the teoyoh...how can you ever go to Omeyocan, or travel safely into Mictlan if you haven't that one simple, most important skill? A god who can't use the teoyoh is hardly a god at all!"

I hadn't even considered that I could go to Omeyocan now that I was a goddess again, and to my shame, the thought terrified me. What if I came upon my grandmother? What would she do? She'd already killed me once, so why not again?

"The Feathered Serpent had no right to keep these things from you," Mextli grumbled.

"No, but then my grandmother didn't teach me much of anything either."

"I will teach you everything you need to know to get along," Mextli said, returning to his hearts.

Good. I was one step closer to getting Ehecacone back then.

I sipped at the blood in my cup while Mextli ate with increasing fervor. When he finished, he tossed the empty basket aside then lounged back against his icpalli, a blood-drunk haze to his eyes. When I finally spoke again, he didn't look at me, lost in his own thoughts, but eventually he turned to me. "What?"

"Who taught you? About being a god?"

"Smoking Mirror," he said with a nostalgic smile, though it soon slipped away. "Most of it, anyway. Some things you have to learn about on your own. But I will teach you everything I know."

I gave him a grateful smile. "Thank you, Mextli."

He started to smile back, but stopped suddenly. "Enough talk. Let's get started. First lesson: how to locate other gods." He sat straighter on his icpalli, reminding me of when my foster mother Nimilitzli gave lectures to her new students at the calmecac. "First, you do know what teotl is, right?"

"Never heard of it," I admitted.

He shook his head, grumbling, but then replied, "Teotl is the essence of everything; it's the very nature of the gods: we are beings of energy at our most basic, and that energy permeates everything and can manipulate both the visual and invisible world." He set both of his hands against his bare chest. "I created this body to house my teotl, just as you created yours, but...this is where it gets tricky. You see, everything living has its own teotl—trees, animals, even humans—but those are different than divine teotl; whereas ours can manipulate and change the world at will, for humans, their teotl is trapped in their bodies until death frees it. That's why we are immortal and they are not. They...taste different than us."

I raised a dubious eyebrow. "Taste?"

Mextli chuckled. "Humans are quite tasty, don't you think? We cannot help but crave their teotl—"

"And that's why we drink their blood, and eat their...." I motioned to the basket lying on the floor.

"Exactly. Divine teotl tastes different; it tastes like...power."

"I don't know what power tastes like."

"I couldn't describe it to you, but I can say that it tingles the senses, and it doesn't trigger the hunger the way human teotl does. When you finally learn to taste it, you will know it immediately."

Now I was thoroughly intrigued. "So how do I learn to taste it?"

"Close your eyes and clear your mind. Focus on your senses. Since you're surrounded by my teotl here in my house, it shouldn't take you long to detect it."

I did as he told me, using my priestly training to focus my mind.

Soon my skin started tingling and a smell began permeating my nose, spreading to my sinuses and filling my mouth—a sweet nectar smell, like honeysuckle in full-bloom. I imagined a garden filled with flowers, teeming with ruby-throated hummingbirds zipping from blossom to blossom. A pleasant feeling—like being wrapped in a warm blanket— swept over me. "I'm not tasting anything but...you smell like flowers! Do we all smell like this?"

"Each god's teotl is unique, and every god experiences divine teotl differently, so perhaps you don't taste it as such," Mextli said.

"The smell is very potent—not unpleasant, mind you—but it's very all-encompassing."

"That's because you're sitting in a bubble of my magic; you are literally surrounded by my teotl."

It sounded so intimate, almost sexual, but given the nonchalance he said it with, I doubted he meant it that way. I finally opened my eyes again. "What do I smell like?"

Mextli shrugged. "I don't experience the world in such a manner, so I wouldn't know how to describe it to you."

"Then what do I taste like?" The desire cackled in my head and my cheeks heated with embarrassment.

But Mextli didn't miss a beat. "Like pain; a victim."

I furrowed my brows. "I'm no victim, thank you. Maybe at one time someone took advantage of my innocence, but that's not who I am."

"Of course not. But whether we like it or not, our pasts leave their mark on us, often in ways we're completely unaware of. It is not a criticism, Mayahuel, just a truth. But you didn't let me finish. Yes, you taste of pain and having been betrayed, but you also taste of ambition and confidence. It is an intriguing mix."

"Then we can change our teotl? You said our pasts mark us, so the present can do the same, changing the way we taste or smell?"

"It never fundamentally changes, if that's what you're asking. The past will always be a part of you, but new experiences will join them, creating a different overall impression. The older the god, the more nuanced the teotl."

I smelled the air again, intrigued. Mextli's scent seemed rather straightforward at first, but the longer I studied it, the more different impressions popped out at me; sunlight, decomposition, water, an unidentified animal smell. *He's quite complicated,* I thought, wondering what it all meant. *And I bet Quetzalcoatl smells like snakes and lies.*

Mextli rose from his throne. "You'll understand more once you meet more gods and goddesses, and once you learn a specific god's teotl, you can find them anywhere on earth or in Heaven. In your case, you would just let your nose lead the way."

"You mean I can smell all the others right now?"

"Of course, but until you know whom you're smelling, it does little good. Come. I'm supposed to address my humans after the meal, to assure them that I'm happy with their offering, and that they need not fear my wrath tonight."

CHAPTER SEVEN

I was startled to see night had fallen when we stepped out of the tent. I hadn't thought we'd been inside for all that long. The humans still gathered in the center of camp, clustered around bonfires eating and laughing, but when Mextli strode out into the middle of the crowd, the priests scrambled forward, prostrating themselves until Mextli motioned them back to their feet. Everyone else looked on with anxiety.

"I thank every one of you for tonight's feast. The Mexica are truly a great and strong people, and all tremble before their might!" When Mextli raised his feathered fist to the sky, the men hooted and raised their fists too. But there wasn't a smile to be found among the crowd. "I know life in the desert is hard and everyone suffers, but continue to invest your faith in me and I will see you and your children elevated to greatness. The day will come when you will finally see the eagle's shadow and look up to see it carrying the sign, and it will lead you home. This I promise you."

The priests said something and the rest of the crowd repeated it, bowing their heads in prayer. Mextli stood silent, listening to the litany, but eventually he told everyone to rise again. "I must also thank you for an unexpected gift." He turned and motioned to me.

After a hesitation, I joined him at the center of camp.

"This is Lady Mayahuel, Goddess of the Maguey. She will be staying with us."

A murmur traveled through the crowd—and I noticed several of the warriors who'd captured me looking like they'd swallowed a leech.

The priests though flung themselves on the ground at my feet, groveling, and though I didn't understand a word they said, the cadence of their voices spoke of fear. Perhaps because they'd planned to give me away as a war prize? "It's quite all right," I assured them, reaching down to help them back to their feet.

But when I touched the nearest one, he shrieked as if I'd burned him. I jumped back, startled.

But he rose to his feet, a look of ecstasy on his face. He babbled incoherently, tears streaming down his face even as he smiled.

"What did I do?" I murmured, backing away still more.

Mextli chuckled. "Humans believe a simple touch from a god means the universe."

I watched the man, feeling foolish. I'd spent much of my mortal life believing myself god-touched because Quetzalcoatl's nahual had bitten me, so why hadn't I anticipated such a reaction? *I need to be more careful interacting with these humans.*

The man stepped toward Mextli but kept his eyes downcast as he spoke. Mextli listened, nodding, but then replied, "She'll need her own tent, and from now on, you will see to her needs. I relieve you of your duties to me."

The priest bowed deeper, his smile nearly reaching his ears. He then spoke to me, keeping his eyes downcast too as he did. When he stopped, waiting expectantly, I looked at Mextli. "I don't understand a word your people say."

"That's because you're still thinking in human language," Mextli said with a gentle ribbing. "Once you relearn the language of the gods, you'll be able to understand anyone who speaks to you, regardless of what language they use."

"How can that be?"

"Because our language is the source of all other languages. I know it probably makes no sense right now, but once you start learning and remembering...it will."

I looked at the man again, who was still waiting on my answer. "What did he say?"

"He asked where you would like your tent set up, and what he can bring you to eat."

"I don't need anything to eat, thank you. As for the tent...?" I looked around before turning to Mextli for guidance.

"Next to my own will be sufficient for now," Mextli told the man. Once the man bowed and shuffled backwards from us, Mextli told me, "You really should eat some more. We have much work to do tomorrow, so you should be fully nourished."

"What kind of work?"

"I will teach you how to use the teoyoh. It is the most important magic a god needs to master in order to get along in life, so that's our top priority. We'll start at dawn."

"Why not tonight?"

"I have other engagements. And you need time to feed; learning to use the teoyoh takes a lot of energy, so don't think that blood alone will suffice. Eat as much as you can and we'll meet up again in the morning."

A couple of warriors came forward with the makings of a tent and the priests directed them where to set it up. Once they finished, my new head priest held the flap open and bowed. I peered inside to find it was just an ordinary tent, like the ones soldiers used while on the march. It would be a tight fit for two people, and there was no way Mextli could come inside. "Kind of small for a goddess, isn't it?" I asked Mextli with a crooked grin.

He waved me off. "I'll teach you how to expand it later, but will it do for tonight?"

"It will be fine."

"I must go then."

"You're leaving?" When he arched an eyebrow at the panic in my voice, I swallowed and added, "Sorry. It's just...I don't know these people—"

"You have nothing to fear, Mayahuel. They will treat you like the goddess you are; they will worship you the way you should have been worshipped all along."

I nodded then added, "Thank you for your kindness, and understanding."

My words seemed to startle him, but once he recovered, he bowed his head. "It is my pleasure." He vanished with a snapping sound.

Everyone was watching, waiting for me to speak. After an uncomfortably long pause, I announced, "Everyone, please, go back to your feast." I had to repeat myself a couple times before the sounds of conversation and music filled the air again.

The priests remained standing in front of me, expectant expressions on their faces. My high priest bowed again as he spoke, but I couldn't hear him over the noise. "I would like to speak with you alone, if possible," I told him. When he motioned to my tent, I shook my head. "Somewhere else; some place quiet, so we can better hear each other."

His face lit and he started towards the north, motioning me to follow him with a sweeping bow. I did so.

The camp was surprisingly large, with many tents; Lord Ten Spines's tribe had consisted of less than fifty people, but this one was easily several hundred strong. The priest wound through the field of tents, leaving the celebratory noise behind.

Eventually we came out the other side of camp, onto a moon-drenched plain dotted with maguey plants. I couldn't help but smile. I reached out with a thread of magic in greeting and the magueys answered in silent excitement, making my chest swell with joy. That feeling only grew brighter when I noticed a few rabbits poking their heads out from holes near the bases of the maguey. "This is perfect!" I whispered.

The priest asked me something, but it sounded like nonsense to my ears. I motioned him to sit down, and once he did, I sat opposite him. I opened my mouth to explain that I didn't understand him, but the desire piped up, *We can't reveal our shortcomings. He must think we are all-powerful and all-knowing, to keep his respect.*

But how can I learn his language if I keep making him repeat everything he says? I protested. But before the desire could growl out a response, the answer came to me. "Do you know any of my prayers, priest?"

He shook his head and muttered a word I assumed meant "no". Perfect.

"I'm going to teach you all the prayers," I told him then started doing so, one line at a time and making him repeat them after me. By the time he'd memorized the first prayer, the fog around my understanding began lifting and when we finished an hour later, I'd taught him twelve different prayers and I could understand everything he spoke, even when I asked him to teach me some of the prayers they said to honor Mextli. I'd always been very good with language—I'd been able to speak in complex sentences before my second year alive, and I'd learned to speak several of the Chichimec tongues fluently within a few months of first hearing them when I was human—but as a goddess, that talent had more than quadrupled. "You've done a wonderful job," I told the priest once we'd finished with the language lesson.

"You honor me, My Most Great Lady of the Maguey," he said, prostrating himself on the ground in front of me. "I will endeavor to serve you with the utmost loyalty and effectiveness."

"I don't doubt it."

He beamed but then turned serious again. "Now that I have learned the sacred prayers, I wish to instruct the people in honoring you. We know His Lord from the South requires the hearts of warriors, but what sacrifices should we make to please you, My Lady?"

Lie down and let me show you, priest, the desire growled, hungry and eager; just imagining it brought a shiver of anticipation. But when I forced the desire back, it snarled, *Mextli said to feed in preparation for tomorrow.*

We have but one priest, and we both know what kind of man he'll become after we bring him to our bed, I reminded her. *We can't feed on him.*

Fine, the desire hissed, petulant, but it argued no further.

"I don't want sacrifices," I told the priest. "But there are a few things you can do to honor me."

"My life is to please you, My Lady. Tell me what you require."

"The normal ritual bloodlettings with thorns are good. But please, *please* don't paint yourself with the blood." I tried not to wrinkle my nose at his blood-smeared appearance but failed. "Just...provide it in a cup for me to drink."

"No wearing the blood," the priest confirmed.

"I'd also prefer you be clean, and wear fresh clothing."

"Then you wish me to make a pilgrimage to the cenote to wash my old life away?"

"No. Just use some of the water from the rain jars and that will be sufficient." He looked puzzled and a bit unsure, so I said, "You have a question?"

"No. It is not important. What the goddess asks shall be done."

I furrowed my brow. "No. Tell me."

"No one uses the water for anything but drinking. Lord Tlaloc seldom pours his jars upon us here, and it is a long journey to the cenote, especially carrying the water jars—"

"Of course," I muttered, embarrassed to not have thought of it myself. "I've changed my mind; no more blood, but no wasting the camp's water. I will bring you water myself." After all, the cenote wasn't far at all if I could use the teoyoh.

The priest nodded, relieved. "What else do you require of me, Most Great Lady of the Maguey?"

Bring me a man to soothe my hunger, priest! the desire growled, but I pushed it aside again. I couldn't think of any way to broach the subject without my intent becoming embarrassingly transparent.

Embarrassing? We don't answer to humans, you fool!

"That's all for now," I replied, feeling flushed and bothered despite my attempts to muzzle the rising desire. "Now, if you don't mind, I'd rather be alone for the rest of the evening."

He bowed. "Of course, My Lady." He started backing away, but before turning to leave, he asked, "Do you wish me to have the men set up your temple out here?"

"Perhaps in the morning." I gazed up into the night sky with a smile. "For now, the stars and the heavens are shelter enough." Especially after so long trapped in the underworld.

¤

Time passed much quicker when I was still human; as a goddess, I didn't sleep, which meant having to find ways to fill the time, and each moment felt like counting the grains of sand upon an infinite beach.

After the priest left, I walked among the maguey, running my hands over their giant, fleshy leaves, pausing to tap my fingertip on the sharp spines and feel the plants' contented energy seep through my skin. It was almost like being home.

Except Little Reed wasn't here with me. Not a day went by where I didn't regret that decision to not see him one last time, to explain to him the truth about myself and why I had to leave. I'd often thought to go back, just to say goodbye to him, but I knew it would be a mistake. Without my love magic distracting him from his wife, I imagined Little Reed would finally have gotten over his aversion to bedding her and that they would now have a handful of beautiful children to carry on the royal legacy in Tollan. I also imagined that Citlallotoc and Little Reed had mended their differences over me, and that Citlallotoc had finally found someone who made him happy and appreciated the man he was. Tollan was no doubt thriving like never before now that her leaders weren't so distracted by silly things.

I tried to feel happy that so many would prosper with me out of the way, but at the same time, to feel thus would be to admit that I deserved no happiness myself, or that others could only be happy in the wake of my own misery. Maybe things could be different here? I was still surrounded by humans, but I was also among my own kind, and I didn't have to hide my true nature anymore. I could embrace it the way I never could back in Tollan. And getting Ehecacone back would go a long way to improving my happiness.

Still, a part of me longed to see Little Reed at least once more....

Footsteps drew me from my thoughts and I looked back toward camp to see a man heading my direction. At first I thought it was my priest, but as he came closer, I recognized him as the young man who'd spoken to the priests earlier, about me. Now that I understood the Mexicas' language, my once again perfect memory provide the content of that discussion to me; he'd asked them for me, to honor his position as the future chief, but the priests had scoffed and said I belonged to the god, and so Mextli would give me to whomever he deemed worthy, which was highly unlikely to be him.

"You call yourself a warrior and yet you've claimed no prisoners," my priest had told him. "First you dare shave your youth-lock without cause, and now you call yourself the most worthy warrior among us? We would give the god your heart in sacrifice, but the taste of your cowardice would insult him." The young man had huffed away after that. I hadn't seen him when Mextli addressed the crowd later, and given his slippery grin and nonchalant demeanor, I doubted he'd heard the announcement of my godhood.

Dinner finally, the desire purred.

But when he pressed too close, I stepped back toward the maguey. He grinned, perhaps enjoying my discomfort—reminding me sharply of Ahexotl. He let me have my space now though, instead pacing like an anxious jaguar. "It's customary for one as lowly as yourself to bow before her new master," he said.

I was about to say the same thing about you, boy, the desire hissed, a sneer sliding onto my lips.

He laughed at my expression. "Are you not honored that the war god gave you to me?"

He reminded me too much of Ahexotl, and how helpless—and ashamed—he'd made me feel; the desire remembered too and immediately supplanted me, laughing with a perfect mixture of derision and seduction. "Maybe he gave you to me instead."

He looked taken aback, but when I stepped up to him, he swallowed hard, his bravado fleeing.

I traced my fingertips over the contours of his lips. "You like to serve the gods?" He stared at me, befuddled and flustered, and the desire chuckled. She loved the opening volleys more than the game itself, loved bringing men to their knees with the slightest touch and a well-considered word. She loved the control.

71

Resistance, on the other hand, irritated her. Not many men cared to resist, but increasingly I thought of Citlallotoc—clinging to his honor with all his might—pitted against this hungry power determined to make him turn his back on it.

And finally succeeding through sheer relentlessness....

My son had no chance against you, Ihuitimal had told me with his last breath. *No man does.*

I wanted to think he was wrong, but I had yet to meet that man.

With this particular one, all the desire had to do was pull loose the knot holding my tattered dress in place at my shoulder and let the rag pool around my ankles, and she had him.

CHAPTER EIGHT

I went back to my tent, leaving the man to sleep off our encounter among the maguey. My rational side felt I should care about him, given what we'd done; prior to taking off on my own, I'd never been intimate with anyone I hadn't cared about on some level. But in the months following my revelation, necessity had forced me to be less discerning. This man was a complete stranger, and nothing about our moments together had convinced me that I wanted anything to do with him beyond that.

Most of the people had retired to their tents as well, the feast finally winding down in the early hours of the morning; only the priests remained awake, overseeing the cleaning-up duties.

When my priest saw me, he hurried over, bowing. "Is there anything I can do for you, My Lady?"

"No, I'm just going to be in my tent until Mextli returns."

"Red Hawk did not disturb you out among the maguey, did he?"

I paused with my hand on the tent flap. "Red Hawk?"

"The chief's youngest son. His brothers are upstanding warriors, but I'm afraid Red Hawk's disposition is one of...entitlement?" He thought on this a moment before adding, "Even his own mother thinks everyone would have been better served if she'd left him in the desert when he was a babe."

Then no one will miss him if we use him up, the desire growled, and I felt sick to my stomach.

"Is something the matter, My Lady?" my priest asked, no doubt seeing the frown on my face.

She's just unused to thinking of your kind as food, the desire cackled. *She'll unlearn her weak human ways of thinking eventually.*

I shook my head. "No, I'm fine, I'm just...I'll be in my tent, and I don't want to be disturbed until Mextli returns. Understand?"

"Of course, My Lady." He bowed as he backed away and I retreated into the quiet of my tent, glad to be alone again.

Except the desire wasn't about to leave me in peace. *We're going to have to tell him eventually how we feed. He must know how to honor us.*

We're not taking our priest to bed!

Of course not. One doesn't slaughter a big male turkey before he's sired his share of chicks to carry on the next generation.

I cringed. "Humans are not turkeys," I muttered.

Oh but they are. Just as the humans raise the birds for their dinner table, we raise them for ours. Do the humans agonize over the moral repercussions of their eating habits even half as much as you do? Even Quetzalcoatl—the self-professed savior of humanity—admitted that no god can survive without blood, and it is folly to even try.

As much as I despised the Feathered Serpent, perhaps he'd shown me the answer to my doubts. He lived exclusively off the blood of his priests, given in earnest devotion, so why couldn't I as well?

Because we have one priest whereas he has thousands. And that one's devotion is up for debate.

"It's one right now, but with some work, I will bring in more," I countered, sitting down.

Why should we emulate the Feathered Serpent anyway? He loves his precious humans so much that he was willing to murder us for their benefit.

"And it's time I return that favor." I lay down and stretched out, staring up at the ceiling of the tent. "And with him gone, someone will need to fill that void in the hearts of humanity, so why not me?"

Now you're thinking like the goddess we are, the desire said with a chuckle.

◻

I spent the rest of the night daydreaming about where Ehecacone and I would go once I had him back, and how I would help him uncover his own magical abilities, so when I heard the telltale crack of Mextli's return, it startled me. I hurried out of my tent just in time to see him duck into his own.

I paused at the flap of his tent, wondering what the appropriate protocol was. There weren't any bells on the hem to attract his attention. I'd never had to worry about such things when I went to visit Quetzalcoatl in the Divine Dream. After a moment of waffling, I called out, "Mextli?" My voice sounded painfully loud in the silence.

"Come in," he answered, so I ducked inside.

He lounged on his throne, quaffing a cup of blood. "You're looking significantly brighter today," he noted. "I trust your priest took care of your needs?"

"He will serve me well." The heat rushed to my cheeks and I had to force myself not to look away lest he taunt me for acting too human. I cleared my throat before saying, "I'm ready whenever you are."

"Eager, I see. Good, because today will be strenuous but rewarding." He drained his own cup then rose. Let's go." He held his feathered hand out to me.

I stared at it instead of taking it though. He'd been nothing but hospitable since I'd arrived in camp, but he hadn't been so in the past; he once put me in bodily jeopardy to satisfy his own curiosity, and then he attacked Little Reed with the intent of killing him—something I didn't think I could ever quite forgive him for.

He didn't attack you though, even when you attacked him, the desire reminded me.

Mextli's face remained neutral as we stared each other down. "I understand your mistrust, Mayahuel, and perhaps it's too soon to ask you to reconsider any judgments you've made, but there are some things I cannot teach you without your trust. Using the teoyoh is one of them. But if you're more comfortable starting with something else, that is fine as well."

Who but Mextli do we know who could possibly teach us what we need to know to defeat Quetzalcoatl? Still, I eyed his hand before taking hold of it.

Mine looked so tiny against it, and the feel of his hummingbird feathers reminded me of those intimate moments Quetzalcoatl and I had shared together in the Divine Dream. To my surprise, my heart raced instead of recoiled.

He closed his fist around my hand, but kept his grip loose. "Are you all right?" His tone was a puzzling mix of concern and disinterest. How did he do that?

"I'm fine." I cleared my throat again, uncomfortable at how often I found myself disarmed around him. "So, what now?"

"I will go with you first, so you can experience the magic, and know what it feels like, so you can do it on your own."

"Go?"

His half-blue lips stretched into a smile. "You'll see. This is how Smoking Mirror taught me."

I cocked my head. "That seems a bit...fatherly for him."

"If you truly knew him, you'd see he is a god of unexpected depth."

All I knew was that anytime Smoking Mirror came around, I ended up in pain.

"These first few times, focus your attention on the pulse of my magic, how it builds, and how it dissipates," Mextli said.

"All right."

"Ready?"

I took a deep breath to calm the sudden flutter of anxiety in my chest. "Ready."

And then all I knew was a throbbing pulse, like the flash of a falling star just before it disappeared in the blackness of night. My own magic surged—

But it all disappeared and I found myself standing out in the desert, clutching Mextli's hand with both of mine while my heart raced. I nearly went to my knees in my light-headedness.

Mextli tightened his grip to keep me from falling over. "The first time is intense."

"Where are we?"

"Not far from the Mexica camp."

After a dazed look around, I spotted the outline of the tents in the distance. "Intense indeed," I muttered, my wits finally returning to me.

Mextli nodded. "When you're ready, we'll go again."

With a couple calming breaths, I said, "I'm ready."

Now that I knew what to expect, I was better able to process the bombardment of sensations and magic encapsulating me. I let it flow over me, making my own magic pulse and throb. Spectral blue hummingbirds played across my vision, crashing into each other and shattering into beams of light that flew away, crashing into other beams and re-coalescing into birds of energy and heat. I landed better this time, and felt my magic shifting and flowing in my blood as it never had before. "Again!" I panted, clamping even harder onto his feathered hand.

His magic coiled around me like a lover's hands, and my own mimicked its every pulse in an intricate dance. Bright balls of light and heat in the shape of rabbits burst from my own glowing aura. They dashed off among the brilliant blue hummingbirds circling me. I looked for Mextli, wondering if he was seeing this too, but before I could find him, my feet hit the ground and we stood surrounded by endless desert. A familiar, pleasant tingle radiated through my body; not the heavy, demanding hunger of my desire, but desire nonetheless; like when I looked at Little Reed. Heat rose in my cheeks and I carefully extracted my hand from Mextli's, unnerved by my unexpected reaction. "I think I'm ready to try this on my own."

Mextli nodded but said, "There is still more you need to know first though. The feel of the magic alone isn't enough. You must believe."

"Believe?"

He nodded. "Faith is an absolute must. To enter the teoyoh, you must *think* yourself a god—teotoca—and to return, you must *know* you're a god—teoti. I find thinking the words themselves makes it easier. Give it a try."

I closed my eyes, letting the magic rise up inside me.

"Say the words in your head," he reminded me.

Teotoca teoti! My magic lurched in my chest, but suddenly the air gushed from my lungs and I found myself lying on the ground, on my back, dazed. "What happened?"

He chuckled. "You came back sideways." He offered his hand to help me up. "Keep your eyes open, so your mind is properly oriented for the landing."

I dusted myself off and nearly launched my tattered dress off my shoulder in the effort. I hurried to right it, glancing at Mextli as I did so, but he had no reaction, making me feel foolish. *He might look like a man, but he isn't one,* I reminded myself. "Let me try again," I suggested, trying not to look too obvious in my learned embarrassment.

"Whenever you're ready."

I took a deep breath—another of those learned human responses I found so difficult to let go of—then let the magic build again. *Teotoca teoti!*

When I rematerialized this time, I landed on my feet, but still stumbled a few steps.

"Better," Mextli said. "But you're saying both of the words together, aren't you? Don't. Say the teotoca to enter the teoyoh then say teoti when you want to come out. Try again."

Indeed when I held back the second word, I remained in the pulsing flames of the teoyoh, letting it flow over me. Saying teoti promptly returned me to the material world. I did it again and again and again, disappearing and reappearing in the same spot, but I quickly got the hang of it. "How do I rematerialize somewhere else?" I pointed to a cactus a few dozen paces from us. "Say I wanted to land over there."

"That is a bit trickier. Come." He strode over to the cactus in five steps whereas it took me at least fifteen. "As I said yesterday, everything around us has its own teotl; it flows all around us like a river, and it's upon the currents of that river—the teoyoh—that we move from one place to another. And just as each of us has a signature energy, so does every material object in the world, and we use that unique energy to know where to rematerialize." He spread his hands in the air above the cactus as if warming them over a fire.

I followed his lead and focused my attention. My magic ebbed and flowed through me, changing yet again.

"Feel it?"

"I don't know,"

Mextli moved over to a rock a few steps away. "Feel over here, so you'll know the difference."

I did so, and my own magic changed yet again. "I feel differently over here," I noted.

He nodded. "That's because your teotl is committing the new signatures to memory, building a map of sorts that you will use to move around the world. You probably weren't aware of it, but you have been building this map all of your life, with every place you've ever walked."

I blinked. "So if I wanted to visit Xochicalco...?"

Mextli smiled. "Go ahead."

"But you still haven't told me how."

"Just will it."

I started to close my eyes but caught myself. I pictured the cistern outside the calmecac, where Little Reed and I had sat next to each other that fateful morning before the ritual ballgame to determine the next king of Xochicalco; how he'd held my hand and told me, "Whatever happens, just remember that I love you, and I always have." I didn't see him for two years after that. The memory brought a bittersweet joy into my heart.

Teotoca! The magic rushed over me, a blur of orange fire dancing across my vision.

When I left the teoyoh, I stood before the crumbling remains of a cistern outside dilapidated stone buildings. Tall grasses and wild flowers thrived between the cracks in the plastered stone ground, and when I turned around, I saw the burnt remains of the Temple of Quetzalcoatl, looking so small in the overgrown precinct. The last time I'd been here, smoke had covered everything in a gray, depressing mist, but today, the sun shone bright and hot, and butterflies bobbed among the flowers while birdsong and monkey-chatter filled the air.

Mextli materialized with a sharp crack and looked around too. "Rather easy, right?"

I nodded, taking in the scene with a heart that vacillated between heaviness and joy. I wished the city still looked as it did when I'd lived here; I wished I'd see Mazatzin coming up the main staircase; see Nimilitzli standing at the door of the great temple, ringing the bell for the afternoon service; see the novice priests and priestesses hurrying through the calmecac's courtyard in their white robes; see the youngest ones carrying brooms to the temple or dragging bags of laundry to the storerooms. But it was all gone.

I walked to the temple and stared at the friezes on the sides—the feathered serpents, the noblemen, the calendar symbols. Only flakes of the colorful paint remained now that no one maintained the art. I ran my fingers over the stone facade that bore Quetzalcoatl's face, remembering how it had peeled off the temple, alive and fierce in protecting me and Little Reed—*no, just Little Reed,* I thought, withdrawing my hand. *That was who the servant had come to kill, after all. I was unimportant, and no one would have bothered with me if not for Little Reed.*

Mextli came over, a frown on his face. "This place has some kind of meaning to you?"

"I lived most of my life here. But then the king burned it down because I wouldn't...." The next thought punched me in the gut. *Because I'd driven him mad. If not for my being here, Xochicalco might still be standing.* "What does it matter?" I muttered, turning away to look down the hillside to the ruins below us. "I destroy everything I touch."

"Whatever happened here, it could have been avoided if Quetzalcoatl hadn't kept secrets from you," Mextli countered. "Our teotls have powerful influence over human minds, so the responsibility rests with him, not you, Mayahuel."

"But your humans don't act so crazy. How do you keep them from doing dangerous things, to themselves and others?"

"Because they know who I am, and what kind of power I'm capable of, and because of that, they avoid contact with me; except my priests, of course, but they are a special breed, willing and able to give themselves over to my power and influence, and so they can speak for me to the people. That is the sole purpose of the priesthood, to act as the safe mediator between the mortal and the divine. The kings and chieftains fancy themselves the most powerful among their people, but they rule only by our grace. The truly powerful humans are the priests, for they speak our will to those who cannot surrender themselves to us without madness."

That explained much about Mazatzin's seeming imperviousness to my magic. "It must be lonely, having to separate yourself from your people."

"Hardly. Humans and I have nothing in common, so they are not *my people* in that sense. I interact often with other gods, both here on earth and in Omeyocan." He sobered as he went on, "Though it will be nice having a fellow god around. We younger ones aren't powerful enough to rule from a distance the way the old gods do, and that often means living separate from our own kind for large swathes of time while we build our own following here on earth." Mextli looked down over the hillside as well, contemplative. "May I suggest a game?"

Now was my turn to chuckle. "Gods play games?"

"Some of us are quite fond of games, like Tlachtli."

"I don't like Tlachtli at all."

"Someday I'd like to play Quetzalcoatl, if he would accept my challenge," Mextli said, standing tall, his hands folded behind him. "I suspect I would be very good at it. But I'm not suggesting we play Tlachtli. I'm thinking something that will help you practice your seeking skills."

"Tell me more."

"I will go somewhere through the teoyoh, and you will attempt to find me." Before I could accept his challenge, he disappeared with a crack, the sound sending the monkeys into startled shrieks in the distance.

I looked around, unsure what to do, but then pulled my thoughts together. *I know his energy, so this shouldn't be too hard.* I let my magic build, and when I thought, *Teotoca!* the orange flames engulfed my senses. I lingered in the teoyoh a moment, smelling for Mextli, and when I finally found it, I thought *teoti!* and the world snapped back into place around me.

I stood in the Mexica camp, at the central fire pit in front of Mextli's tent. The women skittered away at my sudden appearance while the men clutched their weapons, looking nervous.

Mextli chuckled behind me. "Too easy." Before I could turn around though, the crack resounded through camp.

I reached out again with my magic and welcomed the flames of divine energy when they came. I landed this time in a place I didn't recognize—a forest surrounded by trees casting a heavy darkness in the daylight. I looked up to see Mextli's bulky form perched on a large branch above me.

"Not bad," he said, amusement in his voice. "But slow. I could have visited three different places in the same time it took you to get here. Let's try again." He disappeared.

I didn't hesitate this time. I barked the divine word in my head, letting loose the flood of magic, and I registered the barest glimpse of the energy flames before I landed again.

This time I arrived in the market of a bustling city, and shrieks rose as the people around me hurried away, some shouting about witches. I couldn't see Mextli but I felt his presence nearby.

"Better," his voice boomed. "Again!"

We played this game over and over, me getting faster and more accurate with each leap. Soon we were coming in and out of the teoyoh so fast that

I caught only glimpses of the places we landed; a mountain pass with snow swirling through the air; a thick, humid jungle; atop the Temple of the Sun in Teotihuacan; at the bottom of a lake; small seaside villages; the fields outside Culhuacan. We even dashed through Tollan, landing near the treasure houses—where I caught the faint smell of birds and snakes, from the feather and serpent houses nearby.

Eventually I caught up with him though, tackling him as I came out of the teoyoh. He roared in surprise as we rolled through the tall wild grasses, churning up dirt in our wake, and when we finally tumbled to a stop, he tossed me off and I landed with an *umph!*

He laughed as he lay on his back a few paces away from me. "Nicely done, Mayahuel! You're very good at this!"

I rolled over, laughing even as I cringed in pain. "Yes well, I had a very good teacher." The sun hung low. "Have we really been at this for hours?"

Mextli shrugged. "So what if we have? It's not as if time has any meaning to us."

I suppose not. I sat up to find we were in the middle of a field of golden grass with a small city in the distance. "Where are we?"

Mextli sat up too. "Aztlan."

"Where's that?"

"North of the great desert, in the homeland of the Mexica. I was born here."

"Really?"

He nodded. "The Smoking Mirror descended from Omeyocan as a spider and placed a ball of feathers under the idol of Tlaloc in the city's temple. My mother found it, and when she tucked it between her breasts, she became pregnant with me."

Kind of like Little Reed. The thought itched at the back of my mind. "Then you grew up here?"

He cracked a smirk. "In a manner of speaking. My mother—her name is Coatlicue—she had a daughter named Coyolxauhqui, who was a horrible sorceress who terrorized the city, and when she heard that her mother was pregnant with me, she sent the Tzitzimime to murder us both."

"Tzitzimime?"

Mextli pointed to the sky that was turning purple in the dusk. "The Demons Descending from Above. The stars come down to earth to hunt in the darkest hours of the night."

I cast a wary glance towards the sky. "Should we be sitting out here?"

He chuckled. "You needn't worry. They know better than to come anywhere near me. When my sister sent them to kill our mother, I sprang from Coatlicue's womb fully-grown, and fully-armed, and I slew them and sent my sister fleeing into the mountains." He pointed to the dark outlines of peaks to the north of us. "I pursued her up there, to a cave, and for her crimes, I cut her head off and threw her body down into the valley, for all to walk upon." He had the same malevolent gleam in his eyes that I saw when he'd wrenched me off my feet for ruining his basket of hearts. "After that, I led the Mexica out of Aztlan, away from this place."

"Too many bad memories?" I didn't want to even think of the mess he'd left behind after he'd sprang fully-grown and fully-armed from that poor woman's body.

Mextli shrugged. "The Mexica's future is in the south, where someday they will rule all. This I have promised them."

"That's a very big promise."

"I am a very big god," Mextli said with a grin.

I chuckled, surprisingly charmed by his brazen confidence. Pulling my knees to my chest, I said, "So, Smoking Mirror is your father then."

His face turned sober. "He is my brother."

"Whose feathers were they then?"

"Smoking Mirror's, as I told you already. He formed them from his war god essence and placed it under the idol."

I stared at him, puzzled. "But that means he made you from himself, which makes him your father."

Mextli turned his hardened gaze upon me, and I saw nothing of the god I'd spent all day with in those eyes. "As I said, he is my brother."

The acid in his voice made me fidget. "He's your brother." Hopefully that would calm the storm brewing in his eyes. Was this how I looked when the desire took over?

Just as suddenly as it had left, his smile returned. "This was indeed a good day. You did very well, Mayahuel. I'm most impressed."

"Thank you." I still hugged my knees to my chest, watching him carefully.

"We should get back to the camp. You expended a good deal of energy and should replenish before we continue tomorrow."

CHAPTER NINE

When we returned to the Mexica camp, the smell of cooking food permeated the air. All of the women were gathered around the fires, a scene reminiscent of those early days in Tollan when Little Reed and I had lived out of our tent, and Bitter Rabbit and Mitotia would cook our meals under the dark night skies. *I wonder how Mitotia's doing. Are she and Malinalli still together? And has Malinalli adjusted to being the High Priestess of Quetzalcoatl? She never wanted the job to begin with, but I'm sure she's taken to it just fine. She's brilliant and tough, after all.*

Yet I couldn't suppress the guilt for having thrust such a responsibility upon her without explanation, or even saying goodbye.

We can go to Tollan and see how she's doing, the desire said. *We could be there in a blink.*

The thought was so appealing—and I started working over plans in my head—but reality soon dampened my enthusiasm. If I was seen, word would surely get back to Little Reed that I'd been there, and what would he think if I didn't go see him?

Then go see him too!

Except how could I explain to him that everything he felt for me was a lie? My showing up there could seriously undermine whatever happiness he'd finally found with Anacoana, and I'd done enough damage there already. *I can't ever go back to Tollan,* I realized, heaviness settling over me. *I have to let it go; I have to let Little Reed go, for both of us.*

And what about your promise to Ehecacone, to take him to see Little Reed? the desire asked.

I'll have to tell him I can't go with him. The thought felt like a blow to the chest.

"Do you wish to come inside for some blood?" Mextli asked, holding open his tent flap.

I smiled wanly. "Actually, I think I want to go back to my own tent for the night. I'm very drained and...and...."

"And you need to feed." He nodded. "I shall see you tomorrow then." He ducked into his tent.

Looking forward to some alone time, I turned to my own tent.

But it was gone. I looked around, but when I didn't spot it, I went to one of the women tending a nearby fire. "Excuse me, but do you know what happened to my tent?"

She stared up at me, her mouth hanging open. The women behind her—who were mending animal skins—all gasped then scurried away. She remained frozen though, a bewildered look on her face.

I watched, puzzled as the others disappear into nearby tents. "Did I say something wrong?"

The woman clutched her chest, a strange look on her face. "The goddess has spoken to me!" she whispered, breathless. "The goddess has chosen to talk to me!" Her expression shifted to nausea. "What will Yaotl say?"

The memory of Mextli's words from this afternoon came back to me. *Stupid! I mustn't talk to anyone but my priest.* "It's all right," I said, backing away. "I'll find it myself."

But she sprang to her feet, nearly knocking over the cooking pot. She hurried around the fire and prostrated herself on the ground at my feet. "I live only to serve you, My Lady."

"No, really, that's not necessary—"

"Xihuitl moved your temple, My Lady, to the maguey field outside of camp."

"Xihuitl?"

"Your chosen shaman, My Lady."

My cheeks blazed. *I didn't even ask my own priest his name. Seems I'm becoming more god-like every day.* I cleared my throat before replying, "Thank you," then I headed for the north end of camp.

As the woman had said, my tent was set up among the maguey plants. Xihuitl sat outside of it, in front of a small fire where he was burning incense and meditating, but when I entered the clearing, he hurried to his feet then prostrated himself before me too. "Does your new sacred location please you, My Lady?"

"Yes. Thank you."

"If it pleases you, I have moved my own tent to the edge of camp, so I will always be close at hand to serve you." He pointed behind me and I turned to see a new tent erected at the edge of the clearing, along the footpath back to the camp.

And the woman stood next to it, watching us anxiously.

"Why are you lurking back there, Xochitl? It's a grave crime to spy on the gods!" Xihuitl called to her, coming to his feet and lumbering toward her.

"But she spoke to me!" Xochitl called, backing away.

"Lies!"

I rushed to cut him off. "No, I indeed spoke to her. It's all right."

He stared at me with confused eyes but then dropped his gaze. He went to his hands and knees again. "Forgive my outburst, My Lady. I did not know I had failed you."

"Failed me? You haven't failed me."

"Is that not why you've granted Xochitl your grace? You're not disappointed in my service?"

"Omeyocan no! You've been a very good priest," I assured him. "Please rise. I don't like you groveling in the dirt at my feet."

He stood again, looking chastened. "Forgive my displeasing behavior, My Lady."

"Please stop chastising yourself. You've done nothing to deserve it." I looked back at Xochitl and beckoned her over.

She hurried, keeping her own gaze downcast.

"I spoke to Xochitl because...." But the desire stopped me. *We can't admit it was a mistake; gods are supposed to be perfect, otherwise why else would they worship us?*

I floundered a breath longer but then said, "I've decided I need both a priest and priestess. A woman can serve me in ways that a man cannot, just as you serve me in ways that she cannot," I told Xihuitl.

Xihuitl looked at Xochitl—skeptical—then he told me, "But My Lady, she is not unblemished."

"Unblemished?"

"She is not pure of the flesh, as a shaman should be. She has a husband...and she's with child!"

I looked over at Xochitl. It was difficult to see her body under her buckskins, but her cheeks were blazing bright.

I turned back to Xihuitl, my own head swimming with warnings about admitting my own mistakes. "Such things don't matter to me; I'm a mother myself, and it's nonsense to say that being a mother precludes one from being able to serve the gods." *And in my experience, those most concerned about the purity of priestesses are those who are trying to cover for their own lack of bodily purity,* the desire almost growled, but Xihuitl was already looking thoroughly scolded.

I turned to Xochitl. "If you do not wish to serve, I understand and release you of that obligation with no ill feelings."

Xochitl hurried forward, fervor on her face. "It would be the greatest honor of my life to serve you, My Lady. I promise I won't let you down!"

"I know you won't," I said with a smile.

She bowed. "Tell me how to best serve you, My Lady."

"Well, I *am* a bit hungry," I admitted.

"Tell us what you require and we shall fetch it immediately."

The desire started rising up inside me but I pushed it back. *Not yet. I want to try something different.*

Different?

You're not afraid, are you?

The desire bristled but retreated.

Both Xochitl and Xihuitl were waiting with infinite patience, so I said, "Each of you will give me a little of your own blood each day. Not too much, for I don't want either of you becoming ill." I motioned them to follow me over to one of the maguey plants.

I took hold of one of the thorns and bent it back and forth until it broke loose, but when I pulled it off, it brought long, stringy fibers with it. "Take a maguey thorn and put it through your tongue, like this...." I opened my mouth and demonstrated on myself.

It had been so long since last I'd done this that the shock of the pain took me by surprise. And to think there'd been a time when I'd found such sensations comforting. I dragged the damp maguey fibers through my fresh wound then choked back the throbbing sensation in my mouth. "The threads should be dry though, and braided together," I said once I found the will to make my tongue work again. "It soaks up the blood better."

Xihuitl fingered the thorns on another maguey plant. "Then we should not use the thorns tonight?"

"Just use your blade to bleed your earlobes and dribble it into a cup, and that will do for tonight," I said.

Xochitl pulled one of the thorns loose and smiled with pride as the threads came out in multiple long strands. "I will make the ropes and thorns for us," she told Xihuitl. "You get the cup and blade."

He scowled at her orders but hurried away to his tent.

◻

After my priests bled their ears into a small clay cup for me, I gave Xihuitl orders to start training Xochitl in the stories of the Mexica gods, so she would have the appropriate priestly knowledge. The real reason though was so I could listen in as they sat outside my tent and learn all I could about Mexica theology, to know which gods they worshipped and how they told their stories; all knowledge I needed to be an effective goddess for them. I sat drinking the little bit of blood and listened in silence, committing everything to memory the same way I used to in calmecac so long ago.

But the blood was gone all too soon and the hunger still burned bright and petulant. I stared into the empty cup, wondering if I should do something so uncouth as to try the lick the remainder off the sides.

To Mictlan with blood, the desire growled. *We can't live on so little. When we have countless followers giving a little to us every day, like Quetzalcoatl does, then we can live on blood alone. But until then, we need to feed naturally.*

I sighed. I'd hoped this would prove enough, but the desire was right. *But I hate feeding off them...like that.*

The desire hissed, annoyed. *Did you ever give this much thought to the animals you ate when you were still mortal? Did you weep for the turkeys or dogs raised for the slaughter? Did you say a prayer for the soul of the deer filling your tamales? Or did you thank the gods for giving you that food? This is what Omeyocan has given us, and we should be thankful, for without it, we die.*

I set the cup aside to put my head in my hands. *I don't want to kill anyone.*

We needn't kill them. Black Otter lived for many years after.

I wouldn't call that 'living'.

We limit the number of times we take each to bed, just as we have been, but when we're done with them, we banish them. It's the perfect arrangement: we get to eat, they get the pleasure, and no one dies.

I looked up at the tent flap, hesitating. *And what happens when we go through every man in camp?*

We can't do that, of course, for we'd have no one left to worship us. The humans bring Mextli war prisoners; they'll just need to bring some for us as well. When I still hesitated, the desire asked, *Do you wish me to go out there and speak with the priest about our needs?*

"No, I'll do it," I grumbled, crawling out the flap finally.

My emergence startled both of them and they rose to bow to me. "Is there something we can do for you, My Lady?" Xihuitl asked.

"It's getting late and both of you need your sleep. Xochitl, please go home to your husband and get a good night's rest."

Xochitl bowed again then headed back to camp.

"Shall I retire as well, My Lady?" Xihuitl looked ragged and eager for his bed.

"Of course, but first...Red Hawk...."

"The chief's son?"

I nodded. "Tell him I wish to see him, right away."

"Immediately, My Lady." And without a backward glance, he hurried back into camp.

I waited outside my tent, pacing and working over what I'd say to Red Hawk when he came.

He and Xihuitl arrived shortly, and I thanked my priest for all his service and sent him home for the night. Both Red Hawk and I watched him until he disappeared into his tent.

Then Red Hawk turned ardent eyes upon me and drew me into a groping hug. "Then last night was as good for you as it was for me?" he asked, kissing my neck.

His very touch made my skin crawl, so I welcomed the desire when it supplanted me. "If you thought last night was good, you're in for a treat tonight," it purred, pulling him toward the tent.

CHAPTER TEN

The night's activities left me energized and fidgety, reminding me of that time long ago when Citlallotoc had convinced me to smoke tobacco to keep me moving through my exhaustion. I sat among the maguey, practicing manipulating the plants while Red Hawk snored loudly in my tent, but long before dawn, I couldn't take sitting still anymore. I went back into camp, to see if Mextli wanted to get an early start on the day's lessons.

But when I peeked inside his tent, I found it empty; no Mextli, no throne, no vast hall, just a small, empty tent. I stared at it, confused, but then returned to my own.

With Red Hawk sprawled out, there was no room for me inside my tent, so I sat out front, watching a scorpion hunting among the nearby rocks.

A bit before sunrise, Mextli appeared next to me with a snap, making me flinch. "You should have sensed me coming," he chided, a wicked grin on his face. "One mustn't get so distracted by the beauty of the world that one doesn't see danger when it's coming."

I raised an eyebrow. "You're a danger to me?"

He chuckled. "No."

When Red Hawk suddenly started snoring, I cut him off by asking loudly, "Will you show me how to make my tent bigger? Like yours?" I held my breath when I ran out of things to say, but thankfully Red Hawk had fallen silent again.

Mextli glanced back at my tent, but then said, "Very well. Come along." He vanished with a crack and I followed closely behind him.

We materialized out in the desert, next to a rock outcropping. Mextli flexed his left hand and a deerskin tent materialized out of thin air in front of us, already set up.

"How did you do that?" I asked.

"Do what?"

"Make that appear? Did you bring it from the camp?"

He shook his head. "Every god has a special power unique to themselves alone, a power not shared by others. In my case, I can create weapons and military supplies from my thoughts."

"So that's how you summoned knives out of seemingly nowhere?"

"Exactly."

"And every god has a special power that none of the others have? What's Smoking Mirror's?"

Mextli gave me a sideways glance, suspicion on his face, but he answered, "He can see the future."

"Really?" When Mextli nodded, I cocked my head and asked, "Then he must have known he would lose against me at the battle for Culhuacan, so why did he face off with me?"

"The actions of gods are seldom predictable," Mextli answered. "He can see the future as it pertains to mortals, whose behaviors are extremely predictable. Surely you've noticed this?"

I chuckled. "Well, obviously prediction is not my special power, because human behavior is as mysterious to me as that of my fellow gods."

"Experience will teach you otherwise."

"What about Quetzalcoatl? What's his special power?" Such information could come in handy.

Mextli cast his gaze at the sun rising in the east. "He can instill unwavering faith and devotion in the hearts of humans. That is why he has so many followers."

"That is powerful." All of Quetzalcoatl's talk of earning the devotion of his followers felt so very hollow now, and the bitterness welled up anew. He hadn't just lied to me; he was lying to everyone, and growing powerful off that lie.

And you don't? I wondered. *How many men have convinced themselves that they are in love with you and it's all a lie?*

Yes, but we don't reinforce their delusion by telling them that what they feel is real, the desire retorted. *There's a difference.*

"I wonder what my own special power is," I muttered. I invited the desire to give its opinion, but it remained silent, so I said, "I do have that octli magic."

"From what Smoking Mirror tells me, your son possesses that as well, so it is not unique to you," Mextli answered.

That must be why he often fell into spontaneous intoxication, though it seemed that where I could direct it outward, he tended to direct it inward. After a moment's thought, I said, "Well…I can make humans fall in love with me just by being near them."

"A fairly typical ability for a love goddess, Mayahuel," Mextli chided me with a chuckle. "And you aren't the only one around."

"I guess not," I admitted, thinking of Xochiquetzal. "I guess I'll figure out my uniqueness eventually."

"We all do," Mextli agreed.

"So, about making the inside of the tent bigger…."

Mextli nodded. "You create a pocket of the Divine Dream. You're familiar with what the Divine Dream is?" When I nodded, he went on, "Once you've built the pocket, you can then shape it however you like.

Very simple, really."

"But how does one build pockets of the Divine Dream?" I asked. "My experience...well, it always manipulated me, not the other way around. And even then, I could only see it with the help of the Teonanacatl." *Or when you have sex*, the desire reminded me but I bit my tongue.

Mextli crinkled his eyebrows. "You can't see it now?"

"Well, I can *see it*, but I can't interact with it. It's more like...a wash of color over reality. The way you talk about it...you make it seem as if it's a physical thing."

"You're thinking like a human again, Mayahuel."

I creased my brow. "Meaning what?"

"That you think of the physical and mental world as two separate things, unrelated to each other, that there's a clear line between them. The Divine Dream is all around us, in everything, all the time. Humans can perceive both worlds, but they cannot exist in the Divine Dream the way we do. That is how Quetzalcoatl created them—limited. But we gods exist simultaneously in both and so can manipulate both with ease. This is so very basic, Mayahuel." Mextli sighed. "Forgive my criticism, but it frustrates me how unprepared the Feathered Serpent kept you."

"It frustrates me even more than it does you," I said.

"But you shall be ignorant no more. I will make sure of it." He beckoned me to follow him up onto the rock outcrop. "You said you've only ever been able to see into the Divine Dream with the sacred mushrooms?"

"Well, that's not entirely true," I admitted. "When I'd do certain things...things I do now to feed, I could see into the Divine Dream. But now that I'm a goddess, I can see it all of the time, but I have no idea how to interact with it."

"Then you've never changed your form?"

I blinked at him. "I can change my form?"

"Of course. You're not limited to that human body you were reborn into; you can re-fashion it in any manner you wish. If you want to be a rock, then you can be a rock; if you wish to be a bird and fly over the earth, you can do that too. You can even be elemental; sometimes I like to be the sun, at least when Nanauatzin isn't already being it. Quetzalcoatl liked being the wind, and Smoking Mirror plays at being wildfire."

"And I could be any of that too?" When Mextli nodded, I asked,

"How?"

"Just do it."

I frowned. "What?"

"So much of being divine, Mayahuel, is believing all things are possible. The only thing that keeps your thoughts from becoming reality is that you don't believe. You must let go of all that human behavioral training and know that you can do whatever you want—you can *be* whatever you want."

I laughed. "You make it sound easy."

"It *is* easy." He suddenly morphed into a tiny emerald-blue hummingbird, his wings beating so fast they were mere blurs as he hovered before me. "You just must believe." His deep, booming voice sounded comical coming from such a small creature's mouth.

"So if I wanted to become a rabbit—?"

"Don't want; just do it."

I sighed and closed my eyes.

Stop clinging to your own limitations and believe in your potential, the desire chided. *You are a goddess, capable of anything, and more.*

I thought of Ehecacone when he was young, asking me if I ever dreamt of becoming a rabbit, and I imagined the glee on his face as I changed into one right in front of him. As a child, I'd often wanted to be a rabbit, hopping around on all fours, mimicking the rabbits I saw creeping among the bushes in the main garden. Black Otter would play a jaguar, stalking me through the palace halls, and he'd try to pin me in corners or on the floor, but I was better at such games and always eluded him. But now I really could be one, and it would be fabulous to be so fast, so sleek, so fuzzy....

"Not hard at all," Mextli said.

I opened my eyes to find my human hands gone, replaced with delicate, triangular paws covered in brown fur. I pulled them up against my soft white belly to find I now rested on powerful haunches, and the newly-rising sun stretched a long-eared shadow across the desert floor in front of me. I'd done it! I was in the body of a rabbit!

But when I tried to take a step, I went over the edge of the rock outcropping and landed on my back on the ground. My body didn't work at all like I was used to.

Because it's not a human body, silly, the desire laughed. *The joints are all in different places.*

And when I tried to speak, it came out only as high-pitched squeals. How did Mextli manage to speak? I tried again and again, but finally gave up and instead returned to my human form.

Mextli alighted on the edge of the rock outcropping. "Not to your liking?"

"How are you able to speak in that form?" I asked, sitting up and brushing the dust off myself. "When I try, nothing but nonsense comes out."

"Because you're trying to use the limitations of the form," Mextli said. "You really think this tiny body could produce the same deep timbre as my pseudo-human body can? Its mouth can't form speech at all. I speak by projecting my divine voice while moving my mouth in a kind of mimicry; I can simply project if I wish, but I've found that humans have difficulty figuring out where I am without that cue, even if I'm directly in front of them."

I changed back into my rabbit form and tried again. "Like this?" I finally blurted out after manipulating my new mouth a few times.

"You're out of sync. Don't make it difficult. Let your mind move your mouth unconsciously, just as it would if you were in your human form."

"How about now?" I asked, trying not to think about it.

Mextli bobbed his tiny head. "Very nice."

I spent a few moments testing out my new body, figuring out the mechanics, and soon I was loping around in circles. I splayed my claws across the ground and scratched a couple of times, laughing as I did. "This is fun!" Oh how I wished Ehecacone could see me!

Soon he will, and I'll get to teach him all of this!

Mextli turned back into his hulking, half-feathered form and stepped down off the outcropping. "Let's move on to the tent."

I hopped over and sat in front of the flap. "So, how do I start?"

"However you wish."

"Must I be inside?"

He shrugged. "Since this is your first time, it will help."

I nudged my way past the hide flap and sat in the middle. The tent had looked so small before, but from a rabbit-eye view it looked so much bigger.

"Now imagine what you want, and let the Divine Dream build it around you," Mextli said from outside.

I hadn't thought this far ahead, so after a handful of frustrated breaths while I tried to come up with some image in my head, my mind went back to the familiar. With a tickling of magic, the tent melted away.

My old quarters in Tollan slowly formed around me. The curtain leading to the bath yard was half-open, letting the afternoon sunlight drape across my bed of reed mats and animal skins. My wooden idol of the Feathered Serpent stood between it and the next doorway, this one covered with a blue curtain embroidered with rabbits playing drums and reed flutes—the side entrance into Ehecacone's room next door. Just as the first time I'd seen it in the Divine Dream before my son was born, the patterns on the curtain's hem danced about as if alive.

From there I turned to the main doorway into my quarters which was closed off by a curtain. Beyond it, I heard the quetzals calling, and Little Reed's voice, and Citlallotoc's. I returned to my human form then stepped slowly forward, my heart hammering in my ears. Were they really here? Could I talk to Little Reed—interact with him—the way Quetzalcoatl always did with me? The thought sent my heart racing even faster.

But when I parted the curtain, I found the family garden deserted. The pink and orange skies of the Divine Dream were full of fluffy clouds, and fat flakes of Love floated down from above, coating everything in a layer of shimmer. The shapes of birds soared through the air, but they moved with a dreaminess that told me they weren't real. When my gaze found the statue of Quetzalcoatl, I watched it with a growing apprehension that it would start moving and uncoiling, just as the one at the temple had in that long ago visit with the Feathered Serpent in the Divine Dream.

It didn't move, but the face changed; the feathered scales and neck feathers melted away until only a cylindrical pillar remained. *So I can indeed change the Divine Dream however I want.* I switched my gaze over to the light blue curtain covering the doorway on the portico opposite my own, the one emblazoned with Little Reed's royal sigil—a green and white feathered serpent. I imagined Little Reed parting the curtain and rushing to me, to embrace and kiss me. I imagined him weeping as he asked why I'd left and pleaded with me to never leave again. The image left me feeling guilty—for both hurting him so, and for secretly hoping my departure had done just that.

The curtain to his quarters remained completely still. So there were still some things I couldn't make happen here.

I blinked away the disappointment then looked around, sure that Mextli was standing behind me, watching. He wasn't though. I noticed though that the curtain over the door to my quarters had a symbol on it now, a sigil of sorts: a maguey plant with a naked woman crouched before it, holding up a bowl of octli in one hand and clutching a nursing infant to her breast with the other. I recognized my face in the painting, but I'd never imagined I could look so magnificent, so...godlike.

I scrutinized the curtain for a moment until I heard Mextli say, "How are you doing?" His voice sounded distant, as if he were beyond the rooms surrounding the garden.

"Mextli?" I called out, walking around the garden, looking for him.

"Yes?"

I furrowed my brows. "Where are you?"

"Outside the tent. You must invite me in before I can enter your newly-formed pocket of the Divine Dream."

Was that why I couldn't find him last night, and why his tent had appeared empty? "You can come on in," I called back.

He pushed aside the curtain to my quarters and hunched over as he stepped into the garden, to keep from hitting his head on the corbelled arch. As he looked around with curiosity, I was suddenly very glad that the feathered serpent statue had changed to a plain pillar. "Interesting choice," he said. "I wouldn't think you'd like gardens."

I raised an eyebrow. "Why not?"

"The Earth Monster kept you locked up in the one in Omeyocan for eons, and then the Feathered Serpent murdered you in Tamoachan. I'd think you'd have an aversion to such places after all that."

With that in mind, I expected to feel differently as I looked around again, but nothing changed in my heart. "I don't know. Most gardens have been good places for me; even the one in Omeyocan was peaceful, and beautiful, and as for Tamoachan...." *For a while it was wonderful in ways I couldn't even begin to explain,* I wanted to say, but it felt foolish; it had all been a lie. "Aside from Tamoachan, I've always felt at home in them." I smiled. "I used to sit out here on this patio and weave cloth and watch Ehecacone play with his toys—"

"This is Tollan?"

There wasn't any detectable sharpness to Mextli's tone, but I still felt stabbed by the question. "It's the first place I thought of, and it seemed easy to recreate...."

"Understandable," Mextli conceded. "The first few times I made my pockets after Smoking Mirror first taught me, they were just recreations of my mother's—" He stopped, suddenly looking uncomfortable, as if he'd just about divulged something embarrassing. He cleared his throat, resting his gaze everywhere but on me before continuing, "The familiar is always a good place to start, but with practice, you can build completely fresh places that don't exist in the real world. The possibilities are endless."

"I'm beginning to see that." I sat on the patio stones by the pillar and gazed up into the sky where Omeyocan nestled among the clouds. "The other gods...can they see us down here? Right now?"

Mextli looked up too. "They cannot see into your private bubble. You would have to invite them in the same as you invited me in."

"And I have to re-invite you in each time?"

"Every time you form a new pocket, yes. I could leave right now and return on my own, so long as you didn't allow the Divine Dream to reabsorb itself, and so long as you don't rescind my invitation."

"So you form a new pocket every time you retire to your tent?"

"Gods like Quetzalcoatl or Tlaloc keep theirs permanent, but I find it to be an unnecessary expenditure of energy. You and I don't have an endless supply of followers keeping us constantly glutted on sacrifices."

"I definitely don't have that. But we can also invite humans into our private space, right? After all, your priests came into your tent that first night."

Mextli nodded. "Humans can enter and interact with you under the influence of peyotl or the sacred mushrooms. Humans can't *physically* enter the Divine Dream though; they are bound to the physical plane. When you saw my priests inside my pocket of Divine Dream, that was their mental projection of themselves."

"So, if I wanted to interact with my own priest inside my personal space here, he would have to be under the influence of peyotl or the Teonanacatl?"

"And you'd have to invite him in, just as you would with a god," he confirmed.

An itch of excitement rose inside me. I'd sworn off ever going back to Tollan, but I could see Little Reed in my private Divine Dream space the way I used to with Quetzalcoatl long ago. But how did I let him know I wanted to meet him here? "Must a person be under the influence for me to invite them in? I've heard of our kind speaking to humans in their dreams. That could be a good way for me to garner more followers, so how do I do that?"

He laughed. "I'm glad to see you embracing your godhood so eagerly."

The appreciation in his eyes made the desire flare and growl in my chest. A strange contrast to my dreamy thoughts of Little Reed earlier.

"Communicating with humans through dreams is a very powerful tool; they believe the dream world is full of meaning and they take those interactions very seriously. Smoking Mirror came to my sister in her dreams and warned her that her own death was close at hand, driving her to try to kill our mother, and thus releasing me upon herself."

"So how do I do this?"

Mextli sat next to me, taking up the rest of the patio. "It's not very easy, unless you already have a relationship with the person whose mind you're trying to enter. It's best to practice on priests, for they are most open to visions, and they can even have waking ones. Let's try it. Think of a message you want to give to your priest."

"Like what?"

"I don't know, but it should be something you consider worthy of a vision, because once he receives it, he's going to interpret it as such, and it could end up becoming a fixture of your worship."

I frowned. "Maybe this isn't something I should do on an impulse then."

He shook his head. "Just think of something simple but important you want him to do for you. Perhaps you want him to decorate your tent with flowers, or do something related to your feeding needs. Don't over-think it."

After a moment's thought, I came up with something. "All right, what next?"

"Locate him in the same way you would locate me if you couldn't find me."

I reached out with my divine senses. It took only a breath to find Xihuitl's familiar musky smell, almost as if he stood next to me. "Found him."

"When you feel the currents of his thoughts, ride them into his head."

At first I wasn't sure what Mextli meant, but suddenly my own mind became swept up in a gush of images, light, and sound. I saw through Xihuitl's eyes: he was knapping a piece of flint for a blade but he suddenly stopped, as if frozen. "My Lady," he whispered, his voice growing soft and slurred.

"Now deliver your message," Mextli's voice continued from a distance.

Xihuitl, I spoke into the ether, letting the desire's powerful cadence take over. *Bring Lord Red Hawk to my tent each night until I tell you to remove him from the camp. Do you understand?*

"I do, My Lady," he whispered.

And once I'm through with him, you will ensure he is replaced with a new man—or woman, it doesn't matter—to see to the health of your goddess.

"I shall not fail you, My Lady!"

I opened my own eyes, snapping back to myself. "You're right; it wasn't that difficult."

Mextli nodded. "But onto other things now. Let us return to the real world."

I looked around at the garden, searching for an exit. "How?"

"Just dissipate the bubble." When I cocked my head at him, he added, "Tell it to go away."

I gave the silent command and the garden dissolved around me until it was all replaced with the inside of the small tent. When I poked my head out of the flap, Mextli stood outside waiting for me. After I exited the tent, he made it disappear with a flick of his fingers.

"That was rather easy," I said.

"Most things are," he replied. "But other things take quite a bit of practice; like controlling elemental forces. Observe." He stretched his broad arms out and raised his chin towards the sky.

Suddenly, a gentle breeze blew in from the south, rustling the dry leaves of the nearby mizquitl tree. It slithered around me like a lover's caress, and again the desire took to growling plaintively. When he lowered his arms, the breeze died down to hot stillness.

"You…you mean I can control the wind?" I asked, my insides a torrent of lust and excitement.

"All gods can manipulate and control the elements of the world," Mextli said. "I can whip up the wind, make it rain, create brush fires, and make the sun blaze hotter, and so can you."

"You can make rain? But I thought only Tlaloc could do that, and that's why he's the Rain God."

Mextli shook his head. "Tlaloc is the Rain God because he's the best at that skill; I could make it rain here, right now, but I'm not very good at it; I'm still learning to control water. But Tlaloc is a master. He can make it rain anywhere, at any time. And Nanahuatzin is the Sun God because he can make the heat of the sun so hot it would destroy all life on earth in less than the blink of an eye, and Quetzalcoatl can make the wind wipe out the entire countryside. But they can be deposed from their lofty position."

"How?"

"If another god—or goddess—becomes more skilled at controlling and manipulating an element, that god can then vie for their title. If I practice and work enough—and get more humans to worship me as the Sun God, then I could depose Nanahuatzin."

"And if I became better at controlling the wind than Quetzalcoatl...then I'd become the Wind Goddess?"

He nodded. "But you also must be worshipped as the Wind Goddess. That is key."

Had I perhaps found my means of fulfilling my deal with Lord Death? "And what would happen to Quetzalcoatl if I deposed him as the Wind God?"

"He would lose his place in Heaven and become earthbound until he regained his position from you."

"It's perfect!" I murmured.

"The perfect what?"

I hesitated a breath before settling for, "Revenge, for him killing me so long ago."

Mextli chuckled. "Your ambition is admirable, Mayahuel, and we all should have goals, but I must warn you that Smoking Mirror has been trying to depose Quetzalcoatl as the Wind God for thousands of years now. You haven't even learned the very basics of controlling *any* element yet."

When Lord Death said not to take too long, I doubted he meant that he'd wait thousands of years for me to deliver. Still, right now it seemed the best option. "Let's get started, for I think I will be a much better student than Smoking Mirror."

Mextli uttered a deep rumbling laugh and shook his head. "Very well. And since you seem set upon challenging the Feathered Serpent for supremacy of the wind, that's where we'll start."

CHAPTER ELEVEN

"Don't be discouraged, Mayahuel," Mextli said as we walked through camp. "Like I said, controlling elements is one of the most difficult things we do."

"But I destroyed the camp!"

"You did, but they will clean it up."

I watched the women pick through what remained of their homes after I'd accidentally unleashed a massive sandstorm on the camp. Several warriors were hurrying around, directing the re-erection of the tents. "They shouldn't have to clean up after me though."

"It's their job to do it, Mayahuel. We give them things, and they return the favor."

Except I felt like I was only giving them work rather than anything useful.

Shouting drew my attention to the south end of camp, but when women started screaming, the hairs on my neck bristled. Children fled towards us, crying and shrieking as a handful of warriors poured around the lines of tents, brandishing wooden clubs and flint axes, shouting and beating down any Mexica warrior who got in their path.

Mextli roared something before charging into the growing mayhem while I stood frozen.

But when I saw Xochitl fall as the warrior she fled smacked her with his fist, fury rose up inside me like a ball of deadly flame.

"That's my priestess, human!" the desire bellowed, my own heartbeat growing distant in my ears. I didn't resist as my arms rose of their own accord, magic building in my fingertips, nor did I hold back when the throb became a burn, demanding release.

Not that long ago, whenever I used my magic, it sprayed everywhere, hitting more than my intended target, but while teaching me to manipulate the wind, Mextli had taught me how to focus it into a tight stream, the better to avoid damaging my own allies. I'd struggled with it when we practiced out in the desert, but now, in the heat of the moment, I didn't even think about it.

My magic slammed Xochitl's attacker in the chest like a fist and catapulted him backwards into a tent ten paces behind him. I didn't wait to see if he was still alive; every time I laid eyes upon a warrior attacking one of Mextli's men or trying to drag off more women, I unleashed again, sending bodies flying through the air and our own warriors scrambling for cover. The anger in my chest soon gave way to grim satisfaction.

But when I sent one of the now retreating warriors sprawling into the stabbing spear points of our own warriors, that satisfaction turned into intoxicating glee. I laughed as I watched Mextli dispatch two warriors with one swipe of his sword, but when he met my gaze—his own dark and hungry and intense—a desirous shudder rang through me. *He really is a sight to see,* the desire breathed, letting a simmering smile slide to my lips.

He held my gaze for a long moment that left me breathless, but his expression remained unchanged until he turned to survey the mayhem we'd created. I saw it only for a flash, but the subtle smile was burned in my mind. I wasn't sure what to make of it. *Let's find out,* the desire suggested but I shook her away.

I slowly returned to my body to find my skin tingled and my heart raced painfully. Sobbing filled the air. Xochitl still lay on the ground, curled up into a ball, but a man now knelt over her, stroking her hair and whispering to her. *Her husband,* I concluded, and when I came closer, he started to back away, sickening terror in his eyes. But before he could move far, I whispered, "Take care of your wife." The power of my own voice startled me, given how close to shaking apart I felt.

As he returned to tending to her, I approached the man I'd sent flying into the tent. He laid dead, eyes open, milky-white fluid dribbling from the corners of his mouth and out of his nostrils. *As if I'd filled him completely full of octli,* I thought. I looked around, taking in the destruction I'd wrought; unlike the Mexica warriors wrestling their few captives together with ropes, I'd taken no prisoners.

When Mextli came up next to me, he wore a broad grin on his half-feathered face. "You're a most formidable warrior, Mayahuel."

I answered the compliment with a wan smile.

The same darkness still lingered in his gaze, but whereas before I'd thought it viewed me as little more than a buzzing insect when it took him, there was appreciation in there now. "Like I told you that day in Tollan, when you let the inner monster out, you're magnificent."

The desire tried to rear up again, eager to turn that remark into some of the sexually-charged banter she so enjoyed, but his word choice struck me like an arrow. As I looked back down at the dead man lying in the remains of the tent, I felt sick. Monster indeed; I hadn't needed to kill him, or the others, but I'd done it without hesitation.

One of the Mexica warriors came over and prostrated himself before Mextli. "We captured three of the raiders, My Lord, and two escaped into the desert. The rest are dead."

A priest came forward too. "We will begin processing the bodies for you immediately."

"They are Mayahuel's," Mextli answered. "She killed them, so that makes them her sacrifices."

"I don't want them," I sputtered. When he arched his one eyebrow at me, I quickly added, "They're little use to me dead."

He watched me, making me feel intensely scrutinized, but eventually he turned back to his priest. "Do it quickly. I want to eat before I leave with the men."

The priest bowed and backed away, and the warrior hurried away too, barking orders at the other men.

"You're leaving?" I asked.

Mextli nodded. "This was a retaliatory raid, so it must be answered swiftly, especially since some of them escaped."

Mextli shifted into a feathered xicolli over cotton armor and a black feathered headdress appeared on his head. "Do you wish to come along? You'd be a very useful asset."

I shook my head. "No, thank you. War's not to my taste. Besides, I blew down half the camp with that wind gust, so I will stay behind and help the women put it back together."

He nodded, thoughtful. "And with you here to protect them, I can take all the men with me, so we can bring back even more prisoners. This will be good for you; a chance to lead on your own." He flexed his left hand and a flint-bladed spear materialized in his fist. "When I get back, we'll celebrate with a grand feast."

While Mextli ate the hearts of the men I'd killed, I wandered around the camp, seeing if I could lend a hand. But my divine status foiled my every attempt at helpful interaction. People scrambled out of my way, mothers hurried their children into their tents, and the men gibbered in incoherent terror when I tried to help them right a tent pole or asked after the wounded. I wanted to appear unfazed by it all, but when Mextli and the men finally marched out of camp and into the growing dusk, it was a relief to finally duck into my tent and let the built-up emotions pour out.

I sat on my bed in the Divine Dream and wept. Was I becoming exactly the kind of god I despised? I loathed taking human life—I loathed taking anything of them—and yet how could I survive if I didn't?

I had no one I could talk to about this. The humans avoided me out of fear, and even if Mextli were still here, he wouldn't understand; that much was clear from his reaction to my murdering those men today. He probably wouldn't call it murder.

When one plays at war, sometimes one ends up dead, the desire reminded me.

But in my heart it felt little different.

¤

Within a few hours of Mextli leaving, I already started missing him. I'd been alone for much of the time after leaving Teotihuacan, and hadn't minded it much, but ever since my journey into Mictlan with Ehecacone, I'd come to realize just how unhappy I'd been on my own. I liked being around others, particularly those I didn't have to worry about hiding my true nature from. And while I didn't need to hide my divinity from the Mexica, they were poor company compared to Mextli; they mostly avoided me, and the one human who didn't—Xochitl—was all too eager to play servant to me. I could no more talk to her about my troubles or regrets than I could control the wind.

Not that I didn't try working on the latter. I remained at camp during the night hours, to stand guard while the women and children slept, but come morning, I went out into the desert and practiced and practiced, trying to control the wind.

But it seemed the more I tried, the worse I failed. I would have been pleased if I could make the air move just slightly, but every effort produced winds that knocked me over backwards or ripped the gnarled desert trees from the ground.

And when I blew over the camp a second time, I concluded that controlling the wind wasn't my strong suit. Imagining Quetzalcoatl sitting among the clouds, watching me and laughing at my efforts made me rage enough that by the third day Mextli was gone, I decided to give up any notion of becoming the Wind Goddess. I would have to find some other way to make good on my deal with Lord Death.

To pass the time, and keep my mind off my failures, I took to making thread from the maguey for weaving; my dress was little more than scrap cloth anymore, and I might as well have been walking around naked. Once I had enough thread to start, I fashioned a loom from sticks, and fished a smooth bone from the trash heap to use for my shuttle. I then sat in the shade of one of my magueys and worked day and night.

On the afternoon after I started, I looked up from my work to notice Xochitl watching me from the corner of my tent, a curious look on her face. When she noticed my gaze, she straightened but then knelt in supplication. "Forgive my uncouth stare, My Lady."

I waved her off. "Is there something you need?"

She shook her head as she kept it downcast. "No, My Lady. I was just…wondering what you are doing."

"I'm weaving." When she didn't immediately leave me to it, I added, "Do you wish to join me?"

She stammered a moment before blurting, "I would never presume to impose upon the Maguey Goddess."

"You're hardly imposing. I have enough thread for both of us, though we'll have to find some more sticks to make the loom." I beckoned her to come over.

She obeyed, but then hesitated to sit down. When I asked her what was wrong, she finally admitted, "I do not know how to weave, My Lady."

"At all?" When she nodded, her admission struck me dumb; I'd never known any woman who didn't have at least a rudimentary knowledge of weaving—learning to weave was something every young girl had to do, regardless of her social standing. Even Mitotia had learned to weave, and her people had been nomads like the Mexica for many generations before settling in Tollan. I'd always dismissed the claims that Chichimecs knew nothing about weaving as tired prejudice, but perhaps there was something to it. "Your mother never taught you?"

Xochitl shook her head. "My mother didn't know how either, so she couldn't teach me, of course. My grandmother knew a bit about weaving, since she was a girl when the Southern Hummingbird freed us from our servitude, but out in the desert, there is not cotton to make thread, so she never taught my mother how. The story is the same for many of us, so I suppose that's why the art has become lost." She peered down at my loom with intense interest, as if she were looking upon magic.

This was the perfect opportunity to give back to the Mexica for their worship. Xochitl was punctual in her daily offerings, and I'd felt terrible for taking it when I was doing nothing for her in return, but finally I could repay her loyalty, and do something useful for the rest of her people. "Well, that settles it. I'm going to teach you, and the rest of the women how to weave, and how to make thread from the maguey."

Xochitl looked up at me in excitement, momentarily forgetting propriety. "Truly?"

"Absolutely. First though, I need you to gather the best teachers among you, and have them meet us back here. In the meantime, I will go gather sticks to make the looms."

When I returned from the remains of the mizquitl tree I'd blown down the day before, where I'd foraged my own sticks, Xochitl was waiting for me with seven other women ranging in age from barely out of adolescence to one who looked twice as old as Nimilitzli had been when she'd died. They all looked anxious and a little scared, but once I got them gathered in a circle and demonstrated how to form the loom, the work seemed to put them at ease.

And they all proved excellent pupils. Within the hour, everyone sat working and talking as if they weren't sitting in the presence of a feared goddess, and the next morning, they all showed up before dawn, eager to learn how to make the thread.

I took them through the somewhat arduous process that involved beating the maguey leaves with wooden clubs until they split then scraping out all of the pulp until only the coarse fibers remained. We then dried them in the hot desert sun before twisting the individual strands together into thread. I also showed them how to dye the thread with the cochineal bugs found on the magueys and under the broad, paddle-like leaves of the prickly pear. As we all sat around weaving and the women talked loudly amongst themselves, it felt pleasantly like being back in the women's hall in Culhuacan with my mother. Who needed to be the Wind

God anyway? I hadn't felt this contented since becoming a goddess.

CHAPTER TWELVE

Mextli and his men returned before sunset on the sixth day, and they brought with them a line of many prisoners, both male and female. The Mexica women rushed out into the desert to greet their husbands and sons while the children ran up and down the line, gawking at the prisoners.

My own impulse was to hurry out there with them, to greet Mextli, and I was halfway to doing so when I stopped myself. What would I say to him? The women were hugging and kissing their loved ones and telling them how much they missed them, and while I'd indeed missed Mextli these last six days, I was sure he would chastise me for acting so human. So I remained back by the central fire, letting him come to me.

He nodded when he saw me, but he waited to speak until he came to stand next to me. "I trust all was well in my absence?" He didn't look at me as he spoke; instead, he surveyed the camp from his tremendous height.

"Everything was fine." I folded my arms behind my back, trying to match his indifference. "And how was your expedition?"

"Victorious." He pointed to the line of prisoners being paraded into the center of camp. "We burned their camp to the ground."

I blinked. "You wiped it out completely?" When he nodded, I choked, "What about the children?"

He shrugged. "Tlaloc ate well that night."

I thought I might become ill. "Was that really necessary?"

Mextli raised an eyebrow at me. "Our people struggle to feed their own children. We can't afford to take on more burdens."

"Then why bring the women? Why not just kill them too?"

"As the Mexica look out for my needs, I look out for theirs," Mextli said, giving me a curious look. "Children are a burden at the best of times, and taking in their enemy's children would take food from the mouths of their own children. Besides, boys become men who wish to avenge their parents. This is the way of war, Mayahuel. These people don't live in cities, surrounded by safety and plenty; their reality is a harsh one, of death and despair. Many of the men will be dragged off to the sacrifice, but most of the women will perish trying to bring more humans into this world. If the tribe is to survive and fulfill their destiny, more women must take their place. This is reality."

I almost snapped off at him, but even in my own head I understood his logic. Which made it all the worse to me; it was that same logic that had driven Black Otter to murder my son.

"Forgive me," I mumbled, desperate to be alone as tears started stinging my eyes. "I'm tired, so I'm going back to my tent." And without waiting for his answer to my ludicrous claim, I hurried away.

I threw aside the flap and immediately summoned the Divine Dream, surrounding myself in the familiar sight of my old quarters back in Tollan. Its familiarity comforted me; I could even hear Ehecacone making animal noises out on the portico while he played, as he often had; I knew he wasn't really there, but it didn't matter. The memory brought joy to squelch the terrible pain swelling in my chest. Someday soon I would have my son back and that awful hole in my heart would finally heal.

And yet seeing the mural of Quetzalcoatl on the wall before my bed reminded me of just how far off I was from my dreams. My rage grew, and I wished the painting would just go away.

And as if had been commanded, the image slowly faded away until only the white plaster remained. When I looked around, everything that had been imagery of Quetzalcoatl was gone now; no wooden idol, no blankets woven with serpent patterns. Even the obsidian mirror that hung on the wall near the doorway out into the family garden had lost the silver snakes encircling it. The room now was blank and cold.

Let's fix that, the desire suggested, and a painting started forming on the wall opposite my bed, bleeding outward from the center like watered ink on fig-bark paper. I watched with fascination as the colors and lines slowly coalesced into the same image as on my door curtain. All around me, the room transformed in richness and color; stylized rabbits and butterflies danced across the walls, leaving trails of painted landscapes, plants, and animals in their wake; a giant maguey blossom pattern slowly wove into the blankets under me, and a wooden idol of myself sprouted out of the stone floor, the bowl in my hands slowly filling with octli.

But the more images of myself appeared, the more uncomfortable I grew with the self-absorbedness of it all.

This is our temple, the desire chided me. *The humans will expect it to be decorated as such.*

That was true enough.

I lay on my bed, just listening to my son out in the garden for what felt forever before Mextli's voice drifted in from beyond the Divine Dream, asking permission to come inside. It was on the tip of my tongue to tell him to go away, but the desire stopped me. *If we ever want to get Ehecacone back—especially since our other plan is a complete failure—we need help.*

I sat up, pulling my knees to my chest. "Come in."

Mextli pushed aside the curtain from the garden and stepped inside, taking in my Divine Dream with stoic eyes. "Forgive my intrusion...and my earlier insensitivity. I should have realized it would be a painful topic for you."

I smiled wanly, glad for his words. "No, I'm sorry. It was just...difficult to hear...."

"Well, you have spent most of your life drowning in the black-and-white philosophy of the Feathered Serpent, but once you meet the other gods, you'll see his way isn't the only right and just one."

I'd never thought of Quetzalcoatl's ways as being so strident, but perhaps that was why I'd had such difficulty living up to them. "I suppose so."

"Can you forgive me?"

"For what?"

"For never extending my condolences, about your son. I'm sure you know this already but...he won't be dead forever. Gods never really die, not the way humans do."

I nodded.

"He'll come back someday."

"He will, and much sooner than someday." When Mextli cocked his head, I said, "I made a deal, with Lord Death."

Mextli furrowed his brow. "It's never a good idea to make deals with Lord Death."

"I know, but he has Ehecacone, and I want him back—more than I want anything."

"What must you do to fulfill your end of the bargain?"

I sucked in a deep breath then exhaled loudly. "I have to bring him

Quetzalcoatl, to trade for my son."

Mextli shook his head, a frown on his face. "Mayahuel, you've taken on a task beyond your ilk."

"I know, but he wouldn't accept anything less, and I can't renegotiate—I either deliver the Feathered Serpent, or Lord Death keeps Ehecacone forever. He's threatened to take his revenge against Quetzalcoatl on my son if I don't—" My throat constricted, cutting off my words.

Mextli's expression darkened. "Dishonorable."

I nodded. "I thought maybe if I could depose Quetzalcoatl as the Wind God, that would make it easier to capture him, but I'm really quite useless with controlling the wind—"

"Element control takes much practice, but yes, your plan was foolhardy. The Feathered Serpent's mastery of the wind element is legendary."

I looked away, feeling foolish. "You're right, of course, but I have no other plan now, and I thought perhaps with your help—"

"Even the two of us working together can't take on the Feathered Serpent. For all of our power, we are but small gods in comparison. Smoking Mirror, on the other hand, has magic neither of us could ever hope to possess."

The hair on my nape stood on end. "Surely one of the other gods would be willing—"

"And why should they care about Lord Death holding the son of the Feathered Serpent hostage? Quetzalcoatl has taken much from us. If anything, letting Lord Death keep Ehecacone would be a bonus, for then he can't seek revenge for his father losing this war."

"Ehecacone doesn't care about his father. He knows the kind of god he is; he knows what he did to me, and that he didn't care enough to protect him. My son is no threat to anyone."

"Who we are changes over time, along with our experiences, Mayahuel. You—of all people—know that."

I bit my lip. "Then you won't help me?"

"I will help you, but like I said, we can't do this alone."

"But not Smoking Mirror," I insisted.

He sighed. "Very well. We can speak to the other gods, but don't expect anything. Regardless though, I will help you in any way I can."

I smiled, growing warm inside. "Thank you. You're a good friend."

He blinked at me, startled.

"Haven't you any friends?" When he hesitated, I asked, "Not even Smoking Mirror?"

"Smoking Mirror is solitary in nature, and while he did give me his time when he first created me, as you've pointed out before, he never does anything out of kindness, or just to do it; there is a purpose behind every action, every word he utters, which is why it's very wise to not rush into dealing with him. Nor have I had much interaction with the other gods. Being so young and untested, I don't even have a place in Omeyocan to call my own."

"Well, neither do I."

"That's not true. Everyone calls the garden where you were kept the Earth Monster's garden, but in fact it is yours."

"Really?"

He nodded. "You built it with your teotl, so that makes it yours. The Earth Monster was your guest."

I looked up to see the ceiling of my room had become transparent and I could look up at Omeyocan floating among the clouds. "I have a home!"

"Indeed." He looked up too, but with a frown.

"I'm sure you'll get your own place up there soon," I assured him.

"Not likely."

"Why not?"

"Because I would have to depose one of the gods, or marry one of them."

"Marry?"

He nodded. "Among the gods, marriage is a formal sharing of power, but it is an alliance never to be entered into lightly."

"Why not?"

"Because while you inherit the power of your partner, your power is no longer yours alone."

"Sounds more equitable than most human marriages," I said. "But how is it that I have a place up in Heaven and you don't? You're more powerful than me."

"I know I've called you young before, but in truth, you're a very old goddess. You were born before the humans came, when the world was still primordial and going through its first throes of life. You were there from the beginning, in the garden, waiting for that fateful day when the Feathered Serpent liberated you for his own nefarious purposes. I, on the other hand, have been around barely two bundles of years yet."

I turned to study the feathers on the side of his face. "I'm sorry."

He met my gaze. "For what?"

"That things should be so unfair."

He shrugged. "I'm content with my lot; my humans are dedicated and loyal, I have the respect of most of the gods, and now I have a friend." He smiled, proud.

I smiled back. "Indeed you do."

He broke into a grin. "I must admit you had me concerned when you left. When gods speak of sleeping, they mean death, and they don't return from it for hundreds of bundles of years."

"Sometimes I feel like it," I admitted.

"Why ever would you want to do that? You're doing so well here. I noticed you've been teaching the women new skills, and they seem rather happy about it."

"That's one of the admirable things about humans; they're always thirsty for new knowledge."

"And that is why we're here, to give them the things they couldn't get on their own."

His wording gave me pause though. I'd seen both men and women create and destroy of their own free will, and it seemed arrogant to believe that these people couldn't figure out something like weaving if not for me. After all, I'd learned the skill from my own human mother, who had learned it from her mother, generation after generation. Funny, it was humanity who had taught a goddess such an important art form.

"I'd invite you to tonight's feast, but I realize that the accompanying activities will make you uncomfortable, so I won't begrudge you remaining here instead," Mextli said. "I will give your priest your share of the prisoners, and be sure to feed well tonight."

"Why?"

"Because tomorrow I'm taking you to Omeyocan, to meet the other gods."

◻

Once Mextli left, I stepped outside to see Xihuitl hovering nearby with five other men, watching my tent anxiously. When I met his gaze, he hurried forward and prostrated himself upon the ground at my feet. "My Lady, it is so good to see you again!"

"It's good to see you too," I replied, uncomfortable; not so much that he was bowing and scraping to me; as the Queen of Tollan, I'd been accustomed to such behavior, but he exuded anxiety as if he were facing judgment rather than greeting me. "Please, rise and speak your mind," I insisted.

He hurried to his feet again, but kept his gaze downcast. "I'm pleased to inform you that my expedition with the other men went well, and I captured a sacrifice for you." He beckoned to the others—two of them Mexica warriors, one holding a rope tied around the necks of two ratty-dressed warriors with their hands bound while the second man hustled the third prisoner forward until they stood directly behind Xihuitl, so my priest could present his gift with a sweep of his arms.

I looked the prisoner over, the desire slithering up on me. He was larger than Xihuitl, and much more muscular; I couldn't imagine my scrawny priest taking on this man, even bound as he was. He regarded me with wary eyes—one of them blackened—and a hint of distaste. "And you captured him yourself?" the desire asked Xihuitl as an amused smile slid to my lips.

Xihuitl face lit with unabashed pride. "I did, My Lady. Not that he was by any means an easy mark, and he nearly took my head off with his bare hands, but sometimes being small and smart has its advantages." When I didn't reply, he watched me examining his prize with a critical eye for a moment before blurting out, "Does he please you, My Lady?"

"We'll find out soon enough," the desire growled, baring my teeth. "And these other two?"

"Gifts from Lord Mextli."

"Good. I'll start with yours." I stepped aside and held the tent flap open.

The warrior shoved his prisoner roughly inside then retreated quickly back to the edge of the clearing, as if being so close to me scared him. It made the desire chuckle. "When I'm finished with him, bring me another one." Without waiting for an answer, I ducked inside.

From his kneeling position, the man looked up at me with a mixture of loathing and fear, but when I knelt to stroke his cheek lovingly, his resistance melted slowly away. "Don't worry. I'm not going to hurt you; if anything, you're going to feel the greatest pleasure you've ever known." He met my mouth hungrily when I leaned in to kiss him.

When I reemerged from my tent a handful of moments later, hunger still whispered plaintively in my belly and the desire was already thinking about who to have Xihuitl bring next. But then I looked up to see Red Hawk pacing at the entrance to the clearing, looking agitated as Xihuitl kept blocking his way. When he saw me, the frown on his face deepened and his complexion darkened. "What are you doing?"

The desire sneered. "And why would that be any of your business, you insolent little man?"

This time when Xihuitl tried to block him, Red Hawk punched him in the gut, sending him to his knees in surprise. Red Hawk closed the gap between us in a bounding jog but he stopped in front of me, his shoulders heaving as if he were holding back an animal. "You were not in my tent when I returned, as you should be. That is unacceptable. Perhaps men in your old village tolerated such disrespectful behavior from their wives, but we Mexica do not!"

I laughed. "You think I'm your wife?"

"I've taken you to bed; that makes you my wife."

"Then I must be married to the man in my tent, for he's pleasured me too. And he was much better at it than you."

Red Hawk stared at me aghast, but then he grabbed me by the arm. Jealousy oozed off him like a pungent odor, but it only riled the desire more. "I shall have him killed," he hissed between clenched teeth. "You are mine! You hear me?"

Behind Red Hawk, Xihuitl had regained his feet and drew his knife, but I smiled at him, a deadly calm coursing through me. "It's quite alright, Xihuitl," I assured him. "I can handle him myself."

Red Hawk snarled a laugh. "Handle me, will you?" He yanked me by the arm, heading back into camp. "We'll see who gets handled, woman."

Xihuitl lunged forward a step, ready to attack Red Hawk, but I shot him a cold look that stopped him short just before Red Hawk hustled me by.

As we wound through camp, to the tents pitched around the central fire, people stopped their work to watch Red Hawk hurry me along. The desire kept the smile locked on my lips despite the shocked stares and scandalized whispers. When we reached Red Hawk's tent, he thrashed the flap aside and manhandled me inside.

Now alone, he hissed, "How dare you humiliate me in front of another man?" He maintained his stony grip on my arm. "Have you no idea who I am, woman?"

"I know exactly who you are," the desire said with a sultry smirk that gave him pause. I traced my fingers down his chest, sending a shudder through him until he let me go, then I shoved him over backwards onto the ground.

He gasped, appalled, but when I banished my clothing with a flick of my fingers then straddled him, the objections left his eyes. As I started riding him with increasing speed, the desire added, "You're a sacrifice, of course."

Before he could respond, the wave of pleasure and energy surged over me. He gasped in ecstasy too, but as the desire drew more and more out of him, he started writhing and pushing at me, trying to get me off him.

But the desire bared my teeth and drew harder from him, digging my fingernails into his muscular shoulders as I continued holding him down. "Don't close your eyes, human," she hissed. "You *will* look upon the face of the power you disrespected!"

Red Hawk opened his eyes again and when he beheld my terrible glory, the abject horror in his eyes stoked the desire to new heights—especially when I thought of those dreams about draining King Red Flint to nothing. It was intoxicating.

And yet a terrible fear rose in my heart as I watched Red Hawk dying. What was I doing? *Stop!*

The desire only drew harder, and Red Hawk cried out for mercy, his voice weaker with each breath.

I said stop! When she still didn't let go of him, I tried wrestling control of my own body back from her.

She fought me, but only long enough to draw the last gasping breath from Red Hawk, then I snapped back into control. The feel of his cooling flesh between my legs sent a spike of disgust and despair through me and I couldn't scramble away quickly enough. I huddled at the flap, staring at him as he lay deathly still, his skin a sickly pale color. "How could you…?" I whispered.

He manhandled us, the desire spat. *We've put up with enough of that in our mortal life, and I won't let us spend eternity accepting more of it. You have no spine. He got what he deserved, and my only regret is that I didn't do it in front of the whole village, so everyone will know what happens to those who disrespect us.*

"This is not who I am!" The desire growled, annoyed, but before she could say anything more, I added, "You are nothing but a scream in the night, trying to manipulate everyone with fear and threats. And I have no need of you! The world has no need of you!"

If not for me, you would have died a mortal long ago. Intellect is nothing without the primal; men can build great cities and write beautiful poetry, but without the primal to create new life, to protect it, in a generation the earth would swallow it all back, gone and forgotten. For having wasted so much time studying the dualistic nature of existence in that human school, you certainly didn't listen to its lessons, did you?

"You're the reason humans harm each other," I snarled. "You're the reason women live every day in fear for their safety! You're the reason men like Red Flint and Red Hawk think they can do whatever they want, whenever they want, to whomever they want. You are no better than Smoking Mirror!"

The desire bristled. *How dare you—*

"How dare *you* even think you're anything worthwhile when all you do is damage everything you touch. I don't need you; I don't want *you* inside my head, and the world would be better off without you. So be gone already!"

Have it your way. And we'll see just how long you last.

"I will survive just fine," I fired back, but she didn't answer.

I felt strangely empty inside, as if something had sucked the very energy out of me. Much like I'd felt after losing Ehecacone. It left me unnerved, and yet relieved too. So long I'd just wanted her gone, had wanted to be left in peace from her sarcastic taunts and self-serving rapacity, and now finally I was free.

CHAPTER THIRTEEN

When I met with Mextli outside his tent the next morning before dawn, I must have looked as anxious as I felt, for he asked, "Are you all right?"

"I'm fine." My voice cracked a bit though; I was nervous about meeting the other gods, and my anxiety about it only increased now that the time was upon me.

He raised his eye brow at me. "And you fed properly?"

My face flushed with guilt as memories of last night resurfaced. "Sufficiently."

I could tell by the look on his face that he knew I was hiding something, but he let it go. He held his hand out to me. "This first time, I will guide you. Like with using the teoyoh, you need to feel the stream of energy to know where to go."

Logic told me I could trust Mextli—I'd even declared him my friend last night—and yet when I went to take his hand, an inexplicable fear gripped me.

"You're sure nothing is wrong?"

"I'm just nervous…about going to Omeyocan. What if we run into Quetzalcoatl? I'm not ready to face him yet."

"You needn't worry about that happening."

"Why not?"

"The Feathered Serpent has been absent from Omeyocan for a while now, tending to his schemes here on earth, so you needn't worry about encountering him today."

Quetzalcoatl had said we couldn't be together outside the Divine Dream until he'd finished certain business, and the last time I'd seen him, he'd said nothing to suggest that business was complete. Surely he would have come to see me "in the flesh" if he had.

"Don't worry, Mayahuel. The Feathered Serpent can't hurt you anymore." Mextli gave me a confident smile.

I returned the gesture, though without the same confidence. And when I took his hand, that desirous reaction I'd had the first time was completely absent now; his feathers were itchy, and the thought of him touching more of my body with it left me disgusted rather than making my heart race. What did it mean?

"Shall we go now?" Mextli asked, a hint of impatience to his voice.

"I'm ready." As ready as I was likely to ever be, anyway.

ロ

Traveling to Omeyocan wasn't much different than traveling anywhere else, except that it took a great deal more energy. The currents of the teoyoh were strong here, reminding me of lazy summer days spent watching the clouds crawl across the blue sky. The whole landscape felt suspended in time; the water ran over falls slow as honey, and bees and butterflies bobbed through the air as if they hadn't a care in the world.

The place resembled earth and yet looked nothing like it at the same time: there were temples, but they weren't perched atop pyramids, and some were constructed of ridiculous building materials, such as feathers and clouds and smoke. Plants both familiar and alien grew everywhere, sometimes so thick that the buildings were mere flashes of color and light between the trunks of giant trees.

Because my grandmother had kept me locked in the garden, I'd seen none of this when I'd lived here; even when I'd scaled the garden's wall to escape, I'd not bothered to look back at my home when I reached the top. I'd been far more concerned with seeing the face of the mysterious voice that had asked me to leave with him. The familiar energy buzzing in this alien environment piqued my anxiety and I tightened my grip on Mextli's hand.

"Don't worry, I won't let you go," he said, a serious expression on his face. "It takes practice to learn to hold oneself on the divine plane."

"So if I let go of you—?"

"You would fall back to earth."

I blinked. "So we aren't just here in our heads?"

"Omeyocan is the nexus of the material and the spiritual, where the two meet. It is the gateway to the Divine Dream in one direction, and the gateway to the human world from the other. It is the place where we are at our truest divine manifestation, but until you can accept that without the slightest question, you cannot remain here. By holding onto me, my faith will shield you from that."

I looked around, not quite understanding, but tightened my grip on him further. "Would the fall kill me?"

"No, but it isn't fun."

"You fell?"

The feathers on his arm ruffled a bit as he admitted, "Smoking Mirror let me fall the first time he brought me to Omeyocan."

I stared at him, gape-jawed. "He *let you?*"

"He told me the fastest way to gain faith is through fear."

That sounded like Smoking Mirror.

"And he was right; after that I never questioned, I just accepted. Come, let me show you around. Everyone is eager to meet you."

The ground felt solid under my feet as we walked, but when I looked down, the stones dissolved into clouds, and the earth looked so vast and distant below. The sight made my magic tingle unpleasantly, so I resolved to not look down again.

The path wound through a forest of trees painted unnatural blues, reds, and yellows; some even shined with a light all their own. We climbed a flight of winding stone stairs and emerged above a second set of cloud banks. Spread out before us was a village, each house different and all surrounded by gardens. In the distance I spotted the tall stone walls of my garden.

Another house sat near it, perched upon a high hill of rocks and swirling clouds. I couldn't distinguish many details from this distance, but judging from the way the sun hit it, the walls were one continuous curve rather than flat and angular.

It was on the tip of my tongue to ask whose house that was when a woman leaped out of the trees next to the path and landed gracefully in front of us, like a puma springing from a branch. Flowers of every color covered her like a dress, and their aromatic perfume wafted off in visible trails as she moved. Her skin pulsed orange, like my own, and her long black hair swirled around her as if caught in a perpetual soft breeze.

Mextli stopped short, looking annoyed. She smiled coyly and looked around him, searching. "Where's Smoking Mirror?" Her voice was a curious mix of innocent and sultry.

"Not here," Mextli replied, an edge to his voice.

"Pity." Her gaze finally came to me and her pout instantly turned into a smile. "And who's this?"

"Mayahuel, of course." Mextli turned to me to add, "And this is Xochiquetzal."

I opened my mouth to give a greeting, but Xochiquetzal broke into an ecstatic dance and clapped her hands. "Mayahuel! Oh my! You're a love goddess too, aren't you? Oh, what am I saying; you are *the* love goddess!" Her bright smile and gushing admiration irritated me, but I smiled back, as was expected. "We have *so* much to talk about!"

"We do?" I finally managed, polite but confused.

But before Xochiquetzal could answer, Mextli pulled me along. "We haven't time for distractions today, Xochiquetzal. Mayahuel hasn't been back in many years and she's just relearning how to be here, so we can't stay long and we have many people to see."

She skipped to keep up with us. "Then you want to see Xochipilli too?" A swirl of pollen and fragrance enveloped us, making my nose itch, and I suddenly understood Mextli's annoyance.

Mextli swatted it away as if it were a swarm of pesky insects. "Eventually, yes, but not today. I'm taking her to see Nanahuatzin. We have business."

She giggled. "What kind of business?"

"Business that doesn't concern you."

"When is Smoking Mirror coming back?"

"When he feels like it. Now along with you!"

Xochiquetzal twirled like a young girl, her face glowing so bright it hurt my eyes. "You will tell him I asked after him, won't you?"

"He cares not."

"You always say that, you feathery giant, but we both know better. I've seen how he looks at me." She pranced up and took hold of my free arm. "I'll come see you down in the desert, when your dear hummingbird isn't quite so agitated. We have *much* to talk about." She kissed my cheek—a soft, sensual touch that left my stomach churning—then she vanished, leaving behind a shower of flower petals and perfume.

Mextli sighed and walked faster, the better to leave the fragrant precipitation behind us.

"Is she always so...excitable?" I asked.

"Annoyingly so. I don't know how Xochipilli puts up with her."

"Xochipilli?"

"Her brother, the Flower Prince. He's annoying too, what with his dancing and playing music all the time, but he's at least rational. There's no talking to her."

"Meaning?"

"You heard her. She talks about nothing, and does it with near insanity."

"She doesn't strike me as insane," I replied. "Flighty, yes, but not insane. Not everyone is interested in war."

"Nor is everyone interested in the banality of physical attraction and sex."

And one can hardly make judgments without having tried it to begin with, the desire would have said, but without her around anymore, I found myself silently agreeing with him. I was suddenly very aware of the unpleasant itchiness of his feathered hand against mine and had to suppress the overwhelming urge to wrench my hand away.

The path climbed a gentle slope of clouds, up to a temple built on a mountaintop. Up here the sun blazed hot—far hotter than a mortal could stand—and I had to shield my eyes from the glare with my free hand. Mextli seemed unperturbed by the heat and light; if anything, his feathers shimmered all the brighter, and a contented smile tugged at his half-blue lips. Thankfully we soon stepped into the shade of the temple entrance, whose ceiling was held aloft upon giant pillars bearing carvings in the likeness of Tonatiuh the Sun.

Inside, a god nearly as big as Mextli himself sat up on a golden throne, swigging from a gold cup. He glowed pale red, nearly matching the skin that hung in tatters from his body. The room smelled of heat and sickness; not wholly unexpected, given he was a leper.

Mextli knelt, sweeping the fingers of his free hand across the stone floor. "It is a great pleasure to see you again, Lord Nanahuatzin."

Nanahuatzin sniffed and took another drink, but once he swallowed, he peered down at me with contempt. "Well, if it isn't the meddlesome Maguey Goddess. And she doesn't even bow for me."

I looked at Mextli, confused, but when he cast me a chastising glare, I went to my knees too. "My apologies, My Lord. I'm still learning our ways."

"I thought you were teaching her, Mextli," Nanahuatzin said.

"I am, but the process is slow. The gaps in her knowledge aren't always readily apparent," Mextli replied.

Nanahuatzin snapped his fingers and a tiny skeleton scurried out from behind the throne, carrying a golden jug, which he used to refill the Sun God's cup. "Pour for our guests as well, Paynal," the Sun God ordered then returned to swigging.

Paynal hurried down off the dais to us. He summoned two cups and filled them one at time as they floated in the air between us. He then sent them to our hands with a flick of his bony finger. Without a word, he scampered back to his master's throne and disappeared behind it.

I looked down into the cup, thinking it was blood, but in fact it was xocolatl, with a bit of blood mixed in, to give it a deeper red color. I really didn't want it, but didn't want to be rude either—especially given my earlier mistake—so I sipped it politely.

I loved xocolatl, and wasn't sure what to expect with the blood added to it, but I didn't expect to feel as indifferent as I did now. Surely xocolatl made by the gods themselves wasn't so tasteless and uninteresting? And yet each drink had less impact than the last.

"Allow me to be the first to extend you a warm welcome back home, Mayahuel," Nanahuatzin said. "You were kept in Mictlan far too long."

I bowed my head. "Thank you, My Lord."

"Mextli tells me you have a matter to discuss with me."

I glanced at Mextli, confused, but when he mouthed *Ehecacone*, I felt foolish. Of course. That was the entire reason we'd come here today. "I do indeed, and thank you for taking my audience, My Lord," I started, the nervousness swelling again. "I...well, as you might know, I have a son—"

"The one sired by the Feathered Serpent, yes, I'm aware of him."

"Yes, Quetzalcoatl is his father, and...his name is Ehecacone, and...well, right now he's in Mictlan, being held by Lord Death—"

"I'm aware of that as well," Nanahuatzin cut in. "I'm also aware that Mictlantecuhtli is refusing to revive him."

"Well...he's not so much refusing as demanding an exchange to do so. And that's why I've come to speak with you today."

Nanahuatzin chuckled. "I may be the leader of the gods, Mayahuel, but I have no power over Lord Death or his realm, no more than he has power over the living realm." He raised his free hand to gesture around him. "I'm sorry, but I cannot make him resurrect your son for you."

"I understand that, which is why I came to ask your help with fulfilling his demand."

"And what would that be?"

"He will only accept the Feathered Serpent in trade for my son's life."

"And how exactly am I to help you with that?"

The question left me speechless for a moment before I finally admitted, "I don't really know, My Lord. I was hoping you might have some ideas of your own."

Nanahuatzin swigged down more xocolatl then lounged back on his golden icpalli, looking thoughtful. "I'm not unsympathetic to your plight, Mayahuel, but I'm afraid that I cannot help you with this. As the leader of our kind, I must display a certain amount of magnanimousness, and I simply cannot inject myself in a dispute that will see one god imprisoned in order to set another free, especially when that god did nothing to facilitate the other's imprisonment."

I furrowed my brow. "You mean since Quetzalcoatl didn't kill Ehecacone, you won't help me?"

"Precisely."

I stammered a moment before blurting out, "What about what he did to me?"

"I don't know what you mean."

"He fed me to the earth monster!"

Nanahuatzin chuckled. "The earth monster killed you, not the Feathered Serpent. After all, you willingly went to earth with him, so if anyone spurred Tzitzimitl on, it was you."

Rationally I knew I should feel outraged at him blaming me for my own death, but the emotion never came. I felt only guilt and shame, and a further swelling of the fear.

"For her crimes, Tzitzimitl has been Lord Death's guest for thousands of bundles of years, so justice was done. Are you not thankful for that?"

Tears stung at my eyes but I held them back, afraid he would laugh at me further if I broke down. "I am, My Lord."

He set his cup on the floor next to his icpalli then leaned towards me, elbows on his knees. "It is not that I don't believe the Feathered Serpent is beyond reproach; his actions of late make it very clear that he does a poor job of thinking about his fellow gods, about their needs and the grand traditions that our worship among the humans is built upon. Personally, I begrudge his telling me how humans should worship me, as if his way is the only right one. But if I step up and help you with this, I would be thumbing my nose at those who came before you requesting my help with his selfish ways. You are far from the first god to request that I do something about him. I, however, by necessity must stay out of such disputes."

"Even when he's being treasonous against all of the gods?"

Nanahuatzin chuckled then said to Mextli, "I see you've been whispering Smoking Mirror's words in her ears. Perhaps she should ask him for help."

The thought sent a shudder through me. "I don't want his help."

"And I can understand why," Nanahuatzin said, leaning back against his throne. "Do you have any further business to discuss with me?"

I looked to Mextli, but he shook his head. "I guess not, My Lord."

"Then, if you'll excuse me, I have other matters to attend to." Nanahuatzin vanished with a snap.

I sighed. "That hardly went well."

Mextli shrugged. "Nanahuatzin is a politician, so his response is hardly surprising. It was worth a try though." As we walked back outside, into the blinding sun, he added, "A point in your favor though is that he didn't forbid you from pursuing the matter, which means he believes your case has some merit to it. We are then free to continue trying to find others who are willing to help."

"Who else can we ask?"

"There are a few of the older gods we can perhaps sway, like Xipe Totec, or Tlaloc. Though I have reservations about involving the Rain God."

"Why?"

"Because he's flighty at the best of times. His loyalties are easily swayed by whatever will benefit him at the moment."

"An opportunist?" I offered.

"Of the worst variety. He served Quetzalcoatl's plots so long as it suited him, but as soon as support for Smoking Mirror's opposition to this power-grab increased, Tlaloc changed his position. His only interest is in making sure he's on the winning side."

We followed the path down off the mountain, to where it ran parallel to a river, but when we reached the junction, the water suddenly rose up, forming a throne upon which sat a woman in a blue dress that matched her icy glow. She smiled with regal confidence, her back straight and her dress cascading over her shoulders in waterfalls that formed a foaming pool in her lap. "Back again so soon, Mextli? Shame on you! Tlaloc is going to get suspicious of us!"

Mextli glared at her. "There's hardly anything to be suspicious of."

"Always so coy, aren't you?" She laughed then slid off her watery throne. Her smile evaporated when she turned her cool gaze upon me. "This is her then? The Feathered Serpent's little...woman?" Without waiting for an answer, she went on, "You probably know me as Jade Skirt, Goddess of Rivers, Lakes, and the Seas." She held her hand out to me as if expecting me to kiss it.

I stared at it, consumed by inexplicable dread. She smelled of brine and the algae skimmed off Lake Metzliapan that merchants made into cakes to sell in the market. Just being near her set my flesh crawling.

Her smile broadened but she withdrew her hand. "So, what brings you back so soon then?" she asked Mextli while still scrutinizing me like a caiman hunting a small deer drinking at the banks of a lake.

"We had business to discuss with Nanahuatzin, and now we're going to go speak with Xipe Totec."

"And what business would that be?"

Mextli looked at me, as if asking if I wanted to make my case for aid to Jade Skirt, but her piercing stare unsettled me to my very core. I wanted to get away from her as quickly as possible.

When I failed to speak, Mextli replied, "Mayahuel requires some assistance retrieving her son from Lord Death."

"The one her dearest Black Otter killed?" She smiled wide.

Behind her, Black Otter suddenly slunk out of the water and walked towards me, but he stopped next to Jade Skirt and pressed his long body against her leg like a dog seeking attention. His shiny black eyes remained fixed on me though, his lips pulled back in a silent snarl.

To me, Jade Skirt said, "Do you like what I did to your former husband, Mayahuel? His name is so very fitting now, isn't it? He always wanted to be king, and now he is—of all other otters."

Mextli glared at Black Otter as he hissed "Mine" softly.

"And how do you like the hand on the tail addition? As I understand it, he was always a very *grabby* man." Jade Skirt broke into cackling laughter.

Her amusement should have infuriated me, but I felt oddly hollow. "You should have just let him die in the lake."

She pressed on as if I hadn't spoken at all. "I think I shall make more of him. I'm not as famous as my husband, so I don't get very many sacrifices, but with more Black Otters in the lakes and streams—all pulling fishermen from their boats and drowning them in my name—that is most certainly something to consider."

"Can we please go?" I muttered to Mextli, tightening my grip on his hand in my growing anxiety.

He hesitated but then said, "Forgive us, but we must be going. This is Mayahuel's first time back, and so the visit should be short." We then continued on, though when I glanced back at Jade Skirt, she blew a kiss that squirted water into my face.

Once we were far enough away that she couldn't hear us anymore, I asked, "What did I do to her, to deserve that kind of treatment?"

"One doesn't have to do anything," Mextli replied. "It just amuses her to confound the other gods."

"So that's what the whole making Tlaloc suspicious of you bit is about? You two aren't...?" I looked at him questioningly.

He frowned, puzzled. "We aren't what?"

I thought to explain, but in truth I had no feelings whatsoever about it, even if they were a couple. Strange, given my earlier enamored thoughts about him. "Never mind."

"Then let us hurry. Xipe Totec's house isn't far now."

¤

In fact, Xipe Totec's house wasn't really a house at all; it was a maize field that stretched for hundreds of paces, butting up right next to the tall stone walls of my hidden garden. When I again spotted the round house on the mountain overlooking it, Mextli informed me that was Quetzalcoatl's house. He glared at it as we walked, adding to my sense of dread that grew oddly stronger the closer we came to it and my garden. We stopped a ways down the road from them though.

"Before you meet Xipe Totec, there are some things you should know,"

Mextli said. "Like Tlaloc, he initially supported Quetzalcoatl's reforms on earth, but he's since changed his allegiance. I think he might be amenable to helping you because he left Quetzalcoatl's cause out of disillusionment rather than cowardice. He in particular took a significant hit to his power under the Feathered Serpent's reforms."

I supposed that made sense. The cult of Xipe Totec had started to decline in power once Little Reed and I had moved to Tollan, mainly out of a lack of volunteers for the sacrifices. Seems very few people wanted to be driven through with arrows and then have their bodies flayed to honor the God of Agriculture.

We'd stopped halfway up the maize field, and now Mextli stepped down into the ditch where he held the vibrant green stocks aside like a door curtain, inviting me to step into the shaded row. The air was pungent with the smell of peat, and my bare toes sunk a bit into the spongy earth as we made our way towards the center of the field.

Xipe Totec sat upon the ground in a small clearing, bent over a maize seedling like a doting father. He wore a bloody human skin draped over his golden glowing shoulders like a cape, and he whispered cooingly as he let blood from it drip upon the seedling. A smell of fertile earth and water lingered about him. He only looked up when Mextli called out to him, but even then, he showed only mild interest in us. "And what brings you here today, Southern Hummingbird?" he asked as he returned to caring for his plant.

"Someone has come to meet with you." He pulled me forward a bit, so I stood in front of him, and for a moment I thought perhaps I was expected to bow. "May I present Mayahuel, the Maguey Goddess."

"I know who she is," Xipe Totec said without looking up. "Nonetheless, a pleasure to finally officially meet you, My Lady."

After a hesitation, I answered, "Likewise."

Xipe Totec scooped up a handful of dirt and rubbed it between his palms then dusted it away on his thighs as he stood up. He wasn't much taller than me, and under that cape of skin he looked completely human. And though I recognized that he was handsome, I felt nothing about it; not even a slight interest.

"It must feel good to be back home after so long," he said with a smile. He cast his gaze towards the walls of my garden visible above the tall maize stalks around us.

I looked too, but that lack of caring continued. "I suppose."

When no one spoke next, Mextli nudged me.

"What?"

With a pointed look, he asked, "Don't you have some business to discuss with him?"

The thought of having to go through the story all over again—especially knowing it would likely do me no good—annoyed me, but I pressed on anyway. I recapped my dilemma with Lord Death, doing my best to not drag the explanations out, even as Xipe Totec listened patiently, the look on his face as indifferent as I felt inside. Once I finished, I sighed, glad to have that over with.

Xipe Totec scraped the dirt with the big toe of his right foot. "You have my sympathies for your troubles, Mayahuel, but I'm afraid I wouldn't be much help. Because of the reforms you and Quetzalcoatl instituted in Tollan—which have since filtered out into the rest of the Tolteca cities—my power reserves are precarious; it will take years for me to regain what I lost. Not that I'm complaining: I made the ill-advised decision to support Quetzalcoatl's reforms, so now I must reap the crop I planted. However, I'm in no position to go head-to-head with a god as powerful as Quetzalcoatl, particularly when the aim is to give him over to the one god who has the power to trap him indefinitely. I know you wish for your son's return, but I hope you will heed my warning when I say perhaps that isn't worth getting yourself killed by the Feathered Serpent all over again."

He has a point, I thought, but didn't say it aloud. It felt mildly wrong to think like that.

"If you must pursue this, you should seek Smoking Mirror's aid. I think you will find he is the only one who is willing—and able—to take on Quetzalcoatl at this point."

"How would he be able to do anything, really?" I asked, annoyed. "He doesn't even have a place up here in Omeyocan."

Xipe Totec shrugged. "When one has nothing to lose.... And Mayahuel, only fools underestimate Smoking Mirror."

I harrumphed. "May we go?" I asked Mextli.

The darkness crossed Mextli's face—momentarily replacing my indifference with a hint of fear—but then he said, "I suppose that's enough visits for today." To Xipe Totec, he added, "This is her first time back."

Xipe Totec nodded. "I'm sorry I can't be of more help, Mayahuel."

I shrugged, eager to be on my way.

Mextli tightened his grip on my hand enough that it might have crushed it had I been mortal still. "Thank you for your time, Lord Flayed One." Then without another word, he pulled us into the teoyoh.

A blink later we came out back in the Mexica camp and to my relief he immediately let me go. My hand felt unpleasantly itchy from his feathers, and I took to rubbing it against my thigh, as if trying to wipe off the sensation.

"Is everything all right with you?" he asked, watching me with his dark gaze.

"Everything is fine," I replied. I added a bright smile to it to appease the suspicious look on his face.

He scrutinized me a moment more before finally saying, "I'm sorry things didn't go better with the others. At least no one is furious with you; I was concerned that might happen, given your role in the Feathered Serpent's power-grab."

I shrugged.

"Tomorrow we'll go back and see a few more of our kin, but I must warn you that I haven't high hopes that we'll fare any better than today. I thought Xipe Totec and Nanahuatzin were our best chance of success."

"Then perhaps we shouldn't even bother."

"I wouldn't say that. Someone might surprise us. In the meantime, you should go feed, because tomorrow you're going to hold yourself up while in Omeyocan."

Good. Then I won't have to hold his feathered hand anymore, I thought as I walked back to my tent. Rationally I knew the thought was completely out of character given my earlier attraction to him—and that it should worry me—but even that realization produced no emotional reaction from me. Instead I crawled inside and lay staring up at the ceiling, watching the sun's glow travel across the buckskin. I didn't summon the Divine Dream, or even think about the day's events; I just lay staring, letting the time wash over me like hot bath water.

Eventually though, Xihuitl's voice drew me out of my contentedness and dragged me back into the world of annoyance. "What?"

"I've brought you your evening offering, My Lady!"

I sighed. "I suppose I must eat something," I grumbled, then announced, "Bring him in."

Xihuitl open the flap of my tent and the man I'd taken to bed last night—before the incident with Red Hawk—hurried inside. He twitched his head a bit, like those people who sometimes abused the Teonanactl for personal pleasure—and he stared down at me with an eagerness that made my stomach churn.

"Do you need anything further from me tonight?" Xihuitl asked, peering at me around the man.

The growing dread and disgust at the idea of being alone with this man made me want to make up some excuse to keep Xihuitl here, but I could think of none. With a sigh, I said, "No. You're free to go about your business for the evening."

He bowed then left.

I then turned my gaze up at the man he left behind. He had to hunch over as not to tear my tent off its riggings. He didn't say anything, but animal desire oozed off him like a stench. I knew he was waiting for my instructions, so I said, "Well, let's get this over with then." With a thought, I banished my clothing.

He pawed his way out of his own and practically tripped onto me in his eagerness. The feel of his hands on my skin, his groping, licking, biting, sweating—it all repulsed me, and it only became worse once he was panting and grunting and thrusting into me. How had I ever liked this? It was just discomfort and violation; my body didn't want him inside it either, and that made each movement more painful than the next.

Trying to escape the unpleasantness of the moment, I thought about Little Reed, of all of those wonderful intimate moments we'd shared, but to my growing horror, the disgust bloomed even more. My heart didn't palpitate the way it used to when I thought of him, and rather than the memories of his caresses and kisses making me flush with longing, I felt disgusted at myself for even thinking about him like that.

This definitely should have worried me; I'd built so much of my life around my feelings for Little Reed—but the emotions remained absent, as if I couldn't even bring myself to care anymore. I should be fighting to uncover them, but it felt easier to just let them lay buried....

There was no pleasure, but eventually reality bled away and the Divine Dream pulsed and vibrated around me, swallowing me into contentedness. I could stay here forever, unconcerned about the world, about Little Reed, about Mextli or Smoking Mirror. Here I didn't even have to worry about how I was going to get Ehecacone back. I hadn't felt this calm since I'd been dead.

Eventually it faded away though, and I had to shove the man off me. He was cold with death, but this revelation didn't move me one way or the other. He was taking up space in my tent though, so I silently asked the maguey to take him into the earth. Being the loyal servants they are, they obeyed without question, and the world was once again calm.

CHAPTER FOURTEEN

Mextli arrived at my tent early as usual and called out to me, "Are you ready to go?"

The thought of even moving annoyed me, but not as much as the thought of having to go talk to more gods who wouldn't help me with some useless mission that I knew was a complete waste of time. For a moment, I thought to just not even answer, but I knew Mextli wouldn't let that go, so I made myself get up and step out of my tent. "I don't want to go back," I said, walking past him to survey the clearing, if only to look like I cared.

"Why not?"

"Because I'm not going to convince anyone of anything, so what's the use?"

"That's not entirely true, Mayahuel. Smoking Mirror will help you, if you just ask."

I started to laugh, but then sighed, deciding it was too much effort. "Whatever you say."

Mextli came around to look me in the face. "Is something the matter, Mayahuel?"

"Actually, for the first time in a long time, nothing is the matter, and I'm feeling rather content about that."

An expression of puzzlement played over his face, but then he asked, "Do you wish to go talk to Smoking Mirror?"

"Not really," I admitted.

My answer seemed to baffle him. "Do you wish me to bring him here to talk to you?"

"Whatever. I don't care."

He stared at me for a long moment before speaking again. "I shall go fetch him then." He still didn't leave though, an indecisive look on his half-feathered face. "You're sure nothing is wrong?"

"I've never been more sure of anything in my life." I smiled, to make him stop questioning me.

He nodded then vanished with a loud snap that rankled me, but once the morning silence returned, the tension washed away and I thought of crawling back into my tent to lie there, not thinking.

"I thought he'd never leave!" a familiar voice spoke up behind me, and I turned to see Xochiquetzal lurking among the maguey. She hurried over, bits of her dress peeling off her like flower petals in the breeze.

"Why are you here?"

"Like I said, we have much to talk about."

I couldn't imagine what.

Xihuitl—who had been sitting nearby, meditating—hurried to his feet for a better look, and already that annoying glaze seeped into his eyes. He usually didn't become distracted by me, but perhaps the close proximity of two love goddesses was too much for even him. And when I looked around to the women working on their weaving where we usually met by the maguey, they too were watching with dreamy looks on their faces.

Xochiquetzal noticed too and giggled. "Humans are so amusing, don't you think?" She cast Xihuitl a sultry smile but then suggested, "Shall we go somewhere where we won't be distracting them?"

I shrugged but then followed her out of camp, into the desert.

Once we were out of sight of any people, I thought perhaps I should say something. "It's good to see you again."

"Is it truly? For you seem rather indifferent to my being here. Anyway, I've been trying to come see you for hours now, but I wanted to wait until Mextli wasn't around. He finds me annoying."

Before I could think better of it, I said, "Indeed he does."

It didn't seem to bother her though. "He just doesn't *get* us love goddesses; most of the gods don't, which is why I'm so excited to finally meet you. As I said before, we have *so* much to talk about."

"Like what?"

"Quetzalcoatl, of course."

"Why?"

"You're not the only one with a painful past with him, Mayahuel."

I sighed. I had nothing to say about Quetzalcoatl—I'd already wasted enough of my life and energy on him—but I could see she was desperate to talk about him. And besides, maybe if I played along, she would leave me alone sooner. "What happened?"

"He abandoned me, when I needed him most."

When she didn't offer more, I repeated, "And why did you need him so?"

"Well, everyone needs their father, don't they?"

"He's your father?"

"I don't generally call him such," she said. "And I suspect he doesn't call me his daughter either, which is just as well. Someday I will be powerful enough to write my own history and he will be no part of it."

"He has a habit of making children and then not being there for them." I should have felt anger—even irritation at the mildest—for the truth of the statement, and yet I couldn't have cared less.

And it was achingly freeing to feel so.

"I disappointed him," she admitted. "I imagine he thought I would be more like you."

"Why would he think you'd be more like me?"

"Because he took a flower and spilled his teotl upon it, and from that I bloomed."

"Spilled his teotl?"

"Stroked his tepolli until he climaxed, of course."

I grimaced, disgusted.

She cocked her head. "Having lived among humans, surely you're familiar with the practice? Human males do it a lot; the women do it often too, though it looks nothing like what the men do. Both kinds are fun to watch though, don't you think?"

"Can't say I've ever really…watched anyone." The thought made my divine flesh crawl.

She gasped. "Are you serious? Oh! We simply must correct this! We'll go back to camp and we'll have one of the men do it for us. That one near your tent looked more than willing—"

"Heavens no!" When she gave me a startled look, I pressed, "We were talking, remember?" She was far too easily distracted.

"Of course! Forgive me. Where were we?"

I suppressed the urge to snap impatiently at her. "You said that you thought he was disappointed that you weren't more like me." When she nodded but didn't say anything, I asked, "Why would you think that?"

"Because he took the flower from the maguey plant that grew from your bones."

I felt a flash of something—surprise, or perhaps confusion, and a phantom question—*Does that make me her mother?*—floated up from the back of my mind, but it soon flitted away too. *So what if I am?* I thought.

"Perhaps it was just as well that he and I were never close," Xochiquetzal went on, oblivious. "Seeing how he betrayed you to your death. That could have been me!"

"I suppose."

"I'm so very glad you've come to our side in all this nonsense. I was really hoping you would; I mean, I don't care about all the warring stuff—that's nonsense, of course—but the others were talking about putting you back on the Black Lake in Mictlan if you didn't abandon the Feathered Serpent, and quite frankly I'm glad that won't happen now. It's lonely being the only love goddess."

She gazed expectantly when I didn't respond, so I said, "I'm glad too."

"The others just don't understand."

I nodded. "I have difficulty understanding it myself."

"It's not so difficult. War gods think about war and battle all the time, and we think about love and sex. It's who we are, and why should we change that? Especially for the comfort of others? It's not as if our love magic works on other gods, so what do they care?"

"I suppose not." Though given that I had so little interest in sex now—repulsive, disgusting sex—what did that make me? "Is sex the only way we can feed?"

"Well, there's always blood—all gods can subsist on such offerings, but it's nothing compared to a vigorous lovemaking session with a couple of willing men, or even a single woman; women are particularly filling, don't you think?"

I wrinkled my nose. "I've never tried."

She gaped at me. "Oh, how those humans have tainted you! Women are the best, but you must be careful. Unlike men, they can climax multiple times over a short period of time and so it's very easy to drain them to death without much effort."

133

"So it's blood or sex, or nothing?"

"Well, for me, but Xochipilli doesn't really care for sex. He has different tastes."

I perked up at that. "Xochipilli is your brother, right?"

She nodded. "Do you want to meet him?"

"Of course." Hopefully he would have some alternative suggestions to my having to subject myself to tedious, unappealing physical contact to keep myself alive.

I expected her to disappear into the teoyoh and then for someone else to appear, but instead, a cyclone of wind started whipping around her, sending her hair fluttering above her. Her flower-bedecked body came apart a bit at a time until all that remained was a swirling torrent of petals.

Then they started coming back together again. Her delicate body reformed, except the petals didn't coalesce into a dress; they formed a loincloth and a broad, male chest, and when the face reformed, it was a man's. Once the wind died down, he opened his eyes and looked around in wonderment.

But then he fixed his gaze on me. "Mayahuel, right?" His voice was rich and deep, the exact opposite of Xochiquetzal's. He was lean but muscular, and he wore a crown of feathers woven into his hair, which in turn was tied up in an elaborate knot on the top of his head.

"Xochiquetzal?" I asked, confused.

He shook his head. "I'm Xochipilli, her brother. She said you wished to meet me."

"I did, but...where did she go?"

He smiled, patient. "She is still here, just as I am always wherever she is. We are different aspects of a single divine being, and this is how we express that."

"Then you're a *love god*?"

"Most everyone calls me the god of music and flowers, but, in a manner of speaking, you're right. I'm a god of passion." He spread his fingers and a flute of reeds materialized in his hands. "Passion for music, for art, for anything, really." He put the flute to his lips.

To my surprise, the music that came out was beautifully sweet and yet sad. The sound carried on the wind, ringing through the heavens, painting swaths of color across the desert landscape.

My magic vibrated and danced with every note. It had been a long time since last I'd felt so mesmerized by anything; the last time had probably been that night with Little Reed, when we'd nearly disregarded that sacrifice I'd made to save him and let the beans fall where they may, all so we might know each other's love at least once in our lives. I'd so desperately wanted it—so much it pained me now, raw and unfettered and wonderful. I wanted to stay in this moment forever.

When I looked around, I noticed we were no longer alone; Xihuitl stood a little ways off, between me and the camp, a dreamy look on his face, holding his chest as it rose and fell rapidly. Several of the women stood with him, some of them crying, some of them looking more determined than I'd ever seen them. Other people stood still further back from them, watching us in breathless silence.

Xihuitl finally dropped his hand from his chest and, muttering under his breath, he turned and headed back to camp at a swift walk. One at a time, the others followed his example until it was just me and Xochipilli left.

But as soon as Xochipilli lowered the flute from his lips, the feelings of warmth and longing and love faded away again, leaving me empty and incomplete. *What have I done to myself?* I wondered just before the fatalistic indifference sank its fangs into me again, even deeper now than before. I wanted to just curl into a ball on the ground and fall asleep, never to wake again.

Xochipilli smiled then pressed the flute between his palms until it disappeared. "Xochiquetzal creates romantic love, but I stoke the heart's passions for everything else. Without that, there would be no temples, no houses, no statues. Sons wouldn't love their mothers, nor would friendship even be possible."

Xochiquetzal is the primal, and Xochipilli is the rational, I realized. Just as I was once two natures, very much like theirs.

But now I was nothing.

□

Xochipilli/Xochiquetzal left after that, and I soon learned why; within a few breaths of their departure, a loud snap resounded through the still air, and Mextli and an old man dressed in a tattered feathered cloak appeared out of the teoyoh.

"Apologies for taking so long," Mextli said. He then gestured to the old man. "As promised, the Lord of the Smoking Mirror, Tezcatlipoca."

The last time I'd seen Smoking Mirror, he'd been a child—specifically my nephew Night Wind. He'd changed much in the last five years, and I wouldn't have recognized him if not for Mextli's introduction.

Smoking Mirror wobbled towards me with the aid of a twisty walking stick, grimacing and wheezing. "So here we all are, together again at last," he panted when he finally stopped in front of me. The faint odor of burning tobacco hung around him. "Mextli has informed me of the unfortunate situation with my nephew."

The old me would have raised her hackles at him mentioning Ehecacone with his fetid tongue, but I just said, "What about it?"

He gazed upon me with appraising eyes. "I've come to offer you my help, in exchange for an alliance between us against Quetzalcoatl."

I grimaced. "Sounds like a lot of work."

Smoking Mirror chuckled. "Yes, it will require some effort from you, but then your request requires effort from me."

I lifted my gaze to the clouds crawling lazily across the blue sky and scratched my chin. "I appreciate your offer, My Lord, but I'm going to decline."

Now he outright laughed. "Without me, you will never get your son back."

I shrugged. "It hardly matters anyway."

Mextli stepped closer too. "What do you mean it doesn't matter?"

"Nothing matters, really," I said. "Not you, not him—" I pointed at Smoking Mirror—"not Quetzalcoatl, not even Ehecacone. No one—nor anything—matters, when you really think about it."

"It sounds more like you're just not thinking at all," Mextli said, the darkness rearing up in his eyes. He curled his lip, disgusted.

I waved him off.

Now even Smoking Mirror was scowling. "Take me back, Mextli. You've wasted too much of my time here already."

Mextli set his jaw stubbornly but then he took Smoking Mirror by the arm and they disappeared with a resounding snap.

The fresh quiet brought back the intoxicating calm and I returned to my tent to lie upon the ground and stare up at the ceiling.

After considerable debate, I summoned a bubble of the Divine Dream, so I could lie in absolute silence instead of having to listen to the distant noises of the camp, but after a while, that too felt like too much effort to keep going. Eventually I would have to replenish my magic, which meant allowing one of the humans to debase my body for their own pleasure. I craved peace and silence without effort.

I had that when I was dead, I realized. *But that will take so much effort. It's not as if we gods die easily.*

But then it would be the last effort I ever have to make, so it would be worth it, I thought. *Quetzalcoatl killed me once; perhaps I could convince him to do it again.* But then I had no idea where to find him.

An angry snap interrupted my beloved calm. *Mextli. Yes, I'll get him to do it.*

"Come out here now, Mayahuel!" he rumbled.

I sighed, not wanting to move, but then I reminded myself that I wouldn't have to make any more efforts before too long.

I came outside to find Mextli standing there, scowling down at me. "What has gotten into you?" he demanded.

"What does it matter?"

"I put myself out on a limb for you with Smoking Mirror, and now he thinks I'm some kind of fool!"

"Maybe you are."

He flinched. "What did you say?" he hissed.

I tried to think of how the desire would have responded at that moment. "Are you a deaf fool too?"

Mextli flexed his hand, bringing a macuahuitl sword to his grip. "Do you want to die, little goddess?" he snarled.

"If you wouldn't mind," I said and raised my chin to expose my neck for the sword swipe.

But to my disappointment, he didn't accept the invitation. Instead he stared back at me with ill-tempered confusion, but slowly the darkness leaked away. "Why would you say that?"

"Because nothing matters."

He tossed aside the sword, and stepping up to me, he took hold of me by my arms. "What is going on, Mayahuel? Why are you acting like this? This isn't you at all!"

"What does it matter?"

He gripped me a little tighter. "What happened?"

I shrugged. "I told her to go away, and she obliged me."

"Told who?"

"The part of me that revels in performing disgusting, demeaning acts with humans; the part that takes pleasure in striking fear into hearts and takes joy in killing."

He sighed. "Why would you do that?"

"What does it matter, really?"

The darkness crept back in as he said, "Because without her, you're unbalanced. Yes, she's extreme, but then so are you; you just tried to get me to kill you, for Mictlan's sake! But together, you create one stable, balanced being. You need her, and she needs you."

"She's gone, so what does it matter?"

"She isn't gone. Let me talk to her."

"You can't."

"I can, and *I will*."

I scrutinized him, wondering if I could use this to get him to give me the death I wanted, but then he added,

"If you don't let me talk to her, then I'll make sure you never find that peace you're looking for." And judging from the look in his eyes, he was determined to carry out his threat.

I resisted some more, but I knew this standoff wouldn't end until I gave him what he wanted.

"I will speak with her now," he growled.

A familiar heat grew inside me, bringing with it a slew of emotions, just like when Xochipilli had played his flute, but more raw and unfettered. Thoughts of Little Reed rushed into my head, bringing with them tingling feelings of love and desire and devotion. And relief.

But next came memories of Ehecacone, wrapped in a bittersweet blanket of warmth and guilt—I'd turned my back on him, nearly left him to Lord Death's non-existent mercy. I hadn't thought at all of how my death would affect him and his chances of ever getting his life back. My own selfishness horrified me.

A bright ball of rage in my gut soon pushed that aside as the desire rose up powerful and unabashed. She curled my lip into a sultry smile at Mextli. "You are indeed an arrogant little hummingbird boy, thinking you can order me around like that," she said. "You think very much of yourself, don't you?"

He smiled back, sharp and dangerous, sending a mix of anxiety and longing through me. "I have no reason not to."

She laughed heartily but then admitted, "Indeed not."

"It's time to stop playing games."

I leaned in closer and whispered, "Who said anything about playing games?"

"No more telling your other half that they aren't necessary—either of you. This isn't the time for an identity crisis; Smoking Mirror is on the verge of completely dismissing you, and without his help, you'll never get Ehecacone back." When I opened my mouth to protest, he cut in, "And don't try to say that you don't need him, for then who are you to call me arrogant?"

The desire finally started backing down and I put on a stiff smile. "So, we need him. Agreed."

"Then you must make peace with yourself and stop battling over stupid things. You need to be Mayahuel, full and complete, empowered by the passion, and wiser for the rationality. You must find that balance we all find in ourselves, because if you don't...bad things happen."

Fear tickled my gut. "What kind of things?"

"Chaos, and pain. Haven't you had enough of that in your life?"

I nodded.

The color shifted in his eyes, and when he spoke again, his voice had returned to normal. "I will leave you to work this out tonight."

I swallowed the distaste as I asked, "Shouldn't we go speak with Smoking Mirror?"

"He is not in a charitable mood right now," Mextli said. "He was pretty hot with me when we last spoke, so hopefully we haven't completely blown our chances of getting his help. I would give him a few days to cool off before approaching him again."

"I'm sorry if I've made this all the harder."

Mextli sighed. "No, I understand. You're hardly the first of our kind to contend with conflicts of your dualistic nature; we all face that time and again. Every one of us is capable of great extremes and it can be a struggle to maintain the middle ground. Spend some time in the Divine Dream, working this all out. No matter how much either side annoys you, just remember that they are you and you are them, and the sooner you accept yourself—extremes and all—the sooner you'll be able to focus on the truly important things, like getting your son back."

I nodded, but as he started to walk back into camp, I said, "Thank you!"

"For what?"

"For not killing me, for starters. But mostly for being a good friend."

A smile quirked at his lips. "It was my pleasure."

The desire and longing flared up but I just watched him go, a bit of a smile on my own face.

CHAPTER FIFTEEN

When I returned to the tent, I immediately formed a bubble of the Divine Dream and I stood in the calming familiarity of my quarters in Tollan. I settled down on the bed and sat listening to the birdsongs and monkey chatter from out in the garden. When my thoughts wandered to Little Reed, the desire simmered and purred. *I'm sorry I told you that you were worthless,* I thought to her. *I was wrong.*

I shouldn't have let things go so far as they did, she admitted. *I should have stepped back in when you started thinking about death. Stubbornness is one of my faults.*

We both have our share, but we can manage them. Can we agree to work together for now on? For the sake of those we care about, and ourselves?

We can. And we'll embrace who we really are? All of it?

Yes, but will you still berate me as "too human" when I trip?

No.

I smiled. *Thank you.*

One more matter.

Yes?

Mextli. Let's pursue something more serious with him.

Like what? But when images of his feathery hand caressing the bare skin of my belly flashed through my head, my cheeks heated. *He's not interested in such things.*

The desire scoffed. *So he claims, but he just doesn't know it yet. There was a time before we were interested in such things, remember? We just have to teach him.*

It was on the tip of my tongue to ask how I would do that, but it felt too much like our same old arguments. *All right. We'll try. I have a request too though.*

I'm listening.

I want to see Little Reed again.

So do I.

My cheeks flared. *Then it isn't just me?*

The desire chuckled. *No, it's definitely not just you.*

But then how can we want Mextli too?

We are a love goddess; it's in our nature to love, and to do so broadly.

I suppose, I conceded.

Let's go see Little Reed, the desire suggested. When I hesitated, she asked, *Why not?*

I couldn't form into words the fear that the idea brought over me.

But she found them for me almost immediately. *You really think I would hurt him?*

I've had reason for concern, I replied, thinking about Black Otter.

She sighed. *It concerns me too, but Little Reed is different; we've loved him since before he was born, deep in our divine essence. You remember the dream when we were seven. We can't be with him the way we want, but that doesn't change the truth of our love for him, and his love for us.*

But what if his love for us isn't real?

A wave of anxiety and doubt flooded through me. *Let's deal with that when and if it becomes necessary.*

I took a deep breath and nodded. "Yes, let's go see him."

¤

My visit to Tollan required a bit of planning; I couldn't just appear in the palace unannounced, not after being gone for so long. Besides, where would I appear where someone wouldn't see me suddenly emerge from the teoyoh? For all I knew, my quarters were no longer mine, and it wouldn't do to startle someone, be it a servant, a guard, or maybe even Lady Anacoana; after all, my room was the only one that had direct access to the royal nursery.

In the end, I decided on a two-step approach. There were hundreds of rabbits living in the priestly gardens, and their underground burrows would provide the perfect cover for my arrival. I'd need to come out of the teoyoh as a rabbit myself, but then I could find somewhere to change back into my human form unseen.

Not that my sudden appearance among the rabbits in the burrows went unnoticed. The one I appeared next to scurried away, but once I sent out waves of calming magic, it came back and pressed closer in greeting, nose wiggling. As I moved through the tunnels and into the open areas, more of them gathered to greet me, some even rubbing up against my side in affection. I nuzzled each back in turn but then continued up to the surface, eager to be on my way. The thought of finally seeing Little Reed again had my heart pounding.

But when I reached the mouth of the burrows, I smelled humans. I peered cautiously towards the pond in the distance, and immediately recognized Mitotia sitting on the bank, exactly where she and Malinalli had been sitting that day when I'd figured out the truth about them. The stench of anxiety and fear hung in the air, but after a momentary hesitation, I left the burrow and crawled my way through the grass towards the pond. I loped up to the edge of the field grass, but stopped, hiding among the thick patches while still being able to see her.

She looked much as I remembered her: as serious and contemplative as the faded black tattoo of the Feathered serpent on the side of her face, following her jawline.

Another woman came from the direction of the flagstone path from the gate, and Mitotia sprang to her feet. I recognized Malinalli's scent immediately. She wore the high priestess of Quetzalcoatl robes, and her long black hair was tied back in a tidy knot at the back of her head.

"Thank the gods you're finally here," Mitotia whispered as she flung herself into Malinalli's arms, hugging her tight.

Malinalli returned the hug, her sudden anxiety like a miasma in the air. "What's wrong? You're trembling." She took Mitotia's face between her hands. "What's happened?"

"He saw us." Mitotia's voice broke and she began to cry.

"Who?"

"That guard, the one we keep running into in the halls at the palace. He's been following us!"

"You spoke to him?" When Mitotia nodded, Malinalli went on, "Why is he following us?"

"To report about our loyalties."

"What did you tell him?

"That we're loyal to the King and to the God, of course. But then he told me what he'd seen...." Mitotia started sobbing and Malinalli pulled her into a hug again. "He was watching us, not just in the hallways, but in our quarters, and he's threatening to reveal us to the entire city!"

"Then this guard wants something from you, to keep quiet?"

Mitotia pulled away and stood with her back to her, gripping her own arms with both hands. "I think you already know what he wants, but I can't do that—I won't do that. I'll run away from Tollan before I'll stoop to such...such blackmail." She turned back to Malinalli, pleading in her voice as she said, "That's what we should do anyway. We should just leave—"

"And go where?" Malinalli shook her head. "I love you, Mitotia, but I'm the god's high priestess, and I made a promise to Quetzalpetlatl—"

"You owe her nothing! She skipped out on us, with no explanation, with no regard for what it would do to all of us, especially to the King. And Citlallotoc."

Her mention of them in such dire terms made my heart quicken unpleasantly.

"She must have had her reasons," Malinalli fired back. "She wouldn't just up and leave for no good reason at all."

"She could have at least given us those reasons," Mitotia replied. "You've been her best friend all her life, so that was the least she could have done to honor that."

The whole exchange and Mitotia's bitterness poured acid in my stomach.

"You're just saying that to wound me," Malinalli said.

Mitotia sighed and reached out to take Malinalli's hand, but Malinalli withdrew from her reach. "I'm saying it because I'm tired of *her* wounding you. You deserve better than that." When she again tried to press closer and Malinalli again backed away, she sighed. "I'm sorry. I shouldn't have said it. Please forgive me."

Malinalli set her jaw but then said, "I will not let anyone drive me out of my own home—out of the city I helped found."

"What are you going to do?"

"Whatever's necessary."

"I would rather we left than you be killed." She fell silent when a couple of priests walked down the flagstone path, towards the priestly retreat, but once they were out of sight, she said, "I have to go. My temple duties start very soon."

Malinalli nodded but said nothing more as Mitotia hurried away. She stared into the pond for a long moment before heading to the priestly retreat.

I watched her, my heart heavy. My illusions that everything had turned cheerful and bright with my departure were shattered, and all I felt now was intense guilt. Mitotia was right; I had owed them better than to just up and leave with no explanation. And now some unscrupulous palace guard was trying to blackmail them.... *Maybe this isn't such a good idea, coming here and trying to find Little Reed.*

But the desire was adamant. *We've come this far. We can't back out now.*

After a moment more of internal debate, I relented. I hopped closer to the path, to check for more priests or priestess, but the path was clear. I changed back into my human shape, then looked back at the priestly sanctuary again. *Little Reed might be in his meditation room instead of at the palace,* the desire said.

It would be better to announce our arrival at the palace first. We're not the queen anymore, after all.

Little Reed declared us the Queen of Tollan until the day we die.

He did, I conceded. *But let's not be sneaking around any more than necessary.*

We don't need to sneak around at all. Let's just appear and no one will dare question us.

I don't want to reveal our divine nature to anyone here.

Why not?

Because we don't want to ruin the friendships we have. You've seen how people react when they find out we're not mortal.

The desire grumbled a bit but then admitted, *Indeed, we don't want that with our friends. Your way is the better way.*

As the calmecac's noontime bell rang in the distance, I headed up the deserted path, to the gate.

The courtyard beyond was far from empty; novices in their white robes hurried about or lounged on the stone benches around the cistern. No one paid me any attention as I closed the garden gate then wove my way through the crowd. Still, I looked around with anxiety, noticing how different I looked wrapped in the length of plain cloth I'd made for myself while the women and girls wore robes or colorful dresses. Surely someone would recognize me.

But by the time I'd worked my way halfway across the precinct, I realized that no one did, so I strode forward with purpose. I looked around, taking in the buildings and flowers that I'd missed so terribly. Seeing it again in the bright sunlight brought joy to my heart.

The palace looked much as I remembered it. Statues of the gods still held up the ceiling in the Hall of the Gods and the scent of flowers hung heavy in the dry air. There were more guards though than when I'd lived there; they were everywhere, watching everyone with suspicious vigilance, and when one of them caught sight of me headed for the stairs leading into the main foyer, he hurried over to intercept me. "All visitors must be approved by the chief of security," he said, a chill to his voice.

"I'm here to see the king," I replied, matching his tone. The desire growled, restless, but she kept herself at bay. "Anyone may request audience with the king at any time."

The man narrowed his eyes at me. "You can either follow the rules, or you will be escorted off the palace grounds."

"Fine then. I demand to see the Justice of the Peace immediately," I snapped. Citlallotoc would clear this up right quickly.

"If he has time available for you, he will see you," the guard replied. "However, that doesn't change the fact that you must check in with palace security."

"Then take me there already," I hissed.

He hesitated a breath—no doubt debating whether or not to forcibly remove me from the palace—but then he led the way over to a long line of men and women waiting on the opposite side of the vestibule. "Wait your turn and the chief of security will get to you in turn."

The desire sneered in disgust that we should be made to wait—*We're the damn Queen, for Mictlan's sake!*— but I said nothing and kept my place in the queue of people waiting to speak with the security guard twenty people ahead of me.

It took a while, but eventually my turn came. A large man dressed in cotton armor and a feathered xicolli motioned me forward while a scribe sat poised to record my information in a large book of pressed fig bark paper. "Your name, and the reason for your visit," the man rumbled.

I sighed. Earlier I'd been concerned that I would be recognized, but now the fact that no one did had become downright irritating. "Lady Quetzalpetlatl, Queen of Tollan, former high priestess of Quetzalcoatl, sister and former wife to Revered Speaker Topiltzin, and daughter of King Mixcoatl of Culhuacan. And as for my purpose here…I live here, or at least did so five years ago, and I've returned to see my brother."

The scribe stared at me in astonishment, but the chief of security frowned, irritated. "So you're claiming to be the king's sister?"

"I'm not claiming; I *am*," I retorted.

He laughed. "Dressed in that rag? Try again, Chichimec."

The desire wanted to rail back with outrage at being mistaken for a Chichimec, but she agreed that would hardly be productive right now. Besides, now that I listened to myself, I had taken on a northern accent since joining the Mexica. I cleared my throat before speaking again. "If you allow me to see Topiltzin, he will verify my identity."

"We don't allow unidentified people to see the king."

"Then take me before Citlallotoc. He will recognize me as well." When he chuckled dismissively, I asked, "And what is so funny?"

"Citlallotoc is no longer the Justice of the Peace of Tollan."

He wasn't? Citlallotoc had vowed to serve me and Little Reed for the rest of his days, so the fact he was gone made my stomach sink. Was it because of what happened between us at Teotihuacan? "What about Mazatzin, the god's fire priest? Or Malinalli? Either of them would recognize me—"

"I don't have time to continue listening to lies and manipulation—" the chief of security started, but he looked back in irritation when the scribe cleared his throat loudly. "What?"

"The king's standing orders, My Lord?" the scribe offered. "Anyone claiming to be Lady Quetzalpetlatl is to be brought before him—"

"I'm aware of his orders," the man barked back. He scrutinized me a moment longer but then beckoned to the guard who'd brought me here to begin with. When the other man arrived, he said, "Take her to the great hall to see the king. And make sure you stay with her."

The guard bowed then took me by the arm.

"I can walk just fine on my own," I snapped then followed him up the stairs into the Hall of the Gods. We soon passed through the corbelled archway of the great hall.

There were a number of people inside, some sitting on the reed mats reserved for the city's council members, others standing in a line along the wall by the entrance, waiting for their turn to approach the dais. There was only one reed icpalli there—mine was missing—and a man dressed in the royal robes sat upon it.

I couldn't confirm that it was Little Reed though, for he wore a mask. It was a deep ruddy color, the shade of dried blood, and shaped like a beak, the way the god Ehecatl's mouth was often drawn in art. He also wore a tall quetzal-feather headdress. He didn't look up from the man kneeling on the floor before the dais when we entered.

"You'll have to wait for your turn." The guard pointed to the other people waiting for their audience.

But I ignored him. Instead I stared at the eyes of the man behind the mask, willing him to look up at me. Surely when Little Reed saw me, all of this ridiculousness would end.

Yet when he finally did look in my direction, I knew it wasn't Little Reed. They weren't the eyes I'd loved gazing into, and they held no recognition for me either. Who was this man posing as him?

A second man stood next to him, dressed in the mantle of the Justice of the Peace and holding a folding codex for writing in. I didn't recognize him either. The man in the mask never spoke; when he had something to say, he motioned to the other man, who then leaned down and listened at the mask's mouth, then the justice of the peace reported what he'd been told.

I headed for the dais, irresistibly drawn. I had to know who the man behind the mask was.

A hand grabbed me. "Where do you think you're going?" the guard hissed.

How dare you touch me? I let loose a tiny burst of magic and he yelped, releasing me to shake his hand as if I'd burned him. I resumed my journey towards the throne.

Soon enough, the man in Citlallotoc's mantle noticed my advance. Perhaps it was the rage seeping off me, but he started shouting, "Someone stop that woman!"

The council members rose to their feet, making to intercept me, but suddenly Mazatzin broke through the crowd. "My Lady?" he gasped, a disbelieving look on his face. His hair was streaked with silver, and years of worry and stress had creased the corners of his eyes. He rushed to me and pulled me into a desperate, crushing hug. "I was sure you were never coming back," he murmured. "Not after all you said before you left."

"I didn't think I would either," I admitted, tears clogging my throat.

"What is the meaning of this?" the Justice of the Peace demanded, shoving past the man on his knees below the dais. "Who is this insolent woman?"

"The king should know," Mazatzin fired back. He turned to glare at the man in the mask. "Surely you recognize her, Your Majesty?"

I stepped up again, inviting the angry desire to come forward. "Indeed. I was only your wife for seven years, and your sister for seventeen before that." I spread my arms before me. "What's the matter, Topiltzin? Why no hug for the woman you loved?"

The man in the mask rose slowly from the throne, our eyes locked. There was fear and indecision in his.

The Justice of the Peace blocked my line of sight to the other man. "Get this imposter out of here immediately! To the prison yard with her!"

Mazatzin came forward, blocking the guards who'd come to take me. "Enough of this nonsense! Surely you recognize your own sister, Your Grace; she's hardly changed in appearance since last any of us saw her. I recognized her immediately, and at best I can only claim friendship with her. You were her husband, for Mictlan's sake!"

The man in the mask stood stock still before motioning to the guards again, and this time they began clearing the room. It took a few moments before it was only me, Mazatzin, the Justice of the Peace, and the man in the mask. The guards lingered just outside the great hall's entrance, keeping watch.

"What is the meaning of all of this?" the Justice of the Peace demanded, still furious.

"I would ask the same thing." I went around him to step up on the dais. The man in the mask stepped away from me, nearly falling over onto the throne. I glared at him. "You're not Topiltzin."

Mazatzin folded his arms, grim satisfaction on his face while the other two men exchanged looks. "This works on the average citizen, Matlacxochitl, but you can't fool the one person who knows Topiltzin better than anyone in Tollan."

I bared my teeth. "Matlacxochitl! Posing as the king? How dare you?"

His shoulders dropped but then he carefully removed the mask and headdress. I gasped when I beheld his face, not out of outrage, but shock.

I hadn't seen Matlacxochitl since he'd left Tollan to govern Chimalhuacan after Tollan's construction was finished, but even back then he'd worn a mask to cover his facial disfigurement. Rebels had cut off his nose and one of his ears, and for the first time I saw the result: the twisted, puckered skin around the hole of his eardrum and the shriveled pit that was all that remained of his nose. I shuddered to think of what it must have been like to be cut up like that.

"Forgive me for not hiding my hideousness, My Lady." He fumbled with the mask in his hands. "I usually only take the mask off in the privacy of my quarters."

I peeled my horrified gaze away from him. "What happened to your other mask? The one that covers the upper portion of your face?"

"I stopped wearing it since this one covers everything as well."

I suppressed the shudder creeping up on me. "You still haven't answered my other question: why are you posing as Topiltzin?"

"Because the king left me in charge when he himself became incapable of ruling any longer."

Mazatzin glowered. "He left you in charge, but that doesn't give you license to impersonate him."

"We've already been over this, Lord Mazatzin; to admit that the king is on his deathbed with no heir ready to take—"

"Deathbed?" I cut in, my heart jolting. "What do you mean he's on his deathbed?"

Mazatzin set his hand on my shoulder. "Topiltzin hasn't left his bed for almost a year now."

"What happened to him?"

"His accelerated aging...it's finally caught up with him. We expect that he will pass on into Mictlan at any time now."

A pain spread through my chest, so similar to the feeling of not being able to breathe, and for a moment I thought I might faint. I grabbed onto Mazatzin's shoulders to keep it from happening, breathing rapidly. *No! He can't be really dying! Gods, please no! Why didn't anyone warn me?*

But then, what did any of my kind care about the mortal son of their enemy?

"I must see him," I panted. "Right away."

CHAPTER SIXTEEN

As Mazatzin led the way out of the great hall, Malinalli came into the vestibule from the priestly quarters, and when she saw me, she stopped short. We locked gazes for a breath before she rushed to me and flung her arms around my neck. "Dear gods, is it really you?" she whispered through tears.

I hesitated to return the hug but then I let go of the fear of what my aura might do to her and embraced her fiercely. Her conversation with Mitotia came back to me as my own tears began winding down my cheeks. "I'm sorry, Malinalli," I murmured. "I'm so sorry!"

She was all smiles when we finally separated though. "It doesn't matter. You're back!"

I cringed inside. She was so happy, I didn't have the heart to tell her I wasn't staying. Instead, I said, "Mazatzin is taking me to see Topiltzin."

"May I come along too?" she asked, hopeful. When I nodded, she put her arm around my shoulder and we continued on our way. "Has Mazatzin told you about the King's condition?" she asked, her voice turning sober.

I nodded but said nothing more as we headed down the hallway to the royal quarters.

How often had I walked this path, so carefree and without the trepidation that plagued me now? On the surface, nothing about the place had changed in the years I'd been gone, but underneath it all, I felt something sinister and alien lurking about. I looked in every shadow for signs of Xolotl, come to take Little Reed away from me forever.

Anger rolled through me though when we entered the family garden and my eyes found the column statue of Quetzalcoatl on the patio. It grinned at me, enjoying my pain. *His supposedly favored son lies dying and yet he still does nothing. Just more proof he doesn't care about anything but his own power.*

Malinalli escorted me to the light blue curtain emblazoned with a white and green feathered serpent. I hesitated, part of me afraid that I'd step inside and find that in my own self-absorption and fear I'd waited too long and he was already dead. Even the desire shivered inside me, equally afraid.

But I had to see him. I pushed the curtain open, took a deep breath, and stepped inside.

The smell of urine and decay met my nose, bringing forth memories of those couple of days when my mother took me to see my human grandmother where she'd laid abed coughing and wheezing. I hadn't understood any of it back then, why I had to not only tolerate the smell, but had to hold my breath as I had to kiss her sunken cheeks. I hadn't understood why my mother made me sit in there so still while I could hear all my friends' playful shouting from the gardens, and I hadn't understood why my mother had spent most of the visit smiling cheerfully only to burst into sobs once we left the room. I hadn't taken the need to say goodbye seriously and didn't even realize that I wouldn't get the chance to say it again until several days after.

And in the days following Nimilitzli's death, I'd spent a good deal of my bed time thinking about how once again I'd failed to say goodbye properly.

All of this raced through my mind as I stared down at the man lying in Little Reed's bed. I barely recognized him behind the shaggy beard and stringy silver hair. His chest rose slow and shallow under the blankets and furs, his breath rattling. *Still alive.* I sank to my knees next to him, some of the weight lifting from my shoulders. I wasn't too late. I found his skin clammy when I set my hand on his forehead, but he didn't stir.

"He rarely wakes up anymore," Malinalli whispered behind me. "And when he does, he's incoherent and doesn't recognize anyone."

Another daydream shattered; he wouldn't wake up and smile when he saw me again. A hot tear wound down the side of my nose and fell, to soak into the blanket lying over him. "He's made his confession to Tlazotlteotl?" I choked on the words.

"He didn't want to see her," Malinalli answered. "He told Mazatzin that she wouldn't see him anyway, and she's not the one he needs forgiveness from."

What had he meant by that? I couldn't imagine Little Reed needing forgiveness for anything, except perhaps his blindness to his father's true character, but that was hardly his fault.

I took his cool hand in mine and pulled it to my lips for a kiss. *If I did this to you with grief, Little Reed, I'm so very sorry. Please forgive me!*

Tinkling bells drew my attention to the doorway.

Anacoana stood there with a bowl in her hand and a look of shock on her face. "Quetzalpetlatl?" She almost dropped the bowl but fumbled it back under control, sloshing watery atole over her hands. "What are you doing here?" She stared in my direction with venom in her eyes, but not directly at me. When I looked down at Little Reed again, I realized she was reacting to my holding his hand.

My first impulse was to release my grip and apologize, but the desire growled like a cornered jaguar. *We loved him first. We have every right to hold him.* So I didn't let his hand go. "I came to see Topiltzin," I finally replied. "To see how he's been doing."

"Not very well, as you can see," she spat. "His mind has fallen down a dark shaft and he doesn't even recognize his own wife anymore. I fear I shall wake a widow any day now."

Malinalli glared at Anacoana. "That's hardly the appropriate tone to take with Tollan's queen, My Lady."

The color in Anacoana's face flared bright.

I held up my hand to cut off any further arguing though. "I wish I had arrived sooner, My Lady, but I'm here now, ready to pay my respects to Tollan's king...and her queen." I bowed to her.

Anacoana's furious expression softened and her jaw quivered. "You...you honor me, My Lady," she stammered.

To Malinalli, I said, "Would you give us a moment to speak alone?"

"Of course." She cast a hard glare at Anacoana before leaving.

Anacoana stared at the floor, trembling, so I began instead. "I'm sorry I upset you, My Lady. That wasn't my intension in coming here."

She shook her head. "No, please, forgive my harsh words. These last few years have been very difficult, watching the king slowly slip away—not just from me, but from everyone. I try not to be bitter, about being left to care for him on my own, but often it feels like more than I can handle."

I looked down at Little Reed again, my insides aching. "If I'd known this was what would happen to him so soon...."

Guilt now showed in her eyes. "Would you think me evil and spiteful if I admitted that I was relieved when you didn't return from Teotihuacan?"

"I understand why you would have been. I left because...I hoped it would finally let you and Topiltzin be happy together, in the way that seemed impossible so long as I was around."

Anacoana knelt beside the bed next to me, and looked down at Little Reed with a frown. "I thought surely he'd finally start noticing me, but instead he fell into a deep depression and barely spoke to me at all. Before you left, he at least made a perfunctory effort to honor our marriage, if only for appearances' sake, and to keep you from chastising him, but after you left.... I should have known it wouldn't make anything better." She stirred the atole in the bowl, looking on the verge of tears. "I should have known, on our very wedding night, that this marriage wasn't going to be everything I dreamed it would be." She cleared her throat before saying, "The child I was carrying...it wasn't Topiltzin's."

I nodded. "Citlallotoc told me as much."

She squeezed her eyes shut. "I thought maybe he did it out of pity for me—sending Citlallotoc to our wedding bed instead of coming himself—but after you left, it became obvious that I repulsed him."

"Surely not—"

"He still would not bed me, not even to ensure himself an heir after I delivered a stillborn child. I even told him—" She set the back of her hand to her mouth to stifle a sob, the tears coming now. "I even told him that he was obligated by the marriage contract to give me children, and that he was breaking his oath by refusing to do his husbandly duties to me, but do you know what he said to me? 'Then go find one of the guards that sparks your interest, and I'll say nothing about it.' Like I was a common whore!"

I stared down at Little Reed, taken aback. I tried imagining him being so indifferent, so callous, and though I couldn't hear him speak such words in my head, I doubted Anacoana was lying. I'd thought I knew Black Otter well, but he'd hidden his true character exceedingly well. And it cost me my son. "I'm so sorry, My Lady. No one deserves such cruelty."

She wiped away her tears with her wrist. "I might not have taken it so badly had Citlallotoc still been here; after all, for a little while, he and I had been happy with our arrangement. But as you can probably guess, he's too honorable to continue cuckolding his king, even with Topiltzin's permission. I resented him for that, but in my heart I still longed for him, and when he left too...." She shook her head.

When she didn't go on, I cautiously asked, "Why did he leave?"

"I don't know. He never spoke a word to me again after I accused him of turning his back on me when he found I was with child." She sniffled then sat straighter. "Forgive me, but I really must feed the king. Would you help me sit him up?"

I worked Little Reed slowly to a sitting position against the wall while he grumbled and coughed. He opened his eyes, but they were octli-colored, and staring, oblivious.

"Topiltzin, it's me," I whispered near his ear, hoping for a reaction, but he just wheezed and tried to slouch again. I sat against the wall next to him, holding him upright while Anacoana patiently spoon-fed him the atole. Half of it went directly from his lips down into his scraggly beard, and she wiped it away with a cloth, as if he were a drooling infant. Once the bowl was empty, I laid him back down and he drifted off again in a matter of breaths.

I watched Anacoana dab at the mess of atole in his whiskers, making sure he was cleaned up. "If he'd treated me the way he treated you...I don't know that I'd be here now taking care of him, as you are," I admitted.

"It's my duty." She tossed the dirty cloth into the corner where other laundry lay piled. "And for once, I'm actually the most important person in his life."

Indeed. I couldn't look her in the eye though. Instead I focused my blurry gaze down at him. "He doesn't even recognize me anymore."

Anacoana folded her hands in her lap. "I'm sorry, My Lady. This must be terrible for you, seeing him like this."

I wiped my knuckles across my eyes. "Thank you for taking care of him...making him comfortable in his final days. And I'm sorry I wasn't here to alleviate some of the burden for you."

She reached over and grasped my hand. When I looked up at her, she smiled. "You're here now."

The hope in her eyes was too much to bear. "If you'll excuse me, I must speak with Malinalli and Mazatzin." I rose and hurried outside into the garden, welcoming the fresh air after the stifling smell of sickness.

Both Malinalli and Mazatzin stood near the hallway back into the palace. Malinalli hurried over when I stepped out. "I'm sorry about Lady Anacoana's harshness—"

"She's entitled to it," I said. "I left a mess for her to look after."

"Everything has been tough since you left," Mazatzin said as he stepped up too. "For everyone."

"I imagine so. And Topiltzin has been like this for a year, you said?"

Mazatzin nodded. "He's deteriorated a great deal more in the last month or so; he used to respond to our voices, but now...."

"The end is close." I choked on the words and had to clear my throat to go on. "It's a good thing I came when I did."

"Indeed," Malinalli said. "Good both for the king, and the kingdom. We need our queen back more than ever." She gave Mazatzin a pointed look.

He nodded again. "The future of Tollan is in question, My Lady, and much needs your attention."

I bit my lip. "I don't know how much help I can be—"

Mazatzin looked back into the hallway but then took my arm and led me across the garden, to the far side. "Matlacxochitl is poised to seize the throne once the Black Dog comes for Topiltzin," he whispered once we were on the portico.

"He impersonated Topiltzin so he could name himself the next king, since there is no blood heir," Malinalli added. "But now that you're back, you can dispute that claim."

"I don't understand. How has he even been able to impersonate Topiltzin? They look nothing alike," I pointed out.

"After you left, Topiltzin started wearing the mask," Malinalli said. "The one you saw Matlacxochitl wearing earlier."

"Why?"

She glanced at Mazatzin before answering, "He was so depressed...about you leaving...that he didn't want anyone to see his face when he appeared in public."

I snapped my mouth shut.

"Though I'm sure Citlallotoc's departure contributed too," she added. "He didn't leave his quarters for a week after that."

Wonderful. I'd made it easy for Matlacxochitl to step right onto Little Reed's throne. "But maybe this is all for the best. Matlacxochitl was a good governor in Chimalhuacan—"

"He's begun undoing everything you and Topiltzin built," Mazatzin said. "He's removed many of the restrictions on sacrifices, including the requirement that all willing victims register their consent with the royal court. And he's defacing the Feathered Serpent's temple."

I creased my brow. "Defacing it?"

"He's having the columns re-carved, in the likeness of warriors. He claims Topiltzin told him to do this, under orders from the god himself, but Tollan is a city of peace, so why would we place warriors directly inside the temple?"

It was a good question, and my instincts told me this was a bad sign, but the desire growled, *Why should we care if someone is undermining Quetzalcoatl? How is that any different from what we're planning to do?*

I'm not worried about him, I countered. *I'm worried about Malinalli and Mazatzin, and the citizens of Tollan. They don't deserve to get hurt.*

Indeed not, the desire conceded. *And how dare anyone impersonate Little Reed?*

I stood taller. I'd created this mess, and the least I could do for my friends was try to fix it. "I will speak with the Council, and with Matlacxochitl. Immediately."

CHAPTER SEVENTEEN

While Mazatzin went to call the meeting in the great hall, Malinalli came to my old quarters with me, to help me change out of my dull, plain wrapper and into my royal regalia.

"Topiltzin wouldn't let anyone take over your quarters after you left, not even when Anacoana told him she would need its easier access to the royal nursery. He kept it all exactly the way you left it," she told me as she led me inside.

He indeed had; even the cloak I'd abandoned on the bed the morning I'd left for Teotihuacan still lay undisturbed. Surprisingly, there wasn't a layer of dust on everything; apparently the servants still came in and cleaned regularly, if only to keep away the decay. I picked up the cloak, taking me back to that day when I'd looked around with a heaviness born of the knowledge that I might very possibly never see it again, since I was heading into a confrontation with an evil sorcerer god. It felt surprisingly right to be here again, in the actual room rather than in a divine facsimile. I closed my eyes and breathed in the smell of bone flowers drifting in from my own private garden beyond the bath yard patio. It calmed the buzzing anxiety my visit with Little Reed had left me with.

"Do you want to bathe first?" Malinalli asked as she disappeared into my dressing room.

After so many years on the move, the thought of a luxurious hot bath was tempting, but I didn't have time for frivolities. I needed to set things right, and I still had to get Little Reed alone, so I could finally tell him the truth and say my goodbyes. The longer I remained here, the more likely Mextli would notice my absence and question me about it. "Perhaps later," I answered.

She hurried back with a dress and two robes. "So which one do you want? Your royal robe, or your high priestess one?" She held up the latter, as if to encourage me to choose it.

But seeing the gold and silver feathered serpents sown on the front brought an unpleasant heat in my gut. "No, you're the high priestess now. I will wear the other one."

Once I'd changed into the dress and donned my robe, Malinalli brought out my jewelry box for me to pick pieces out. Among the gold and turquoise necklaces and bangles, I spotted the silver feathered serpent bracelet Citlallotoc had given me. I stared at it a moment, a flux of guilt and self-loathing fighting in my stomach before I settled for the feather and turquoise necklace that had once been my mother's. Malinalli then fixed my white heron-feather headdress on my head.

"I swear, it looks like you haven't aged a day since I last saw you," she commented as she examined her work. "Wish I could say the same about myself."

"There's nothing shameful in growing older. Besides, I think it looks very good on you, and I bet Mitotia thinks so too."

Her lips twitched, making me wonder if I'd hit a tender nerve, but she then smiled. "You're all ready."

◻

Most of the Council was already in the great hall when I arrived. Some of them recognized me and came forward in greeting, but at least half of them were unknown to me. Those ones kept their distance, whispering amongst themselves. Curiously there were no women on the council as there had been when I had still been Tollan's queen. Matlacxochitl had indeed been switching the pieces around on the patolli board.

With the greetings finished, I crested the step onto the dais and looked down at the reed-woven icpalli throne before me. "I would like to know where my throne is," I announced, turning back to the crowd.

Matlacxochitl's older brother Blood Wolf stepped forward, looking very grizzled and frail, a far cry from that fiery-tempered young man who had whisked my mother and I off to safety in Xochicalco so long ago. "The King had it put away in storage a few months ago, My Lady. He'd given up hope of your return and it pained him too much to have it sitting empty next to him every time he held court."

I scrutinized Blood Wolf, wondering if he didn't know of his brother's machinations, or if he took me for an ignorant fool. Until I learned the truth, I decided it best to play the part of the fool. "I suppose this will do for now." I sat down, which brought a wave of confused—and hostile— whispers among the men.

I took my time settling in then looked around. Not seeing Matlacxochitl, I sighed. "Oh, where is my dearest brother? Surely someone told him I wished him to be here for this meeting?"

"I informed him myself, My Lady," Mazatzin answered from where he stood next to the doorway. "I assured him that you very much wanted to speak with him."

Just then the Justice of the Peace strode through the doorway, followed by Matlacxochitl dressed as himself in his old half-mask.

When Blood Wolf saw his brother, he started and rose to his feet again. "Brother? When did you come to Tollan?"

"He's been here for several years now," Mazatzin answered.

"Several years?" The surprise and hurt on Blood Wolf's face told me all I needed to know.

Without answering his brother, Matlacxochitl approached the dais and bowed, sweeping his fingers across the ground at my feet. "Forgive my tardiness, My Lady, but I had to change clothing before the meeting."

"Indeed. I certainly would have been displeased if you'd shown up dressed *inappropriately*." When he started rising, I snapped, "I did not dismiss you yet."

"I beg your pardon, My Lady."

"You should be begging more than my pardon, Lord Matlacxochitl, considering your crimes against the Crown."

The color drained from Blood Wolf's face. "Crimes, My Lady? What has my brother done?"

I sat straighter, watching Matlacxochitl with intense eyes. "Yes, Lord Matlacxochitl. Please tell everyone what you've been doing for the last few years since your arrival in Tollan."

This time he looked up to meet my arrow-like gaze. "I was doing my duty to the Kingdom, and Lord Topiltzin, My Lady," he retorted.

"And what duty requires you to pose as my brother and fool not only Tollan's citizens, but the city's own Council?"

Blood Wolf started coughing in distress. "What is she talking about, Brother?" he choked out.

I stood, letting the rage and indignation carry me to my feet. "Lord Matlacxochitl has been pretending to be the king while Topiltzin has lain bedridden and dying, all with the intent of naming himself Tollan's heir once my brother passed on to Mictlan."

Matlacxochitl shot to his own feet, fists clenched. "It wouldn't have been necessary if Tollan's queen hadn't run out on her own responsibilities, and if the king had been of sound enough mind to think to name an heir after his wife miscarried. Someone had to think about the people and their future."

"A future that turns its back on everything Topiltzin and I built here? How dare you undo the founding principles of Tollan, and do it in Topiltzin's name!"

"The changes you and Lord Topiltzin made are admirable in theory, My Lady, but they are impractical in practice—"

"*Do not trifle with me, human,*" the desire snarled but I caught myself before I could say more. I breathed deeply and stood straighter, smoothing my hands down the front of my robe. "It doesn't matter what you think, because you will not be king once my brother passes on to Mictlan; in fact, you will leave Tollan tonight, and you will never return."

Matlacxochitl pursed his lips, his face darkening. "You're exiling me?"

"Would you rather I hand down a death sentence? After all, what you've done could be considered high treason."

My words brought a confused murmur to the crowd. Matlacxochitl set his jaw and didn't respond.

Maybe we should kill him anyway, the desire growled, but I held firm. There was no capital punishment in Tollan, and no matter how much I thirsted for Matlacxochitl's blood in the name of justice, I would follow the law, out of respect for Little Reed. My disregarding it in the past hadn't turned out well.

I motioned to the guards, who stepped forward. "You will escort Lord Matlacxochitl from the city."

They hesitated, looking at each other and then the Council.

"You heard your queen," Blood Wolf barked. His jaw quivered as if he might break into tears under his furrowed brows. "Now carry out your orders."

The guards took Matlacxochitl by the arms and escorted him from the great hall. He held my gaze while I lanced my own angry one right back at him, daring him to say anything. But he left without protest or resistance.

Blood Wolf came forward and knelt on the floor before me. "I must apologize for my brother's conduct, My Lady. As his blood relation, I share in his shame."

"Of course you don't, Lord Blood Wolf. I have known you to always be an honorable, loyal man, and whatever your brother chose to do, he alone bears the burden of that guilt," I insisted. "Please rise."

He didn't stand, but he did raise his head to meet my gaze. "Then let me take this moment to renew my fealty to you, as Tollan's queen."

"And I gladly accept it. Please rise, Lord Blood Wolf."

He finally came to his feet, slowly, matching his frail appearance. "Is it indeed true that Lord Topiltzin is dying?"

I nodded. "I have seen him myself, and he is indeed expecting the Black Dog any time now."

Blood Wolf looked around at the others. "Why were none of us told of this?"

Mazatzin stepped forward. "Both Lady Malinalli and I were sworn to secrecy under the threat of death, as was the king's wife. The guards who were privy were loyal to Matlacxochitl, and so kept his secrets." He cast his glare at the Justice of the Peace, who had imperceptibly moved towards the doorway out before then. "As was Lord Timaltzin."

Timaltzin froze, his distressed gaze locked with mine.

I glared at him, my fists clenching. "Guards, seize him as well."

"I had no choice, My Lady!" Timaltzin cried, struggling against the guards. "Lord Matlacxochitl threatened my family if I didn't go along with him!"

My gut was to distrust him—he'd been rather snappy with me when I'd arrived—but I didn't know him at all, had never even met him, so maybe he was telling the truth. "Your involvement will be investigated and put to trial. In the meantime, you will reside in the prison yard."

He wept as the guards removed him from the great hall.

"Lord Blood Wolf." When he turned to me again, I stood and motioned him up onto the dais. "As a loyal subject of Tollan, and a man I know personally to be of high character, I wish to offer you the position of Justice of the Peace. I beg you accept this honor."

He bowed. "I am both pleased and humbled by your faith in me, My Lady. Thank you." When I sat again, he took the position at my right, where Citlallotoc had always stood when that rank had belonged to him.

"Your first duty as Justice of the Peace will be to identify who is still loyal to Topiltzin and bring those who have turned their back on him to account before the throne." I looked around at the other Council members as I spoke, taking in the diversity of reactions, ranging from stern nods of agreement to darting gazes and stiff frowns. I addressed the crowd. "I know that I have been missing from Tollan for a number of years, and many of you have doubts and fears about where we all go from here. But know this: I will personally see to Tollan's future and ensure that there is no struggle or unrest when the time comes for Topiltzin to leave us. There will be peaceful transition from one king to the next, and that king will carry on the important works that Topiltzin and I started here."

Many of the men nodded and hooted their approval. I made note of who remained silent, for Blood Wolf to question later.

"Let us feast to honor your return, My Lady," Blood Wolf suggested. "It will not be a grand feast, given the short notice, but we can still celebrate in good order."

I nodded. "You will see to it for me?"

"Absolutely. And perhaps tomorrow we can prepare something much larger and invite all of the nobles?"

"A good idea. The citizenry should know of the situation, so they too can rest easy knowing their future is being looked after with utmost care."

Blood Wolf bowed and stepped down from the dais to address the crowd. "Let us adjourn until nightfall, so we might prepare ourselves and our spouses for tonight's festivities. If you wish to renew your pledge of fealty, please arrive an hour prior to the feasting."

As the crowd dispersed in a flurry of conversation, I motioned Malinalli to me. "Please bring Mitotia tonight. I'm looking forward to seeing her again."

She nodded and turned to leave too, but then stopped to ask, "Should I invite Amoxtli too?"

"He's here in Tollan?" The last I'd heard he was the fire priest of Quetzalcoatl back in Culhuacan.

"He returned shortly after you left, to assume guardianship of his niece when Lord Black Otter and Night Wind went missing." She frowned. "Such a tragedy for her; she's lost so much of her family."

I gritted my teeth against the guilt grinding in my gut. "Tragic indeed. Yes, I would like him to attend, and Cuicatl as well."

She bowed then finally left.

By then, only Mazatzin remained behind, smiling at me with brotherly affection. "I cannot tell you how relieved I am that you've returned home, Quetzalpetlatl."

"It is so very good to see you again, my friend." I hugged my arms against my chest as I looked around. "So much has changed."

"As have you as well."

I started. "How have I changed?"

He shrugged. "I cannot put it into words, but your presence feels very different than it used to. Have you come to terms with whatever it was that made you leave in the first place?"

Now was my turn to shrug. "Come to an acceptance, perhaps, but some things can't be moved beyond...at least not just yet."

He nodded. "I must admit that...after all you said that morning, about the god and being through...this was the last place I ever expected to see you again."

"I hesitated for a long time, but in the end, I had to see Topiltzin one last time. And I had to make sure that you and Malinalli were all right. Seeing what Matlacxochitl was doing...I'm very glad I did come back. He would have returned us to the days of Ihuitimal, which is why finding the right successor for Topiltzin is a top priority."

"Do you have someone in mind?"

I smiled at him. "Well, you would make a very fine king."

But he shook his head. "And it is a job I would not accept. There are leaders, and then there are servants, and I'm afraid that in my heart, I am the latter."

"One can be both," I corrected him.

"Yes, one can. Both you and Topiltzin exemplify that. I, however, am not that kind of man."

I chuckled. "Always so modest. But don't worry, I know the temperature of your heart when it comes to ruling. I have someone else in mind."

"Who?"

"Citlallotoc, of course. He is Topiltzin's best friend, and best man, and he was an integral part of Tollan's founding and keeping the law. What better candidate could there be?"

Mazatzin frowned. "While I agree he is the best man for the throne, I don't know that you could convince him of it. He and Topiltzin haven't spoken in five years. I don't believe they parted on good terms."

"That may be, but surely he wouldn't deny his queen's summons?"

"Probably not, but he might well deny your more important request."

"We won't know until we ask him, will we? I need you to journey to Acolman and bring him here, so I may convince him that there is no better man for this job. And tell him that I won't accept *no* for an answer." I cringed almost as soon as I said it; I hadn't accepted his repeated *no*'s that night on the sacred precinct in Teotihuacan either, and now look at how things were. "Tell him I would be eternally grateful to him if he would come see me to discuss this important business."

He nodded. "Should I leave right away? If I hurry, I could likely get passage with a trade caravan heading out tonight."

"It would be for the best. We can't let disorder in the throne's succession continue much longer. Your having to leave so abruptly won't cause trouble with anyone close to you? A wife or a lover?"

Smiling bashfully, Mazatzin replied, "My devotions rest only with the god, and my king and queen. As always, my house is otherwise empty."

I smiled back, wistful. "I suppose not all of us are made for that kind of life, are we?" *And yet some of us feel incomplete without it.* I gave him a hug, taking in the solid, muscular bulk of his body, and the presence of the hump on his shoulder; he was so like his father physically and yet so very different in every other way. "Be sure to hurry back."

"If all goes well, I should be back within the week, with Citlallotoc."

"Thank you."

As I watched him go, I indeed felt grateful that I'd finally found the courage to come back.

CHAPTER EIGHTEEN

Most of the Council came early to renew their vows of fealty to me, and a few more showed up late, as the servants brought the food out. They apologized for their tardiness and promised to make their pledges on the morrow, when it wouldn't interrupt the feasting and celebrating. I noticed five of the men who had been at the earlier council meeting didn't show up for the feast at all, and when I mentioned this to Blood Wolf, he promised to investigate their whereabouts after the meal.

I didn't give much more thought to it though. As an immortal, I didn't worry about things like assassins or kidnappers plotting against me anymore. I could set any attacker to rights with a mere flick of my finger. I'd seldom thought myself fearful when I was still a mortal queen, but that had been an illusion created by the constant presence of armed guards protecting me. Blood Wolf had assigned me guards but I found their presence more annoying than anything.

But I would let that go for everyone else's sake. It was best to play my role and not let it known that I was anyone but the woman they all remembered.

The high priests and priestesses of the various religious orders came as well, and though I was unfamiliar with the new high priest of the Smoking Mirror, the Chichimec woman Yaretzi was still his high priestess. She greeted me with an unsettlingly amused smile, though perhaps my reaction had more to do with the faint odor of guano that lingered around her. I didn't recall her ever smelling so repugnant, but maybe she'd been sacrificing bats to her dark god. It was a relief when she finally moved off to join the other priests in conversation; though I had the distinct feeling she was still watching me from afar.

Mitotia smiled politely when she came into the great hall at Malinalli's side and I embraced her heartily, squeezing her tight. The tattoo of the feathered serpent along her jawline looked newly freshened with ink and I tried to avoid looking at it if only to keep from letting a distasteful frown find its way onto my own face. Another reminder that my feud with Quetzalcoatl had nothing to do with those who worshipped him in blissful ignorance of his true character. Still, like always, my eye was drawn to it whenever I looked at her face.

"You're looking very well," I remarked as I escorted her to the two mats near the throne, which I'd reserved for her and Malinalli. "The fire priestess robes suit you."

"Thank you, My Lady. And you're looking very well too." When we stopped at the mats, she looked me over, a puzzled look on her face. "In fact...I could have sworn you used to have silver in your hair."

"I've been pulling them out whenever I find them," I lied. I hadn't given much thought to my own appearance for a while now, and in my mind's eye, I didn't have silver hairs. Given how many times I reformed my body from my teotl each day, it made sense that I'd unconsciously changed how I looked.

Malinalli smiled, accepting my explanation, but Mitotia continued studying my face with a suspicious eye. I smiled back, unsure what more to say.

Malinalli cleared her throat, finally distracting Mitotia. "Some people age more gracefully than others. There's no need to stare so, Mitotia."

"It's all right," I assured her. "I have been gone a while."

"Where were you?" Mitotia asked.

"Travelling. I never stayed in one place for long."

"And you found what you were looking for?"

I furrowed my brows. "Why do you think I was looking for anything?"

"Why else would you leave? If not to look for something you were missing?"

My face heated with a mixture of discomfort and anger. Why was she interrogating me so?

"That's quite enough, don't you think, Mitotia?" Malinalli cast me an apologetic glance. "What matters is she's back."

"Are you?" Mitotia asked, not letting me off that easily.

Thankfully I saw Amoxtli enter the great hall, saving me. "If you'll excuse me, my cousin has arrived and I really should go greet him." Without waiting for an answer, I hurried over to the entrance where Amoxtli stood, looking around.

A misty-eyed smile broke out on his face when I called out to him as I cut through the crush of men and women. He hurried to me and pulled me into a crushing hug. "Dear gods, I was sure you were gone for good," he murmured, tears in his voice. It was strange to see him so emotionally vulnerable; he was a plumper version of his father Ihuitimal, but he had a weary, weathered look about him. It was readily apparent these last five years had taken a heavy toll on him.

"It's so good to see you again, cousin," I whispered, unable to stop my own tears. "How have you been?"

"Busy. Always busy." He wiped at his cheeks then turned to a young woman standing behind him. "You remember Cuicatl?"

Cuicatl stepped up, an ill-tempered boredom hanging about her. She looked a good deal like her mother Jade Flower, but she had Black Otter's intense eyes. Standing next to Amoxtli, they looked very much like a troubled family.

"I do remember." The look on her face said that touching was off-limits, so I gave her a bow. "I suppose you often hear that you look like your mother."

She cast me an annoyed glance but then looked away before saying, "Sometimes."

"You're what...seventeen summers now?"

She sniffed in the affirmative.

"Did you take the trials to become a priestess?"

"She decided the priestly life isn't for her," Amoxtli answered. "Right now she's apprenticing with the feather worker who provides all of the king's banners."

"You enjoy it?" I asked Cuicatl.

She shrugged. "I suppose."

As we walked towards the head of the great hall, Amoxtli whispered, "Please pardon her, cousin. She's had a rough time: first she lost her mother, and then her father walked out on her, taking her brother with him."

Was that what they thought? "That's...horrible. No wonder she's so surly."

"I tried to do right by her, being that I'm all that's left of her immediate family, but I'm afraid I know little about children. I undoubtedly made mistakes along the way. She barely talks to me either."

"I'm so sorry."

"Perhaps I did the wrong thing by pushing her to embrace faith in the Feathered Serpent to help get through her losses, but I guess, after losing so many people, doubt feels a little more useful than faith."

I glanced back at Cuicatl as I climbed the dais. She was me; bitter and disenchanted and angry at having been a chisel others used to transfer blows. It soured my gut to know that I'd been a part of making her that way.

◌

After the feast, Malinalli escorted me back to my quarters. When we turned down the hallway from the vestibule, I noticed Mitotia watching us, a conflicted look on her face. She quickly turned and disappeared down the hallway to the priestly quarters when she realized I'd seen her.

"Is all well with you and Mitotia?" I asked as we walked.

"Of course." Malinalli didn't look at me though.

"I hope my being here isn't causing problems—"

"Why ever would you think that?"

I snapped my mouth shut. I couldn't admit that I'd overheard their conversation earlier today. Eventually I said, "I don't know. She didn't seem entirely comfortable when we talked, as if she doesn't trust me or something." When Malinalli didn't answer, I added, "It's understandable. I have been gone a long time, so naturally she'd be skeptical of why I've come back."

This time Malinalli smiled. "It's her skepticism that will make her a very strong high priestess when I step down."

"You're not going to stay the high priestess?"

She shook her head. "As much as I enjoy the work, she's the one you were grooming to take your place, and I bow to your superior knowledge of the matter, as the god's chosen high priestess."

"Mitotia will make a good high priestess someday, but my choice was just as political as anything else, Malinalli. Don't throw away your future because of a decision I made long ago in order to appease an offended ally."

"You know it's a position I never aspired to."

I sighed. "I know."

When we reached my room, she turned down the blankets for me and asked if I wanted to take a bath before bed. I told her I was fine, and so she bade me good night and started to leave. But she stopped at the curtain, hesitating.

I was eager to return to the Mexica camp; I'd stayed later than I thought prudent, but seeing her indecision now, I couldn't just send her away. "Do you want to talk?"

After a tense pause, she finally said, "I wish I could say Mitotia and I were happy, but...things that must happen in secrecy rarely ever remain good for long."

"Indeed not. It often becomes a burden difficult to bear."

"I love her as much as ever, but I've started to think that's just not enough, especially when it could cost us everything."

"Is someone threatening you?"

Malinalli fumbled with her hands as she turned to look at me. "Let's just say that the royal court isn't as let-live as it once was. Matlacxochitl's methods of rule weren't your brother's, and he surrounded himself with people who think just like him. He instituted an outright ban on relationships like mine and Mitotia's, and one of the guards found out about us and has threatened to expose us before the entire council...." She started shaking, tears flooding down her cheeks.

I hurried over to embrace her. "You don't have to worry about that anymore. Matlacxochitl isn't the law in Tollan, and I won't let anyone like him take the throne. In fact, I've already sent Mazatzin to Acolman to bring Citlallotoc back, so I can name him Tollan's heir."

She wiped her tears away. "Then what everyone says about you and Citlallotoc...it's true?"

I furrowed my brows. "What is everyone saying?"

"That you two were in love, but Topiltzin couldn't stand his best friend taking you to wife, and he forbade it, so you ran away, and Citlallotoc did the same a few weeks later, to be with you."

"I haven't seen Citlallotoc in five years."

She nodded. "It's just...the guards who went with you to Teotihuacan told stories, about you and Citlallotoc...on the steps of the Temple of the Moon."

A heated flush crept up my neck and I withdrew back to the bed. "Well, that much is true."

She sat next to me on the blankets. "Is that why you left?"

I didn't answer, but I couldn't meet her eyes.

"But if the two of you didn't run off to be together...then where have you been?"

"It's not important. What matters is that I'm going to fix all the messes I made, and then I will leave everyone in peace again, hopefully for good this time."

"You're not staying?" When I nodded, she sputtered, "But...but we need you! Tollan needs her queen, now more than ever!"

I shook my head. "I set this life aside five years ago, Malinalli. I can't come back to it."

"Of course you can!"

"You don't understand; I'm not the woman I was back then."

"Why not?"

"Because too much has happened; too much has changed for me, and I can't ever be that...that woman again."

Malinalli set a hand on my shoulder. "What really happened to you in Teotihuacan? Mazatzin said you cursed the Feathered Serpent and warned me not to trust him."

I shook my head, the words caught in my throat and the threat of tears stinging my eyes.

"Please tell me what went wrong, Quetzalpetlatl."

"I found out the truth, and it was more than I could handle," I finally sputtered.

"The truth about what?"

I shook my head. "If I told you, it would change everything between us."

"Surely not—"

"No, truly. If you knew the truth about me...we wouldn't be able to sit here talking like friends anymore."

"What could you have possibly done that would make me turn so absolutely against you?" she asked, worry in her eyes.

I laughed. She'd read that completely wrong. "Well, I did execute Black Otter, for murdering my son."

She stared at me, her mouth agape. "Black Otter killed Ehecacone?"

"In a jealous rage over Topiltzin. He just couldn't let go...."

"I'm so sorry, Quetzalpetlatl." She pulled me into a fierce hug.

I hadn't wanted the contact—in fact I was so strung up that the thought of anyone touching me made my magic pulse angrily—but as soon as her arms closed around me, the cloak of rage and fear slid away, replaced with a calm heat of gratefulness and safety. I hugged her back, burying my face in her shoulder. She stroked my hair, not saying anything, just being there.

But when I finally looked up at her again, the warmth grew into a pulsing heat. We were leaned in so close together that her breasts pressed against mine, soft and enticing in a way I'd never allowed myself to consider. Pain and longing lurked in her dark eyes, bringing a hitch to my chest and a throb to my ears. I thought of that time long ago when I'd nearly asked her to join me and Black Otter in my bed; of all of the times I'd seen her body when we'd shared a steam bath when we were just priestesses; the feel of her fingers dragging through my hair when she'd brushed and fixed my hair for me. *Women are the best,* Xochiquetzal had told me, and in that moment, finding out if she was right seemed eminently important.

I didn't have to make the first move though. Malinalli closed the small gap between us, but unlike the countless men I'd known, she didn't try to devour my mouth with hers, imposing her will. Instead she brushed her lips against my own, as if begging permission, and only when I moved mine against hers did she commit. She enveloped me in the sweet fragrance of jaguar flowers, making my mind drift, but my blood pulsed with raw, joyous desire, drowning out the sorrows plaguing my heart. She slid her hands up to my neck, to my cheeks, kind and comforting— something I hadn't felt in so very long and missed so very badly.

My hands wandered down her sides, taking in the softness of not just the robe's fabric, but of her body underneath. My own shivered, and she deepened the kiss. When my hands reached her hips, I bunched the cloth in my fists, kneading and pulling at it with increasing desperation. And growing hunger.

But you must be careful. It's very easy to drain them without much effort.

Xochiquetzal's warning broke through the fog in my head and I tore myself away from Malinalli, my heart thudding. She stared back at me with a worried look, almost as if she couldn't see me anymore but sensed my presence, like an apparition. As the haziness faded from her eyes, replaced by bewilderment, I turned away, gulping down fear and guilt. What in Mictlan was I doing?

"Quetzalpetlatl—"

"I'm sorry. I shouldn't have...we can't...."

"Why—?"

"I don't want to hurt you, Malinalli...or Mitotia."

She squeezed her eyes shut, balling her fists at her side. "Dear gods, what have I done?"

"You didn't do anything. I did it—"

But she shook her head. "I have to go. I'm sorry, but...I have to go." She hurried out into the garden, tearing aside the door curtain in her hurry.

I ran after her. "It's not your fault, Malinalli! Please! Come back! There's something I must tell you!" What did it matter now if I told her the truth of my nature? I'd already irrevocably changed everything for us.

But by the time I reached the portico outside my door, I saw only the tail of her robe just before she vanished down the corridor back into the palace. When Anacoana appeared at her own door curtain, blurry-eyed, I ducked back inside my room.

When I looked up to see the Feathered Serpent mural grinning back at me, I scooped up a small wooden idol next to my bed and threw it at it. The hollow idol split neatly in half but the plaster in the middle of Quetzalcoatl's face broke off all over the ground. "You must find it so funny, watching me fail at not hurting those I love," I panted.

The bells on my door curtain jingled. "Quetzalpetlatl?" Anacoana called. "Are you all right?"

Anguish stoked the plaintive pulse of hunger in my gut. I couldn't stay here and risk causing more trouble, so I jumped into the teoyoh without answering.

CHAPTER NINETEEN

When I returned to the Mexica camp, I slumped on the floor inside my tent, heavy with dread. "Why do I wreck everything I touch?" I muttered, sniffling back tears. Was I making a huge mistake involving myself in the succession issue in Tollan? Was I just helping Quetzalcoatl continue his lies? And would Mextli see my actions as a betrayal?

We can't go back, the desire agreed, even more surly than usual. *We'll only make things worse if we do.*

But we promised—

Let them work it out on their own. We've exposed Matlacxochitl, and Citlallotoc will come back and take the throne. They don't need us; humans are resilient in ways we never will be.

But what about what happened with Malinalli? Don't we owe her an explanation? But I felt only defensiveness when I thought of what happened.

It doesn't matter, the desire scolded me. *We can't change what happened. We need to stop hemming. Ehecacone is waiting for us to rescue him, so let's get on with this. We must convince Mextli to take us to see Smoking Mirror and we'll finally be done with the Feathered Serpent, once and for all.*

On that I could agree without hesitation. It was time to put aside my distaste for Smoking Mirror for the good of my son.

But when I reached Mextli's tent, he wasn't there, nor was he hiding out in a private bubble of the Divine Dream—or if he was, he wasn't answering me. I reached out with my divine senses.

I smelled his presence in the streams of magic coursing everywhere, but I hesitated to follow it. What if he didn't want to be bothered right now? Privacy was just as important to gods as it was to mortals, and it would be intrusive to show up unannounced.

Then let's go somewhere nearby, so we can at least know where he is, the desire suggested.

I reached out with my divine senses and a blink later I stood at the mouth of a path leading into a moonlit forest. Mextli must have been somewhere up the path, but where exactly was I?

It wasn't until I looked around and saw the tall stone walls of my garden outlined against the sky behind me that I realized I was in Omeyocan. A second path—this one of jagged stone steps—wound up a nearby mountainside to a circular building with clouds swirling serenely around it. Off to my right a third path led to the fields where Xipe Totec lived among his rows of maize.

I stared down the wooded path before me, but soon my gaze wandered back to the building on the mountain. It was Quetzalcoatl's house, as Mextli had told me. I didn't want to go up there.

And yet an irresistible impulse drew me towards the stairs. It wasn't as if Mextli was expecting me, after all, and he had said that Quetzalcoatl hadn't been back to Omeyocan for years. Part of me needed to go up there, almost as if seeing where he lived would somehow explain why the god I'd once loved so deeply could betray me.

After another glance towards the woods, I instead trekked slowly up the ragged steps carved out of the boulders and dirt.

I reached the top with surprising speed. Even though it was the middle of the night, the clouds were startlingly bright, and they slithered like snakes across the ground, coiling around my feet, encouraging me forward to the plain white door curtain hanging in tatters. I pulled it aside and peered within, my heart pounding.

I half expected to see Quetzalcoatl coiled up in his feathered serpent form, shaking the rattle on his tail just before striking me with his silver fangs, but the interior was completely empty. There was no hearth, no water jars, no blankets. The white walls were smooth, interrupted only by curtainless windows every few paces. The inside was massively large—much larger than I would have thought, given the size of the exterior. I stood in the center of the room and looked around, my hair ruffling in the gentle breezes twisting in through the unobstructed windows. It was a surprisingly calming place.

Feeling less apprehensive now, I went to one of the windows and looked out, over the buildings and fields below me. The path through the woods wasn't visible in the dark, but a glow of light filtered up through the forest canopy a ways into it. I spotted Xipe Totec tending his patch of maize and beans by the light of a bonfire in the clearing where we'd talked, dressed in his ragged old cape of human skin. Next to his field came the tall walls of my own garden. If it had been daylight out, I probably could have seen into my garden from this high vantage point, but it was shrouded in cold darkness now.

"It's really a very spectacular view, isn't it?" an unfamiliar voice spoke up behind me, and I jumped. I whirled around to see an old woman in the doorway, a halo of faint white light pulsing off her. Her eyes crinkled when she smiled at me. "My apologies. I didn't mean to startle you."

"Who are you?" I asked, taking deep breaths to slow my throbbing pulse.

"I'm just a very old creator goddess," she replied, coming inside. She didn't have a staff, but she walked with a slight hunch. "The humans call me the Snake Woman."

"Cihuacoatl," I whispered, awed. She was one of the very oldest of the gods, *the* mother goddess of all mother goddesses.

She nodded. "Then you're familiar with me?"

"I learned all about you in calmecac—that's the humans' priestly school—"

"I know. It was I who suggested to Quetzalcoatl to inspire the humans to create the schools to teach future priests and priestesses our stories." She shuffled over to my side and she too looked out over the fields and gardens below. "I'm also the one who taught him the secrets of creation; the same knowledge he in turn taught to you. You've done some very interesting things with it."

I furrowed my brow. "What do you mean?"

She chuckled. "Before you and Ehecatl formed that tree in Tamoachan, sex was no different than eating or drinking; a bodily necessity, but nothing more. But you took that knowledge and you stirred it around in your own nature and turned it into something completely new, something the world had never seen before. And it changed everyone. It changed civilization itself."

I shrugged. "It just happened. It's not as if I set out to change anything."

"It's the ones no one intended that end up mattering the most," Cihuacoatl replied. "Even we gods cannot fully comprehend how our choices can change the world, and even ourselves." She scrutinized me for a moment then said, "I hear you've been trying to recruit other gods to help you in some conflict with the Feathered Serpent."

I returned the considering gaze. "I was. And everyone but Smoking Mirror seems to want to stay out of it."

Cihuacoatl laughed. "When it comes to Quetzalcoatl, of course Smoking Mirror can't help himself. That conflict started at the dawn of time and it will continue long after humanity has disappeared. Listen to an old goddess, Mayahuel: you'd do best to stay out of that yourself."

"I can't. My son's life depends on it."

She shook her head. "My poor dear. One of the things they don't teach in the calmecac is that when it comes to the gods, it is our greatest gifts that are also our greatest weaknesses."

"Meaning?"

"Your love for your son is a means to an end for ambitious gods looking to increase their own power."

My temper flared. "Am I just supposed to abandon him, then?"

"Of course not. Just know that whatever choice you make, you will have regrets, so make sure they are ones you—and humanity—can live with." She then shuffled back out the way she came in.

I stared after her, both furious and baffled. What was I supposed to do with such vague advice?

When I returned to looking out the window, the sun had started creeping above the horizon, painting swathes of orange across the heavens.

"I didn't imagine I'd ever find you up here," Xochiquetzal suddenly spoke up. I jumped, startled yet again, but before I could turn around this time, she stood next to me at the window sill. The sensual scent of her flowers carried on the gentle breeze flowing by me.

"I was just…curious," I said.

"What did Cihuacoatl have to say to you?"

I glanced back at the door curtain again before replying, "I can't quite figure it out, to be honest."

"She's a weird old woman, isn't she?"

"Actually, she reminds me of the woman who raised me when I was a human being, and she turned out to be mostly right about everything."

"Then you're not going to accept Smoking Mirror's help, to get your son back?"

I frowned. "I think at this point, since no one else is willing to help me, I have very little choice but to go to him."

"Why haven't you asked me to help you?"

I blinked at her before admitting, "I don't know. I guess I just assumed that, since I have very limited powers…."

"That I would too?" She giggled. "I'll admit that I probably don't have much to offer, but I want to help however I can. Individually, we might not be as powerful as the old gods, but with enough of us working together, that's an entirely different matter."

I smiled. "You're absolutely right. Thank you."

The last time we'd talked, I'd been so deep into my depressive state that I hadn't given much thought to Xochiquetzal—and Xochipilli—nor really internalized that they were my children as much as Ehecacone was. But the thought sent a mix of joy and terror through me now. I wondered what she would want, or expect from me given this truth, and was I ready for it?

Xochiquetzal leaned her delicate elbows against the sill and uttered a contented sigh. "Isn't Omeyocan just beautiful?

"It is." I leaned against the sill too, taking in the fresh colors revealed by the rising sun. "And the view from up here is exceptional."

"It's the most magnificent one in all of Omeyocan."

"You come up here often?"

She shrugged. "When the Feathered Serpent isn't here, which has been a whole lot lately. I don't like to talk to him when he is here. Not that he would talk to me anyway." She frowned.

I frowned too. "He's not worth fretting about. Believe me; I know."

"It's just so unfair; he gets to have the most beautiful view of the world and yet he doesn't even care enough to be here to enjoy it. Nor does he share it. Do you know that he set up magic to keep Smoking Mirror out of here?"

I shook my head.

"Smoking Mirror is just as entitled to this beauty as him, and yet he denies him. He's awful!"

This wasn't the first time she'd mentioned Smoking Mirror with the dreaminess of a young girl in the thrall of infatuation, but still I raised an eyebrow in surprise. How could anyone feel anything but contempt for Smoking Mirror? He was beyond self-absorbed, and took great joy in hurting others, both humans and gods alike. I suspected she didn't know the real him at all. Still, it seemed rude to start lecturing her. "You really like him, don't you?"

She smiled. "Someday I'm going to make him my husband."

I couldn't imagine Smoking Mirror marrying anyone and having to share his powers, least of all with a good-hearted daughter of his nemesis. "Well, he'd be a fool if he refused you."

"Indeed he would be."

With the daylight growing, I could finally see down into my walled garden. There was the copal tree I once spent years and years sitting next to, watching the hummingbirds and the bees, and the top of the cave where my grandmother spent her time sleeping. Had Quetzalcoatl stood here watching me, plotting and scheming to steal me away from my grandmother, or had it just been a whim?

"Why haven't you gone back into your garden yet?" Xochiquetzal asked.

"I don't know. I guess I just didn't feel the need."

"If I had a house in Omeyocan, I would never leave it. That's why I want to be Smoking Mirror's wife. It's one of the only ways for us younger gods to have a place here in Omeyocan, since the old gods have scooped it all up and claimed it for themselves."

"But Mextli said that Smoking Mirror doesn't have a house here in Omeyocan either."

"He doesn't," Mextli suddenly answered from the doorway behind us.

"Well, Mictlan!" Xochiquetzal whispered under her breath, vexed. "Now he's going to make me leave." But then she switched on the smile and asked him, "Have you asked Smoking Mirror about my proposal yet?"

He frowned. "Of course I haven't. He hasn't time for such nonsense."

"It isn't nonsense!"

"He has much on his thoughts right now, and much to accomplish before he can even think about forming such alliances. Your time would be better spent offering your powers to service his plans. He will not forget those who stood with him when this is all over."

Xochiquetzal bunched her shoulders and smiled like a shy young girl. "He won't?"

Mextli's frown deepened in annoyance. "Of course not. And why are you doing that?"

"Doing what?" She batted her eyes at him in mock ignorance. I stifled a grin.

He harrumphed. "Both of you are love goddesses, and yet you don't see Mayahuel acting so ridiculously childish, do you?"

"That's because the best parts of love aren't for children," I said, the desire seizing my tongue. Heat already smoldered in my chest, and began pulsing throughout my body when he locked gazes with me. I couldn't tell if he was befuddled by my words or disgusted—for his hard, darker-self lurked in his gaze—but the desire didn't care; she just smiled back at him, sultry and daring.

"Indeed not." Xochiquetzal giggled but then told me, "I should go. I'm sure you two have much to...talk about." She flicked a trail of flower petals across Mextli's cheek as she strolled past him out the door. She laughed when he swatted it away, annoyed, then she disappeared down the stairs.

"If she thinks Smoking Mirror will have anything to do with her, she's fooling herself," Mextli muttered, scratching his cheek as if the petals had irritated his feathers. "He has even less patience for nonsense than I do."

The desire narrowed my eyes. "So we love goddesses are nothing but nonsense?"

He laughed. "Of course you're not, Mayahuel. Xochiquetzal, on the other hand, is pushy and impulsive and annoying. And completely predictable. You, however, are a mystery...and a challenge."

This time the desire purred, the heat building again. "And you like challenges, don't you?"

He pinned me with his gaze—leaving me even hotter and breathless—but instead of answering the question, he said, "There is someone I wish you to meet."

"Who?"

"It's a surprise." He gave me a secretive smile.

We walked back down the mountain, to the crossroads, and from there he turned down the path leading into the woods.

"I'm pleased to see that you're back to yourself," Mextli noted as we walked. "I was worried about you."

My face heated at the admission. "Thank you, for helping pull me out of my own stupidity."

"I suppose it can be difficult living with such stark duality when you not only don't understand why you're that way, but you've been told to view that part of yourself as evil."

"No one ever told me that it was evil," I said. "Quite to the contrary, it was an important part of life, to be taken seriously and nurtured. It just...made things difficult when I chose a life that was supposed to forsake it, as a sign of my devotion to Quetzalcoatl."

"It doesn't surprise me that the Feathered Serpent would demand such nonsense. He would reduce all of us to half-beings if he could. But you needn't forsake anything anymore. You are free to be yourself, unabashed and unashamed."

His words made my heart race.

The path soon led us to a small stone house tucked among the trees. "Wait here, while I make sure it's a good time to visit." He pulled aside the curtain and stepped inside, letting it fall behind him. The sound of sweeping came from within.

As I looked around, I noticed a man standing at the corner of the house farthest from me, a pipe clenched between his yellowed teeth. He wasn't giant, like Mextli, but he had the same hard look about him. Red and white stripes decorated his aura, and he wore a feathered cloak over his left shoulder. His stare was piercing.

I cleared my throat, swallowing back the strange anxiety and discomfort his mere presence instilled in me. He smelled of blood and lightning. "Hello."

He chewed his thick pipe stem before answering, "Mayahuel."

I looked at the curtain again, hoping Mextli would come out soon, but I jumped back when I returned my gaze to the man to find him standing closer to me, almost within arm's reach. "What are you doing?" I demanded.

He studied me with cold, calculating eyes. "Do I scare you?"

I stood taller, both put-out and embarrassed. "Of course not."

"You're twitchy, like a deer...no, like a rabbit." He smelled the air. "Yes...definitely a rabbit."

The curtain turned aside and Mextli stepped outside again. He too started when he saw the other man. "Mixcoatl. Coatlicue said you were out hunting."

Mixcoatl flashed a clever grin at him. "I'm always hunting." He turned his appraising gaze back on me. "Yes...most definitely a skittish little rabbit."

I couldn't help staring back at him. This god had my human father's name, but thankfully the resemblance ended there. After all of the stories Mitotia had told me about her people's patron god—how he'd raped his way into power, and maintained that control through a ritual reenactment of that first violation year after year—if this Mixcoatl had looked like my mortal father, it would have been more than I could stand.

Mextli frowned. "You've met Mayahuel, Goddess of the Maguey?"

"I've acquainted myself with the Feathered Serpent's collaborator."

Before I could say anything, Mextli stepped right up to Mixcoatl, hulking over him like a bear, his feathers puffed. "Watch your forked tongue, Cloud Serpent. Funny you should throw around accusations of treachery given your own children's collaborations with my sorceress sister."

"And yet your mother still became my wife." Mixcoatl grinned as he returned the pipe stem to his mouth.

That made Mextli's feathers ruffle even more, but before he could retort, the curtain came aside and a woman stepped out between them. "There will be no battles outside my door curtain."

I would have expected Mextli's mother to be a giant, like her son, but in fact she was slight of build. Nor did she resemble her son in the ways that human children often took after their parents. Her skin was smooth and colored a hue typical of humans, and she wore her long hair tied back in a tidy knot. No feathers grew from her body like they did on Mextli; she looked completely human, even dressed in a plain dress that resembled the robes worn by novice priests and priestesses. She had no divine glow to her, but she smelled like the serpent house in Tollan.

"I was just leaving anyway." Mixcoatl tapped out his pipe against the corner of the house and the ashes turned to clouds as they fell. He then tucked the pipe into his jaguar-skin belt.

"Why don't you make yourself useful and go hunt the Feathered Serpent?" Mextli barked.

Mixcoatl grinned at him. "Now that would hardly be sporting, would it?" He darted a glance at me but said nothing as he walked away, down the path back the way we'd come just moments before.

Mextli watched him, eyes narrowed, but then he turned to the woman. "Mother, this is Mayahuel."

When she turned her gaze upon me, I felt a strange dread, like she was a snake and I was a mouse she was watching. "A pleasure to meet you at last," she said, bowing her head to me. "I'm Coatlicue."

With her name being Snake Skirt, perhaps her smell wasn't so strange after all. "It's very nice to meet you as well." I returned the bow.

Her appraising gaze swept over me a breath before she announced, "Let us go inside. I'm eager to hear all about you, Mayahuel." Without waiting for an answer, she went past the curtain.

I looked up at Mextli but he only smiled and held the door curtain open for me.

The interior of the house resembled the inside of a temple. A wooden idol that was a pretty good representation of Mextli sat against the back wall, clutching a sword in one hand and a serpent scepter in the other. Several reed mats sat in front of it, and Coatlicue sat upon one of them. She motioned Mextli and me to take the other two. "Can I offer you something to eat?" The water jar sitting in the corner floated over to her outstretched hand.

"Thank you," I murmured when she handed me a clay cup filled with blood. Mextli accepted one as well and downed it in one swallow while I nursed mine politely.

"Mextli tells me my people have welcomed you into their community," Coatlicue said, sipping from her own cup. When I nodded, she went on, "They were always a very devoted people, very respectful of their gods. It's such an honor that they have accepted my son as their leader. Treat them well, and they will always return the favor. I understand that you too were a priestess."

I tensed a little at her words but nodded. "For most of my life, yes."

"Me as well, as you can probably tell." Coatlicue motioned at our surroundings. "Did you enjoy it?"

"For the most part, yes."

She nodded. "I loved it; a much better life than most slaves could claim, and then for the Smoking Mirror to choose me to bear Mextli...." She sighed longingly. "I was truly a blessed mortal."

I blinked. "You were fully human?"

"As mortal as any Mexica."

Mextli answered, "Smoking Mirror turned her immortal moments before my birth, and later I brought her back from Mictlan."

Both my rational side and the desire gasped simultaneously, and it was all I could do to not blurt my thoughts out loud. *It's possible to turn mortals into gods? What if we could turn Little Reed immortal?* I had to make myself listen to the conversation again.

"And he avenged me against my wretched daughter." Coatlicue beamed. "No mother could ever hope for a more perfect son."

"Mextli's impressive on multiple fronts," I said, hoping my distraction hadn't been obvious. "He's taught me much, and I owe him a great deal."

"As do we all," she said, her smile careful again. "I understand you have a house here in Omeyocan."

I nodded. "It's the garden back at the crossroads, next to Xipe Totec's fields."

"You're so lucky. I had to marry Mixcoatl to gain a place here in Omeyocan."

"You could have remained with the Mexica, Mother," Mextli said. "You are welcome among them."

She waved him off. "I know I complain about Mixcoatl and his ways, but I am quite content, my fierce hummingbird. It isn't as if he demands much of me; he has no mortal cravings, and so in that regard, we are well-matched. Besides, the nomadic life is not to my liking; I much prefer high stone temples to meager tents. But someday, when you've settled them somewhere and they can build me a permanent temple, I'll come stay with you on earth again."

He nodded, seemingly disappointed.

"Besides, you have much on your plate right now, with the war with Quetzalcoatl and other political matters. I'd just as soon stay out of it, and I can't really do that if I'm down there right now." She shifted her gaze to me again. "If I might ask, Mayahuel, where do you stand in the current conflict?"

"She is with us, Mother," Mextli said before I could answer.

When she raised an appraising eyebrow at me, I said, "In fact, Smoking Mirror and I are close to an agreement. I'm most definitely not on the Feathered Serpent's side anymore. I learned from my mistakes."

"We all make them." Coatlicue held up the blood jar. "Would you like a refill?"

"Actually, I think we'll be on our way, Mother," Mextli said, rising to his feet. He had to hunch over to keep from striking his head on the ceiling. "Mayahuel was going to show me her garden today."

That was news to me, but since he seemed eager to leave, I declined another cup of blood and thanked her for her hospitality. "It was very nice to meet you."

"Likewise." She watched me all the way to the door curtain—which Mextli was holding open for me—and again I felt like a mouse being stalked by a snake. It was a relief to be out into the open again, away from her.

CHAPTER TWENTY

As Mextli and I proceeded back down the path, I said, "Your mother seems...nice."

He laughed. "You needn't mince words, Mayahuel. I know she's intense. Even I find it difficult to be around her for more than a few moments at a time. And I sensed you were becoming uneasy with her questions."

Then it wasn't just me. "Regardless, she thinks the world of you."

"She does."

We walked in silence for a moment before I finally mustered up the courage to say, "So...I didn't know we can change mortals into immortals."

"Technically speaking, only three of us can," Mextli corrected me. "Lord Death has the ability, of course, as does Smoking Mirror."

"And who's the third one?"

"Quetzalcoatl."

My newfound hope fell back to earth. "And it's not something that can be learned?"

He gave me a curious look as he answered, "It's a power that you either have or don't. It cannot be taught."

"But how do you know if you have it or not?"

"You just do." He cast me a curious look. "Why?"

I couldn't admit that I would use such a power to save Little Reed's life, so I shrugged and answered, "It just sounds like a really nice power to have."

"I suppose it could be useful under the right circumstances."

After a moment of walking silently, I asked, "Was there a particular reason you wanted me to meet your mother?"

He shrugged. "She heard I was helping you, and she was curious. She asked to meet you, and so I obliged her."

"Like the obedient son," I said with a laugh. "Do you think I passed her test?"

"Test?"

I laughed some more but waved him off. "Never mind. Are we really going to my garden?"

"It was an excuse to bow out gracefully but...you haven't been back in thousands of years. Don't you think it's time you looked in on it?"

By then we'd reached the crossroads again and the massive walls stood before us. There was no door anywhere in sight, so I peered up at the top, squinting against the sun shining bright in the sky. "Any idea how we get inside?"

"The same way you got out?" he suggested.

Back then, strange magic had tried to convince me that I'd never reach the top, and I didn't relish battling it again. It had taken days for me to reach the top—and my freedom. There had to be an easier way....

I approached the wall and ran my fingers over the gaps in the stones, searching for signs of a hidden doorway. As I'd predicted, the magic that had tried to keep me inside still pulsed in the walls, but this time it lit up my own in all new ways. The wall magic shrank away from me like a leech from a flame. I pushed harder, forcing it back, and my fingers started sinking into the wall as if it were blocks of honey rather than stone. Once I'd submerged myself to my elbows, I pushed outward, like parting a curtain.

The walls gave way, revealing a tunnel leading to the garden within. I stood holding the walls open, taking in the strange perspective.

Mextli gazed over my shoulder. "Well, aren't you going to go in?"

Indeed, what was I waiting for? The tunnel was empty and the only life visible beyond it was the bees, butterflies, and hummingbirds puttering around the flowers and trees. Mextli had said that the Earth Monster had been exiled from Omeyocan, and the garden's stillness reflected that.

I finally stepped inside and went to the mouth of the tunnel, where the hard dirt gave way to lush grass and beds of vibrant flowers in black, fertile soil. The air smelled like summer in the gardens back in Tollan, and it should have made my heart swell, but there was another odor here, one of foreign yet familiar magic. And it was everywhere.

Unlike Quetzalcoatl's house—which was bigger on the inside than the outside—mine was smaller on the inside than I thought it would be. The patch of garden was maybe twenty paces across at its longest side, and the copal tree took up most of that space. The rest of the garden was dominated by the tunnel, which I now recognized as the cave where my grandmother had always slept. I'd never found the garden exit because she'd been guarding it all along, keeping me inside.

And it had been her magic that had tried to deter me from climbing the walls—that tried to convince me that attempting to leave was futile. None of the magic around me was my own. This garden wasn't mine; it was built completely from my grandmother's jealousy and anger.

And I wanted it gone.

As if I'd given a silent order, the walls began melting away. The flowers shriveled in on themselves, regressing slowly back into their seeds and the cave vanished. The ground turned to clouds and now Xipe Totec's fields were clearly visible, as was the crossroads and the path into the woods. Xipe Totec emerged from the rows of maize, and leaned on his digging stick, looking like a human farmer in spite of his blood-red face and cape of skin. He didn't say anything as he chewed a stick of grass and watched me intently.

Mextli looked around at my blank clouds with mild interest. "Not to your liking?"

"It wasn't mine," I said. "I didn't build it, and it's just a reminder of things I'd rather forget. I'd rather start over fresh."

"A good idea. What are you going to build?"

"I don't know. What would you build, if this was your house?"

He raised an eyebrow as he looked around. "I've never really given it any thought. I suppose it would have to be someplace that makes me feel safe. Xipe Totec has his field of vegetables, and Tlaloc submerges himself in water, and my mother lives in the temple where she served Nanahuatzin during her mortal life."

I nodded. "You make your tent look like a palace hall."

But he shook his head. "That is not where I feel safest." When I cocked an eyebrow at him, he went on, "My priests and warriors have certain expectations of me and who I am; that is reflected in what I choose to show them when they enter my temple. Where I spend my own time...that is a different matter."

"Where do you go?" When he hesitated to answer, I said, "I promise not to judge, no matter what it is."

Mextli gave me an earnest look before admitting, "My mother's womb."

His answer shocked me, but I trained my face to not show it. I had been certain it would be something like an army camp, surrounded by soldiers and weapons—all of the things he ruled as a god—and yet instead he longed to return to the cramped quarters of a human woman's womb? It seemed so strange.

"It's the only place I have ever felt truly safe," he said, the earnest expression set in stone upon his face. "Ever since I was born, I've been in a constant state of vigilance, never able to relax my defenses. I wish I could find that kind of peace again."

Every time I spent any time at all with Mextli, I found myself surprised by the new depths he revealed to me. *And here I promised not to judge him, and yet I did it anyway,* I thought, ashamed.

"So, where do you feel safest?" he asked me.

I turned my attention back to my empty space. I always chose my quarters in Tollan for the Divine Dream, but after yesterday, that didn't feel quite so safe and happy anymore. But the area outside the Mexica camp hardly felt like home either.

But there is one place that's always felt like home to me. I closed my eyes, imagining the sacred precinct where I'd spent so many years of my life— far more than anywhere else I'd ever lived since being reborn. I thought of all those evenings sitting in Nimilitzli's house, eating dinner and discussing religious philosophy with her. It was one of the few memories I could look back upon without regrets.

When I opened my eyes, the blank clouds had been replaced with a dreamy replica of Xochicalco's sacred precinct, complete with temples, priestly houses, calmecac, and the vast staircases. Mextli and I stood in front of the doorway to Nimilitzli's house, in the shelter of the side of Quetzalcoatl's temple.

Seeing the painted bas relief of the feathered serpent on the side used to fill me with joy and purpose, but now I felt only a sad sense of loss. I moved my hand across it in my field of vision and the carvings disappeared, replaced with a flat plaster surface, waiting for new decoration. For now I left it blank.

Mextli gazed around with interest. "You have very powerful magic, Mayahuel."

I chuckled. "Hardly."

But he shook his head. "Only the most powerful gods create such elaborate magical renderings, so yes, you're definitely quite powerful."

"This isn't elaborate; I just copied that place we visited, when you taught me to use the teoyoh."

"Still...to be able to not just create this, but to hold it together so flawlessly.... That's not something most gods can do. Very impressive!"

I looked around some more, not sure how to take this compliment. I was hardly powerful compared to the likes of Quetzalcoatl or Smoking Mirror. Even Mextli's magic seemed to dwarf my own. But I was just beginning to learn, and it often surprised me what I was capable of. Maybe I was underestimating myself.

And wasn't that what Quetzalcoatl said, that people tended to underestimate me?

And since when should we believe a word that comes from his split tongue? the desire hissed.

Mextli walked across the precinct, towards the calmecac, taking in everything with an unnervingly awestruck expression. I followed but sat on the stone ring of the cistern, remembering all those afternoons when Malinalli and I would eat our lunches there between teaching classes. Back then I never would have thought of doing anything like what happened last night, but I wondered if even back when we used to sit here sharing lunches, had she felt that tickly feeling in her stomach whenever she looked at me? I felt it a bit myself now when I thought of her, remembering the softness of her robe and the curve of her hips, the taste of her tongue....

"That's Quetzalcoatl's temple, isn't it?" Mextli was staring back at the temple now, a contemplative look on his face.

"It was, but I stripped all of the carvings from it, so now it's just a temple. I haven't yet decided how to redecorate it."

He nodded then turned back to me. "I can't say I'm surprised that you chose this place. It was obvious when we visited the earthly site that it meant a great deal to you."

"It's the only place I've ever truly felt at home."

He knelt in front of the cistern and set his unfeathered hand on the stone. He didn't say anything, as if feeling the heat left behind by the sun blazing overhead.

But strangely I felt as if he were touching me instead; it wasn't a tactile sensation, but rather a caress of energy deep inside of me, and it only intensified when he ran his hand back and forth over the stone surface, feeling the contours and texture.

"Your magic...it's...so very strong, Mayahuel," he murmured, admiration in his voice.

When he looked up at me, his eyes intense, it was more than the desire could take. Throwing all caution aside, I leaned forward and put my lips to his, desperate to have him close to me. I even bunched my fists in the front of his feathered xicolli and tried to pull him to me, but he was so immovable that I ended up pulling myself to him instead.

And yet he didn't return my gesture in the least; in fact, he seemed completely unaffected by my attempt to kiss him and when I pulled away, confused—and not without an angry flame of frustration—he stared back at me, puzzled. And a bit suspicious. "What are you doing?" His voice was a whisper yet it sounded like a booming shout to my ears.

I withdrew from him, swallowing back embarrassment. I couldn't find words that wouldn't sound ridiculous.

But he set his hand on my arm, keeping me from scooting further away. "I meant...what does it mean?"

I gaped at him before finally saying, "Well, it doesn't have to mean anything—"

"Then why did you do it?"

"Because...I don't know." And it was the truth. "It's just one of those nonsense things we love goddesses do, I guess," I stammered.

He frowned, skeptical. "You're angry at me for what I said about Xochiquetzal."

I shook my head. "I'm not angry at you. It's just...I don't know how to explain it to you so you would understand."

"Perhaps you should try anyway."

A flush crept up my neck. *Get back here and help me!* I scolded the desire. She was so much better at this than my rational side. But she remained aloof, and Mextli was watching me expectantly, so I pressed on as best I could. "You've...you've been very good to me...and...and I like having you around, and...you make me feel...."

When my words stalled, he raised his one eyebrow. "I make you feel what?"

"Lots of things; dizzy, hot, a bit fluttery in my stomach—"

"I'm sorry."

I laughed. "It's not unpleasant. If anything, it's quite wonderful."

"I'll have to take your word for it because it sounds disturbing to me."

"Then the kiss...it was unpleasant for you?"

"No. But frankly, I don't understand why the humans do it so much."

Now the desire butted me aside, indignant. "That's because you did it completely wrong! You sat there like a stone statue!"

Mextli cracked a smile. "What was I supposed to do?"

I scooted closer again, right up to him, the desire pulsing defiantly through me. "Just do what I do, and you'll see." I then leaned in and kissed him again.

This time he mimicked my every move, parting his lips when I did, setting his hands on my shoulders when I put mine on his, and offering his tongue when I offered him mine—

"Oh!" I pulled back, startled.

He looked at me with uncertain eyes. "What did I do? You told me to follow your lead—"

"You have feathers on your tongue!"

He frowned. "Of course I do. The entire left side of my material body consists of feathers."

"The entire?" My gaze started wandering down to his loincloth but I caught myself. "I guess I just wasn't expecting them, that's all."

"If they bother you, I can make them go away—"

"No, no, it's all right." I pressed closer again, the desire calming the nervous thudding of my heart. "I think they're...interesting." I took his mouth to mine again, greeting his half-feathered tongue with enthusiasm.

I'd expected a distinct—even unpleasant—taste, thanks to the feathers, but in fact he had none at all, except perhaps a trace of heat and sunlight. When I deepened the kiss, he followed suit, his hand movements copying my own as I let my fingers venture lazily down the contour of his chest. When he started massaging my left breast through my dress because I did the same to him, I knew I could easily get him to do whatever I wanted him to. I needed only to move my hand on him wherever I wanted him to touch me. *Just think of the wonderful purposes we could put that half-feathered tongue of his to,* the desire purred, sending a shiver through me— a motion he mimicked as well.

But the more closely he copied me, the more my enthusiasm waned. While the pleasure he was giving me was wonderful—and disturbingly reminiscent of my more intimate moments with Quetzalcoatl—it all felt hollow when I considered that I wasn't giving him the same. With humans, it was always readily apparent that they were enjoying themselves as much as I was, but by all appearances, Mextli was merely going through the motions and not feeling anything himself. There was no passion in his kiss, no longing in his touch. I might as well have been touching myself for all the good this was doing either of us. I didn't even know how to react to him being so completely unaffected by me. I'd never encountered such a reaction.

He just needs to learn, the desire chided, a hint of desperation to her voice. *What did we know of such things before the Feathered Serpent taught us the secrets of creation? We just need to teach Mextli too.*

The thought wasn't without appeal. And really, wasn't this what I'd wanted all along? Someone that I knew my magic didn't affect, so I'd know his or her feelings for me were genuine?

But what about Little Reed?

Little Reed is dead, the desire growled.

No, he isn't.

He might as well be, for all the help we can give him.

The truth of her words sent a spike of anguish roaring through me. I didn't want to believe that it was truly over for good, but I suspected I was just deluding myself.

Mextli pulled away, worry in his eyes. "Something's wrong."

I shook my head. "No, nothing is wrong. Absolutely nothing." I just hoped it didn't sound like the lie it was.

"You're sure?" When I nodded, he said, "There is something I wish to ask you."

"What would that be?"

He looked charmingly nervous now as he rubbed the back of his neck. "Would you be interested in an alliance...with me?"

I smirked, puzzled yet amused by his nervousness. "An alliance? But I thought we already had one, of sorts."

"I mean an *official* alliance, before the other gods, and before the Mexica."

I still wasn't sure what exactly he meant, but then it dawned on me. "Are you proposing marriage to me?"

He sat up stiffly. "If that is how you wish to think about it, then yes, I am asking you to be my wife."

I raised an eyebrow, unsure what to say. "This is rather sudden, isn't it?"

He furrowed his brow. "I'm not sure what timing has to do with anything. It's readily apparent that we complement each other quite well, and as you said, we've already agreed to an unofficial alliance."

"I suppose."

He looked nervous again as he added, "Besides, you know things about me that I've never told anyone...not even Smoking Mirror. And I believe I've proven my good intentions, have I not? We are friends, right?"

"We are," I agreed. "And you did save me from myself the other day. I could never thank you enough for that."

He smiled, pleased. "See? It seems only rational that we take this to the next step, by solidifying it into an official alliance recognized by both gods and men."

"I suppose it does, but Mextli...." Too flustered to know what to say, I finally settled on, "I need time to think about it. This is a big step...a huge step, really."

Mextli nodded. "I understand. I do not wish to rush you to a decision, so please, take whatever time you need."

An awkward silence fell between us, and after a few moments of looking around, Mextli said, "I should go back to the camp. I haven't spoken to my warriors yet today, and I'm sure they're waiting for my daily address."

I nodded. "I'm going to stay here a little while longer, do some more work around my new house."

"I shall see you later today then?" he asked.

I nodded, but when he rose to leave, I asked, "This alliance...is that why you wanted me to meet your mother?" I couldn't keep the grin from quirking at my lips.

"That is standard practice, isn't it? To introduce a potential new spouse to the rest of one's family?" he asked.

I laughed. "It is. I just never took you for the...traditional type. At least not when it comes to these kinds of things."

He smiled back at me. "You're not the only one who can surprise, Mayahuel." He then leaned down and gave me another kiss, this one completely his own, and startlingly wonderful. It left me feeling pleasantly numb and floating, as if we were standing on a cloud—which I suppose we were. I hadn't felt this disconnected from pain and sorrow and worry since....

Well, since that first time that Little Reed had kissed me next to the temple the night before he left for the army.

CHAPTER TWENTY-ONE

Once Mextli left, I wandered around my recreation of Xochicalco, trying to focus on how I wanted to rework the little details, but my mind kept wandering back to those moments next to the cistern. This new development was exciting, for sure, but all the same, it felt a bit like a betrayal of everything Little Reed and I had.

We can't keep clinging to what never was—and never can be. It's time to move on, the desire chided me.

But he's not even dead yet! How can we just jump into anything more serious than friendship with Mextli while Little Reed is still living? Don't we at least owe it to him to wait until he's passed on to Mictlan?

No, we don't. We owe nothing to anyone but ourselves. We've spent all of our life catering to the needs of others; it's time to give some thought to our own happiness, and take some action towards achieving that.

It just...feels so wrong.

The desire sighed. *I feel it too, but what if we hem too long and we lose our chance with Mextli?*

It feels like we're trying to replace Little Reed.

No one could ever replace him. We both know that. But Mextli could be very good for us too, if we just give him the chance. We could finally be happy.

Or we might not be, I countered. *He finds our physical needs ridiculous.*

But with a little time and effort, we can change that, the desire replied. *He's already taken to the little bit we've taught him about love.*

I stared wistfully at the cistern across the precinct from where I sat on the bottom step of the temple. *He has. But what if he finds our need for sex repulsive and disgusting?*

Then we know he's not worth our time. But if he isn't...?

"Then it could be something very good," I murmured, the courage and sense of purpose building.

All this thinking is just wasted time until we know whether or not he's willing to meet our needs, so let's go talk to him.

"Agreed."

¤

When I arrived back in camp, I found several priests standing outside Mextli's tent with the morning offering of two hearts in a reed basket. They started at my sudden appearance, but they soon bowed. "Good day, Lady Mayahuel."

"I realize it's offering time, but I have important business with your master and it will require some privacy. I need you to come back later." I didn't want Mextli distracted by his stomach.

The priests exchanged nervous glances before the lead one replied, "His Grace becomes very...edgy when his offerings aren't delivered on time."

"I will make sure he knows that it was I who told you to wait, and I promise that he won't take any frustrations out on you."

He bowed. "Thank you, My Lady. We shall wait over by the fire." He and the other two priests retreated.

I faced the tent flap but hesitated, nervous now that the moment was upon me. *I want you to do the talking for us. You're better at this.*

The desire grabbed control of my tongue and some of the anxiety melted away. "Mextli! May I come in?"

"Of course," Mextli called, so I stepped inside.

Mextli sat on his icpalli throne, but he'd turned it around and sat staring into a garden off a patio behind the dais. It hadn't been there the other times I'd visited him, nor had he ever struck me as the kind who appreciated flowers and gardens.

But as I approached, I realized he was watching a swarm of hummingbirds dueling each other with their pointy beaks, their movements a carefully choreographed dance of violence and blood. I stood at his side, watching it too, fascinated. "Are they your nahuals?" I asked after a while.

He nodded. "Very fierce, aren't they?"

"Most definitely. One wouldn't think so to look at them, as tiny as they are."

"Size has little to do with one's fierceness. After all, you stood up to me multiple times in the past."

I chuckled. "I suppose I did."

"And I hear your nahuals are not to be taken lightly either," he said with a grin. "As individuals, they might not look like much, but as a group, driven to protect their mistress, even the fiercest of nahuals wouldn't stand their ground against them."

"They are a force to be reckoned with," I replied, the smile falling from my face at the memory of all those rabbits swarming over Smoking Mirror's nahual, trying to save Ehecacone. And I'd rewarded their efforts by killing them under a flood of octli magic. Even now, the memory of that jaguar grinning at me set my heart thudding and the magic tingling in my fingers. "And yet it still wasn't enough."

Mextli set his hand on mine and gave it a warm squeeze. "We will get your son back, Mayahuel. And soon. I promise."

The determination in his eyes made my heart race even faster, but pleasantly so. Just another reason to give serious consideration to a formal alliance with him.

I'd only ever imagined myself married to one person—Little Reed, of course; even when I'd stupidly pursued matters with Red Flint, I hadn't thought at all of what our marriage would be like but rather how it would wound Little Reed. And though I'd tried to make myself embrace my marriage to Black Otter, my heart knew all along that Little Reed wasn't really dead and so had refused.

But now things were different. I'd had the marriage to Little Reed, and though it hadn't been everything I'd always dreamed it would be, my heart finally accepted the inevitable. That dream was over, and it was time to find new ones. I could see a future with Mextli, the two of us together leading the Mexica into a bright future, with him continuing to teach me how to be a goddess while I taught him how to be more than just a war god. I'd settled for much before and came to resent it, but with Mextli, there would be none of that. He would accept the whole me, or we would just be friends.

Mextli leaned towards me, his elbow against his knee, his hand still on mine. "Do you wish to talk about something?"

I nodded. "Very much so."

He summoned a second reed throne, next to his own. "Then let us talk." He motioned for me to sit too.

I did so, the nervousness creeping up on me again, but this time I was determined. "I want to accept your proposal."

"I'm glad to hear it."

"But I must make certain that we're in agreement about expectations and...needs, on both sides." I withdrew my hand from his to smooth my dress across my knees. "In the past, I've given up things I wanted, and I cannot do that again."

"I do not wish you to give up anything on my account. I wish for this alliance...this marriage to be mutually beneficial."

"What would be your expectations of me in this?"

"Loyalty, of course. That would be paramount. As is support for my decisions, though I would also want your input on matters, such as how we deal with our humans, our enemies, and our allies. I won't expect absolute agreement in matters of war, but I would expect that if there were disagreement, you will respect my decision and not undermine me with your own actions."

"I would expect the same of you," I said. "I imagine there will be things we both feel strongly about and that we can respect each other enough to come to a consensus about how to proceed."

"I imagine so as well. Other than that...." He thought for a moment before saying, "I won't expect you to be friends with Smoking Mirror, but I must ask that you understand that my relationship with him is important, and I will not abandon it, not even for you."

"I understand, and I request the same of you regarding the people of Tollan. They may live in the Feathered Serpent's sacred city, but they must be left alone. And that includes Topiltzin."

Mextli looked at me with sad, pitying eyes. "Mayahuel—"

"This is not negotiable. Without that promise, there will be no alliance."

Looking annoyed, he opened his mouth to argue more, but then he sighed and nodded. "You have my word. Is there anything else?"

I nodded and took a deep breath. *I can do this.* "As gods, we both have our own special needs, things that are just part of who we are. You're a war god, so it's only natural that you should need to wage war, both offensive and defensive, right?"

"On that we can agree."

With the desire in charge, I'd expected a bit more confidence in all this, but she was surprisingly nervous as she spoke. "As a love goddess, I have...certain interests...certain *needs* that are just part of who I am. It's as inescapable for me as your need for war, and any meaningful relationship we're to have...it must include it. I can get some of what I need from humans, but I want it with you as well."

Mextli stared at me, confused. "Perhaps you should just state what it is you require of me."

My mouth felt dry, making it so easy to stay silent and stall by trying to find the perfect words to say.

He sighed then took my hand in his again, his grip warm and calming. "Is this something the humans taught you to be embarrassed about? Like your feeding habits?"

"Yes. No. Yes, maybe, I don't know. But...they are one in the same." When he wrinkled his brow at me, I said, "When I have sex with humans, it nourishes me, the way that eating hearts nourishes you. I was never taught that my appetites were shameful—not systemically, anyway—but I figured out early on that my desires and urges were not like other women's, and trying to live my life as a celibate priestess in the face of my divine nature was...soul-wrecking in ways that it wasn't for humans. It was a relief to finally understand why I am the way I am, and to not wonder anymore if I was crazy."

"Then why all of the evasiveness about your feeding habits? Why did you hide it from me?"

"Because you kept saying I was acting so human, like that was a bad thing, so why should I think you would react any other way to this?"

Mextli's grip tightened a bit. "My apologies for making you think that," he murmured. "It wasn't my intention to make you feel it necessary to hide your true self from me."

"If we're to be husband and wife, I want to share everything with you." I reached up to touch his feathered cheek with my free hand. "Everything."

But the look on Mextli's face was mystifyingly unreadable. "I'm honored that you think so highly of me, Mayahuel, but...you feed through sex and yet you wish to have sex with me; that would be like me wishing to eat your heart, if you had one."

It was on the tip of the desire's tongue to tell him I did have a heart, but I held the words back for her. *He seems so sure that we don't have one. Are hearts something most gods don't have?*

And if so, what did my having one mean?

Let's not share everything all at once, the desire agreed, cautious. *One step at a time.*

"I realize it sounds strange, but I don't believe it works the same way with gods," I finally answered. "The first person I was ever intimate with was Quetzalcoatl, and he didn't suffer any ill effects. He's the one who taught me the art of creation."

Uncertainty lurked in his eyes, along with hints of that darkness. "Will you be teaching it to me then, if we do this?"

The desire grinned. "Does that frighten you?"

The darkness supplanted him and he bared his teeth in a careful grin.

"Nothing scares me."

"I didn't think so." My smile melted to seriousness though. "But let's be clear on one thing: in the past, I've put my own needs aside for the sake of convenience, but I won't do that again. I require not only consummation of our marriage, but also regular intimacy after that. If these are things you don't wish to provide then let us dismiss any notion of an official bound alliance."

Mextli leaned back in his icpalli, a thoughtful look on his face. "This sex you wish for us to engage in...is it like what we did this afternoon, in your house in Omeyocan?"

"It's even better," the desire purred.

He smiled back, a predatory look in his eyes. "I'm definitely interested."

I set my three-fingered hand on his feathered one. "It would be wise for you to try it first before making a decision, for it just won't do for us to bind ourselves before the other gods only to find out afterwards that sex is not to your liking."

He turned his hand so he gripped mine. "That would be wise."

Now that I knew we were in agreement, all of the nervousness slipped away, fueling my growing courage—and libido. I abandoned my throne to straddle him on his, and I ran my fingers through the feathers of his xicolli, imagining they were the ones hidden beneath. "There's no time like now to give it a try."

He answered with a deep kiss. A quick learner indeed.

I pressed myself against him, luxuriating in the passion. It wasn't the slow, lazy kind Quetzalcoatl and I had always practiced in the Divine Dream, but it also wasn't the desperate, animal longing that took over humans when I let them touch me. It was a pleasant in-between, especially with his feathery hand rubbing my arm, sending chills through me.

But now that we were entwined, something felt wrong. He barely had to shift his hand at all to move from my shoulder to my elbow, and though I wanted to sit in his lap, I had to stand upon my knees, but even then, he hunched over to reach me. We were so disproportionate in size, I worried that the situation would become not just uncomfortable but painful once matters progressed far enough.

You worry too much, the desire chided.

I feel like a child in his lap, I fired back, and even the desire couldn't rumble past that thought. In response, my teotl began building beneath my skin, expanding outward, and my body grew to accommodate it. Once it ended, Mextli was still larger than me, but the size difference felt more natural now. *Is that better?*

Much. At least now he wouldn't crush me when he lay atop me.

We continued wrestling tongues, the desire growing increasingly impatient with his constant mimicry rather than taking command. I tore my lips away long enough to growl, "Undress me," before savaging his mouth with mine again.

And though he took my enthusiasm as a challenge of tongue strength, he still didn't heed my command. Eventually I pulled away, flustered.

"What is the matter?" he asked, puzzled.

"I asked you to undress me, but—"

"I cannot do that, Mayahuel."

The desire bared my teeth. "Why not?"

He furrowed his brow at me, as if he didn't comprehend the question. "Why are you looking at me that way?"

"You do realize that your clothing is a part of your physical manifestation, and it's no different than your fingers and ears?"

I stared back at him. "Why would I know that?"

He opened his mouth to answer, but then thought better of it.

I laughed. "You mean I didn't have to make myself a new dress? I just needed to summon a change of clothing?"

"I thought you just preferred to wear that rag you came here in."

I drew back enough to look down at myself and with a thought, my simple white dress was transformed into a delicate feather-woven one, similar to the one I'd worn to my wedding to Black Otter when I was just a girl. I changed it again, this time so I wore a warrior's xicolli—just to see if I could make one. "And you can do the same?" I asked, astounded.

In answer, he made his own xicolli disappear, and a black feathered headdress appeared upon his head.

My gaze was drawn immediately to the neat seam of feathers running straight down the middle of his chest and down his stomach. I set my hands against him, one on his fleshy pectoral, the other on the feathered one, then slowly drew them down his chest, tracing the contours of his muscles. As I pushed my fingers further down, my gaze wandered to his loincloth. "And the feathers...they go all the way down?" When he nodded, the desire said, "Show me." I slipped off his lap and knelt on the floor, waiting.

He grinned as he rose, that intense darkness engulfing his eyes. Once he stood fully upright, he banished his loincloth just as he had the xicolli, and my wonderings about whether that part was in proportion to the rest of him was finally answered. A flush of longing crept up my neck as I stared. "Why feathers anyway?"

He shrugged. "Why do you choose a clothed human form? It's not as if we must wear clothing."

"I don't like people staring at me; I don't like them seeing only my body and not me." I tilted my head to look up at his face finally. "Why do you wear clothing?"

His grin grew darker. "One must be able to hide some weapons from their opponents."

I furrowed my brow. What did he mean by that?

He settled on the ground next to me. "If your clothing will interfere, just make it go away."

Initially I balked at the idea, but eventually I made all of my clothing just disappear. My memories of Little Reed undressing me in the throes of passion were some of my most erotic, but Quetzalcoatl and I had almost always skipped over the whole undressing part, so maybe this was just how we gods did this.

Mextli scrutinized me, but as if assessing my magic skills rather than as a man admiring my feminine beauty. There was no lust in his eyes, no signs of arousal at the sight of my nakedness. I'd said I'd wanted people to notice me, not my body, but now it felt strange and wrong, and not even the desire knew what to do.

He took my right hand and gazed upon it as if it were an interesting stone he'd found in the bottom of a brook. "You can grow your fingers back now, you know?"

"But I gave them up in sacrifice—"

"In your mortal life. That life is over, and you can change anything you want now, remold, re-fashion it all. You can even leave this completely human body behind if you so choose."

I had been a caiman-like creature in my previous incarnation, but I had no desire to go back to that. Yet I couldn't imagine abandoning this body I'd spent all of my mortal life in. *It would be nice to have my fingers back though....*

Two small buds sprouted from the empty space next to my middle finger on my right hand, slowly expanding outward into the ones I'd cut off long ago. A sob stuck in my throat when I started wiggling them. *I can feel them! Actually feel them again for the first time in so many years!*

"And the scars, they needn't stay either," Mextli murmured, rubbing his thumbs over the faint streaks on my hips and belly.

I stared down at them. For years after having Ehecacone, I'd mourned the loss of my skin's flawlessness, but now they were the only evidence that I'd once been a mother. And if I never got my son back, they would be all I had left of his existence. "No, I want to keep those. Someone dear gave them to me."

Though now that I looked at my fingers again, it felt so wrong to keep them. I'd given them up to save Little Reed, and though I'd often seen their absence as a bitter reminder that we could never be together, now they had become symbolic of my love for him. Even knowing what I would have to give up by making that sacrifice now, I wouldn't hesitate to do it again; he was worth it. So I made the fingers disappear again, and when Mextli raised his eyebrow, I said, "I don't need to change anything about myself. This is who I am."

He smiled. "You are very wise, Mayahuel."

I pulled myself onto Mextli's lap again and took his mouth with mine. I moved his hands across my bare skin, along my ribs, over my breasts, and back down to cradle my rear. It never took more than a mere touch to get mortal men ready, but Mextli remained unaffected even by my firm strokes on his half-feathered tepolli. "You need to be harder," the desire whispered in his ear as I stroked him still more firmly. The feathers themselves felt intriguingly smooth no matter which direction I stroked them.

"Why?" But when I whispered the details in his ear, he pulled back to give me a puzzled look. "You really wish me to do such things to you?"

A hot mixture of desire and embarrassment lit my cheeks. "It's not as painful as it sounds, really."

"You're sure?"

"Of course."

Within a blink, the darkness lurking in his eyes took over, and his gentle grip on my arms turned crushing. He pushed me over backwards, pinning me to the ground, but when he turned that stone grip onto my legs, pushing them apart, the desire fled, leaving only the fear to take the brunt of his hard thrust into me.

I reacted only with surprise on the second one, but when the third brought pain blooming in my abdomen, I finally reacted in self defense; I let loose a blast of magic against his chest, singeing some of his feathers and flesh.

It stopped him, but the darkness intensified. "What did you do that for?"

"Why are you suddenly being so rough with me?" I fired back. "That hurts!"

He narrowed his eyes, irritated. "You said this is what you wanted...that it doesn't hurt as much as it seems...." But then the darkness fled his eyes, replaced with concern, regret, and confusion. "I'm sorry. I should have known...."

"Known what?"

"That it was crazy to use a weapon of war on you for your enjoyment."

Now was my turn to feel stupid. "Forgive me for not being more precise; it didn't occur to me that you'd be...familiar with some of sex's unpleasant uses."

"I should have asked for more clarification."

An uncomfortable silence settled between us as an even more unpleasant question rose in my head. "You haven't...used this weapon against anyone, have you?" His answer could very well change everything between us.

He shook his head. "Other options are more effective at achieving my goals."

"Thank goodness," I murmured. When he cast me a puzzled look, I said, "When I was mortal, I had some...bad experiences involving that."

"I am sorry."

I waved him off. "I'd rather not talk about it."

"What should we talk about then?"

Growing brave again, I took his hand. "The proper way to make love."

He still looked uncertain though. "Make love?"

"It's called that because it brings people closer to each other, on an emotional level." I drew closer to him again. "It sows love and affection."

"I don't experience such feelings."

I straddled his lap, pressing my body against his. "Just because you haven't yet doesn't mean you can't." I kissed him again.

He hesitated before carefully wrapping his arms around me. When we finally parted lips, he whispered, "Teach me, Mayahuel."

I sunk slowly down onto him, luxuriating in the sensation of flesh and feathers, delightfully familiar and yet also disturbingly reminiscent of someone else. I moved methodically, making sure to keep my gaze locked with his, the better to chase away the thoughts of Quetzalcoatl. "The basics are the same, but you move with a different purpose."

"And what is the purpose?" he asked, watching me intently.

"To give pleasure." I kissed him, the desire overcoming me.

He tipped me onto my back, laying me gently on the stone. "Like this?" He moved carefully inside me, a stark contrast to earlier.

"Perfect." Everything was coming together so well, and the pleasure began blossoming in my abdomen.

But opening my eyes again chased away all notions of perfection. I was used to seeing pleasure-induced disorientation in the eyes of my lovers, but Mextli might as well have been doing some menial but necessary task for all the passion in his eyes. *He's not enjoying this at all.*

But he does not dislike it either, the desire argued. *You were indifferent the first time too, remember? Quetzalcoatl had to teach us to feel pleasure. We just have to teach Mextli.*

But I had no idea how Quetzalcoatl had done any of that....

There will be time enough for that. Let's just enjoy this for now.

The pleasure rose in a wave over me, making me gasp, but when Mextli stopped moving, I panted, "No, don't stop!"

"But I'm hurting you again—"

"You're not. Don't stop." He picked up the pace even more when I begged him to. I clung to him, a tense storm roiling inside me, waiting for the first lightning strike to start everything. My magic pulsed and throbbed, and my body felt on the verge of flying apart and unleashing my raw, unfettered teotl out over the world. Like I had when those raiders attacked our camp. For that thought alone, I resisted the growing urge to let go and let the pleasure overtake me.

Nothing bad will happen, the desire whispered, a pleading to her tone. *We've done this before, remember? And no one got hurt.*

I gazed up at Mextli. He looked like a man focused on a task requiring great mental concentration. *If only I could share with him what I'm feeling right now, so he can understand....*

I couldn't hold back forever though. The wave of pleasure finally crashed over me, and the Divine Dream flexed around us before everything became blinding light. Even Mextli glowed, as if I was gazing upon his uncontained teotl. He pulsed bright turquoise, and his magic swirled around him in a flurry of glowing hummingbirds. I'd never seen anything more breath-taking, more beautiful.

My own body had given way to an intense, burning orange, and my magic reached out in tendrils, forming leaping rabbits. They danced around the birds, which darted away, uncertain, and the streams of our magic mingled together, sliding and twisting around each other. This all felt very familiar.

Yes, this is just like when Quetzalcoatl and I came together in Tamoachan. His magic had been the softest purple, almost white, and it spectral serpents had speckled feathers, and eyes that were a deep—almost black—purple. My own magic hadn't formed anything recognizable from its tendrils, but when the serpents had coiled themselves around the tips, time seemed to slow and pulses of pleasure and contentment took over everything; Quetzalcoatl's thoughts and emotions had flowed over and through me, like he was an ocean I was swimming in. I'd wanted to stay there forever. I couldn't wait to feel like that again.

Overcome with anticipation, my glowing magic rabbits bounded after Mextli's skittish hummingbirds. The birds darted and flitted among our entangled tendrils as if playing a chase game, but when one of my rabbits pounced upon one, the bird burst into a spray of light. A heavy pulse of magic throbbed up my orange tendrils, bringing with it a strange, sudden flash of memory.

I was somewhere dark and warm, and safe, huddled like a sleeping infant, but then suddenly everything turned to light and wetness. I wiped liquid from my eyes to see beastly creatures with dog-like faces, needle-like fangs and glowing red eyes surrounding me, hissing as they pressed forward, thick spines raised upon their backs. But I had macuahuitl swords in both of my hands—one of them covered in countless tiny blue hummingbird feathers.

These are Mextli's memories! Of his birth, perhaps?

The ebb of magic grew in intensity as more of my rabbits caught the birds, and more of Mextli's memories flowed into me with it. I chased his sister Coyolxauhqui into a cave in the mountains until I'd trapped her and she huddled against a wall, a look of utter hatred on her face. The copper bells on her cheeks tinkled preternaturally loud when my sword took her head from her neck. Then there was the adoration and devotion on Coatlicue's face when she first saw me after rising from the dead; it warmed my empty chest. But then came the stinging pain when Smoking Mirror glared at me and hissed, *Don't ever call me Father again, Mextli.*

I was overflowing with power now, and Mextli's magic shifted hues with growing rapidity. His birds took frightened flight in every direction, pulses of fear ebbing like icy water through me. This was nothing like with Quetzalcoatl, and I had no idea what was happening.

What do we do? I shot off at the desire, my own panic rising.

I don't know. Her voice was uncharacteristically anxious.

I dug through my memories, trying to find the answer. With Quetzalcoatl, the magic had flowed like a whirlpool between us, but what was happening now felt more like a one-way flood. Would I kill Mextli if I kept at it much longer?

When I have too much magic, I get rid of the excess, so I pushed magic back up my tendrils. Maybe I could start the perpetual flow.

But Mextli resisted. He tried to retract his tendrils, but my own pursued him even more aggressively, latching onto them as if they had actual physical substance. More of his magic flooded in and I started to truly panic. I couldn't control my own magic and didn't even know how to break this bond we'd created. *Let him go!* I shouted, not knowing what else to do.

The rabbits paused their pursuit of the birds as if suddenly frozen, but then they joined the tendrils in a slow retreat. The influx of magic abated but I was still flooded. Even as my physical body re-coalesced to contain my teotl again, it oozed out of me like slime from a salamander's skin.

The world reformed around me to reveal Mextli's tent was gone. I lay on the ground, completely naked while many men and women stood at a distance, watching me. Mextli, however, stood staring down at me, his chest heaving, a confused, almost terrified expression on his face.

Dear gods, I'm sorry, Mextli! was on the tip of my tongue, but as soon as I stumbled to my feet, he struck me full-force in the chest with his fist, returning me to the ground. The shock of the raw pain made me gasp as I clutched my sternum, my mind reeling.

But when I heard his first heavy footstep towards me, instinct took over. I sprang back to my feet, magic pouring from my hands, ready to throw it at him if necessary.

The angry, vengeful darkness dominated his eyes, but he suddenly stopped, an air of uncertainty hanging over him. When I followed his gaze, my heart started racing.

I held a lightweight macuahuitl sword in each hand. Where did these come from?

But when I flexed my right-hand grip, the sword changed into an obsidian-headed spear. *How am I doing this? I'm not a war goddess; I've never created such things before.*

The humans whispered, and Mextli bared his teeth. "Thief," he growled, low and dangerous.

I tightened my grip on both weapons. "I don't know what's happening."

"Liar!" His voice shook the ground and everyone looked around as if deciding whether to run away.

"You're scaring me, Mextli!" Tears clogged my throat. "Please stop."

"Don't play coy with me, Mayahuel. You knew exactly what you were doing, didn't you?"

"What are you talking about?"

"It was all a lie, wasn't it? You not knowing how to use your magic and having me teach you...." He looked around, as if suddenly realizing that we weren't alone, and when he returned his glare to me, shrewdness had replaced the anger.

"Listen well, everyone," he announced, his voice booming over the silent camp. "Mayahuel is leaving us."

My heart dropped into my stomach.

"Every one of you has been trustworthy, loyal servants, both to me and her, but she's chosen to betray what trust you've put in her. So she is leaving us now. And henceforth, anyone found worshipping her— whether it is by praying or offering sacrifices—shall be put to the eagle stone in my name."

Trading out his predatory posture, Mextli stood straighter, as if he dared me to attack him. "Run on back to your precious Topiltzin, Mayahuel. He's going to need your protection more than ever now."

My magic thrummed hot at the threat, but when I spotted Xochitl standing next to her husband with a look of utter confusion on her face—and both hands gripping her round belly—the anger cooled. Whatever was transpiring between me and Mextli had nothing to do with the Mexica, and the best thing I could do for her—for all of them—was leave.

I slowly lowered my weapons. "I'll go, but you owe me an explanation, Mextli. Once you've had a chance to calm down."

"Oh, we *will* see each other again soon, but I won't be any calmer than now," he replied. The image of his hateful glare followed me as I disappeared into the teoyoh.

PART THREE
THE YEAR NINE HOUSE

CHAPTER TWENTY-TWO

I didn't think about where to go; I just wanted to be somewhere safe, away from Mextli and the new threat he posed. But it didn't surprise me when I materialized in my private quarters in Tollan, fully dressed in my royal robes and neatly groomed. Inside though, I was a complete wreck. I sunk down on the bed and tears I didn't even realize I was holding back came flowing down my cheeks. My head was a muddle of confusion and embarrassment. Things had definitely gotten out of hand, and I'd done nothing to help it.

Not true! the desire insisted. *We tried to break the bond when we realized we were hurting him.*

I stared down at the spear in my left hand, watching it change to a dagger, then to an axe each time I flexed my grip on the handle. *Actually, we only made it worse,* I realized when it dawned on me how I was suddenly able to make weapons of war. *All of those power surges when we were bound together, filling me up to the point of bursting...it was his war magic. We were pulling it out of him!* Feeling sick, I let the weapons drop to the ground, my hands now sweating. No wonder he called me a thief.

I'm sorry, the desire said, her voice small and shaking in my head. *This is my fault.*

Hardly, I replied. *We both agreed to pursue this with him.*

But you were right, to be concerned about him accepting us. I should have known that he wouldn't, especially after how he talked about Xochiquetzal. I was just...just so desperate...I'm sorry. Fresh tears rolled down my cheeks and a terrible ache reverberated through my chest as the desire took over my tongue. "I just wanted to not feel this terrible pain anymore," she whispered. "Very soon, the time will come where we can't ever see or speak to Little Reed again, for eternity, and when I think about it—"

I blinked back the tears and nodded.

"I let our hopes get up when we found out that Coatlicue had once been mortal," she went on while I wiped the tears from my cheek with my fist. "And seeing that dashed yet again…I'm sorry. I thought moving on into a new relationship would help soften the blow, for both of us."

"I don't think we need to soften the blow," I replied, taking my own turn to speak aloud. "I think we need to feel it, and always remember it."

"But it hurts so much!"

"I'd rather feel that than nothing at all. At least then I know I'm still alive and there's the potential to feel happiness again."

The desire sniffled. "What are we going to do about Ehecacone now? We can't take on Quetzalcoatl on our own."

I finished drying my tears then looked around my empty quarters. "I don't know. I haven't thought that far ahead yet. But I'm not sure that we should stay here. When Mextli comes for us…."

"No one will be safe," the desire finished.

"But we made a promise, and we haven't finished it."

You're right, the desire agreed, retreating back into my head. *And we can't just up and disappear again, knowing how many people we hurt doing so last time.*

"We stay to help install a new king, then we go again, and this time we explain our reasons, so the people understand and accept."

We're going to tell them the truth about us?

"Eventually. We owe them that much."

The bells on my door curtain rang. I scooped the spear and sword under the blankets on my bed before asking, "Who is it?"

"It's me, My Lady." Anacoana's voice. She poked her head past the curtain when I told her to enter, but the smile fell from her face. "You've been crying?"

"It's nothing." I took another swipe at my cheeks, to wipe away what I'd missed. "I was just…thinking about Topiltzin."

"Sometimes I cannot help my own tears. But I imagine this is very tough for you, seeing him like he is after so long."

"It is."

"I came looking for you earlier, to ask if you wanted to take over some of the duties of caring for him—I know you were closer in his heart than I could ever hope to be—but I couldn't find you. I even had the guards search for you, but no one knew where you were."

I faltered before replying, "I'm sorry for sneaking off as I did. I was in the priestly gardens, meditating. I should have told my guards where I was going, but I've grown used to coming and going as I please."

She nodded, appeased.

"I thank you for your offer, and I'm happy to take over your duties to the king, if it would please you. I know it's been a burden on you, shouldering so much, but I'm happy to give you a much needed break from such matters."

She stiffened, and after a brief struggle for words, she said, "You're most kind, My Lady, but it wouldn't feel right for me to completely burden you with his full-time care. You have other important obligations to the kingdom whereas I only have my obligations to the king himself."

I sensed it was more of a defense of her usefulness than any sense of obligation, perhaps fearing I'd take away whatever value she had for Little Reed. But then I'd felt that same way when he would ask me to relinquish some of my priestly duties to others so as to lighten my own burden.

I smiled reassuringly at her. "I understand, My Lady. I'm at your disposal should you need me for anything. You look exhausted, so perhaps I can take the night shift for you, so you can catch up on your sleep? I don't mind in the least."

"I am tired," she admitted, letting some of the tension roll off her shoulders as they sagged a bit again. "I thank you."

"I'm happy to help. Sleep well."

She smiled and started to leave, but then she turned back again, embarrassment on her face. "Forgive me, My Lady, but the reason I came to speak with you in the first place...Lord Citlallotoc has arrived from Acolman and is with the king as we speak."

I blinked. "But I just sent Mazatzin out last night!"

Anacoana nodded. "They both arrived no more than a few moments ago."

When I departed my quarters, Anacoana at my heels, I found Mazatzin leaning against the wall outside Little Reed's quarters. He stood straighter then bowed when I approached.

"What is this I hear about Lord Citlallotoc having arrived already?" I asked, my voice barely above a whisper in the silent garden.

He nodded. "I got a few hours down the road when I came upon him, headed for Tollan."

"He was already on his way here?"

"He told me he received a summons a week ago, saying he needed to appear before Lord Topiltzin as soon as possible."

Someone sent for Citlallotoc before I arrived? Surely Malinalli would have told me if she'd done so, and it seemed unlikely Matlacxochitl would have—for Citlallotoc would have immediately known he wasn't Little Reed. "He's in there with Topiltzin?" I pointed to Little Reed's quarters.

Mazatzin nodded. "He insisted on seeing the king right away."

I paused at the door curtain, wondering if I should wait, but decided it would be best to speak with him in private. Taking a deep breath, I parted the curtain and stepped inside.

Citlallotoc knelt on the floor next to the bed, holding Little Reed's frail hand in his one remaining one. He looked up when I entered. "Quetzalpetlatl!" He started to his feet, but I motioned him to stay put. After a hesitation, he settled again. "Mazatzin said you just came back yesterday."

I nodded as I sat opposite him. "I thought I'd been away long enough."

His gaze lingered on mine, his jaw tightening a fraction, but then he returned his attention to Little Reed. "You're looking quite well, My Lady."

"As do you." It was just a politeness though; while he might not have changed much physically, there was tiredness in his eyes and posture, and not just from the journey from Acolman. "I'm glad you came back."

"When my king calls for me, I try to be there."

"He needs you now more than ever; as do I."

This time he did look up at me.

"As you can see, Topiltzin hasn't long before beginning his journey to Mictlan, and he left no heir for the throne. The future of Tollan is in question."

"But you're back now."

"I'm only here to make sure that my brother's interests are looked after properly, and to ensure that someone of dedication and integrity takes the throne upon his death."

"And then you're going to leave again?" When I nodded, he asked, "Why?"

I hesitated before saying, "I'm not capable of being Tollan's queen anymore, so it's time I moved on, for the good of her people."

I wasn't sure if he accepted my vague explanation, but he didn't argue. "Who do you have in mind to replace Topiltzin?"

"You, of course."

Citlallotoc shook his head. "I cannot accept that honor, My Lady."

"You must."

"Surely there is someone else, someone the King trusts—"

"I don't trust Topiltzin's judgment in this matter," I replied. "The man he entrusted with the care of the city went on to deceive the Council and her citizens, and overturned many of our most sacred laws. I don't believe Topiltzin was in a well state of mind when he chose him, and he's even less so now."

Citlallotoc furrowed his brow. "Whom did he name?"

"Matlacxochitl. Until yesterday, he'd spent the last three years impersonating Topiltzin with the intent of naming himself Tollan's heir. He forced me to send him into exile for treason."

He frowned. "Blood Wolf always said his brother was ambitious, but I doubt even he had any idea of its extent."

"I had just sent Mazatzin to Acolman to ask you to come take Matlacxochitl's place here in Tollan, so I'm relieved that you arrived so soon. Topiltzin could leave us any day now."

He sighed. "I am honored by your faith in me, My Lady, but I am not the right man for the throne."

"Why not?"

"Because I betrayed Topiltzin's friendship. I betrayed his trust."

I cast my gaze down at Little Reed lying on the bed between us. "He said as much to you?"

"He didn't have to. I know what I did, and it was dishonorable."

"And it was a request that he had no business making of you in the first place, Citlallotoc. Our lives and happiness were not his to bargain with. What happened in Teotihuacan...it is a matter between you and me, and only you and me."

"I promised him—"

"And he promised *me* that he would never treat me as a commodity to be traded upon, the way so many other noblemen have treated their wives and sisters and daughters. He broke that promise when he made you promise to not pursue me, and you are not a man to abide false promises, so your honor is clean."

He hung his head, flummoxed. "I don't even know how to respond to that, My Lady," he finally said.

"My brother isn't perfect, and I can forgive his flaws. Just as I wish you would forgive yourself for this one little thing. He loved you, and I know that if he could, he would tell you as much, to set your heart at ease. If my brother's friendship meant anything to you—"

"It was everything to me," he cut in, an edge to his voice.

I nodded. "Then you will honor it by embracing this responsibility."

"I did swear my fealty to him for the remainder of my life." A pained expression crossed his face as he stared down at Little Reed's sleeping form. "Very well, My Lady. I will do this, for both you and Topiltzin."

"Thank you." I wanted to reach out and squeeze his hand in mine, but I fought the impulse. After what I'd done to him in Teotihuacan...that was a privilege I'd thrown away. Instead I brushed Little Reed's hair off his forehead with a gentle sweep of my fingers.

Citlallotoc watched me. "I can't believe he's really leaving us."

I bit my lip before saying, "Neither can I, and so soon. His aging seemed to slow down there for a number of years...."

He nodded, his jaw quivering. "Do you think...our leaving...do you think it did this to him?"

"I don't know." When my voice broke, I paused to collect myself. "Maybe...or perhaps it's just his time."

Citlallotoc nodded, fighting back tears. "I'll do my very best to give justice to your legacy, my friend, and I promise I'll stay true to your laws, philosophies, and your chosen god." He kissed Little Reed's hand then got to his feet. "I suppose I should meet with the Council. I'm sure they have many questions for me."

"A good idea. The sooner everything is settled, the better."

To my surprise, he offered me his hand to help me up. I hesitated before accepting, but I let go of him as soon as was polite. "Thank you."

"My pleasure, My Lady," he murmured, avoiding my gaze.

¤

Citlallotoc's arrival in the great hall was greeted with much enthusiasm from those members who'd served while he'd still been Justice of the Peace. Those who were newer hung off to the sides, watching the laughing and heartfelt greetings with uncertainty. I, in turn, watched them closely from the dais, my discussion with Blood Wolf from the night before lingering forward on my mind. Purging the Council of Matlacxochitl's supporters would need to be a top priority.

Citlallotoc finally made it to the dais and I invited him to stand next to me. A hush fell as I turned to address the crowd. "Thank you all for coming to council in this most mournful time for Tollan. As many of you are aware, Revered Speaker Topiltzin didn't name an heir prior to his falling ill, so the task of deciding who should rule Tollan once he leaves us has fallen to me, as his closest living blood relative. And I've chosen someone whom I think that, if Topiltzin were still with us now, he'd heartily approve of. I speak of course of Tollan's former war chief, Justice of the Peace, and my brother's best man, Lord Citlallotoc of Acolman."

Hoots and whistles rose in the crowd.

Last night I'd ordered my old icpalli brought out of storage and it now sat next to Little Reed's; the servants had even decorated the back of it with stalks of bone flowers, as they used to. I settled onto my throne, silently rejoicing at the familiar contours the years of council meetings had molded into it. I motioned Citlallotoc to take Little Reed's throne.

He looked at it, uncertain, but when he went to sit down, a voice shouted out, "Halt!" He did so and turned to look out into the crowd.

I saw red when Matlacxochitl strode up the middle of the great hall towards the dais, the crowd parting for him and murmuring in confusion. A handful of soldiers came with him, clutching spears in their hands.

My guards exchanged unsure looks, but when they saw the deep-set frown on my face, they rushed forward to block Matlacxochitl's way. Tension mounted in the room.

But Matlacxochitl stopped well before the dais, and glared back at me behind his half-mask, his mouth matching my own frown.

"What in Mictlan are you doing here?" I growled, rising to my feet. "I sentenced you to exile!"

"And I don't recognize your authority," he fired back.

"I am the Queen of Tollan—"

"Anacoana is the Queen of Tollan. You forfeited your crown when you left Tollan five years ago, vowing never to return."

Blood Wolf stepped from the crowd. "Enough of this foolishness, brother! Topiltzin never revoked Lady Quetzalpetlatl's claim to the throne! You know that!"

"It wounds me that my own brother doesn't stand with me. She left a mess for the rest of us to clean up, and now she swoops in here as if nothing happened and names a traitor as heir to the throne!"

I laughed. "Ironic words coming from the mouth of an actual traitor."

"The king himself kicked *him* out of Tollan five years ago for disloyalty." He jabbed a finger at Citlallotoc.

Citlallotoc stiffened. "Topiltzin didn't kick me out. I left of my own volition."

"And would you care to tell everyone why?"

Citlallotoc set his jaw.

Matlacxochitl flourished his cape as he turned to the crowd. "Was it because the King discovered that you were sleeping with his wife and he couldn't be sure the child she carried was truly his?"

Confused murmurs spilled through the crowd.

"Very reliable sources tell me that you were paying late-night visits to Lady Anacoana's quarters on a regular basis for months after she married Topiltzin—"

"You imply deception where none existed," I said. "Topiltzin was fully aware of the situation, and in fact, he not only encouraged it, he suggested it. The sad truth is that my brother couldn't bear any more children of his own. He and I were lucky to be blessed with Prince Ehecacone, but that is the only blood offspring the gods saw fit to grant us. Tollan needed an heir, and Topiltzin couldn't produce one himself, so he asked his best friend to father a child for him, for the good of the kingdom." It felt dishonorable to blatantly lie, but the truth would not only damage Little Reed's reputation and legacy, but also humiliate Anacoana in front of the entire court.

Matlacxochitl glared at me. "I thought Topiltzin sought a divorce from you because *you* were the barren one."

"Our reasons are none of your business, nor do they have any bearing on the situation at hand."

"But if the affair had nothing to do with anything, then why did Lord Citlallotoc leave?"

"To make sure Tollan's future was safe and secure, of course."

"Meaning?"

"Already Prince Ehecacone had been murdered, and rather than risk another tragedy, Topiltzin planned to send his new child to Acolman, to be raised there in King Huemac's household. And to be blunt, he had good reason to be concerned, considering the lengths you went through to slither your way onto the throne. And your defying my orders now suggests you've made a concerted effort to fill the Council and the king's guard with your own little loyal, yipping dogs."

He smiled, smug. "If you had seen to your duties in the first place, it wouldn't have been necessary for me to step in. But I will not just step away now. I earned the throne with my loyalty—"

"You have a very warped definition of loyalty," I fired back. "You've overturned the very laws the god handed down through myself and Topiltzin—"

"And Quetzalcoatl isn't the only god in the heavens."

I narrowed my eyes. "Smoking Mirror put you up to this, didn't he?"

Matlacxochitl turned to the crowd again. "For twelve years, Topiltzin has turned his back on the other gods, creating laws to weaken the other cults while elevating the Feathered Serpent. He attempted to name Quetzalcoatl *the only god*, but that is a lie, and we forget that at our peril. Already we've seen evidence of the other gods' discontent—the mudslides last autumn, followed by the almost complete lack of rain this year. We're living on the stored grain thanks to drought devastating our crops. The gods have abandoned us because we've turned our backs on them!"

An angry murmur rolled through the crowd.

"Citlallotoc will continue Topiltzin's disastrous policies—*her disastrous policies*—" He pointed at me—"and it will lead to Tollan's destruction!"

"Will you continue Lord Topiltzin's policies, Lord Citlallotoc?" a voice asked from the crowd.

Citlallotoc stepped up to the edge of the dais. "Topiltzin's laws have seen peace reign in Tolteca lands for the first time in many bundles of years, so yes, my intention is to continue them, for the health and well-being of Tollan's people."

"And what about your allies? How do you intend to run this empire that Topiltzin built?" This voice I recognized as Lord Mozauhqui, the son of the king of Tepanec. He turned a glare onto Matlacxochitl. "In the last few years, while impersonating the king, Lord Matlacxochitl had grown increasingly demanding of his allies, exacting tribute where Topiltzin expected nothing of us but peace."

"I intend to continue respecting our allies' sovereignty."

"And when the food is gone and the people are starving in the streets?" Matlacxochitl demanded. "When the poor are tussling at your palace gates, what will you do then?"

"I will ask our allies for their assistance, not demand it," Citlallotoc growled.

"And we would gladly give it," Mozauhqui replied, defiant.

"The empire was built upon mutual trust and respect, not power plays and fear," Citlallotoc told Matlacxochitl. "Your way would see the empire crumble and the cities fall into constant war again."

"And your way would have it fall into war with the gods. These last few years were just the beginning. And curiously Quetzalcoatl has done nothing to stop it."

"As if you'd know anything about the ways of the gods, little man," I snarled.

Matlacxochitl frowned. "Then by all means educate us, My Lady. You are, after all, a high priestess of the Feathered Serpent."

"I am not anymore. Nor would I claim to know anything about Quetzalcoatl's motivations, but just because one side appears to be winning doesn't mean the other side is doing nothing. Only a small-minded individual would think so, and small minds have no place on thrones."

His shoulders rose like a bristling jaguar, but then he turned away to address the crowd again. "In the end, it doesn't matter what she thinks; what matters if what the Council thinks. She can name whomever she wishes to the throne, but without the support of the Council, that man would have no power. The Council should decide who will take the throne."

"That would be fair if you hadn't loaded it with a majority of your supporters," Mozauhqui replied. "And who knows what you've done with the king's guard."

Matlacxochitl smirked. "Then perhaps it would be best for everyone if Lord Citlallotoc stood aside, to avoid unnecessary conflict."

I glared at Matlacxochitl while the desire growled deep in my chest. "And perhaps it would be best if you don't forget what I did at the battle for Culhuacan."

His smirk dropped and a worried whisper raced through the crowd. Even Matlacxochitl's guards looked ill-at-ease.

I reclined, grinning. "The Council will not determine who rules next. And while it is my birthright to name the heir myself, I too will stand aside in this matter. Instead, the citizens of Tollan herself will determine whom to entrust their future to. Let there be public debates between the candidates, so each can make their case for why they should rule Tollan, and then let the people cast their lots. At this juncture, it's the only truly fair way to determine the throne's future."

"I will agree to that," Citlallotoc said.

Matlacxochitl mulled a moment before replying, "I have no objections either." To Citlallotoc, he added, "Though perhaps you should reconsider, My Lord, lest your transgressions with the Queen become revealed to the entire city."

"And I would be forced to divulge your treason," I cut in, narrowing my eyes at him. "Which one do you think will cause the most stir among the citizenry? Are you sure you wish to remain a contender?"

Matlacxochitl nodded stiffly, returning my glare. "I trust that you will extend your royal hospitality without my having to fear for my safety, the same as you're giving to Lord Citlallotoc?"

Now was my turn to mull. I didn't like him having such easy access to his rival, given his treachery.

Smirking, Matlacxochitl told Citlallotoc, "Surely you're not afraid of me, My Lord?"

Citlallotoc laughed. "Hardly. I have no fear of you remaining here in the palace. I trust in Quetzalcoatl to protect me from whatever evil you might be plotting against me."

It was on the tip of my tongue to warn him not to place faith in the goodness of the Feathered Serpent, but with everyone listening, now wasn't the time to cast doubts on the city's patron god. I didn't want to give Matlacxochitl credibility in anyone's eyes. "You shall be assigned quarters in the western wing, but you are not allowed into the royal quarters for any reason. And I shall assign my own guards to watch over you, for the sake of the palace's other residents."

"Are *you* afraid of me then, My Lady?"

"Don't attempt to shame me into foolishness, Matlacxochitl. I make a habit of not underestimating the cunning of my enemies. And yes, you are my enemy."

Matlacxochitl bowed. "It's good to know where I stand with you."

"It is lucky for you that both Citlallotoc and I are more honorable than you. I doubt we would be as lucky as you if our positions were reversed."

He sneered. "I don't need deception to win this competition. I am the better man for the throne, and the people will see that in the end."

"Then let us reconvene this business tomorrow morning, when everyone is rested. Dinner is growing cold while we duel over words that make no difference today. Forgive me for not inviting you to join the feast though; this is in honor of Citlallotoc and your very presence is an affront."

"I will eat in my own quarters, My Lady." Matlacxochitl gave me a mock bow then stormed from the great hall, his guards following, bringing a rush of conversation.

"And anyone else who doesn't wish to honor Lord Citlallotoc's return," I called over the noise, bringing a hush, "you are free to join your chosen leader. No one will harass you for doing so."

The crowd remained silent as everyone looked around, waiting to see who would leave. No one did, though several councilmen looked distinctly uncomfortable as everyone took to the reed mats spread about the floor.

As the servants filled our dishes, Citlallotoc searched the room from Little Reed's icpalli. "Where's Anacoana?"

"No doubt sleeping," I said. "She needed to catch up on her rest."

He let out a ragged breath. "At least she wasn't here for Matlacxochitl dragging her name through the muck. She deserves better than that." He shook his head. "I never should have agreed to Topiltzin's request."

"He asked it out of loyalty to you. Flame Tongue put him in an impossible situation but he still felt guilty for getting between you and Anacoana. Undoubtedly he thought it the best reparation he could make to you."

Citlallotoc nodded. "My feelings for her clouded my judgment in that regard."

Lowering my voice, I said, "Things didn't go well for you two in the past, but...Anacoana will be widowed soon—"

But he shook his head. "It is much too late for that."

"You're already married?"

"No." He picked at his food. "Too much has passed between us since then."

"The past can be forgiven."

"Perhaps." He still wouldn't look at me though as he started to eat.

I ate a few bites myself, letting the silence linger until it became too much to bear. "We need to talk."

"About what?"

"About what happened between us...in Teotihuacan."

He stopped mid-chew but made no move to look at me.

"I know this isn't the right time or place, but...it could be beneficial, for both of us."

"And if I don't wish to talk about it?"

"I won't force you to." As soon as I said it, my choice of words tasted terrible in my mouth. "I understand the...awkwardness of all of this, and if you feel the need to...excise some of that, I will listen to whatever you need to say."

He chuckled guardedly. "Maybe you have some words in need of saying to me as well?"

"There is only one thing I can possibly say, and that is I'm sorry for all of the damage I have caused you."

"Am I damaged now, since you rejected me?"

"That's not what I meant."

"It is all right, My Lady. I have much practice with rejection, so you haven't hurt me anymore than anyone else has."

I'm not so sure about that, I almost said, but instead frowned. "Still, if there's anything you wish to talk about, come find me, at any time." I handed my plate off to one of the servants and rose.

Citlallotoc raised an eyebrow. "You're done eating already?"

"I'm not hungry, but I should feed Topiltzin. The servants will ready your old quarters for you; I'm sure you're tired from your journey." I nodded and left the dais.

But he called back to me, "Wait." He handed his own plate off to a servant then came over to me to whisper, "I'm not ready to talk about that night yet, but perhaps tomorrow, after I've rested...."

"Then I shall see you at breakfast?"

"Yes." He looked as if he wanted to say more, but then lowered his head into a bow. "Sleep well, My Lady."

CHAPTER TWENTY-THREE

The halls were quiet at this late hour, and only a few guards lingered at their posts. I stopped by the royal kitchens and brewed up a small bowl of atole for Little Reed before continuing on to the royal living quarters. I checked on Anacoana, who was sleeping soundly, and ordered the idle servants to fix Citallotoc's old room for him.

Little Reed was sound asleep in his bed, his breath wheezing and rattling. He muttered and grumbled when I struggled to sit him up, but eventually I propped him up against his Feathered Serpent idol. I shot scathing glares at it between spooning the watery atole into his mouth.

Once I'd emptied the bowl, I wiped his messy beard. He looked so unkempt and rumpled, and a feculent odor grew stronger around him. "You need a good bath and some grooming, my love." I kissed his cheek then went to the bath yard to fill his wash tub.

I set the first pot of water on the brazier, and was about to return to the room to fetch a stick of fire from the hearth, but then I thought of that first battle between Mextli and I long ago now, how he'd set my maguey roots on fire to escape. Now that I had his magic, could I too make fire myself? I bent next to the bundle of sticks under the tripod and flicked my fingers at it.

To my delight, tongues of blue flames sprang from my fingertips, igniting the lumber faster than normal flames. "I could get used to this," I murmured as I watched the water begin to steam. Once I'd filled the tub with water and heated it with the hot water from the fire, I went to fetch Little Reed.

He was much heavier than he looked, and I struggled to lift his frail body out of bed. There wasn't any way I could carry him to the bath yard myself.

How easily you forget you're a goddess. My face heated with embarrassment. Draping Little Reed's arm over my shoulder, I took us both into the teoyoh then into the bath yard.

In that brief instance in the fires of the teoyoh, strange white wisps of unidentified magic curled among mine, and I had the unsettled feeling that I wasn't the only one of my kind in the stream. Was Smoking Mirror spying on me? "Teoti," I murmured aloud, eager to be back in the material world. I filed the feeling away for future reference then laid Little Reed on the mats to undress him.

Under his robes he was wasted away, everything shriveled and sagging. He lay completely limp while I worked, oblivious even when I wrestled his naked, bony body into the tub then rubbed copal soap over his loose, spotted skin. *And to think he's only lived thirty-five years. The curse of being only half divine, perhaps? How can there be nothing beneficial about having one divine parent? No special abilities or magic, just a shortened lifespan?*

One of the few reasons to be thankful for Quetzalcoatl being Ehecacone's father rather than Black Otter, the desire said, uncharacteristically sober.

I trimmed Little Reed's shaggy beard so it wasn't so unruly, and contemplated shaving it off, but when I nicked his jowls with his obsidian shaving blade, I decided it best to leave it be. I combed the tangles from his long silver hair and trimmed it a too, so it looked well-kept. *At least he'll look kingly and dignified when Xolotl comes for him.*

But as I leaned over to scoop him up under his arms, I noticed he was staring at me. "Little Reed?"

He didn't respond, but continued staring.

I waved a hand in front of his face, and though he didn't blink, I was certain he was looking at me. I searched for the right words to say, but I knew they would never come if I didn't just start talking.

"I don't know how much longer you have, Little Reed, and I don't even know if you can hear or understand anything I'm saying, but I may not get another chance to tell you any of this, and...you have the right to know the truth." I took a deep breath, committing. "I'm not who you think I am, Little Reed. I'm not even who *I* thought I was. You see...oh, where to start? With what happened at Teotihuacan five years ago, I guess.

"I was very angry about what happened to our son—so angry I summoned Smoking Mirror, so I could confront him, but it turned out it wasn't his doing." Pain rose in my chest. "I was wrong about Black Otter. I should have known...I shouldn't have trusted him...." I wiped hot tears from my eyes. "He murdered Ehecacone, Little Reed. He tried to drive a wedge between you and me, and in that regard, he succeeded, since everything fell apart for us after that. But even that's not the worst of it. He sold his soul to the lake goddess and turned himself into a hideous monster, so he could continue pursuing me; even now, after I killed him for his crimes, he's still after me.

"But I can blame him only so much, for I caused his insanity, just as I caused Red Flint's." I stared down into the dingy water, dreading most what I had to say next. "And I fear I've caused it in you too."

When I looked up at him again, there was still no change in his expression, so I went on.

"During my confrontation with the Smoking Mirror, I discovered something so...devastating that I couldn't come home again, not with knowing what damage I was doing to everyone around me."

I took a deep breath. The moment was finally upon me. "There's no easy way to put this, so I'll just say it: I'm not a human being, Little Reed. I'm the goddess Mayahuel. I feel so foolish, for when I think about it, I should have known long ago, but then who would believe it was anything but ego? I was sure it was just in my head, but now that I know the truth, everything makes sense. Just being around me drove both Red Flint and Black Otter insane.

"And it kills me to say this, because I love you so much...." I choked but made myself go on. "What you feel for me isn't real, Little Reed. I made you waste your life on me when you could have been happy with someone else, and I'm so very sorry for that. If I'd known what I was doing to you, maybe I could have spared you...."

I balled my fists, rage flooding over me. "But I didn't find out until it was too late, and I know this will be even more difficult to hear, but your father knew the truth but he kept it from me, out of spite. I had to find out from Smoking Mirror, of all gods!"

I rested my forehead on the edge of the tub, the anger boiling away until I felt only grief. "That's why I didn't come back from Teotihuacan. I had to leave because I loved you too much to continue poisoning your mind. The one good thing that will come of you passing on into Mictlan will be that I won't have this hold over you anymore. You'll finally have peace again."

When I looked up again, Little Reed was slumped against the lip of the tub, asleep again. A strand of drool wound down the corner of his mouth onto his chin. I wiped it away with a rag. "I want you to know though that my love for you is very much real and having you in my life has meant so much. No matter what your father did, you are the one thing I cannot thank him enough for."

Once I returned him to his bed, I dressed him in a clean sleep xicolli and tucked him under his blankets. He didn't rouse during any of it. I bent to kiss his forehead and whisper good night, but stopped. For all I knew, just touching him strengthened those false bonds between us. *I should avoid touching him unless absolutely necessary.* Instead I patted the blanket over his hands. "Sleep well, Little Reed." I then left his quarters.

But when I stepped out on the portico, I heard sandals scraping on flagstone followed by the rustling of bushes. Beyond the torches on the portico, I couldn't make out anything in the moonless night. "Who's there?" When no one answered, my tension rose. Fearing an assassination attempt against Little Reed was eminent, I flexed my hand, bringing an obsidian-bladed dagger to it. The handle felt just like the buckhorn one of my mother's sacrificial blade, bringing with it deadly confidence. "Come out, now! I am not defenseless!"

The silence continued for a breath, but then came movement in the bushes. I tightened my grip on the knife as a shadow moved to the flagstone patio in the middle of the yard, but I relaxed it when the figure moved into the dim torchlight. "Malinalli? What are you doing lurking out there?"

She stared at me with a frightening dead look, her face ashen.

I stepped towards her. "Are you all right?"

But she sprang away like I was a hissing jaguar. Her shoulders heaved with heavy breath.

I stopped. "We should talk, about what happened when I saw you last—"

"Did you make me this way?" she asked, her voice barely above a whisper.

Make her what way? "What are you talking about?"

"Did you make me an abomination before the eyes of the gods?"

"Why...what...why would you think—"

"I heard you talking to Topiltzin."

My heart thudded painfully in my ears. "Malinalli—"

"Is this why I am the way I am?" she fired at me, anger supplanting the fear.

After a hesitation, I admitted, "I don't know."

"All these years I could have been normal, if not for you," she muttered, looking bewildered.

"You're not abnormal, Malinalli. Please don't say that about yourself!"

"What else can I possibly be? Why else would I choose to live a life of lies, a life of shame where I can't show my true self outside the privacy of my own quarters? If I was normal, I wouldn't have to hide anything from anyone; I wouldn't have to worry that I will be killed if anyone found out whom I share my bed with. Why would any normal person choose to live under such conditions?"

Her words alarmed me. "I don't have answers right now, Malinalli, but if we just talk about it, rationally—"

"I can't be rational, not right now. I mean, you're a...a...." She backed away, shaking her head vigorously.

"I know this is a lot to take in, but deep inside, I'm still the woman you've always known. In my heart you're still my best friend, but if I've lost that...." I choked, tears finally breaking free. "Please, Malinalli. It was never my intention to hurt you and I'm so very sorry that I did. Please forgive me."

But Malinalli continued shaking her head. "I don't know that I can. At least not right now; I need to think, and pray for guidance." Now she switched to nods. "Yes, I'll seek the guidance of the Feathered Serpent. He will know what to do."

You can't trust anything Quetzalcoatl tells you. But before I could say anything, she ran off into the dark. "Malinalli!" I came down onto the flagstone patio, but she was already gone. I slumped to the ground, holding my head in my hands as I wept.

"My, my," a creaky voice cackled. "For a creator goddess, you're sure good at destroying things, aren't you?"

I looked up to see Smoking Mirror standing on the portico outside Anacoana's room, leaning his frail, shriveled body against his gnarled staff. He grinned at me.

Anger dragged me to my feet. "How did you get in here?"

"I have a standing invitation. I'm the royal chemist."

"Why are you here?"

"The queen often has trouble sleeping, and suffers head pains. I provide medicines as needed."

"And what about to Topiltzin?"

"I *am* the royal chemist, my dear."

Magic roiled in my fingertips. "Then you did this to him? You made him into an invalid with your evil medicines?"

Smoking Mirror laughed, a rickety sound that didn't carry far in the still night. "You think so little of me, Mayahuel. But no, I didn't do any of that to him. If you're looking for someone to blame, that rests squarely with the Feathered Serpent. You should take up your complaints with him."

"If I knew where he was, I would," I snarled.

He hobbled down off the portico. "I'm pleased to see that you're back to your normal temperamental self."

I stared at him, suspicious. Had he not yet spoken to Mextli about what happened earlier today? Maybe it wasn't too late to strike a deal with him. "I have...regained my balance."

"An unbalanced god is a dangerous god," Smoking Mirror replied.

"What brings you here?"

"It's come to my attention that you are meddling in affairs with the humans here."

"You mean the royal succession?"

"Precisely! I'm sure it wasn't your intention to step on my toes, but you're meddling in things you shouldn't."

"So Matlacxochitl is your man?" Just as I'd figured.

"The healing process after Quetzalcoatl's treachery will be a long and difficult process for the humans. Matlacxochitl will return them to the correct path quickly, with far less pain than the alternative."

I narrowed my eyes. "Is that a threat?"

"What do you care of the humans anyway? You're not one of them."

"I have friends among them, people I care about; people whom Matlacxochitl would harm."

"And so long as they stand with the Feathered Serpent, they are my enemy, and I will show them as much mercy as they showed my followers in Culhuacan."

I shook my head. "He will harm people I love."

"As will you if you stay. In fact, you will end up with much more blood on your hands if you don't walk away."

I stood straighter, my indignation rising. "You underestimate me, Smoking Mirror."

He grinned wide. "And you think too highly of your own abilities."

"I will help them, and they will thank me for it," the desire snarled.

Chuckling, Smoking Mirror started down the path towards the hallway back into the palace. "Let's just hope you come to your senses before it's too late, Mayahuel. Come see me again when you're ready to put your ego aside and deal in reality."

I followed him to the hallway but stopped where my guards were posted. I watched him shuffle down to the main hallway then disappear around the corner.

"No one but myself, Anacoana, Citlallotoc, Malinalli or Mazatzin are allowed in the royal quarters without my express permission. Understand?" I told the guards. "And make sure the daytime guards know as well."

I returned to Little Reed's quarters, anxious. I didn't trust Smoking Mirror's claims of innocence concerning Little Reed's current state; having unfettered access to his enemy's mortal son, why wouldn't he try something? It gave me chills to think of that sorcerer plotting over my beloved's bed while he lay unaware. *The royal quarters aren't safe for him anymore.*

But where could I take him?

The priestly retreat, the desire suggested. Nobody but priests had access to it, so Smoking Mirror couldn't just walk in there without an escort in his current form. It wasn't perfect, especially since it relied on the Feathered Serpent's mood as to whether or not he would extend his protection, but if I told only a few trusted people and one of us always stayed with him, I would feel much better.

I gathered as much of Little Reed and his bedding into my arms as I could then moved him through the teoyoh to the private mediation room he and I used to share at the priestly sanctuary. My anxiety rose when those same white wisps of magic infiltrated the stream with me, along with a faint reptilian smell. Was Coatlicue nearby? If our enemies were indeed monitoring my movements through the teoyoh, I couldn't risk taking Little Reed through it anymore. I didn't know how to defend him if Mextli or one of Smoking Mirror's other allies attacked us in there.

We arrived to pitch blackness, but I recognized the soothing odor of the copalli incense Little Reed and I always burned on the plate in our meditation room. I had to fetch wood from the store rooms, but once I had the fire burning bright in the hearth, I found the room looked much like I remembered it; murals of Quetzalcoatl on the walls, and a large stone idol sitting against the garden-side. But unlike my quarters, there was a thick layer of dust over everything; no one ever came in here anymore, it seemed. I swept the area in front of the hearth clean and set up Little Reed's bed there, then spent the rest of the night turning the room into a livable space for him to pass his remaining days.

At dawn, I fixed a warm bowl of atole for his breakfast in the priestly kitchens, but when I heard footsteps out in the main garden, I peeked out from behind the closed curtain.

Mitotia headed to one of the meditation rooms opposite mine.

I gathered up the bowl and hurried out after her. "Mitotia!" When she started, I added, "I'm sorry. I didn't mean to frighten you."

She smoothed her dress, looking distinctly uncomfortable. "It's all right. I'm just used to there being no one here this early."

"Are you busy?"

"Do you need my help with something?"

I nodded and motioned her to follow me. "I've moved Topiltzin out of the palace for safety's sake."

"Has someone threatened him?"

"Not directly, but with the conflict over the throne, I'd rather he be somewhere I know to be safe." When we reached the door to my meditation room, I pulled aside the curtain for us.

Mitotia looked around when we stopped next to the bed. "However I can help, you can count on me."

"Thank you." I knelt next to Little Reed to sit him up for his meal. "It's vitally important that only trusted individuals know he's here. My intention is to only inform you, Malinalli, and Mazatzin."

She knelt to help me. "What about Anacoana?"

"I'll tell her, but she's not permitted in here anyway, since she's not a member of the priesthood."

"But Mazatzin said you quit the priesthood when you left."

"I quit Quetzalcoatl's priesthood. I don't think that in my heart I could ever really stop being a priestess. It's in my nature to serve."

"Whom do you serve now then?"

"The people of Tollan, regardless of their spiritual hearts."

I wasn't sure if my answer appeased her, but she didn't say anymore.

"I must attend the public debates today, so I need someone to watch over Topiltzin while I'm gone," I said. "Would you do this favor for me?"

"Of course, My Lady."

I handed her the bowl. "Thank you. I should get going before I'm late." When I reached the door curtain though, I said, "I'll talk to Mazatzin, but if you could tell Malinalli for me, I'd greatly appreciate it."

"I will."

"And please let her know that whenever she's ready to talk, I'm willing to sit down and listen."

Mitotia cocked her head, confused. "Is something the matter?"

"We just had a misunderstanding last night, that's all. I upset her, and I want to make it up to her anyway I can." Feeling the intensity of her gaze, I added, "I realize I betrayed our friendship when I left as I did, and she has every right to be angry, but I will do my very best to be a better friend—to be a better person this time."

After mulling on my words for a breath, Mitotia asked, "Are you going to leave again?"

"I will likely have to," I admitted. "But I promise a full explanation when the time comes. No sneaking away this time."

Mitotia nodded, but her expression was guarded. "I will speak with Malinalli when I see her next."

"Thank you. I will return at lunch time."

It was a relief when I finally stepped out into the garden.

But when I left the retreat and started crossing over the bridge, splashing in the river below caught my attention. I stopped to gaze over the wooden railing, expecting a fish.

Instead, inky black eyes peered back at me from the water.

I backed slowly towards the middle of the bridge.

"Mine!" Black Otter hissed below.

My heart hammered steadily as I glanced to shore. It wasn't far but Black Otter was fast, and long when he stretched himself out. Hearing clicking on the wood, I darted my attention back to the river.

Black Otter was climbing up onto the bridge, water cascading off his fur in rivulets. When we locked gazes, he bared his teeth into a grotesque grin. "Mine!" he hissed softly.

I ran.

He lunged after me, stretching out to rake his claws at me, but he missed as I cleared the bridge for the mainland. But with the next bound, he tackled me by the legs, tripping me to the ground. To my horror, when I looked back, he was completely out of the water, not a bit of him touching it. How could that be?

There was no time to dwell on that though. I flexed my right hand, to bring a dagger to it, but nothing materialized. Mextli's magic still tingled in my hands, but it felt weak compared to what I had become accustomed to. I flexed my fingers over and over again, cursing each time nothing happened.

But just when I was sure I would have to rely on my own octli magic, the blade appeared in my palm. I rammed it down between Black Otter's shoulder blades and twisted.

He cried out and let me go then retreated back to the water at a painful limp. He eased himself into the river then disappeared from sight. I stared at the water, waiting for Mitotia to come running from the retreat to ask what all of the noise was, but no one came out. Black Otter resurfaced though and glared at me, a petulant look on his monstrous face. "Mine!" he whined.

I hurried to my feet and scrambled further into the garden, almost tripping as I looked over my shoulder as I ran. He came up onto the shore, and the dagger was missing from his back, but he didn't pursue me. I would have to be careful coming and going from the retreat from now on.

I'll just have to use the teoyoh to get in and out, I decided, then with a final glare at him, I vanished into thin air.

CHAPTER TWENTY-FOUR

Anacoana was still sleeping when I returned to the palace, so I let her be and left a message with the guards to let her know to come find me when she woke up. From there, I ate breakfast with most of the council—including Matlacxochitl—but then we all adjourned to the sacred precinct for a day of debating.

Workmen had built a platform at the base of the Feathered Serpent's temple with a canopy to shield us from the sun, and by the time we'd arrived in the precinct, a very large crowd of citizens had already gathered to hear the debates. Blood Wolf had done a wonderfully efficient job of setting this up on such short notice.

An icpalli had been set out for me while everyone else was given a reed mat to sit upon. Mazatzin greeted me with a bow when I came up onto the platform, but I noticed Malinalli wasn't there. She hadn't been at breakfast either. "She's feeling ill this morning," Mazatzin informed me when I asked. "Do you wish me to send someone to fetch Mitotia in her stead?"

"No, I have her doing other things for me today. We'll just proceed as is."

Once the rest of the council and the two candidates had taken their mats upon the dais, I rose from my icpalli and addressed the crowd, which had grown twice as large since our arrival. "I cannot put into words just how happy it makes me to be here in Tollan again, back among the countless good people who have made this city the greatest in the empire. Nor can I adequately express just how much I have missed my home city; missed the sounds of her market, the smell of her citizens feeding their families every night, and the joy her people take in living within her loving embrace.

"Many of you no doubt wonder as to my whereabouts these past five years. All I can say is that I embarked on a much-needed journey of personal discovery, so I might better serve the needs of each of you. When I left, I was not fit to be your queen."

A murmur of confusion swept through the crowd.

"And when I left, Tollan was in good hands; the king was well and strong, both physically and mentally. But that has changed. It saddens me to announce that Topiltzin, King of Tollan and Emperor of the Tolteca, has fallen gravely ill and will pass on into Mictlan very soon."

The confusion turned into a tide of distress. "He didn't look ill when I went before him yesterday!" one voice called out, and another cried, "But there is no heir! What are we to do?"

I raised my hands for calm and slowly the noise level in the precinct fell low enough so I could be heard again. "It is true there is no blood heir to carry on his legacy—"

"But what about you, My Lady?" a woman shouted. "You carry the king's blood."

"That is true, but I've come to understand that I am not worthy of ruling you." As the noise rose again, I called out over it, "But it is my duty to make sure that someone of grace and character takes up the mantle of rule in my absence, and that is why we are here today.

"Two contenders have stepped forward, willing to take on the tremendous responsibility of overseeing Tollan's future, and as her citizens, you will choose who will lead you next. They will each make their case for why you should name them your next king and when all the debates have been heard, each adult citizen—both male and female—will cast their lot in favor of their desired candidate, and the winner will be crowned Tollan's new king upon Topiltzin's death."

An interested whisper passed through the crowd, but no one shouted any questions or objections, so I went on. "Let me introduce the candidates. First—" I motioned to Matlacxochitl— "I present Lord Matlacxochitl, the younger brother of our own Lord Blood Wolf. He's served a good number of years as the governor of Chimalhuacan."

Matlacxochitl stepped forward and raised a hand in greeting, which was met with a healthy round of hooting and cheering.

Once the crowd calmed down, I motioned him back to his mat then summoned Citlallotoc. "And second—and more familiar to most of you, undoubtedly—Lord Citlallotoc, brother to King Huemac of Acolman, former Justice of the Peace in Tollan, and Topiltzin's most trusted advisor."

When Citlallotoc stepped up, the hoots and shouts were louder, and they lasted long after I'd retired back to my icpalli to let the debates begin.

The speeches and arguments didn't hold my attention though. I'd heard most of it already, and soon my mind drifted back to the conversation between me and Smoking Mirror last night. Would he try to disrupt the debates today? I scanned the crowd for signs of him—or his allies—but I saw nothing to give me pause.

I did notice that both Citlallotoc and Matlacxochitl avoided criticizing each other during this opening volley. They discussed their policy plans, what they would change and what they would maintain. Matlacxochitl was downright respectful compared to last night.

I wondered how long that would last.

The crowd dispersed for the afternoon at lunch time and I returned to the palace to check on Anacoana before bringing Little Reed his meal. When I came to her room, she was awake but still in her bed, looking bedraggled.

"I'm so exhausted," she complained as she struggled to sit up. "How late is it?"

"Lunch time."

"It is? Did the king get his breakfast?"

"I took care of it. You needn't worry."

She laid back again, letting out an exhausted breath. "I'm sorry to set so much at your feet like this. You already have so much to deal with as it is."

"I don't begrudge it at all. You've been doing it for much longer, and it's time you had a break from it, to look after yourself." When she started to protest, I set a gentle hand on her shoulder, to keep her from trying to sit up again. "You've been so busy caring for Topiltzin that you haven't taken care of yourself. I insist you rest now, for you still look as if you need more sleep."

"That does sound wonderful," she replied, rather dreamily. "You're sure it's all right? You don't think Topiltzin will mind?"

"I think he would want you to rest," I said as I helped her slide back under her blankets. She sighed as she settled in.

A gourd pitcher half-full of dark liquid sat next to her bed. The sleep tonic Smoking Mirror had mentioned last night? Suspicious of his intentions, I smelled it, and while it did have a pungent aroma and a bitter taste, I didn't detect any magic in it.

"Can you pour me a little tonic?" she asked, her voice already sluggish.

"Are you sure you need it?"

"I can hardly sleep without it anymore."

So I poured a cup for her. Soon after she finished it, she was snoring softly.

I retreated into my own quarters before jumping into the teoyoh and I came out in the store room at the priestly retreat. I materialized behind the stack of copal wood, to hide my arrival if anyone was in there, but I found myself alone. After a quick trip into the kitchens for some atole, I went to relieve Mitotia.

When I parted the curtain, she wasn't alone. Mitotia worked on her weaving while Malinalli read through a priestly codex. They both looked up when I cleared my throat.

"I've brought Topiltzin's lunch," I announced as I stepped inside and pulled the curtain closed behind me. I glanced at Malinalli—who didn't meet my gaze—before addressing Mitotia. "Any trouble while I was gone?"

Mitotia shook her head. "After his breakfast, he slept peacefully." She too glanced at Malinalli before saying, "I have some things I must do back at the calmecac, so if you don't need me further right now...."

"Yes, of course you may go. And thank you for your help."

She hurried from the room, leaving me alone with Malinalli and Little Reed.

Malinalli said nothing, and though she'd bowed her head as if to return to her reading, I could tell she wasn't. I wondered if I should say anything, but I decided it was best to let her start the conversation, so I knelt next to Little Reed and sat him up for his meal.

But as I struggled to pull him upright, Malinalli came over to help, kneeling across from me. Once he was sitting up, I murmured, "Thank you."

She nodded but remained kneeling, a determined expression on her face. Still, it took a handful of breaths for her to finally speak. "I have questions."

"And I will provide all of the answers I can."

"So you're Mayahuel?" When I nodded, she asked, "Can you prove it?"

"I can perform feats of magic, if that's what you mean."

"I already knew about the magic. How do I know you're really who you're claiming to be?"

I thought about it while I spooned atole into Little Reed's mouth. "I don't have any way of proving it definitively to anyone but myself. What we were taught in calmecac doesn't mesh with what I remember of events before my death."

Malinalli furrowed her brow. "But you're not dead."

"I was, for many hundreds of bundles of years, but Quetzalcoatl brought me back."

"Why?"

So many bitter thoughts raced through my head that I had to take a moment to compose myself. "I don't really know. I wish I understood it myself; sometimes I wish he hadn't, if only so I wouldn't feel so lost and betrayed." I choked on the words, and Malinalli waited patiently for me to continue. "Long ago, the Feathered Serpent orchestrated my death so humanity would have octli to commune with the gods." I was shaking so badly I had to put the bowl down.

After a long pause, she said, "You were in love with him." There was pity in her voice.

I nodded. "I thought he felt the same way about me, but I was foolishly wrong."

"But if he didn't care, why would he bring you back from the dead? That doesn't make sense."

"Probably because it serves his needs to have me here now. But he never loved me; for thirty-five years he kept my true identity secret from me, and any number of times I could have died a mortal and been gone forever; he gave me a son but then did nothing to save his life; and he's condemned Topiltzin to an early death." I gazed at Little Reed with teary eyes. "We're all nothing but beans for him to roll while he plays his grand patolli game."

Silence fell between us while I dried my tears and resumed feeding Little Reed. Most of the atole went into his beard, but I pressed on anyway.

"Is that why you left?" Malinalli finally asked. "Why you didn't come home from Teotihuacan?"

I shook my head. "If that was all, I could have seen fit to continue on as the queen of Tollan, but...my own divine nature...." I closed my eyes against the sting of fresh tears. "My divine nature was poisoning Topiltzin's mind, driving him slowly crazy, just as I'd driven Red Flint and Black Otter to madness. I couldn't stand the thought that I was hurting him so much—or that I was hurting you or Mazatzin, or Citlallotoc. Every one of you means everything to me; I couldn't continue doing that, so I decided I couldn't come home. I'm sorry I didn't share my reasons with you, Malinalli. I thought everyone would be better off not knowing the truth about me."

She nodded. "We need to talk about what happened in your quarters the other night."

"I do owe you an explanation," I conceded.

"Do you have...feelings for me?"

I hesitated before saying, "You are extremely important to me, Malinalli; so important that I've resisted certain impulses out of fear of ruining our friendship. But yes, I love you, and my life is richer for having known you. Maybe it could have been more than that, but...." I looked down at Little Reed. "I've loved Topiltzin my whole life, even before he was born. I had a vision of him before my mother became pregnant with him, and even then he made my heart dance as no one else ever has."

"Like it was destiny?" Malinalli offered.

"Perhaps." I wiped the dribbled atole from Little Reed's lips. "But it feels immensely cruel of Heaven to let me so completely love someone I cannot even be intimate with without killing him."

"You and Topiltzin never—?"

I shook my head.

"But what about Ehecacone?"

"He's Quetzalcoatl's son. I became pregnant when he possessed me on the battlefield at Culhuacan. Topiltzin married me so he could claim Ehecacone as his own son, since we could never be intimate after I pledged my body and heart to the Feathered Serpent to save his life." I sighed. "And to think that I used to curse that sacrifice I made, when in fact it probably saved him from me." Seeing Malinalli's puzzled expression, I added, "I feed by having sex."

A weird look came to her face. "Only with men?"

"I can feed on anyone," I admitted. "Which makes what happened between us all the more...regrettable."

Malinalli stared at me, the color drained from her face. "You were intending to feed upon me?"

"That's what stopped me. I don't want to hurt you."

"Then why would you even let it start?"

The betrayal in her voice stung me. "I don't know," I whispered. "Topiltzin is on his deathbed, and despite all of my powers, there's nothing I can do to save him. I...I wanted to feel something other than pain and hopelessness...I'm sorry, Malinalli. I should have been stronger." I covered my eyes with the back of my hand. "I should have been stronger for Citlallotoc too. I was careless and I almost killed him. And my actions only exacerbated an already tense issue between him and Topiltzin. It's my fault he left; if I'd respected his wishes, if I hadn't pressured him to forget his honor...." Seeing her staring at me with wide eyes, I bowed my head in shame. "It's something I can never be forgiven for."

"That's his decision, not yours," she said.

I nodded. "But I have much to answer for."

"Is that why you came back?"

I chuckled dejectedly. "It didn't start that way; I wanted to see Topiltzin one last time, but finding what a mess I created here in

Tollan...I must make amends for my past misdeeds and ensure Tollan's future."

"And when all of this succession business is over?"

"I will leave again, for the good of everyone. I still have so much to learn about being a goddess and controlling my divine nature, and I can't risk exposing Tollan to my mistakes along the way. Until I learn to use my powers without hurting anyone, I need to keep a distance from humans."

"That is understandable," Malinalli conceded.

Neither of us said anything while we situated Little Reed back down in his bed, but once the uncomfortable silence took over, I said, "You asked me last night if I made you the way you are—"

"You didn't," she said. When I looked up at her, she hung her head this time. "I've thought a great deal about it, and I've realized that in all of my years, I've never felt for any man what I've felt for Mitotia...or you. The one time I was with a man...it felt completely unnatural. But with Mitotia...I don't have to even try. It doesn't matter; this is who I am, and I feel at peace with that."

I smiled, relieved. "I'm happy for you. Learning to accept ourselves fully is often a long and difficult task, with many setbacks and mistakes."

She returned the smile but without as much enthusiasm as I'd hoped. "Do you wish me to watch after Topiltzin while you're at the debates tonight?"

"That would be helpful, but tomorrow you should come while Mazatzin watches the king. It's important that you, as the high priestess of Tollan, be present for at least some of it." After passing another moment in tense silence, I said, "I should go. The debates will start up again soon."

She nodded, but when I stood, she said, "Thank you for answering my questions, My Lady."

"Thank you for giving me the opportunity to explain," I said.

"I'd hoped that talking to you would give me a sense of where to go from here, but...I feel even more befuddled than before."

"As do I." After a pause, I asked, "Did you tell Mitotia...about me?"

"No, and I don't know that I will. At least not before I know how I feel about all of this. Though since she's going to be the next high priestess, perhaps she ought to know regardless."

I bowed my head and nodded.

In the distance, the copper gong on the temple of the Feathered Serpent rang, signaling the beginning of the new hour. "You should go," Malinalli said. "You're probably already late and it's a long walk back to the palace."

"Distance doesn't matter anymore," I said. "I can be anywhere I want in the blink of an eye, but yes, I should go, so I don't keep anyone waiting. I'll be back at dinner time."

She nodded.

I fumbled my hands together as I said, "Thank you for everything you've done for me, Malinalli." Then I muttered "teotoca" and disappeared into the flames of the teoyoh.

CHAPTER TWENTY-FIVE

For the next two days, I spent my days sitting on the reed icpalli in the sacred precinct, thinking about my conversation with Malinalli and paying very little attention while Citlallotoc and Matlacxochitl argued over policy. Both men were still careful not to fling accusations of treason and disloyalty, but it became increasingly obvious that Citlallotoc's arguments were winning. Even the recent drought and food shortages couldn't dampen the memory of so much prosperity under Little Reed's rule, and when the time finally came for the casting of lots, the number of jars containing Citlallotoc's chips grew faster than Matlacxochitl's. Even Matlacxochitl knew he'd lost long before the final lot was cast, for he'd looked bewildered most of the day while we sat watching the citizens toss their painted stones into the jars for their chosen candidate. I left before the final voting was done, confident that Citlallotoc would be crowned king, and my work here in Tollan would soon be over. I decided it called for a nice hot bath, my first in years.

As I walked into the palace trailed by my guards, I saw Mitotia walk into the Hall of the Gods, heading out from her own quarters for her priestly duties. We really hadn't spoken much since my return, and even now we passed each other with only a silent nod for a greeting.

But as I turned down the corridor leading to the royal quarters, I glanced over to see that the guards at the entrance to the foyer had stopped her. I backed up, my own guards following me.

One of the men—the guard who'd escorted me into the great hall the day I arrived back in Tollan—was talking to Mitotia. I couldn't hear his words, but the slimy smile on his face raised the hairs on my neck. I headed back down the stairs towards them.

Before I could reach them, Mitotia shouldered her way past him and continued on her way at a brisk walk, her head down and fists clenched. He laughed to his compatriot. "Pretty soon I'll have both of them in my bed."

When he saw me coming, he dropped the smile and went to his knees. His friend followed suit. "My Lady."

"What is your name?" I demanded.

"Patli, My Lady."

"You weren't a palace guard five years ago, were you?"

He shook his head.

"And you're no longer one now."

He looked up at me with wide eyes. "My Lady?"

"You will leave this palace this very moment and never cast your shadow upon its floors ever again."

"I don't understand—"

"Do not play coy with me, Patli. I'm well aware of the nature of your discussions with Ladies Mitotia and Malinalli, and frankly, men like you are disgusting, vile excuses for human beings. It's indicative of what kind of king Matlacxochitl would have been that he allowed men like you to not only operate under his rule but flourish."

His face now flushed, Patli said, "You're obviously unaware of the abominable behavior those two engage in—"

"The only abominable behavior is being displayed by you," I shot back, and on the wave of rage rising inside me, the desire took hold of my tongue. "If I weren't trying to be a better person, I would devour you one screaming, begging breath at a time, just to see the look on your face when the reality of your foolishness hit you just before the Black Dog dragged his cold tongue over your eyes."

That flush turned pale and I smelled fear oozing off of him. The scent was unnervingly enticing.

The desire receded slowly, leaving me feeling jittery. "Fortunately your resignation will suffice," I said. "You will make a better farmer than a guard."

He returned to his bowed position, hunched all the way over. "Yes, My Lady."

"But if I hear of you so much as speaking to either Mitotia or Malinalli, I will not be as merciful anymore." I then turned and swept away to my quarters.

¤

"Many congratulations on your victory," Lord Mozauhqui told Citlallotoc with a hearty clap on the shoulder.

The council was gathered in the great hall for breakfast, and though the voting results hadn't yet been publicly announced, word of Citlallotoc's definitive triumph had already spread through the noble ranks.

Matlacxochitl was there too, watching sullenly from the corner while the others gathered around Citlallotoc, alliances already shifting. He stiffened when I approached him, a cup of xocolatl in my hand.

"My condolences on your defeat," I said. "I must commend you on not running a dirty campaign; perhaps you are not as treacherous as I originally thought."

"Thank you for your generosity, My Lady." He said it with acid in his voice.

I smirked. "There is perhaps a lesson to be learned in all of this. We cannot return to a past where most people suffered under the ambitions of the elite. Tollan's citizens have made it clear that they will not accept anything less than a king who will move them into the future instead of returning them to the past."

"The people know not what is good for them," he muttered.

Is Smoking Mirror now speaking with your tongue too? I almost asked. "I was going to suggest that we let the last two years be bygones and that you return to your position as governor of Chimalhuacan, but I think perhaps you're not made for political office. You've been listening to all the wrong people."

"Those are big words coming from the mouth of the woman who helped Topiltzin turn humanity down the dangerous path of opposing the gods, and you'll regret it all when the gods bring you to justice for your sacrilege."

"As if you'd know anything about the gods, you mealy-mouth—"

But before I could finish, Citlallotoc came over and extended his hand out to Matlacxochitl. "I wanted to congratulate you on a hard fought battle, My Lord."

Matlacxochitl contemplated the gesture before slowly taking it, clasping Citlallotoc's forearm with his own hand. "Congratulations on your ascension. It must be a tremendous relief knowing that now you can fuck not only the king's sister but his wife as well without the burden of conscience."

An outraged gasp rose in the crowd gathered around.

Citlallotoc narrowed his eyes, and judging from the bulge of his arm muscles, he tightened his grip on Matlacxochitl's arm. "Do not mistake my congeniality for weakness. Speak one more disrespectful word about Lady Anacoana or the Queen, and I'll remove your tongue, as those rebels should have when they cut off your nose and your ear."

Matlacxochitl stared back, defiant, but the strain in his own arm told the real story.

Citlallotoc finally let him go, practically pushing him away. "You would do well to listen to your queen and leave Tollan now, for I will not be so forgiving of your behavior once the throne and its powers have passed to me."

After a brief glare at everyone standing around, Matlacxochitl retreated from the room.

"I know the law in Tollan is exile, but my arm longs to divide him in half with a sword," Citlallotoc admitted, watching him leave.

I didn't want to talk about Matlacxochitl anymore, so I looked around. "Have you and Lady Anacoana had a chance to talk since your return?"

He shook his head. "Every time I've tried to call upon her, she's been resting. Her servants tell me she's been ill the last few days."

I hadn't seen much of her either, and I'd hoped she might have recovered from her exhaustion by now. Citlallotoc might believe the past was too much to contend with, but I suspected they could repair their fractured relationship if they just sat down and talked. I would have to look in on her after breakfast.

Yet when I returned to the royal quarters, I found Anacoana's bed empty. I was just about to ask the guards if they'd seen her, but as I started down the portico, I heard girlish giggling coming from Citlallotoc's room.

I pulled the door curtain aside to find Anacoana sprawled out on the bed, looking unusually provocative and sensual. She giggled like a young girl, whispering under her breath, and even when I cleared my throat, she merely glanced at me, uninterested.

"Are you feeling all right, My Lady?" I asked, stepping up to the bed.

"I'm just wonderful, thank you." She hid her smile behind the back of her hand when she started giggling again. "Oh Quetzalpetlatl! I've never felt better!"

I raised an eyebrow before saying, "I'm glad to hear it."

She stroked her hair with one hand, my own presence seemingly forgotten again.

"I'd hoped you would come to breakfast this morning," I said. "Much has happened since yesterday."

She just shrugged and still didn't look at me. She stared into the far corner of the room, as if someone were standing there talking to her, but when I looked, the area was empty.

"Citlallotoc wants to talk to you," I offered.

Anacoana laughed. "As if I don't know. Why do you think I'm lying here?" She sat up and began sliding her dress off her shoulders. "Why didn't you bring him with you?"

Taken aback, I grabbed her hand before she could expose more than just her shoulders. "Are you crazy? You're Topiltzin's wife and he's not even dead yet!"

"Topiltzin gave me permission long ago to seek out other men, so what does he care?" She let me push the dress back into place though. "In fact, he gave both Citlallotoc and I permission to carry on to our hearts' content."

"Yes, but discretion is necessary, My Lady—"

"To Mictlan with discretion!" she snapped. "Citlallotoc couldn't abide the secrecy, so no more of that nonsense. I will take him in front of the whole city! Mark him as mine now and forever, so everyone knows he's off limits!" She gave me a pointed look.

"A queen doesn't behave so lewdly," I chided her. "What would your father think?"

She laughed. "Where on earth have you been? My father is dead, thank the gods. My mother put a knife through his skull for hitting her one too many times. The priests garroted her for it, but my brother said she refused to show any remorse, even when they showed her the flowery garland."

I stammered before settling on, "I understand your wanting to move on with your life, but I really think you should wait until Topiltzin passes on to Mictlan."

"Why?"

"Because it's the honorable thing to do."

"I don't care a wit about honor."

"But Citlallotoc does."

Anacoana pushed past me to pace in front of the hearth. "Blast it, you're right! But I've waited so long, and Topiltzin just isn't dying quick enough!"

I suddenly felt like she was squeezing my heart. "Don't say that."

"We should poison him, to speed things up."

"Maybe I should poison you, you little—" the desire roared, but I pushed it back. I felt dizzy with rage, but managed to keep my tone calm as I said, "You're suggesting treason, Anacoana."

She laughed. "Don't tell me you don't want him gone just as much as I do. I see it in your eyes: it tortures you to see him rotting away like a corpse. You wish he'd just die so you can move on with your life too. Don't deny it."

I snapped my mouth shut. Yes, I'd thought it, but not for the reasons she accused me of. The selfish part of me didn't want him to ever die; if I could turn him immortal, I would, without hesitation, even if it meant I still couldn't have him. The thought of losing him forever was like a swarm of ants trying to eat its way out of my insides.

"I've loved him all my life, so don't even suggest that I would want him dead," I snarled. "He's everything to me: my family, my best friend, and my husband. I'm sorry he was never any of that for you, but that gives you no right to say something so horrible."

To my chagrin, Anacoana laughed. "You're so funny, Quetzalpetlatl."

Now I was thankful that I hadn't yet told her where I'd moved Little Reed. "There's nothing funny about any of this. Frankly, I'm appalled that you'd behave like a defiant, selfish little girl. This is completely unlike you."

"What would you know about me?"

"Quite a bit."

Anacoana narrowed her eyes at me. "I know what this is about." She jabbed me in the chest with her finger. "You want Citlallotoc for yourself!"

"Stop this nonsense—"

"First you stole away Black Otter, then you made sure Topiltzin would never love me, and now you're trying to keep Citlallotoc from me too!"

"You couldn't be further from the truth—"

"He's mine! And if you try to take him from me, I swear to the gods I will kill you!"

She had such a wild look in her eyes that I stepped away, but her yelling brought my guards into the room. While one of them stood in front of me, the other one held Anacoana back with both hands.

"I see exactly what you're up to, you shameless whore!" Anacoana shouted, drawing the other guards into the room too. "All this time I thought you were my friend, but now I see the truth: you're an evil witch, plying innocent men with love potions to turn their hearts against all other women! But I will stop you!" Two of the guards grabbed her by the arms and she thrashed against them. "Let me go! You should be arresting her, not me!"

"You're not under arrest," I assured her. "But you're obviously not well."

The guards took her back to her quarters, and after some more struggling, they forced more of the sleep tonic down her. In a matter of minutes, she lay motionless on her bed, fast asleep. There were many of the medicine gourds lying scattered around her room.

"Has the royal chemist been back to see her?" I asked the guards.

"Not that we know of, My Lady," one of them said. "We've kept most people out of the royal quarters in accordance with your orders."

"I think My Lady sent her servants to fetch her medicines for her though," the other guard added.

I had little doubt that Smoking Mirror was behind Anacoana's sudden strange behavior. His seeming lack of action since last I saw him had indeed been too good to be true. "Watch her very closely. Don't let her leave her room," I told the guards then I left, my own guards following closely behind.

¤

My guards led me to the house of the royal chemist in the jaguar neighborhood, and to my shock, when I rang the copper bells,

Xochiquetzal answered the door curtain. I immediately sensed my guards' growing distraction, so I ordered them to remain outside then I pushed my way past her and yanked the curtain closed behind us. "What in Mictlan are you doing here?" I hissed.

She glared at me. "Smoking Mirror had need of a love goddess's talents, so I offered him my services."

"You're working for Smoking Mirror now?"

"Don't complain; you had your chance and instead you chose the Feathered Serpent over the rest of us."

"I didn't choose Quetzalcoatl!"

"You betrayed Mextli!"

I snapped my mouth shut, my face flushed. Seems what happened was no longer a secret. "What happened between me and Mextli...that was an accident. I didn't know that would happen."

"He's very mad at you," she warned. "And so am I! Do you realize that now Smoking Mirror will never trust me?"

"Why shouldn't he trust you?"

"Because of you and Quetzalcoatl, of course! He was willing to forgive me one parent, but both?"

Hearing her acknowledge my being her mother brought a hitch to my throat. I tried to speak, but nothing could get past it.

"I'm having to work really hard to show him that I'm not treacherous like you." She gestured to the row of gourd bottles lined up on the shelf next to the hearth. "I've been working day and night trying to make sure we have enough love potion for Topiltzin's wife."

I blinked. "You've been drugging Lady Anacoana?" When she nodded, I demanded, "Why?"

She folded her arms. "Wouldn't you like to know?"

"Xochiquetzal, you can't trust anything Smoking Mirror promises you—"

"You have never given him a chance! You've already forgotten that without him you wouldn't even know you are a goddess, and you'd still be under Quetzalcoatl's thumb."

"I haven't forgotten anything, including all the terrible things Smoking Mirror did to me. He's no more innocent than Quetzalcoatl is, and I'd be a fool to believe he is."

"Mextli is right. All you care about is yourself."

Standing straighter, I replied, "And you should care more about yourself than you do."

She gasped but then said, "What does it matter to you what I do and don't do?"

"I am your mother."

"And you're terrible at it."

Now was my turn to feel slapped. "It's not as if I've had much of a chance to prove myself to you."

She pushed past me to stand glaring into the hearth. "I don't owe you anything. I got along just fine on my own all of these many years, and I'll continue to do just fine for many more to come."

Irritated that I'd let her draw me into childish arguing, I sighed. "All I'm saying is that you deserve someone who won't use you for their own selfish purposes, someone who won't hold things over you that you have no control over." When she still wouldn't look at me, I hung my head. "You have much to be angry at me about; I haven't been there for you anymore than Quetzalcoatl has, but in my defense, I didn't know I had a daughter—and a second son—until just a few days ago, but even then, I didn't know how you felt about my being your mother, and I don't know if you wish to acknowledge it, but regardless, I am here now and I'd like to build on that, for both of us, if it's possible. I'm willing to try, if you wish."

She finally looked at me, an arch to her eyebrows. "Would you be willing to support me where it concerns Smoking Mirror?"

I pursed my lips, mulling before replying, "I am, but please, please, go into it with open eyes. It's his nature to exploit innocence and invoke fear in the name of power, and I don't want to see you become just another tool in his quest for more of it."

Xochiquetzal sniffed, frowning, then turned away from me again. "Xochipilli and I will give it thought. In the meantime, I believe we're done talking, so go."

I nodded but as I started to turn back to the door, I again spotted the gourd pitchers lining the shelf on the wall. "You should know that I won't let Lady Anacoana consume anymore of your love potion."

She shrugged. "My job is to make the potion, not to make sure anyone drinks it."

"If you ever need to talk, about what we've discussed here today, or anything else, just send word to the palace and I'll come meet you."

She harrumphed in reply, so I ducked back out onto the street, a brand new regret weighing me down. I had far too many of them these days.

CHAPTER TWENTY-SIX

At midday, the Council and the high priests of all of the orders met upon the wooden dais in the sacred precinct. A considerable crowd of men and women had gathered, all eager to hear the election results, and when I came to the front of the dais, the crowd took to cheering. I let them go for a moment before raising my hands for silence.

"I'm pleased to announce that the people have spoken and a new heir to Tollan's throne has been selected by an overwhelming majority. Thank you everyone who participated in this most unusual but important duty to your kingdom. Everyone should be proud of their contribution to Tollan's continued success.

"But now, without further ado, I present the next king of Tollan." I stepped aside and motioned Citlallotoc forward.

He stepped up from behind the dais and raised his arm in greeting as the crowd burst into cheers. The applause and cheering continued for a long time before he was finally able to calm the crowd enough to address them.

"I thank each and every one of you for placing your trust in me to see us all into the future. I promise to serve Tollan to the best of my ability, and continue the traditions lay down by both Lord Topiltzin and Lady Quetzalpetlatl. While the circumstances of my ascension leave me with a heavy heart, we shall make it through these unfortunate times and come out the other side stronger than ever!"

More cheering erupted.

"And to those who didn't cast their lots for me, I will work extra hard to earn your respect and trust. Your concerns and wishes for the future are as important to me as any, and together we will make sure Tollan remains on the forefront of the Tolteca Empire."

"Big words for a one-armed mortal!" a familiar voice shouted from the crowd.

My joy at hearing Citlallotoc's impassioned speech died in my chest. I scanned the crowd, and it didn't take long to locate Mextli standing near the very back of the crowd. He stood twice as tall as anyone, and it amazed me that I hadn't noticed him before. He was dressed for war, but he held no weapons in his large hands.

I glared at him. "What are you doing here?"

"I think you already know, My Lady." He gave me a malicious smile.

"You!" Citlallotoc grabbed his sword from his belt. "One would think that having been handed defeat twice at the hands of Tollan's queen you'd know better than to darken this city's stones with your shadow!"

"And one would think that after having to be saved twice by a woman, you'd keep your mouth shut," Mextli fired back.

Citlallotoc made to leave the dais, but I grabbed his arm. "He's baiting you."

"You were warned to stay out of matters of royal succession," Mextli said. "But you didn't listen, and now it's time to pay the price."

He turned to the crowd. "The days of Quetzalcoatl's rule are at an end, and the time of the Smoking Mirror is beginning, and those who stand in his way will be trampled under the feet of change. For twenty years, Tollan's king and queen have blasphemed the other gods, have changed the laws passed down on earth by Heaven itself, and have led you all astray.

"The Smoking Mirror is merciful though. He recognizes that you all are just humans, easily manipulated and fooled into acting against your own interests. It isn't too late to redeem yourselves and spare Tollan from ruin. Forsake Topiltzin and his ways, and refuse to accept his successor, who shares all of his fatal flaws. You will only be given this one chance!"

A murmur of confusion spilled through the crowd, but eventually that turned to shouts of, "Who are you to tell us what to do?" and "Treason against the crown!"

"Calm down everyone!" I called, trying to be heard over the shouts, but the rumble from the crowd only grew in intensity. The people nearest Mextli had stepped away from him, and most of the faces in the crowd were frowning or twisted in anger. Many shook their fists at him as they shouted. The guards around the precinct readied their spears, looking around with unease but making no move to control the crowd.

"Let them tear him apart," Citlallotoc muttered, a stiff sneer on his face. "It's what he deserves."

Magic tingled nervously in my finger tips. "It could well be our men who get torn apart."

Suddenly the shouts turned to cries of surprise as Mextli's hands turned to blue fire balls. He grinned at the people shrinking away from him. "You humans like to learn the hard way, don't you?" He launched the fireballs into the crowd.

Screams echoed through the precinct and people ran in every direction. Those closest to Mextli burst into flames, and those fires jumped into the fleeing crowd like men doing acrobatics.

Cut off from escape by the fire and the crowd, the people nearest the temple flooded the dais, knocking Council members and priests aside. The flow separated me from Citlallotoc and surrounded me with screaming and cursing.

But a hand clamped down on my arm and I turned to see Malinalli. "We must get out of here!" she shouted. Mazatzin stood with her, looking harried.

"But what about Citlallotoc?" I shouted back, but then I saw several guards hustling him through the crowd, knocking over anyone who got in their way.

"Let's go!" Mazatzin shouted.

But someone ran into me, knocking both me and Malinalli over. Someone stepped on my hand and Malinalli cried out in pain as more and more people stepped upon us. Fearing she would be trampled to death, I let loose a concentrated burst of magic at those nearest us, knocking them backwards. Mazatzin hustled Malinalli—bruised and tender—to her feet, and I hurried after them, letting off a few more bursts of magic to make sure the way was clear.

But just as I laid out the last man heading for me, the blue flame warriors jumped up onto the dais. They thrust and jabbed flaming swords and spears at us, and the wood beneath their feet caught fire with preternatural speed. I brought the magic pounding up into my fingers as they ran in circles, building a growing ring of fire around us.

Malinalli looked around with wild eyes, and Mazatzin yelped when one of the flaming warriors jabbed his neck with its spear, searing his skin.

I blasted magic at the flame warriors, but instead of quelling them, the fire flared high and hot, as if I'd thrown fuel onto them. Mazatzin shrieked as flames engulfed his left hand and started eating up the sleeve of his robe. Malinalli pounded at it with her hands, trying to put it out, but the smell of burning flesh grew heavier with each breath.

With the wall of flames completely encasing us now, I had no choice but to flee. I swept my arms over both Malinalli and Mazatzin and yelled, "Teotoca!" over the roar of the flames.

¤

The air was deliciously cooler when we emerged from the teoyoh, but I had no time to feel relief. We were greeted by a gasp and the sound of something breaking, but I didn't bother looking away from Mazatzin. The jump had extinguished the flames eating up his robe, but the flesh on his hand was blistered and red.

"The water jar!" I shouted as I rolled his scorched robe sleeve up, checking the skin underneath. The hairs were burnt and the skin irritated, but nothing like his hand.

It took a second shout for someone to finally get the jar. I caught Mitotia's stunned gaze for only a breath before pouring some of the water over Mazatzin's hand, to stop his flesh from continuing to cook. He howled in agony.

"Get me some clean rags," I panted. "We'll need to wrap his hand."

Mitotia hesitated again but this time went before I could snap at her.

Malinalli stared down at Mazaztin with wild eyes. "Can't you...can't you just heal him?"

I shook my head. "I wish I had healing powers, but I don't." I smoothed Mazatzin's graying hair from his forehead as he lay panting after the dousing.

Mitotia hurried back into the room bearing bandages. I wet the first one quickly and started wrapping it around Mazatzin's hand. "Get the next one ready for me." And for the next endless minutes, Mitotia kept the wet bandages coming while I wrapped them around Mazatzin's hand. By the time I'd finished, he was delirious with pain, so I gave him a small dose of my octli magic through my fingertips to put him to sleep.

Mitotia looked bewildered but she said nothing as she knelt next to him, Malinalli across from her. I took the water jar back to the corner and remained there, trying to gather my thoughts in the face of overwhelming guilt. I should have gotten Malinalli and Mazatzin out of there instead of trying to stop the flames. I'd been an arrogant fool, and now Mazatzin's hand would never be the same, and I couldn't stop thinking about Smoking Mirror's warnings.

"How did you—how did you suddenly appear, out of nowhere?" Mitotia finally spoke, her voice shaking

"It's how we...gods travel from place to place."

"Gods?" The color drained from her face as she looked at me.

I nodded.

"She's the goddess Mayahuel," Malinalli provided.

Mitotia stared at her, a look of utter shock on her face. And hurt. "You knew?"

"She found out just a few days ago," I said. "I imagine the news was too shocking to talk about with anyone right away."

After a hesitation, she asked, "Is that why you left?"

"I had to. I can't stay among humans for long without causing them harm. Already things are going sour, and I haven't even been back a week. Maybe I should have stayed away. It might be best for everyone if I just left again now—"

"But you said you would stay and help us," Malinalli said.

"I did, but I fear I'm doing more harm than good."

She stood up, her posture defiant. "You promised. You can't just up and leave again, especially now. You heard that...that creature in the sacred precinct; we need you now more than ever."

Mitotia looked at me expectantly.

"And what if my staying makes everything worse?" I asked. "Besides, I'm but one goddess, here on my own, and Smoking Mirror has allies. I'm no match for that."

"One goddess on our side is better than none," Malinalli countered. "None of us have any reason to believe Quetzalcoatl cares anymore. You can't abandon us too."

Her words filled me with shame. "Very well, I'll stay." It cut me to be compared to Quetzalcoatl, but I truly hoped I wouldn't come to regret this decision.

I looked to the door. "I really should go make sure Citlallotoc got out safe."

Malinalli nodded stiffly. "And I'll fetch the royal chemist to see Mazatzin—"

251

"Absolutely not!" When both women gaped at me, I rushed to add, "The royal chemist is Smoking Mirror."

"How can that be?" Mitotia asked.

"He took over the body of Black Otter's son and used him to infiltrate the royal court. He's also been plying Lady Anacoana with love potion."

"For what reason?"

"I don't know," I admitted, though I suspected that I would find out before long.

"I'll walk back with you," Malinalli offered, but I held a hand up.

"It would be better if you stayed here and helped Mitotia watch after Topiltzin and Mazatzin. Until I know what's going on, I think both of you will be safer here."

"All right, but let me walk you out." She wasn't taking no for an answer this time, and without waiting for my response, she walked out of the curtain into the garden. I cast a hesitant glance at Mitotia before following her out.

Malinalli was waiting for me a dozen steps away from the door, where we wouldn't be overheard if we whispered. "I must say thank you," she said. "You saved my life back there."

"Your welcome, but surely you know it's not something I'd ever hesitate to do, Malinalli. You're my best friend."

She nodded. "I know that. It's just...I was pretty tough on you in there."

"You had every right to be. I'm trying not to mess up things, and yet everything I touch...."

"Everything will be fine."

"I should have acted quicker back there in the precinct."

"Mazatzin's alive, and I'm sure he's grateful for that. At least it didn't burn his dominant hand."

I shook my head. "I never should have set my magic on the fire."

"What did you do?"

"I shot it with my octli—" I slapped my forehead, feeling stupid. "By Mictlan, I actually poured fuel on it! I'm an idiot!"

"Anyone could have made the same mistake," Malinalli said, setting a supportive hand on my shoulder. It was the first time she'd touched me since that night in my quarters, and though I wondered if she realized what she was doing, I felt on the verge of tears. Such a small gesture, but for that moment, it was as if we were still best friends and nothing had changed between us. "I'll do my best to get us safely out of this," I said past the tears clogging my throat.

"I trust you will."

"I'll be back soon with news," I said, finally pulling away, to make sure I didn't pull her into the teoyoh with me.

She gave me an encouraging smile and I held onto the hope it gave me as I vanished into the flames of the teoyoh.

◻

"One hundred and fifty-three dead, all burned to death," Blood Wolf informed me when I reached the great hall. "And hundreds more are wounded. When I couldn't find you in the melee, I was sure you were dead too."

"Malinalli and Mazatzin got me out," I told him.

He exhaled a ragged breath. "Thank the gods! The last thing we need right now is for the queen to be killed, for that would surely instill panic among the people."

I nodded. "Citlallotoc is all right?"

"His guards removed him very quickly, but I'm furious how your own guards didn't do the same for you. I will immediately assign a new set to protect you, My Lady."

"That won't be necessary. I'm sure they just became disoriented in the commotion." And it wasn't as if mortal guards could protect me from Mextli; he would get at me if he truly wanted to.

"I would feel more comfortable if you'd indulge me on this, My Lady."

I shrugged. "Whatever makes you feel better. Where's Citlallotoc?"

"He went to check on Lady Anacoana. He was very worried that she might have been out in the crowd, but I assured him that she had been abed all day. Still he insisted on going to see her."

I tapped my fingers on my knee as I sat on my icpalli, debating whether I should go check on her too. The love potion had made her sleep almost all day, so she was probably all right....

"I've sent warriors out into the city to hunt down the man who started all this rubbish," Blood Wolf went on. "I aim to have him and that treacherous Matlacxochitl standing here in front of the throne by tomorrow, answering for their heinous crimes against Tollan. This I swear to you."

I shook my head, alarmed. "No, call them all back. That will only make matters worse, and more lives will be lost."

"But My Lady, we can't just let them—"

"Trust me, all the soldiers in Tollan couldn't bring Mextli in. I don't want more bloodshed."

"Then what are we to do?"

"I don't know yet, but I'm thinking about it."

Blood Wolf motioned one of the guards over and issued orders to bring the rest of the guards back in from the city. He then returned to his spot next to my throne. "You're probably right. The fire that man set...it moved with unnatural swiftness."

"We are dealing with magic now, and only more magic can answer it."

"You will call on the god, like you did in Culhuacan?"

"I will do what's necessary." The words haunted me though; the last time I'd said that, I'd hesitated, and Nimilitzli ended up dead and Little Reed very nearly joined her.

A servant suddenly clamored towards the dais, panting as if he'd run far. "My Lady! My Lady! Come quickly!"

"What is the meaning of this?" Blood Wolf demanded.

"Lord Citlallotoc—he's been stabbed!"

I shot to my feet and pushed my way past Blood Wolf. "Stabbed? By who?"

"Lady Anacoana!"

CHAPTER TWENTY-SEVEN

I arrived in the royal quarters to the sounds of screaming and cursing coming from Anacoana's quarters, but a number of guards were gathered around the doorway to Citallotoc's quarters. They blocked my entrance, but once Citallotoc heard me calling to him, he ordered they let me by.

He sat upon his bed, his personal physician tending to wounds on his arm, hand, and his chest. The one on his chest was a glancing blow, leaving a shallow cut, but the ones on his arm were deeper, with the worst of them on his palm; one looked as if the blade had gone completely through. "What on earth happened?"

"Lady Anacoana attacked me with a knife," Citlallotoc replied, his face stoic as he watched his physician started winding a bandage around his wounded hand.

"Why?"

After some hesitation, he finally looked up at me, and though he said nothing, the message was clear in his eyes; he didn't want to talk about it in front of his men. I nodded then retreated to the corner, staying out of the way while the doctor finished his work, and when it was done, Citlallotoc announced, "I would like a private moment with Lady Quetzalpetlatl."

He remained on the bed while everyone filed out, but once the room was clear, he went to the curtain and told his guards to step out into the garden, away from the door. He then closed the curtain but remained standing there, holding the seam together with his bandaged hand.

"What we discuss here...you must promise you will tell no one," he said, his voice lowered.

"Why?"

"Because it would ruin me in the eyes of the Council, and destroy my reputation among my guards and warriors."

"What happened?"

He finally moved back towards the bed, but he didn't sit down. "I went to make sure that Anacoana was all right. I was worried that she might have gone to the precinct to see the announcement. But she was awake in her room, and so I stayed to talk to her...." He turned his back to me, distress seeping off of him like a choking smoke.

I sat down on the bed and waited for him to continue, my own anxiety elevated.

After a handful of deep breaths, he said, "We were just talking, and it was going very well—better than it had in years—but she...she became...."

He sucked in a nervous breath and set the back of his wounded hand against his forehead. He turned to face me again, slowly, and the look on his face was one of shame and fear. "She became very aggressive...sexually. She climbed on my lap and made me...she made me touch her—" He looked ill. "I told her we couldn't act like this, no matter what Topiltzin might have allowed in the past, but she kept insisting, and demanding...."

"It's not your fault, Citlallotoc."

He laughed, uneasy. "I must have said something, or done something to provoke her—"

"You did nothing."

"You weren't there—"

"I know you well enough to say with certainty that you would never be anything but honorable with another man's wife, no matter how close to death her husband might be."

Citlallotoc turned away again. "I told her I don't feel the way I used to, but that I would always take care of her, out of respect for Topiltzin. That's when she pulled out the knife." He stared down at his bandaged hand. "If I hadn't seen her move for it when I did, she might have stabbed me right in the throat. Instead, she impaled me through the hand when I tried to shove her away. Then she was on me like a jaguar, ripping at me with her fingernails...." He dropped his hand to peer at me over his shoulder. "Is this what I did to her, Quetzalpetlatl? Did she become like this because of what happened between us?"

I stood, shaking to hear him bearing the blame for any of this. "She's not in her right mind, Citlallotoc, and you didn't cause it. Smoking Mirror has been plying her with love potion."

Citlallotoc turned to me, the fear deep on his face now. "The Smoking Mirror is here, in Tollan? He's actually here, in the flesh?"

"I'm afraid so."

He looked ready to pass out, so I grabbed onto him and helped him settle down onto the bed. "Mextli was telling the truth!" Bewilderment on his face, he panted, "The gods *have* turned against us!"

"Only some of them."

"And Mextli...he's one too?"

I nodded. "He's a war god."

"Dear gods, and I've tried to fight him—twice!"

"And you survived him twice. That's nothing to sniff at," I said.

He brayed with manic laughter. "Yes, but I only survived because...." His strained smile dropped as he turned to look at me. "You...you're one of them too, aren't you?"

Given the desperation in his eyes, I wondered if he could handle the truth right now, but eventually I said, "For many years I didn't know it, but...yes, I am."

He turned away, that sick look on his face again. "And Topiltzin?"

I shook my head. "Regrettably, no. He's mortal as any human."

He nodded slowly. "But you are....are you Xochiquetzal?"

"Actually, I'm Mayahuel."

"I thought surely you were a love goddess."

"I am. I've just never been worshipped as one."

"No wonder Topiltzin didn't want to let you go."

"I'd like to hope it was because he truly loved me as I love him, not because I made him feel something that wasn't real," I said.

Citlallotoc tightened his jaw. "I feel so foolish now, about those things I said to you in Teotihuacan. No wonder you ran away."

I started reaching for his hand but stopped. Those days were over. "We must talk, about what happened that night in the sacred precinct."

"You mean when I was weak and betrayed my best friend?"

"You weren't weak. You were exceedingly loyal and strong, and I...." The desire slithered up to take my tongue, a strange spike of regret coming with her. "If anyone is to blame, it's me. You said no, but I continued pushing...and arguing with you."

"We didn't do anything I didn't want to. I'd wanted it for a long time."

"Except maybe it was my divine essence that made you want it."

He shook his head and stood, putting distance between us. "I don't want to go down that path, Quetzalpetlatl."

"Citlallotoc—"

"No! I know what you're getting at, and I won't even entertain it. I mean, think about it. I'm twice your size!"

"My power is not in my size, Citlallotoc—"

"Enough! This is ridiculous, and if my guards overheard this nonsense.... I've suffered enough indignity answering for my conduct with Anacoana years ago, but if they thought for a moment that I couldn't defend myself against a woman—"

I shot to my feet. "We both know I'm no mere woman. That's mitigating."

"It doesn't matter; either way I come out looking weak. You asked me here to be Tollan's next ruler, so I beg you to not undermine me with this."

"I don't want to undermine you, but that doesn't change the fact that I owe you an apology for my own conduct, and…and for nearly killing you in my carelessness. I know that no apology will ever be enough—"

"If it will make you stop pressing the issue, I accept your apology. And now we'll never speak of it again."

I looked away, cursing myself for making him feel pressured yet again. "As you wish."

"I do," he said, curt.

After another pause, I asked, "And what about Anacoana? If there's a trial, the truth will come out."

He stared into the hearth, his voice stiff. "As the queen, that decision rests with you."

"She is under the influence of dark magic and I'd just as soon let her recover from that before deciding what to do about all of this."

He nodded, an air of relief coming over him. "Now if you'll excuse me, I wish to rest." He held the curtain open.

Without further argument, I headed for the door, but when I neared, Citlallotoc whispered, "Where is Quetzalcoatl in all of this? With so many gods here in Tollan now, surely he's here as well, so why didn't he stop Mextli? Why has he let any of this happen? Has he abandoned us? In our time of greatest need?"

It was on the tip of my tongue to rip into Quetzalcoatl, to say that he was no friend to anyone, but in these trying times, sometimes hope was better than bitter truth. "I don't know about the Feathered Serpent, but the people of Tollan have at least one goddess on their side."

¤

After I left Citlallotoc's room, I crossed the garden to Anacoana's quarters. Eerie silence had replaced the cursing and screaming, and when I peeked inside, she was asleep again.

"We gave her some more sleep tonic," one of her guards told me. "It was the only way to calm her down."

I snatched up the remainder of the love potion and threw it out into the flowerbeds in her private garden. "She is not to be given any more sleep tonics or other medicines," I said. "Nor is she to eat anything that isn't brought to her by me. Is that clear?"

The guards snapped straighter and nodded. "Yes, My Lady," they said in unison.

"And I want anything that could be used as a weapon removed from her quarters immediately. If she becomes unruly again, bind her. She is not to leave her quarters, and one of you will stand guard at the doorway into the back passage, so she cannot slip out that way. I'll be back later to check on her."

CHAPTER TWENTY-EIGHT

With the Council, I visited the sacred precinct to assess the damage left by Mextli's attack, then we went around to the homes of some of the victims, to deliver my condolences and supplies of food and clothing to those left behind. Women and men alike cried and wailed for their lost loved ones, imploring me for answers as to why this happened and why I hadn't called on Quetzalcoatl to protect them. By the time we returned to the palace, all I wanted was to leave Tollan and go into hiding far from everything, but I'd made my promise and no matter how much it pained me, I would keep it.

I sat on my throne and listened while the Council members discussed what to do now. A small number of them—mostly those who had supported Matlacxochitl—said this was a sure sign that the elections had been a mistake and that the high priests should consult with the gods to name the next king. Most people scoffed at that notion though and called those who said it traitors to the crown. I let them argue and instead focused my own thoughts on what I could do myself. *Smoking Mirror warned me, and I didn't listen. Maybe it's not too late to go back to him and try to make a deal.*

"I don't understand why the search for the culprit in this morning's tragedy was called off," an unfamiliar councilman piped up. "What if this barbarian does this same thing in the noble quarters, or in the Chichimec quarters—"

"He wouldn't do it in the Chichimec quarters," another man rebutted. "No doubt he's one of them!"

"We will not turn upon each other now," Citlallotoc said. "That is exactly what the enemies of Tollan want: for us to tear ourselves apart from the inside. We can't make their ambitions so easily achieved."

"And perhaps we shouldn't make it so easy for our enemies to justify our destruction!" another man called. "We should listen to the warning given us today!"

"Topiltzin built this city on faith, not fear—"

"To Mictlan with Topiltzin!"

An outraged rumble carried through the room, and Citlallotoc rose to his feet, hand poised to take his sword, but then he cringed in pain. Gritting his teeth, he hissed, "Anyone who is so bold as to slander the king has no place in this hall, or this city."

"And you should listen to his warnings, little man," a deep, familiar voice spoke up. Everyone turned and many gasped to see Mextli standing in the great hall's entrance, palace guards holding him by the arms as if they'd taken him into custody.

Citlallotoc strode to the edge of the dais, this time putting aside the pain to take his sword in hand. "So, the villain has been brought in for justice after all!"

My divine instincts told me Mextli wasn't here against his will. I launched to my feet too and barked at the guards, "Do not touch him!"

Mextli grinned. "Oh, never fear, My Lady. I have indeed come to face justice for my crimes against you and the future king. I will not harm these innocent men who are merely doing their jobs." He looked over his shoulder at the guard to his right. "Aren't you going to march me before the Queen for judgment?"

"They will do no such thing!" I said, stepping down off the dais. "You will come no closer."

"You aren't afraid of me, are you?" He started walking up the center of the great hall towards me.

I retreated back up onto the dais, and the guards rushed to stop him, but when they reached him, my warnings to not touch him must have re-entered their heads. They didn't grab hold of him but walked the rest of the way with him, their spears at the ready.

Mextli stopped before the dais and dropped to his knees. He gazed imploringly up at both Citlallotoc and I, a smile on his face, but the darkness lurked in his eyes, staring me down. "So, what is my punishment, My Lady?"

"In Tollan, exile is the proscribed sentence for your heinous crime," Citlallotoc said.

"That is no punishment at all, for I will just come back and do it again," Mextli said. "For the safety of your city, the Queen must put me to death."

"I am more than happy to oblige you." Citlallotoc started to step down, his sword ready.

But I grabbed his arm. He stiffened at the touch, but didn't move to free himself. However, the sour odor of his discomfort compelled me to let him go.

"What's the matter, My Lady? Don't you want justice for those I murdered?" Mextli asked.

I glared at him. "You're too eager for us to kill you."

"Perhaps I'm contrite and believe I should pay for my evil deeds."

I laughed. "Or maybe you're inviting all of us onto your web."

He grinned wider. "I guess you'll just have to find out, won't you?"

I looked to Citlallotoc, but he appeared just as frustrated as I felt. A tense unease emanated from the crowd before us.

To Mextli, I said, "We will not be rushed to a decision, so you will spend the night in the prison yard while the Council discusses what to do about this situation."

Mextli grinned. "As you wish, My Lady."

"Guards, escort him to the prison yard." I then moved to return to my icpalli.

Citlallotoc did the same, but before he'd gone more than two steps, Mextli asked, "Did you enjoy Smoking Mirror's gift, little man?"

Citlallotoc froze.

"Though I wonder what kind of man—or future king, for that matter—refuses a beautiful woman when she offers herself so freely? Perhaps you just don't like women, what with all your talk about how much you 'loved' your king."

Citlallotoc's face burned deep red.

"Ignore him," I warned Citlallotoc, then to the guards, "Get him out of here already."

The guards grabbed onto Mextli's arms, but he ignored them. "But that's not really the problem at all, is it, My Lord?" He closed his eyes and drew in a deep breath between his clenched teeth, as if tasting the air for something. "It was fear, and shame; the same things that drove you from Tollan five years ago. It was happening all over again, but this time, the Council would find out the truth: that you are so weak that you can't keep a woman half your size from having her way with you, like when the Queen ignored your pleas of honor and instead ravaged you on the steps of the Temple of the Moon in Teotihuacan. They'd finally see that you're no man at all, but rather a scared little boy crying in the corner of his mother's room—"

Before I could say anything more, Citlallotoc whirled around and buried his sword between Mextli's neck and shoulder blade.

Mextli stared down at it then broke out laughing. "A nice blow, for a one-armed man." Golden dust began oozing down the feathered half of his chest.

"Give my regards to Lord Death, you Chichimec dog," Citlallotoc hissed, and he yanked on the sword handle with all his strength, making the dust gush out like a blizzard.

"You can tell him yourself." Mextli fell over backwards, a cloud of shimmering dust floating in the air around him.

The guards backed away, expressions of horror on their faces. "What is this...sorcery?" one of them asked, his voice shaking.

Citlallotoc waved the dust away as he looked back at me, no doubt expecting me to answer.

But the dust's golden hue shifted to moldy-green, and he began coughing and gagging, his eyes bulging. The guards started folding over with hacking coughs as the smell of putrefying flesh swelled. Even my own eyes started stinging.

The green dust soon spread all over the great hall, sending people into coughing and vomiting fits. A strange buzzing noise rose and a black cloud of flying insects swarmed out of Mextli's dead body, attacking the crowd. Terrified screams joined the already chaotic noise. The concentration of insects and dust soon grew so thick I couldn't see more than an arm's length in front of me.

I clambered about, calling for Citlallotoc, but after only a few steps, I fell over the edge of the dais, crashing to the floor. I found Mextli and the bodies of the guards, both dead. I crawled until I found Citlallotoc; he lay face down, his eyes bulging and bloodshot, his final gasp for air still locked on his purple face like a ghastly scream. The sight was a punch to my chest.

I never should have brought him here. What was I thinking? He was happy back home in Acolman, but I brought him here to die!

The cries soon fell quiet—evidence of the swiftness of Mextli's toxic death—but still more rose from out in the Hall of the Gods. I looked down at Citlallotoc again, my heart heavy and my fear ramping up.

There's nothing you can do for him now, the desire reminded me. *He's already gone, but that doesn't mean you can't still save others.*

Yes. Now wasn't the time to dwell on my own shortcomings. The palace needed to be evacuated.

I stumbled through the cloud of dust and insects, tripping over bodies strewn upon the floor, but eventually I found the entryway and clamored out into the Hall of the Gods.

The pestilence had infiltrated the vestibule, but I soon emerged from the cloud to find people fleeing through the public gardens while others sat on the steps, trying to catch their breaths and coughing the noxious dust from their lungs. The guards shouted in the confusion, herding as many people out as they could, but when one of them saw me, he hurried over, looking beleaguered. "Are you all right, My Lady?"

"I'm fine, but the people in the living quarters need to be evacuated. Take a couple of your men and go to the east wing, and take anyone you find out through the emergency corridor. Be sure to cover your nose and mouth before venturing into the green mist." I then turned and started back into the cloud myself.

But the guard grabbed my arm. "Where are you going? You must evacuate with everyone else!"

"I'm going to the royal quarters to get Lady Anacoana, and then we'll leave together through the passage to the priestly gardens."

"I can send some men to do that—"

"No, there's more people needing your help in the east wing. I will take care of Lady Anacoana. Now go!" I slipped his hold then plunged back into the cloud of dust and whirling insects. I heard him shouting for me to come back, but now that I was concealed from view, I jumped into the teoyoh.

I materialized in the hallway to the royal quarters. The guards that usually stood watch were gone—no doubt drawn away by the sounds of commotion deeper in the palace—but when I stepped out into the garden, one of Anacoana's guards still maintained his watch at her doorway. In his harried state, he forgot to bow when I approached. "What is going on, My Lady?"

"Is Lady Anacoana awake?"

"She wasn't when I last checked on her." He opened the curtain to let me inside.

We both stopped short when we found the bed empty. "Perhaps she's in the water yard," he suggested, and hurried towards the private garden ahead of me.

But she wasn't there either. And when we went through the doorway leading out into the back passageway, we found the other guard lying on the ground. A makeshift garrote made from a dress was still wound around his neck.

"I'll mount a search for her immediately, My Lady," the guard said, looking exceptionally pale.

I shook my head. "No. Go help evacuate the palace, and be sure to wear a cloth over your nose and mouth before you go."

"But what about you, My Lady?"

"I'm going to the priestly gardens."

He fidgeted a breath before saying, "I would be negligent in my oath to the crown if I left you unattended as you are. Where are your guards?"

"I don't have time for this. Follow my orders or I will relieve you of your duties!"

He hesitated only a moment more before bowing and heading back into the palace at a jog. Once he was out of sight, I leaped into the teoyoh, following the sweet fragrance of Anacoana's mortal teotl.

¤

I rematerialized in my meditation room in the priestly retreat, in almost complete darkness; someone had quelled the fire in the hearth. I saw a shadow knelt next to Little Reed's bed, but when my divine eyes adjusted, I saw it was Anacoana. She held a dagger, poised to stab Little Reed as he slept.

I dove over him and tackled her, knocking the blade from her hands. She grunted but clawed at my face with both hands. I pushed back, pinning her arms to the ground at her sides.

"Get off me!" she shrieked. "I want him dead, and you're not going to stop me!"

Magic tingled in my fingertips but I resisted releasing it. "I don't want to hurt you, Anacoana!"

But she kneed me in the stomach and wiggled away. When she reached for the blade on the floor, I shot a blast of magic at it, sending it skating across the room to hit the far wall.

She jumped after it, but I grabbed her ankle and she crashed to the ground with a grunt. But then she kicked me in the face, breaking my nose, and I let her go. My magic mended my wound quickly, but the pain-induced tears still clouded my eyes. I brushed them aside and blinked to bring my vision back into focus.

Anacoana had grabbed up the knife again and came around the other side, the blade held aloft to deal the killing blow to Little Reed. I reached out my hand, ready to blast her over backwards with my octli magic.

But someone came up behind her and slid a blade across her throat. The action itself was silent, but Anacoana choked. She dropped the blade to clutch her throat, gasping and sputtering before falling to her knees, blood gushing over her fingers. She slumped over, her breath rattling as her blood flowed out onto the floor.

The door curtain stood open now, and at first I couldn't make out the figure standing there, set against the early evening light pouring in from outside, but as my eyes adjusted, her features came into shape. "Yaretzi?" The high priestess of Smoking Mirror.

She turned her cold gaze upon me. "Are you all right, My Lady?" Her voice lacked surprise or anxiety, almost as if she were asking me my breakfast order instead of inquiring about my health after a deadly struggle.

"I'm fine, but...." I moved around to Anacoana, to feel for a pulse on her neck. It was thready and fading, and her pooled blood soaked into the reed matting of Little Reed's bedding. Her pulse ceased before I pulled my fingers away. "You didn't have to kill her," I panted.

"Of course I did," Yaretzi replied, dispassionate. "She was poised to kill Topiltzin.

"You could have disarmed her."

Before she could answer, Malinalli rushed into the room and slid to a stop with a gasp. "Omeyocan save me, what happened?"

"Lady Anacoana attempted to murder her husband," Yaretzi replied. "But I stopped her, and now the Queen is upset with me."

I glared at Yaretzi, but Malinalli hurried to me and fell to her knees. "Forgive my negligence, My Lady! I left for only a few moments, to go to the water yard, but I shouldn't have left the king alone. I beg your forgiveness!"

The way Malinalli prostrated herself unnerved me, and Yaretzi was watching with a curious smirk on her face. "Would you please give us a moment alone, Lady Yaretzi?" I asked.

Her smirk stretched further. "Of course."

"But wait out by the store room, for I wish to speak with you further," the desire hissed.

She bowed her head, still amused, then she disappeared out the curtain, closing it behind her.

"Malinalli," I started, but when she didn't move from her prostrated stance, I nudged her shoulders with both hands. "Please, sit up and look at me."

She finally did so, gazing at me with watery eyes.

"This isn't your fault."

"I shouldn't have left him alone! Dear gods! What if you hadn't come back—"

"He's all right."

"I let you down."

"Not at all. It wasn't fair of me to leave so much on your shoulders. I'm sorry."

Malinalli cast her forlorn gaze down at Anacoana. "I can't believe all of this. Everything has turned to madness!"

I hesitated to say more, but she had to know the full situation. "Citlallotoc and the entire Council are dead."

She covered her mouth with both hands, fresh tears welling in her eyes. "How?"

"Poison. You mustn't go back to the palace; it's completely uninhabitable."

She blinked, a lost look on her face. "What are we going to do?"

"For now, we stay here until it's safe to go back, so please, go get some sleep in your meditation room. You very much look like you could use the rest. I've asked too much of you these last few days."

"But what about Anacoana?"

"I'll take care of her." I stood and held my hand out to her. "I'll take care of everything, but right now I want you to take care of yourself."

She accepted my offered hand and I helped her to her feet. "You're right. I need some sleep. I'm useless if I'm exhausted."

I walked her across the garden to the meditation room she and Mazatzin shared, then I went to where Yaretzi stood by the store rooms. Her smug smirk made my magic roil.

"You didn't have to kill her," I hissed.

"Topiltzin would be dead if I hadn't."

"I was taking care of the situation—"

She laughed.

I squeezed my fists and set my jaw hard. "Have you something you wish to say to me?"

"You're like a dog that doesn't realize it's actually a jaguar and can't understand why it keeps eating its companions, Mayahuel, and frankly, it's amusing."

I stared at her, my mouth hanging open. "What...why did you call me that?"

Her grin stretched sharply up her cheeks, and when she spoke again, her voice had changed to a high-pitched, shrill sound, like a bat squeal. "I've been watching you for a long time, She of the Maguey."

I drew in a sharp breath. "Who are you?"

In answer, wings of obsidian blades sprang from her back, shredding her human flesh. As more of her bladed body tore loose of its fleshy prison, her skin and flesh dropped around her clawed feet. "You know me as Itzpapalotl, the Obsidian Butterfly," she hissed, her eyes glowing green like the rest of her newly-revealed aura.

I backed away, bewildered. "You...you possessed Yaretzi?"

"And limit myself and my magic? I wouldn't be so foolish."

"Then you've....you've always been here?"

"Among the tasty morsels? Of course. Smoking Mirror needed eyes inside the priestly orders, and I've served him well."

I looked back at the doorway to my meditation room. "But then why did you save Topiltzin? He's Quetzalcoatl's son."

"It's not his time yet."

The matter-of-fact way she said it raised the hairs on my neck. "What's that to mean?"

She smiled smoothly. "Just that it isn't his turn."

"His turn for the same terror and death Mextli's been wreaking over the people of Tollan?"

"And there's that puppy whine again. Why should anyone care about the humans?"

"The dispute is with Quetzalcoatl, not with the humans."

"When it comes to the Feathered Serpent, they are good bait."

"Really? Because I don't see him anywhere."

Itzpapalotl smiled but said nothing.

"Leave these people alone!" I insisted

She shook her head. "They must see what happens when they blindly follow charlatans like the Feathered Serpent, so they will know never to make that same mistake again. They must realize that they will be held accountable with their blood and very lives. We must imprint the penalty on their consciousness, so they will teach their children the sad tale of their misstep, and their children will teach the lesson to their children, generation after generation, so we never again have to come to such crossroads.

"And Topiltzin must be there to the bitter end, so his name will become the warning echoing through time: this is the consequence of defying the gods."

Her words made my magic sizzle in my limbs. "Enough already! Smoking Mirror has won; Quetzalcoatl fled the battlefield and continuing this is just cruel."

"It is, isn't it?" Itzpapalotl cooed. She disappeared with a crack.

CHAPTER TWENTY-NINE

I stood there, anxiety settling over me. What was I to do now? I'd promised Malinalli that I would protect everyone, but it was obvious I wasn't up to the task. The only one who could stop this madness was Smoking Mirror, but was it in anyone's best interest for me to crawl back to him now, begging forgiveness for my foolishness?

We could lead everyone away from Tollan, I thought, but the desire rebelled.

We built this city; it's ours, and it's cowardly to just hand it over to Smoking Mirror's sycophants—

A strange music drifted in from above, soft at first but growing in intensity. I looked up, half expecting to see its source floating above me, but I saw only the sunset streaking orange and red across the sky. It sounded like a bone flute, sweet and trilling like a quetzal bird. If I weren't feeling so anxious, I might have sat down and listened to its haunting melody. I closed my eyes though as the tempo picked up, relishing the sudden distraction from my worries.

Hearing curtain bells tinkling, I turned to see Malinalli glide out of her meditation room, twirling and stepping in time to the music. The sight brought a lazy smile to my face.

But while her movement was fluid and graceful, the anxiety and fear was plain on her face.

My growing concern shattered my mysterious contentment, and I immediately moved to intercept her. But when I reached out to grab her, she twirled out of my reach, heading for the bridge leading out into the main priestly gardens. "Quetzalpetlatl! Help me! Please!"

I ran after her and this time grabbed onto her arm, but she yanked me around with her, not missing a beat. I almost lost my grip but instead matched her steps to keep my balance and stay with her. "Stop dancing!"

"I can't!" she cried. "No matter how hard I try, my legs just won't stop moving!"

I dug my heels into the ground, hoping to slow her momentum, but there was no stopping her. She wrenched free, flinging me backwards into one of the walls. I hit with such force that the white plaster crumbled off behind me.

"Help me!"

I looked back to see Mazatzin dancing out of my meditation room, his face looking as if he was barely awake in spite of his body moving with strength and precision. He too swung around in time with the strange music playing on the wind. "What dark magic is this?"

I looked back at Malinalli; she was nearing the retreat's entrance, with just the gate and the bridge standing between her and the gardens beyond. If I couldn't stop her with physical force, my only alternative was magical force. Perhaps a little burst of octli magic could incapacitate her.

But dear gods, what if I killed her in the process?

Just be extra careful in how much you shoot at her. Taking a deep breath, I fired a small burst of magic.

I hit her square in the back, and her head lolled down against her chest, but her body kept moving, completely unaffected. I thought to increase the dosage, to overpower the music magic, but my fear of accidentally killing her stayed my hand.

Bind her, the desire suggested. *There's ropes in the store room.*

I ran up behind her and jumped on her back. The moment I wrapped my arms around her, I leaped through the fires of the teoyoh into the store room. When we rematerialized, she danced us right into the wall, knocking us both over, but as she started struggling to her feet again, I grabbed a length of rope from a nearby shelf and wrapped it around her legs. They kicked, trying to stop me, but I bound them together so all she could do was fishtail back and forth. I also bound her wrists together behind her then stood back to check my handiwork.

She wiggled around on the floor, but couldn't go anywhere.

I rushed back into the garden to see Mazatzin heading out to the bridge, but I grabbed him from behind too. We landed in the store room in the same manner, but Mazatzin kept his balance and I had to trip him with the ropes to make him go over.

"What is going on?" he cried, terrified. "How did I get in here?"

I finished binding him then rolled him over to lie next to Malinalli. "I'm sorry about this, Mazatzin, but it's for your own safety."

His legs flailed around as he asked, "Am I hallucinating?"

I shook my head. "No, you're awake, and I will explain everything to you, I promise, but first I must make this music stop. If it's affecting you and Malinalli like this, it could be affecting everyone else the same way."

Mazatzin still looked panicked but he nodded. "Do what you must."

"I promise I will be back to free you as soon as it's safe. All right?"

"Yes. Please hurry," he panted, his body thrashing around.

¤

I arrived in the sacred precinct to mayhem. Some people stood watching while other people danced frantically, screaming for help. City guards shouted for everyone to return to their homes and tried to stop some of the dancers, but just as with Malinalli and Mazatzin, the dancers tossed them around and aside as if they were nothing. I climbed up the steps of the temple of Quetzalcoatl to get a better look at the scene, and to my horror, I realized that it was only the white-robed priests of the Feathered Serpent's order who were affected by the enchanted music.

I rushed to a group of priests of Tlaloc who were watching the whole scene in befuddlement. "Go to the storerooms and bring as many ropes as you can carry," I shouted over the din. "The only way to stop them is to tie their legs together so they can't move anymore." When they stared at me, even more dumbfounded, I added, "Hurry up and do as your queen commands!" Only then did they run for the calmecac.

I went from group to group and gave them the same instructions, but soon I realized that this was taking too much time; people were already dancing beyond the sacred precinct. I cut through the milling and dancing crowd, following those leaving the precinct and out into the city.

Eventually the line of dancers wove outside the city walls, out among the canals. I stared up the path between the fields, following the line of people dancing up into the hills where the turquoise and silver mines were.

"Mine!"

Before I could move, hairy arms with clawed hands snapped around me, and I went over backwards into a nearby canal. I thrashed, but a strong, coil-like appendage wrapped around my legs, binding me the same as I'd bound Mazatzin and Malinalli. The world grew dimmer as we sank deeper into the canal, the day's dying sunlight now only splashes of color at the water's surface.

Unable to break free by physical means, I jumped into the teoyoh, taking my captor with me.

I came back on dry land, but he still clung to me, hissing and howling in my ear. I jumped back into the teoyoh again then came out midair, so I knocked the breath from him when we hit the ground. He still didn't let go though, so I did it again, dropping from an even higher height. This time he unlatched his limbs from me when we hit the ground. I rolled away, dizzy.

But I fell back into the water again. I clung to the bank once I resurfaced and looked around, blinking the water away from my eyes.

Black Otter lay on the ground away from the water, thrashing around in pain. The hand on his tail clawed towards the canal, dragging the rest of him with it. I hurried back ashore as he slipped tail-first back into the water, cutting off his pained cries. I sprang into the teoyoh, intending to take myself up the path, safely out of his reach.

But a bolt of magic knocked me back out of the stream, dropping me back where I was. As Black Otter popped his head out of the water to snarl at me, I tried again, but with the same results, except this time I fell into the next canal, at the opposite side of the maize field.

"Mine!" Black Otter shrieked then disappeared from sight. I jumped into the teoyoh again but when I landed, I was all the way back at the beginning of the fields. What in Mictlan—?

Laugher filled the air, and a geyser of water rose up from the nearest canal. The goddess Jade Skirt sat upon it as if it were a throne. "Oh my, you *are* amusing to watch, Mayahuel!" She slapped her knee as she broke into even louder laughter.

"You're the one blocking me?"

"As if I would waste my precious time with such trivialities," she replied, her mirth now forgotten. "I'm not afraid of you!"

"I never said you were."

"Because I'm not." She bent forward and the water of her geyser shifted to form a shelf for her to lean upon. "Though I wish I could say the same about Mextli. Seems you gave him quite the scare."

The desire flared with pride.

"Besides, if we were to battle, I have my own army that serves my every whim," Jade Skirt went on.

Black Otter popped up in the water in front of her geyser, showing me his silvery fangs. "Mine!" he hissed.

I laughed in spite of myself. "He's you're army?"

She grinned caiman-like back at me. "No. This is my army."

As she stretched her arms out, more creatures just like Black Otter began popping up in the waters of the canals; hundreds of them, all with otter-like heads, and shrieking and hissing in a terrible cacophony. Some slunk up onto the bank, keeping the fingers of the hands on their tails dipped in the water while still others swam up and down the canals.

Jade Skirt lounged back on her throne of water. "I think they turned out quite well, don't you?"

"They're lovely," I replied, dryly.

She glared at me. "How very rude you are. I think you need a lesson in politeness." She flicked her fingers.

Suddenly the water in the canals started rising and the creatures' frenzy grew louder. I darted a quick glare at Jade Skirt but then ran as fast as I could, heading for the hills. The creatures shrieked and lunged from both sides, but the road was wide enough to keep them from reaching me.

But as the water seeped over the banks, running out onto the road, I lost that advantage. I wove back and forth between the dancing priests, dodging slashing claws and snapping fangs. Behind me cries rose then fell to gurgling, but I couldn't stop. I had to reach the end of the fields, where the ground was higher. Only when I reached the incline did I look back.

The fields of half-dead maize were flooded and the creatures dragged the dancers and farmers into the canals. They vanished under water to gushing bubbles, but then re-emerged not as humans anymore but rather as more of the beasts, all of them covered in slick fur and staring with ink-black eyes.

As I stood staring in horrified silence, the water crept closer and closer to the hills, bringing the creatures with it. They would reach me any moment, and swallow up all those people I'd ran past.

In that instant, I made a decision.

I rushed back towards the water, firing small bursts octli magic to knock back the creatures at the head of the advancing water. Already I was feeling my magic waning from overuse, so once the water ran over my sandaled feet, I knelt, submerging my hands, and I pushed a hefty dose of magic out of my fingers, hoping it would finally stop Jade Skirt and her army of monsters.

It took a few breaths, but soon the creatures began shrieking in pain and confusion rather than excitement. A milky cloud of white spread out from me, and the further it went, the faster it infiltrated the water, overrunning the canals and the fields. The creatures thrashed around in the water-turned-octli, gurgling and crying, and they began collapsing by the dozens, their bodies twitching in their death throes.

"You...you...you treacherous serpent!" Jade Skirt shrieked, standing atop her geyser. Black Otter stood at her feet, pressed against her legs like a frightened child. I felt her magic pushing back through the octli, trying to keep it from infiltrating her geyser.

Fearing she would overpower my magic, I fled up the path into the hills, cutting in between the dancing priests. Her curses and screams echoed up the canyon after me.

I didn't run more than a few moments before I found the source of the music.

Xochipilli sat on a tall outcrop of rocks and Mextli stood next to the edge of the road, overlooking the quarry below. When a priest danced within reach of him, Mextli grabbed them by the front of the robe and hurled them over the edge where they crashed to the rocks below. The pile of bodies at the bottom was already significant, and the line of remaining priests was alarmingly short.

To my horror, I spotted Mitotia and Amoxtli among the dancers heading to their deaths. I sprinted to the head of the line, and just as Mextli reached for Mitotia, I hit his hands with a burst of magic, making him snap them back to his chest with a muffled yelp. Next I unleased a strike against Xochipilli, who howled in surprise and dropped his flute, ending the enchanted dance. The line of dancers collapsed to the ground, panting and crying in exhaustion.

When Xochipilli made to retrieve his flute, I held my hands out and warned him, "Don't make me hit you again, son." I doubted I had enough magic left to disarm him again, but to my relief he stopped, staring at me in amazement.

"I wondered how long it would take you to get here." Mextli shook his hands as if they still stung.

When Mitotia looked up at me, I said, "Get the others, and lead them back down to the city."

She nodded then crawled to the others lying sprawled upon the ground.

"And what makes you think I'll let them leave?" Mextli asked.

I turned my hands on him, and he winced ever so slightly. "Let's end this. I wish to speak to Smoking Mirror."

"For what purpose?"

Hearing the priests hurry back down the path behind me, I waited until they were out of earshot before speaking. "He said when I was ready to accept an agreement that I should come see him, and well…I'm ready to talk."

"And what makes you think he'd be interested?"

After a hesitation, I said, "I could still be useful to him."

I expected laughter, but instead Mextli studied me with a hint of appreciation.

A sudden wave of water hit me from behind, and when I turned around, another hit me in the chest, nearly taking me off my feet. I stumbled backwards until I ran into something, and when I looked up I saw it was Mextli.

"Jade Skirt, enough already," Mextli snarled.

The river goddess stood in the middle of the path, a puddle of water spreading out under her feet. Black Otter stood with her, his handed-tail thrashing back and forth as he crouched to spring. "Hand her over, Mextli!" Jade Skirt roared. "She destroyed my servants!"

To my surprise—and utter unease—Mextli wrapped his feathered arm around me, clutching me to his chest. "No."

Jade Skirt narrowed her eyes at him, and as if that were a silent order, Black Otter lunged at us.

But Mextli grabbed him by the neck and dangled him out over the ravine. Black Otter choked and thrashed, slashing open wounds on Mextli's arm, but the war god maintained his grip.

Jade Skirt's eyes bulged. "How dare you—?" But when Mextli squeezed harder, making Black Otter gag and writhe, she shouted, "No! Please! He's the only one I have left!"

"Then you will listen when I speak," Mextli replied. "Otherwise I will dash his brains out on the rocks below."

She held her hands up. "Fine. She's yours. Just don't hurt him."

With a hint of amusement, Mextli said, "She's Smoking Mirror's, not mine."

"She's Smoking Mirror's and I promise not to touch her. Now please, give me back my servant!"

Mextli threw Black Otter back at Jade Skirt, knocking her over. "Off with you then. The treacherous thorn bush goddess and I have business to discuss."

She glowered at him, but then wrapped her arms around Black Otter's neck before disappearing into the teoyoh.

Mextli shoved me away. "I'm declaring a temporary truce while you negotiate with Smoking Mirror. I suggest you hurry." He then too disappeared with a snap.

Only Xochipilli and I remained, but when he reached for his flute again, I scrambled to my feet. He held his hands up in surrender though. "I won't play it. There's a truce, remember?"

I slowly lowered my own hands to my sides. "I had to be sure."

"I understand." He picked up his flute and pressed it lengthwise between his palms until it disappeared.

"I must admit...you were the last person I expected to find helping Smoking Mirror," I said, disappointment blooming in my chest.

"I don't have much choice in the matter. Xochiquetzal was adamant about joining the cause, and I couldn't really stop her, so here I am."

"Enchanting the Feathered Serpent's priests with your music," I finished.

"It's all I have to offer the cause. Frankly, I'm glad you showed up and finally stopped me. Killing isn't one of my preferred art forms." He jumped down from the rocks. "Did you mean it, when you called me your son?"

"Of course I did."

He smiled, boyishly charming. In some ways he reminded me of Ehecacone. And it made my heart sting.

"I know Xochiquetzal is really mad at you, but I...I'd rather let the past be the past, and move on into the future. Nothing good ever comes of dwelling on things we can't change."

"I hope we can move forward too," I said.

He started to say something more, but suddenly the cyclone of flowers started whipping around him. Within a moment, he was gone and Xochiquetzal stood in his place. "Don't count on it, Mayahuel," she spat, but she then too disappeared in a burst of flowers.

CHAPTER THIRTY

I stood outside the door curtain to the royal chemist's house for a long time, hesitating to jingle the bells. Going inside was admitting defeat, and I feared that even then it was too late. I imagined Smoking Mirror laughing when I told him I wanted peace; laughing so hard his frail human body couldn't stand it and he keeled over dead. But what choice did I have? I was practically powerless in the face of so many gods working against me, and Quetzalcoatl hadn't even the decency to stay and protect the people of Tollan.

I reached to tug on the curtain, but before I could touch it, Mextli yanked it open from the inside. "For someone who claims to have had enough of war, you sure take your time making it to your meetings," he rumbled.

"I couldn't go through the teoyoh like you did, since you didn't lift the magical barrier before you left," I replied, glaring at him. "And even then, I can't sense where Smoking Mirror is."

He smiled smoothly. "Of course not. In his current state, he's highly vulnerable to his enemies, so we took measures to protect him." He stepped aside, inviting me in with a silent gesture.

The house felt overcrowded even with just me and Mextli—who was hunched under the low ceiling—but Smoking Mirror wasn't there.

"Get any silly ideas and I will scatter your teotl to the corners of the universe," Mextli said.

Before I could ask what he meant, he put his stony grip on my shoulder and we disappeared.

The familiar sensation of rushing energy swallowed me, and Mextli's magic twined around and through me for half a breath before we landed, each of us returned to our physical forms. My heart thudded drunkenly, with a twinge of loss and yearning.

We stood in a cavern lit by a single bonfire in the middle. Itzpapalotl crouched next to it, the firelight reflecting off her angled obsidian body, and Xochiquetzal sat off by herself at the edge of the fire light. Jade Skirt was there as well, pacing the back wall as she glared at me.

Smoking Mirror sat with his back to us, but when Mextli went to him, he turned to look at me over his shoulder. Mextli whispered before moving off, letting Smoking Mirror ease himself to his feet with the aid of his knobby walking stick. I remained standing beyond the firelight, too nervous to approach, so he came to me, hobbling slowly.

He looked little better than Little Reed; octli-whiteness had engulfed one of his eyes, and several more of his teeth were missing now. "So, you've come to your senses," he said, his spirit as fiery as ever.

I didn't answer until he stopped a few paces from me, and even then, I kept my voice low. "You warned me, and I've seen the error of my thinking."

"I know how difficult it is for any god to admit their mistakes, so I commend your humility now. Please, come join me at the fire. You're most welcome among us here."

I looked over at the others—and judging from the frosty looks all around, I knew it was a lie—but I doubted any of them would dare countermand him, so I followed him.

Smoking Mirror returned to his spot in front of the fire and held his hands out to warm them. "This body...its blood doesn't circulate very well anymore; too much stress on the heart inside of it, I'd guess. Luckily I need only put up with these tiring inconveniences for a few more days at best." When he noticed me still standing, he patted the ground with his gnarled hand. "Sit down, so we may talk."

I obeyed but kept at an arm's length.

Once I sat down, Mextli did too, on Smoking Mirror's other side.

"I'm pleased that you've finally joined us," Smoking Mirror said.

"I don't know that I'm at that particular juncture just yet," I replied, not looking at him.

"What is it now that's still holding you back?"

"I don't like what the others are doing, specifically to the people of Tollan."

The other gods chuckled, except Xochiquetzal, who harrumphed and stared into the fire.

Smoking Mirror cleared his throat for silence. "I understand. You spent many years among these humans, living as one of them. It's difficult to completely sever those ties of brotherhood so quickly. But the events of the past day were absolutely necessary, for the future of the city."

"I understand your reasons, but please, enough is enough! You've made your point."

Mextli exhaled a laugh. "Those are big demands for someone who's on the losing side."

"Yes, you've won," I went on. "Anything more is completely pointless, and likely will work against your endgame anyway. If you continue killing off all of the humans in Tollan, who's going to be left to pass on the lesson?"

Smoking Mirror nodded. "There is certainly logic to your argument, Mayahuel, and I'm not a god to disregard good sense. But you're rushing ahead of yourself. I haven't in fact won yet; Quetzalcoatl is still out there, not answering for his treachery. So long as he is free to contaminate yet another human community with his mutinous reforms, the war is far from over. And—" He held up a shaky finger— "Your son—my nephew—will continue languishing down in Mictlan. That is why you're here, really. Am I right?"

I hadn't even had time to think about Ehecacone these last few days since everything started falling apart, but now that I thought of him trapped in Mictlan forever, waiting for a rescue that might never come.... "Then it's not too late? You'll still help me?"

"Of course I will, but in return, you must help me."

"What can I do?"

Pressing his fingers together as if praying, Smoking Mirror said, "I want Quetzalcoatl's teotl."

I furrowed my eyebrows. "What do you mean?"

"His magic, I want it, and you will deliver it to me. I will tell you where to find him, and you will take his magic from him, and then you will give it to me."

That didn't clear anything up. "And how exactly am I supposed to do that?"

Smoking Mirror grinned wide. "Mextli told me about your...special ability."

I turned to glare at Mextli. "I don't know what you're talking about."

"Come now, Mayahuel," Smoking Mirror said. "You should be

thankful; if not for that, you and I would have nothing to discuss right now and I might in fact have decided to deal with you permanently. But instead you're useful to me."

"Let's not speak in puzzles," I said. "Just tell me exactly what you expect me to do."

"I expect you to seduce the Feathered Serpent into your bed where you will use your special ability to extract all of his teotl and then you will transfer it to me, through the same method."

The hairs on my neck bristled. "You want me to have sex with you?"

Xochiquetzal looked up from the fire, a panicked look on her face.

"Precisely," Smoking Mirror said, his own face eerily neutral.

Even the desire recoiled, and my magic pulsed most unpleasantly. "And for doing this, I get what?"

"Quetzalcoatl, of course. Once you've drained him of all of his magic, he's yours to do with as you please. I presume you'll take him to Mictlan to trade for your son's life, but that is entirely up to you."

"That's hardly good enough. You're asking me to do something I find physically repulsive, and expose myself to you and your magic at my most vulnerable. You haven't exactly been trustworthy in the past."

Smoking Mirror chuckled. "Indeed not. But you can rest easy; any deals we make will be sealed with a vow before Heaven, to protect both of our interests against treachery."

"I still need more than just Quetzalcoatl."

"Then tell me, Mayahuel, what unfulfilled desire can I offer you to make this deal acceptable to you?"

Little Reed, the desire purred, desperate, and my pulse jumped. Yes, if I could have anything, it would be him, with me forever, the husband at my side in Omeyocan. I couldn't turn him immortal myself, but Smoking Mirror had the power. I was suddenly too excited and hopeful to speak.

But surely Smoking Mirror won't agree to give his mortal enemy's son immortality and magic that he could someday use to avenge his father; magic he might use against me if he found out about my part in it.

He will understand our reasons, the desire said.

And if he doesn't?

He will.

"Well?" Smoking Mirror pressed.

The thought of letting Little Reed disappear into oblivion outweighed the thought of any potential risks. I drew in a deep breath, preparing for battle. "You will make Topiltzin immortal, the way you made Coatlicue a goddess."

Jade Skirt burst into hysterical laughter. "Omeyocan save us, you're such a fool—" But she snapped her mouth shut when Smoking Mirror cast a scolding glare at her.

After clearing his throat, Smoking Mirror returned his attention to me. "I must admit that such a thing doesn't sit well with me."

"No better than the idea of what you wish me to do with you does for me," I replied. "One compromise begets another."

"And if I say no?"

"Then we have nothing more to discuss. This point is not negotiable."

Smoking Mirror scrutinized the fire, deep in thought.

Across from him, Xochiquetzal looked devastated. *Perhaps this isn't such a good idea, especially if we want a relationship with her and Xochipilli in the future.*

But we're so close to everything we've ever wanted, the desire warned. *What do we owe her, really? It's not as if we knew about her, and she doesn't even want to be our daughter.*

That could change.

We're not throwing away our one opportunity for true happiness because she can't see what a lout Smoking Mirror is.

Smoking Mirror finally turned from the fire. "Fine. I accept your terms." He held his hand out to me.

But I eyed it warily. "Let's be absolutely clear about the details. When you turn Topiltzin immortal, he's not going to be the way he is right now. He will be clear-headed and healthy."

"Of course he will."

"Nor will you enslave him to me or you or anyone else. He will be his own god, bound to nobody."

Sighing, Smoking Mirror said, "Agreed."

"And you and your supporters will allow him to take his supporters and leave Tollan, unharrassed and unharmed."

Mextli frowned, but Smoking Mirror answered, "Very well. No harm shall come to any of your precious humans by my hand, or anyone else's here."

"Or your human allies," I insisted.

"Or my human allies," he agreed.

"And to show your good faith in this agreement, you will deliver Topiltzin's immortality immediately, before anything else."

Smoking Mirror narrowed his eyes at me. "Now you're just becoming demanding."

"Take it or leave it," the desire hissed.

"Very well. You get Topiltzin, then I will deliver Quetzalcoatl's location, upon which time you will then bed him, either willingly or through force, draining him of all of his teotl, then you will initiate the transfer of his teotl to me. Once that is complete, I will give you what's left of Quetzalcoatl and we will go our separate ways." He held his hand out to me again. "Now let us make the vow before Heaven, to solidify our deal."

Deep inside I felt as if I was missing something important, but the desire scoffed. *I've got all contingencies covered. Let's do this now, before Smoking Mirror changes his mind.*

I took Smoking Mirror's frail hand and clasped it. His skin was papery and cold.

"I promise to make Topiltzin immortal, to deliver Quetzalcoatl to Mayahuel, and to protect those humans loyal to Topiltzin from physical harm," he said, his voice raspy with exhaustion. His hand grew warm with magic though. When I didn't say anything, he said, "Now state your promise."

"I promise to deliver Quetzalcoatl's teotl to Smoking Mirror." My own hand grew hot too as my magic surged.

"Now state what the penalty will be for me if I break my end of the bargain," Smoking Mirror said.

"If Smoking Mirror fails to deliver on any of his promises, this deal will be broken and I don't have to deliver on any of my promises to him."

Smoking Mirror tightened his grip on my hand. "And if Mayahuel breaks her promise, she shall be forever bound in servitude to me, using her magic to serve my needs." He then dropped my hand as if it were a snake that might bite him if he held it any longer.

"That's not fair!" I said.

"Are you intending on not fulfilling your end of the bargain?"

"Of course not."

"Then stop your complaining. The vow is made, so let us get started." He motioned to Xochiquetzal. "Take your mother back to the house. I will join you once I've relieved my infernal bladder."

Xochiquetzal glared at me but rose to her feet. "Let's go already," she growled when I stood to join her. She grabbed my hand and before I could get in my next breath, we stood in the middle of the small chemist's house.

She tossed my hand away and stood facing the hearth, arms folded across her chest.

"Xochiquetzal, I'm sorry I must do this—"

"You didn't have to do it at all!" she fired back.

"Was I supposed to just let Ehecacone linger forever in Mictlan? Lord Death threatened to torture him if I don't bring Quetzalcoatl to trade for him. And while I know this isn't ideal, you must know that I'm not looking forward to doing this with Smoking Mirror. The entire notion makes me sick to my stomach."

"I don't care! You know how I feel about him!"

"Yes, I do, but he knows too, and yet he still insists on doing this. It just shows he doesn't care. You deserve better than that!"

She whirled on me. "What I deserve is a better mother!" She shouldered me aside and disappeared out the curtain, leaving the bells tinkling.

◘

I walked back to the priestly retreat, so I could see the state of the city and the sacred precinct, but also because I didn't have enough magic left to use the teoyoh. Every human I looked at made the desire simmer and growl, but luckily most people seemed to be hiding in their houses, afraid to come out. Not even the guards were present at the palace gates, and by all appearances, the inside was dark and uninhabited. It reminded me of the

Empty Days before the beginning of the new bundle of years, like the night Little Reed was born in Xochicalco.

The sacred precinct looked much the same, though when I went by the calmecac, it looked as if it had been ransacked and the classrooms' contents strewn about the courtyard. Someone had locked the gates into the priestly gardens, forcing me to jump to the other side through the teoyoh, but at least the gardens themselves had been spared from the chaos. Still I hurried to the retreat at a run, and dashed across the bridge when I saw Black Otter lurking in the water of the canal. He didn't try to pursue me though.

Inside I found Mazatzin and Malinalli had already been freed by Mitotia and Amoxtli and they were all gathered around the basalt slab outside the kitchens, eating and looking bedraggled. Malinalli hurried over. "Thank Omeyocan you're all right!"

"I'm sorry I had to tie you up like that."

"If you hadn't, I might be dead. Mitotia and Amoxtli told us what happened at the quarry."

Seeing both of the men watching me, I approached the table. To Mazatzin, I said, "I promised that I would explain everything to you when I returned—"

"It's all right," he said. "Malinalli told us while you were gone."

I nodded, unsure what to say then. Eventually though I said, "Smoking Mirror has agreed to a ceasefire for now, so we need not fear further attacks tonight."

"And you trust his word?" Amoxtli asked, incredulous.

"In this case, yes. There are consequences if he breaks it."

"Does Citlallotoc know of this?" Mitotia asked.

After a hesitation, I said, "Citlallotoc is dead."

She gasped. "Oh my gods! This is all my fault!"

"Mextli killed him in the attack on the palace. You had nothing to do with it."

Tears welled in her eyes. "But I called him here, before you came back. I sent him a message in Acolman, asking him to come see Topiltzin. I was hoping he'd see what was going on with Matlacxochitl and he'd intervene for all of us."

"That still doesn't make you responsible. If you hadn't called him here, he would have received my summons. But in the end, it was Mextli that took his life, not you, and trying to take blame upon ourselves isn't useful right now."

She nodded, wiping the tears away. "My apologies."

"It's all right," I said with what I hoped was a comforting smile.

"So how dire is the situation right now?" Mazatzin asked.

"The entire Council is dead, as are a good number of Quetzalcoatl's priests. Most of the city's population appears to have gone into hiding. For all intents and purposes, Tollan has fallen to Smoking Mirror."

A shocked silence settled over the garden. Malinalli looked especially stunned.

"I need each of you to go out into the city and find all of the remaining priests of Quetzalcoatl and bring them back here, packed and ready to march. Tomorrow we're all leaving Tollan."

"Leaving?" Mitotia asked, astonished.

I nodded. "I won't make anyone go who wishes to stay, but I have every reason to believe that Smoking Mirror's followers will execute anyone who doesn't leave."

"I don't understand," Amoxtli stammered. "Where is the god? He aided Topiltzin in Culhuacan, so why not now?"

"I don't know," I said. "Perhaps he's abandoned us. I tried to protect the city in his absence, but...I failed you all, and I am sorry. It pains me to lose everything Topiltzin and I built here, but cities can be rebuilt while lives lost cannot be replaced."

I'd hoped my words might fortify their resolve, but both Amoxtli and Mazatzin still looked befuddled and distressed. Even Mitotia looked troubled.

"We should hurry," Malinalli suggested, putting on her leader voice. "Morning isn't all that far off now."

The others nodded but as they went out the main entrance, she hung back. "We're taking Topiltzin with us, right?" When I nodded, she asked, "Do you need help putting the litter together?"

I shook my head. "I can do it on my own."

She nodded and turned to leave.

"I'm sorry I let you down, Malinalli," I called after her.

She paused, resting her hand on the archway leading out to the bridge.

"I thought…I thought too highly of my own abilities, and now Tollan is in ruins—" I choked back tears.

"You didn't let me down," she said, not looking at me. "You tried, which is more than Quetzalcoatl can claim. This is his city, but he hasn't even bothered to defend it."

"The people of Tollan deserve better gods than any of us," I whispered.

Malinalli looked back at me, tears in her eyes too. "That may be, but I'm still hopeful that my faith will pay off in the end," she said and walked out.

I stared at the archway a long time, mulling over her words before turning my gaze to the doorway to the meditation room where Little Reed was waiting for me to turn him immortal. "Yes, your faith will pay off in the end, Malinalli," I whispered. "Humanity will finally get the god they deserve."

CHAPTER THIRTY-ONE

I needed to replenish my magic before proceeding, but I didn't have time to find someone to appease the desire. It was already dark and sunrise would come all too soon, so instead I went to each of the meditation rooms and pilfered what blood I could find from the various idols. I must have been a monstrous sight, sucking dried blood from the maguey thorns and their rough ropes, and eating the dried grass balls. It was hardly filling, but it took the edge off my hunger and the magic simmered in my fingertips again. I'd take care of filling myself up once Litle Reed was safe and immortal.

After that, I fetched a fresh jug of water from the river, watching Black Otter carefully. He glared at me as he swam back and forth, but he kept his distance, abiding by the ceasefire. Still, I filled it quickly then went to my meditation room where Little Reed was.

I paused to touch his neck, my heart dancing nervously while I checked to make sure he hadn't passed away while I'd been gone, but his pulse was strong as usual. I pulled over the tray with his gold-plated pitcher and cup.

He must drink every bit of the potion, Smoking Mirror had told me. *So mix it in a container that it won't stick to.*

I pulled the leather pouch of powder he'd given me from the pocket of my dress and poured it into the pitcher.

Next, add water and mix it well.

I poured the water slowly into the pitcher then stirred it with a lacquered xocolatl stirring stick, being sure to tap it clean afterwards.

Finally—and this is most important—change the water mixture to octli with your own magic. That way you can control how young the potion will make him. Picture him as you'd like to see him, and so it shall be.

I set my hand over the opening of the pitcher and let a slow dribble of magic ooze off my fingers. I then stirred it again, for good measure.

The potion to make Little Reed immortal was now ready.

I poured the first cup but hesitated. By feeding this to him, I was fully committing to the deal with Smoking Mirror, no backing out no matter what. *Are we absolutely sure this is the right thing to do?*

Little Reed will be twice the god his father ever was, the desire chided me. *We're doing humanity a favor by revealing Quetzalcoatl for the fraud he truly is. No longer will he lead them down the path to destruction for his own selfish purposes. Little Reed is the god humanity deserves. He's the god they* need *now more than ever.*

My mind set, I put the cup aside so I could sit him up. "Wake up, Little Reed. It's time for some drink."

He roused enough to take a swallow, but he cringed and tried to push the cup away. I held his hand down and gave him some more, against which he struggled vehemently. I was stronger than him though. It was slow going, but eventually he drank the entire cup of the potion. He grumbled while I refilled the cup.

"I know you don't like octli, but it will make you feel much better," I said as I put the next cup to his lips. He struggled again and tried to move his head away, but eventually he relented. Once he finished off the last of it, I laid him back down and he went to sleep.

I wonder how long it will take. Smoking Mirror hadn't said, but he wasn't coming to see me again until daybreak, so it should do its work by then. *It better,* the desire rumbled.

I gathered some rags and used the remainder of the water from the jar to make sure Little Reed was fresh and clean when he woke up, and I changed his clothing. I'd hoped I would start seeing signs of him changing by the time I finished, but he still looked exactly the same, and he breathed with the same rattle as normal.

Unsure what else to do, I settled against the wall between the bed and the hearth, and waited. No one was ringing the hourly bells tonight, so I had no idea what time it was, but the sky beyond the half-open curtain was the deep bluish-purple of night. Malinalli came by after a few hours, to update me on their progress fulfilling my orders, then she retired to her meditation room to get some sleep. I spent the rest of the night watching the stars crawl maddeningly slow across the heavens.

The first sign that something was different came when the rasp in Little Reed's breath faded away to the sound of healthy, steady breathing. I watched him closely then, my magic dancing joyfully under my skin.

As still more time passed, the age spots on his hands and face faded away and the wrinkled skin around his eyes smoothed out. His silver hair steadily reverted to brown, his whiskers retreated back into his chin, and his withered muscles grew in volume. Seeing him returning to health overwhelmed me, but I couldn't look away. I didn't want to miss a single moment of his transformation.

By the time roundness replaced the skeletal thinness of his face, the first signs of the approaching dawn had turned the sky gray. I hadn't seen Little Reed in those years between his leaving for the army and when treachery had forced him to come back to Xochicalco, but I'd always imagined that he had looked this vital and strong.

And when he finally opened his eyes and I saw they were clear and focused again, I had to hold back a sob. There was only one question left now: was his love for me true, or had it all been a painful illusion?

Little Reed looked around, confused, but when his gaze met mine, a heartbreaking expression of disbelief crossed his face. "Papalotl?" he whispered, his voice shaking.

I couldn't hold the tears back any longer. "Yes, Little Reed. It's me," I choked, holding my arms open in welcome.

Without hesitation, he sat up and accepted my embrace, almost crushing me. He buried his face in my neck. "Dear gods, I thought I'd lost you forever," he whispered, tears muddling his voice.

I returned his hug with just as much ferocity. It hadn't been a lie at all; he really did love me. I wept as a wave of relief and regret and guilt washed over me. How could I ever have doubted his true feelings for me?

He pulled back to touch my face. Anguish plagued his dark eyes. "I'm so sorry, Papalotl—"

"No, it's me who owes you an apology, leaving like I did, without talking to you. I promise I'll never do that again, ever."

"Then you forgive me?"

"There is nothing you need to beg my forgiveness for; not even for demanding Citlallotoc to stay away from me. It was for his own good anyway." I stroked his cheek. "Besides, I couldn't have married him, not given how much I've always loved you."

He squeezed his eyes shut. "You truly still love me?"

"Forever and always, Little Reed."

He pulled me into a passionate kiss that sent the desire soaring so high that I felt intoxicated. It had been a long time since it had affected me so; not since I was a young woman and gave little thought to the truth behind my own intense reactions. And just like back then, I let it flow over me.

He trailed his lips over my chin, down to my neck, his hands on my back urging me closer still, so I climbed onto his lap. When his lips neared the collar of my dress, I made it melt away, making way for his achingly wonderful progression down my body. I remolded my clothing to give way as he slid his hands under my dress and kneaded my divine flesh with his strong fingers. Under his night xicolli, his already firm tepolli pressed against my thigh.

I understood now why the desire never took over when I was with Little Reed: we were always of the same mind when it came to him. And we both decided we'd held back long enough.

"Make love to me, Little Reed," I panted, desperate.

"Now?"

"Yes. Now. Please." I pulled his night xicolli up, to keep it from blocking him from me, and as soon as he'd properly positioned himself, I joined us together with a plaintive gasp.

My whole body tensed, but my magic was so primed and ready for what promised to come next that the pleasure built of its own accord, rushing to it without either of us moving. I tried to resist but it was beyond my control.

Warnings of what happened with Mextli flooded my mind. Omeyocan save me, what had I been thinking? I hadn't even told Little Reed what he was now, and I knew nothing about controlling my power; I could kill him without any effort. "Little Reed!" I gasped in panic as the pleasure roared up on me, unstoppable.

But he only held me tighter. "It will be all right, Papalotl," he whispered. "Just don't resist." He thrust hard into me, his own body shuddering in time with mine, but then the world melted away into blinding light.

I saw my own orange teotl first, but there was no other glow to give any indication of where Little Reed was. Had Smoking Mirror lied to me and hadn't turned him immortal at all? I should have known better than to trust anything he promised.

But then I noticed a shifting of shadows, forming what I realized was the barely visible outline of tendrils. They slithered among mine, my teotl rabbits watching them with cautious curiosity. It was only when the tendrils crossed paths with my own that I could see they were the purest white I'd ever seen, and shaped like serpents. *Like his father,* I thought.

Until I saw they each had a familiar ring of wispy feathers around their necks. Like Quetzalcoatl had.

It can't be! Quetzalcoatl's teotl had been purplish, and the serpents had dark, almost black eyes. The eyes on these were only discernible when they passed over one of my rabbits, when my orange teotl shown clearly through them, as if they were empty. *Little Reed is the son of the god, not Quetzalcoatl himself—*

But when one of my curious rabbits jumped up and clasped one of the feathered serpents between its paws, a flash of memory unfurled around me; of me—not human me, but the earth monster I once was—lying on my back on a grassy bank, gazing longingly up at me, as if I were watching myself through someone else's eyes. My coils—no, not mine—slid and caressed my scaly body, making me laugh with a toothy smile that filled the headspace around me with a desperate heart-like thudding.

Every god gives at least one gift to the world, I whispered, my pulse humming in my belly. *Isn't it time you shared yours?*

Earth monster me gazed back at me in earnest. *But how do I do that?* In my own head, my voice back then had been harsh and snarly, but through ears not my own, the sound was sweet like honey.

Close your eyes and I will show you.

Omeyocan save me, Little Reed is *Quetzalcoatl!*

And he'd captured me again, wrapped me up in his divine coils and would crush me, just like last time. I'd been so worried about harming Little Reed, but here I was, the fish trapped in that very same net. I was such a fool, *again*! And would I end up on the banks of the Black Lake in Mictlan all over *again*? My panic soared.

But instead of attacking my rabbits, the feathered serpents retreated. The throb of magic all around me waned and the material world slowly leaked back in its place. I was once again on Little Reed's lap—*no, Quetzalcoatl's!*—his body still inside mine, but neither of us moved.

I stared at him, rage and devastation sparring in my gut while I struggled to find the right words.

Quetzalcoatl saved me the trouble though. "Papalotl—"

I shoved him away, finally separating us and I retreated beyond the second bed where Mazatzin had slept. The rage choked me before I blurted, "Don't you dare call me that! You have no right! How dare you?"

"But I thought you knew." He started moving towards me but he froze when I raised my hands as if to throw magic at him. "When you said I didn't need your forgiveness, I thought—"

"You thought I could ever forgive you? When all you've ever done is lie to me?"

"Please, Mayahuel, let me explain. It isn't what you think."

I shook my head, tears flowing down my cheeks as the devastation finally won out. "It was bad enough that you refused to tell me who I was, and that you fed me to my grandmother, but to then hide yourself from me like this...to make me believe you were someone else—someone I loved so much it hurt.... How could you do that to me?"

"It wasn't my intention to hide from you, you must believe me. I tried to tell you, in a letter, but Ihuitimal intercepted it and you never—"

"That was one time—one! What about the other twenty-odd years we lived together?"

"I should have. I'm sorry." He hung his head.

I seized the opportunity to leave. I didn't want to talk about any of this. I slashed aside the curtain and stumbled into the garden.

Luckily I was alone, for I'd forgotten my nakedness. I reformed my dress with an errant thought, unsure of even where I was going now.

I wasn't alone for long though. Quetzalcoatl hurried out after me. "If I had it all to do over again, I would have had my nahual tell you that I had incarnated into this world as Chimalma's only son. My vision was always the two of us leading humanity into a new future, side by side not as humans but as the gods we really are."

I was striding toward the entrance, but at his words I whirled on him. "And this was somehow going to be accomplished by keeping me ignorant of my own divine nature?"

He stopped a few paces from me, a contrite look on his face. "I wasn't allowed to tell you the truth about yourself. You had to figure it out on your own."

"What is that even supposed to mean?"

"When I made the deal with Lord Death to resurrect you, part of the bargain was that I couldn't tell you who you really were."

"Why?"

"Because he despises me; he's never forgiven me for winning the bones of humanity from him. And since there was a good chance that you would never figure out you were a goddess and you'd die a mortal death...what better revenge than making me suffer losing you forever?"

An unexpected twinge of guilt rose inside me. "And what would happen if you told me?"

"You would return to the Black Lake and I would be enslaved to Lord Death for eternity. Though I don't understand...how did Smoking Mirror tell you when the deal prohibited anyone from telling you, lest you return to the Black Lake as if the deal never took place?"

"He didn't actually tell me," I admitted. "I figured it out on my own;

he just confirmed it."

"That does explain why you're still alive."

I folded my arms. "So you weren't withholding that information out of malice. But why didn't you just tell me who *you* really were all along?"

He hesitated, looking uncomfortable, but then said, "Because I thought if you knew from the start that I was a god that we couldn't have the close relationship I wanted. I thought it would add a barrier between us that you might not be able to overcome."

"But we were lovers, in the Divine Dream—"

"The Divine Dream isn't reality for humans, and by the time that happened, you'd thought of me as your brother for ten full years. After that...the fear of losing what we already had...it all just accumulated and grew, especially when you told me why you stopped coming to see me in the Divine Dream."

I swallowed a wad of guilt building in my throat. "I can see how that would present difficulties."

He nodded. "But in the end...I was just cowardly. I should have told you and accepted the beans as they fell, and for that I am sorry, Mayahuel. The last thing I wanted to do was hurt you all over again."

The *all over again* part re-hardened my heart. "And now we come to the matter of Tamoachan, and my *gift to humanity*."

Quetzalcoatl bowed his head. "Indeed."

"You let Tzitzimitl kill me!"

"I did," he admitted.

His words struck an arrow through my heart. "But...how could you? After everything we shared...?""

"The why is hardly relevant," Smoking Mirror suddenly spoke up behind me.

I turned to see Mextli leading his decrepit form by the arm across the bridge from the gardens. Itzpapalotl, Jade Skirt, and Xochiquetzal followed behind, the first two looking rather smug while the latter looked distressed.

"Brother?" Quetzalcoatl walked closer, but then he stopped short. "What is going on?"

Smoking Mirror smiled wide. "Your coup is over, and you've lost.

Tollan has fallen and the humans have turned against you; even as we speak, packs of people are roaming the streets in search of captives, and soon the blood will run freely down the temple steps. Things are finally back to how they should be."

Quetzalcoatl turned his incredulous gaze to me. "Is this true?"

"I couldn't stop them," I said. "I tried, and it cost a lot of people their lives." After a tense pause, I added, "Including Anacoana and Citlallotoc."

The distress on his face deepened. "No!"

"Yes, many, many lives, all because you wouldn't come out and face me, brother," Smoking Mirror wheezed. He and Mextli finally stopped a dozen paces from us. "When the game became contentious, you ran away like a coward."

"I didn't run anywhere," Quetzalcoatl replied. "My mortal body broke down, temporarily trapping me between worlds, but I was always here."

Smoking Mirror grinned. "Here, yes, but completely useless when it really counted." He turned his cold gaze upon me. "I confess surprise that you haven't yet upheld your end of our bargain, Mayahuel."

"Bargain?" Quetzalcoatl asked me, confused.

The panic welling up inside of me rendered me mute.

"She's going to use her special magic—you know the one I'm talking about—to drain you of all of your teotl and give it to me," Smoking Mirror answered for me.

Quetzalcoatl stared at me, incredulous and wounded. "Is this true?"

"I...I didn't—" I choked on tears.

"Why?"

"Because you killed her in Tamoachan, of course," Smoking Mirror said. "You told her that her death was her gift to humanity!"

Quetzalcoatl took a step closer to Smoking Mirror, but Mextli moved to stand between them. "Funny how you leave out your part in it, *Brother*," Quetzalcoatl said.

I switched my gaze back and forth between them. "What does that mean?"

"Since we're all revealing truths today, I believe it's your turn." Quetzalcoatl motioned to Smoking Mirror.

Smoking Mirror's smile broadened. "The truth hardly matters at this point. The deal has been struck."

"Tell her how you know about her special power."

"Mextli told him," I said. The shocked expression on Quetzalcoatl's face brought heat to my cheeks.

"Yes, he indeed shared with me what you two did—and for now on I think he will heed my warnings when I tell him not to do something, won't you?" He cast a spear-like glare at Mextli, who bowed his head, looking embarrassed.

"He knew about your ability long before that," Quetzalcoatl said.

"How?"

"Because you've been with him before."

I snapped a glare at him, taken aback. How dare he accuse me of something so…distasteful? "I have not! The very thought…."

Though we'll have to do it soon enough, the desire reminded me. Even she shuddered.

Quetzalcoatl nodded. "You have, when he and I were still Ehecatl."

"That doesn't make sense. Ehecatl is just one of your many names."

"No, it was my very first name; before there was the Feathered Serpent and the Smoking Mirror, there was one god who was both the darkness and the light, and he was called the Wind.

"But he lived in constant internal conflict; he went to the underworld to steal humanity's bones because he wanted to be important and worshipped by all humanity, but he ended up learning what it meant to be human." He reached out and gently took my hand in his. "And he brought you from Heaven to bring Love to the people, who were living in constant fear and violence. But you also brought Love to his heart, and you changed him forever."

The look of adoration in his eyes overwhelmed me. It was the same look that had confused my heart about the god and Little Reed, and now the reason why seemed so glaringly obvious that I felt a fool for not having realized the truth before.

"Yes, and it was all just sickening," Smoking Mirror spat. "Ehecatl could have been the most powerful of all the gods—he wanted it so very badly—but then came Love; his one big mistake. Every time the darkness moved to fulfill his destiny, the light—with its infernal sense of conscience and fairness—ruined everything, and Love was making it even worse. There was only one possible course of action." He focused his hard, hate-filled gaze squarely on me. "You had to die and be made to serve the darkness—to serve me."

I stared back at him, a feeling of clarity flowing over me. "I remember you now," I whispered. "When my grandmother came, Ehecatl...he changed. He turned cold and disappeared, and I was all alone...." Rage bubbled up inside me. "It was *you* who buried my bones so the maguey would grow, and the humans could brew octli. *You're* the one who said my real gift was my death!"

Smoking Mirror smiled smugly.

I looked at Quetzalcoatl again, my rage dwindling away. "It wasn't you at all."

Tears shone in his eyes. "I'm just as culpable. I didn't stop him."

"Why not?"

"Because I was weaker than him; so much weaker that he nearly consumed me entirely. I'm only here now because of an act of faith by my first priestess. Her sacrifice severed Ehecatl into his two halves, and I became Quetzalcoatl—"

"And he became the Smoking Mirror," I finished.

The hatred flamed in Smoking Mirror's eyes. "That priestess cost me everything; she gave the Feathered Serpent all of Ehecatl's strongest magic and left me with practically nothing. I spend hundreds of bundles of years starving on the fringes of human civilization, gathering my own followers when and where I could while he sat here in the midst of so much adoration, so many offerings. It should have been me!"

"But I've reaped my revenge, Brother. All of that magic is coming back to me, delivered with delicious irony by the very goddess who started this whole sorry ordeal with us." To me, he smiled wide. "Time to deliver, my dear."

"And if she doesn't?" Quetzalcoatl asked, challengingly.

"Then she becomes enslaved to me for the rest of her existence, and I use her to take what I want from you anyway."

When I saw Mextli glaring hatefully at me, a new angle came to me. "It's not going to work, Smoking Mirror. The magic I take from others, it fades away, so even if you get your paws on Quetzalcoatl's teotl, it won't last."

Smoking Mirror laughed. "Perhaps if you were trying to give me any other god's magic, but Quetzalcoatl's teotl is the same as my own, so it will just be coming home in a new body." He stepped closer to me. "Time to make your decision, Mayahuel."

CHAPTER THIRTY-TWO

I stepped away from Quetzalcoatl, overwhelmed and panicking. "Omeyocan save me, what have I done?"

"Assured victory for me no matter what you do," Smoking Mirror replied, delight painting his wrinkled face.

Quetzalcoatl took me by the shoulders. "You can't listen to him, Mayahuel. He lies."

I shook my head. "No, he's right. No matter what I do, I can't stop him from hurting you!"

"There's always an out on these deals—"

"There is," Smoking Mirror admitted. "But it will do her no good because I've upheld my end; all of her precious humans remain unharmed, and I gave you to her, just as she wanted."

I whirled on him. "This is hardly how I wanted anything!"

"And it's my fault that you were too dense to realize that Topiltzin was already immortal?"

"So the potion was all just for show then?"

Chuckling, Smoking Mirror said, "Actually, that's my favorite part. It was indeed a magic elixir, one that when activated with your magic will bind whatever god consumes it into human flesh."

My heart skipped a beat. "You turned him human?"

"Of course not. That would break our bargain; after all, I promised you immortality, and he's indeed still immortal. Mextli, give Mayahuel a demonstration."

Mextli summoned a knife to his feathered hand and advanced on Quetzalcoatl.

I flung myself in front of him. "What are you doing?" When he didn't slow, I threw a burst of magic at him.

But he slashed the knife at it, bouncing it back at me. It hit me in the chest, knocking me over backwards, dazed. I looked up just in time to see him plunge the blade into Quetzalcoatl's neck. "No!"

Quetzalcoatl clutched at Mextli's hand on the blade jutting out of his neck, but when Mextli yanked it out, sending a geyser of blood spraying across his feathered xicolli, Quetzalcoatl collapsed into a heap. I sobbed as I crawled to him. He twitched, his eyes wide and staring, but when I set my hand on him, he fell still, his final breath escaping him with a rattle. I stared at him, my breath stuck in my throat.

But suddenly he gasped as if emerging from a very deep lake. He stared around in terror, but he clutched onto me with both hands when he saw me. He was still covered in blood, but when I checked for his wound, it was gone.

Smoking Mirror grinned. "See? He's still immortal. But he feels everything the same way he always did as a human being, but he'll never die from any of it. I'm sure Lord Death will find this an added bonus when you trade him for your son."

I stared down at Quetzalcoatl, my insides curling. "I can't do this to you!" I whispered.

"Are you refusing to uphold your end of our bargain, Mayahuel?" When Smoking Mirror spoke, a tightness formed around my throat, as if someone was placing a slave collar on it.

I started reaching for my throat, but Quetzalcoatl grabbed my hand, holding it tight. "Just do it," he whispered, his voice raspy.

"What?"

"It's going to happen either way, but don't enslave yourself to him for me. If you're still free, at least there will be someone who can oppose him."

"But I'm so weak, and when he has your teotl too—"

He squeezed my hand. "You're stronger than you know, Papalotl. Have faith."

A sob escaped me.

"Time to make your decision, Mayahuel," Smoking Mirror said, impatient.

I turned to glare at him.

And found Malinalli standing behind his hunched form. All of the shouting must have woken her. I drew in a startled breath when she raised her sacrificial blade aloft.

She brought it down in what seemed like slow motion, burying it between Smoking Mirror's shoulder blades, then yanked it out and stuck him again, this time from the side, under the ribs. She gritted her teeth as she twisted the weapon.

Smoking Mirror's gasping cry brought the other gods whirling around. Xochiquetzal shrieked as if she were the one being stabbed, and Mextli knocked Malinalli aside as he moved to shield his master from further attacks. Smoking Mirror crumbled to his knees, cringing in pain as he pawed at the knife handle with his gnarled hands. "Who in Mictlan dares?" he choked, blood dribbling from his frail lips.

Itzpapalotl bared her wings of obsidian blades with a loud clacking. "Treacherous human!"

"Stop!" Mextli boomed.

But too late. Itzpapalotl drove the end of her wing through Malinalli's back, impaling her all the way through.

Malinalli gagged, but when Itzpapalotl withdrew her blades, she stumbled away to lean against the copal tree, clutching her bleeding chest.

"Dear gods no!" I rushed to her, arriving just in time to catch her as she fell over backwards. "No! No! No!" I heard other hysterical screaming, but I focused on lowering her gently to the ground and resting her head in my lap. *Omeyocan please, don't let it be as bad as I fear it is!*

"You idiots!" Smoking Mirror roared between wet coughs. "I had everything...exactly as I...wanted it!"

I smoothed the damp hair from Malinalli's forehead. "Why on earth did you do that?" I cried.

She gazed up at me with pained eyes, her chest heaving with each difficult breath. "Now he has nothing to force your hand with."

Indeed, the tight feeling around my neck had gone away completely. The deal was broken. "Oh Malinalli!" The tears came thick.

In the midst of the growing commotion in the garden, Mitotia collapsed to her knees next to Malinalli and clutched her hand to her chest. "Just stay still. If we can get a doctor here quickly—"

But Malinalli shook her head. "It's too late for that, my love." She reached up to caress Mitotia's tattooed cheek, tracing the feathered serpent there with her fingertips.

"Don't say that!" Mitotia said, tears winding down her cheeks.

"I'm not afraid," Malinalli assured her. But when she looked up at me again, her eyes widened. "Oh my! Have you any idea how...glorious you are to behold?" When Quetzalcoatl crouched next to me and looked down at her too, she whispered, "My Lord!"

He touched her hand. "Faith will see you on from here, my friend."

"I know it will," she said with conviction. "It's always led me."

I couldn't hold in the sobs anymore. "Why did you do this?"

She wrapped her hand around mine where it clutched her shoulder. "Because you're the goddess the people need right now. You just need a little help to prove it to yourself."

"Get your hands off of me!" Smoking Mirror shouted, and Xochiquetzal shrank away from him. "You're all idiots!"

"Death is my gift, to all of you." Malinalli shifted her anxious gaze to each of us in turn, but when she came back to me, she whispered, "You can do this, Quetzalpetlatl. I have faith in you. Take my gift, and find that faith within yourself." Her chest then fell still.

Feeling empty and numb, I looked up to see Smoking Mirror watching me, a sneer on his face. "Mextli," he said. "I'm done with this body."

Without a word, Mextli drew his macuahuitl sword from the air and took Smoking Mirror's head off with a single hack. He and the others then hurried away, taking shelter under the archway entrance of the priestly retreat.

The sight made my magic jitter, but it turned into hysterical pulses when smoke began swirling out of Smoking Mirror's headless body.

Quetzalcoatl rested his hand on my shoulder and gave it a gentle squeeze. "Remember faith. Trust in it."

The ground started rumbling under me, and the billowing smoke formed a gigantic black cloud, obscuring the body. It twisted and roiled into the form of a giant wildcat, and when it opened its eyes, they burned like hot embers. It opened its flame-filled mouth with a scream that rattled the stone bricks of the building, sending cracks snaking across the plaster walls.

I stared up at the smoke-jaguar with wide eyes, my mind racing. What should I do now?

Suddenly my magic surged; the world bent around me and I could see the teotl flowing through everything and everyone. My own whipped around me, just like in those moments with Mextli and Quetzalcoatl, the tendrils reaching out, orange spectral rabbits bursting forth to dash around the garden. They bounded among the other gods, Mextli with his turquoise hummingbirds, Itzpapalotl's green bats, Jade Skirt's blue fish, and Xochiquetzal's yellow quetzals. Smoking Mirror's were jaguars, dark purple, almost black, and they swatted their paws and hissed at my rabbits when they came close.

Does this work the same way as before? Deciding to find out, I targeted Itzpapalotl first. For Malinalli.

My rabbits changed direction and ambushed the goddess's gliding bats, pouncing on them or snatching them out of midair with their long teeth. She screamed. Her magic pulsed up my tendrils, but it wasn't very powerful; she had even less magic than I did. All I could do was change my hands into obsidian swords; perhaps useful in a physical altercation with an army, but hardly so in a battle of magic. I let her go and she disappeared with a snap of green light, taking her petrified cries with her.

Jade Skirt wasn't much better. Her little fishes tried fighting back by flipping their tails at my rabbits' faces, but they were quickly subdued. She tried throwing water at me to break the connection, but I blocked it with hardly a thought. I made the water in the canal beyond the retreat's walls rise up, but flooding the garden would only endanger Mitotia. I let Jade Skirt go too, and just like Itzpapalotl, she fled.

My rabbits moved towards Xochiquetzal's birds, but I called them off with a silent command. She was my daughter, and I still hoped that someday that we might be able to put the past behind us and have a relationship. "Leave, Xochiquetzal," I said. "This situation isn't about you."

She looked from me to Smoking Mirror, seemingly unsure, but then she said, "I'm sorry, Smoking Mirror," and she too vanished.

"You're completely useless anyway!" Smoking Mirror roared, churning up more smoke as he pawed the ground. He kept his distance though.

Mextli still remained, watching me warily.

"You should leave too," I said. "Despite everything that's happened, I haven't forgotten the kindness you showed me."

I'd hoped to see the compassionate side in his eyes again, the side that I could have fallen in love with under the right circumstances, but the darkness refused to yield. "I don't flee from battles, and I won't abandon my brother. I pledged my very existence to him."

"Just know that I won't hesitate to drain you of every bit of your teotl if necessary," I said. "Don't make the mistake of forcing my hand."

He sneered but remained where he was, his hummingbirds hovering close to him.

I turned to Smoking Mirror finally. "You can still leave—"

"I will see you in Mictlan before I will leave!" His teotl jaguars attacked my rabbits, and his smoke rushed at me, its fangs bared.

We collided with a crash that blasted the plaster from the walls around us, and we both lost physical form. I pulled in as much magic as I could, intending to throw it back at him, but as soon as it flowed into me, it flowed back out. The more I tried and failed, the more my rage grew, and soon we were caught in a whirlpool of flowing magic, his jaguars tangling with my rabbits while my rabbits bit and scratched madly.

I know all of your tricks, Mayahuel, Smoking Mirror hissed. *You can't win this battle!*

And neither can you! I tried to pull still more of his magic, determined to kill him with a sneak attack, but the flow's intensity only increased. We were deadlocked, and the only way out was death, for both of us. *Good! I'd rather be dead than let him win!* I thought with a suffocating ferocity.

Death is my gift, to all of you, Malinalli's voice echoed in my head, and for a moment it calmed the uncontrolled rage. *Surely this isn't what she made this sacrifice for,* I thought. Nothing I tried did any good; he was more than equal to my most powerful magic—

Rage and hate isn't my most powerful magic, I thought. All of my mistakes of the past, all of my missteps, they came back to me now, from

Red Flint, to Black Otter, even Quetzalcoatl. All of it had been born of anger and the need for revenge. *I am a goddess of love, not hate.*

And yet all this time, I'd been fighting hatred and anger with more of the same, dragging Smoking Mirror's dark, sinister magic through me, whipping my own negativity and loathing to new heights. And it only seemed to make him stronger.

Let's give him a dose of what he came here to destroy.

The desire hesitated, but only for a breath before I let my own love magic leak into the flow, and I stopped fighting back.

Smoking Mirror shrieked loud, his voice a mixture of jaguar yell and human scream. *Oh no you don't!* He tried pushing more of his dark magic back at me, but it just opened the flood gate on my own. Smoking Mirror hissed and gurgled, waves of hatred and fear coursing through us, but I countered it with memories of everyone I'd ever loved: my father, my mother, my aunt Eloxochitl, my uncle Nochuatl, Nimilitzli. Black Otter, Jade Flower, Citlallotoc, Mazatzin, Amoxtli. Even Mextli. But most especially Malinalli, and Little Reed, and Ehecacone, who'd all given me so much and made me who I was. Who proved the transformative nature of my greatest gift.

Maybe I can change Smoking Mirror too.

My rabbits had disappeared, but his teotl jaguars now glowed with a hint of orange, and they pawed at themselves as if something had captured them by their heads. Smoking Mirror howled. *Never!* His teotl writhed as if in pain, but he made no attempt to withdraw. *You won't defeat me! You aren't powerful enough!*

I don't want to defeat you, I said. *I just want you to see that there's more to life than hate.*

I am the Darkness! Smoking Mirror screamed. *You cannot change me!* His teotl grew to new, reality-bending levels, bent on destroying us both.

Have it your way. I released one last blast of love magic into the flow then immediately severed the connection between us. I vaguely heard him roar as my teotl reformed my physical body, but then a blast of wind knocked me over backwards. Loud crashing and chaos filled the air, but then everything fell still and silent. When I looked up, gold dust fell from the sky like snowflakes.

The garden had been wiped out, the trees uprooted and the bushes bared of leaves. The buildings had been leveled to the ground too. Mextli stood where the entrance had once been, looking stunned.

Beyond him, out in the priestly gardens, Mazatzin and Amoxtli stood at the head of a large group of priests and priestesses and their families. They too stared at the rubble agape.

Mextli reached out so the glittery dust gathered on his feathered hand. He rubbed a pinch of it between his fingers before putting it to his tongue. He gagged then shook the dust from his hands, a bewildered look on his face. "Smoking Mirror?" he whispered. He looked up at me, his eyes wide. "You killed him?" He backed away a couple steps, as if I might come after him next, but then just like the other gods, he disappeared with a snap.

CHAPTER THIRTY-THREE

With Mazatzin's help, I found Quetzalcoatl and Mitotia under the remains of the copal tree. They'd been saved by virtue of one of the walls not fully crumbling when the tree hit it, though Quetzalcoatl had been impaled through the shoulder by a branch while he'd shielded Mitotia when the tree came over. The branch had to be cut from the tree and it took both Mazatzin and Amoxtli to pull the branch out of his chest. They stared in amazement—and fear—when they witnessed the sucking chest wound heal by magic.

"I think it's time we told everyone the truth, about both of us," I told Quetzalcoatl once we were alone while the rest of the priests were combing through the wreckage for whatever they could scavenge.

He nodded. "I will address the crowd in a few minutes." He gritted his teeth in pain as he raised his arms to let me slip a new xicolli one of the priests had given him on over his head.

I cringed. "Not fully healed yet?"

"I'm all right," he assured me.

When an uneasy silence fell between us, I whispered, "I'm so sorry. You have every right to hate me—"

"I don't hate you. I understand why you did what you did."

"But you're trapped in that body thanks to me."

Smiling, he said, "So it'll just be like the last thirty years, except I won't grow old anymore. I definitely won't miss the aching bones."

I tried to smile but it came out as a frown.

He set a hand on my shoulder. "Everything is going to be all right."

Nothing will ever be all right again, I almost said, but it was too painful to admit aloud. I'd done all of this to get my son back, but I didn't even have that as a consolation in this disaster. How would I ever get him back now? "You're far too easy on me."

"You're tough enough on yourself for both of us."

Mazatzin and Amoxtli gathered everyone in the field beyond the river, where long ago I used to take Ehecacone to play and where I'd practice my magic with Malinalli; bittersweet memories of everything this war with Smoking Mirror had cost not just me, but everyone.

The chatter of conversation was already muted, but when Quetzalcoatl and I approached, the crowd fell silent, waiting.

"Thank you for coming here today," he began. "I know many of you have questions, the least of all being why I stand before you right now rejuvenated as I am. And that is as good a place to start as any."

He took a deep breath before continuing, "For years, you've been told that I am the only legitimate son of Mixcoatl, the former king of the city of Culhuacan, and many of you fought at my side to help me reclaim that throne after Ihuitimal murdered him. But I have to tell you today that that is not the truth. I have no blood relationship to Culhuacan's former king."

A confused murmur built in the crowd but fell silent when he raised his hand.

"And still others of you were told that though I wasn't Mixcoatl's blood son, I was instead the mortal son of the god Quetzalcoatl, placed by the god himself in the belly of a mortal woman so I could see the Feathered Serpent's reforms actualized here on earth. But again, this is not the truth. I am not the son of Quetzalcoatl."

"Then who are you?" someone shouted.

He looked at me, the anxiety plain in his eyes; it wasn't the supreme confidence he'd always shown me in the Divine Dream, but rather the very human look of doubt I'd sometimes see in Little Reed's eyes. I'd always seen Little Reed and Quetzalcoatl as separate beings, but now I realized they were just like me: different masks joined by their shared teotl, and that I'd always loved each of them equally, and I always would. I took his hand in a show of support.

He gave me a grateful smile then said, "The truth is…I *am* Quetzalcoatl himself. I bore myself into the mortal world as a human being so I could live among you and show you a new path of worship that would see an end to human sacrifice."

The people in the crowd looked at each other in confusion, and some in outrage.

"I know many of you will question this claim," Quetzalcoatl went on. "And no doubt believe me sacrilegious for making it, but I've lived a lie for the last thirty-five years, not just to all of you who put your faith in me as the god you chose to commit your lives to, or the people who put their faith in me as their king, but also to those who loved me as a friend—" He motioned to Mazatzin, who had a bewildered look on his face. Quetzalcoatl then turned to me. "And the one who loved me first as her god, and then her brother, and later as her husband. I deeply regret how my deception has hurt everyone around me, and, in the wake of what has transpired here over the last day, how I failed every last citizen of Tollan when they needed me most. I am so very sorry."

The tempo of conversation picked up, quickly growing to a dull roar. "How do we know you're not lying now?" someone shouted, and still another person asked, "Can you prove that you're truly who you claim?"

"Yes! Where's the proof? If you're truly the god, you can prove it!"

"Show us your divine form!"

He held his hands up for silence, and though the crowd didn't completely quiet, he was able to say, "I understand your reticence, but unfortunately I can't—"

The rise of angry shouting cut him off, and no amount of calling for quiet could convince them.

Mazatzin stepped up and shouted, "I've known this man almost my entire life, and I've served the god almost as long, and as one of the

Feathered Serpent's highest servants, I believe—" But the crowd only grew more insistent.

I leaned in to whisper to Quetzalcoatl, "Raise your hands to the sky."

He cast a doubtful look at me but then did as I said.

I reached into him with my tendrils of magic and pulled a strand of his wind magic out, letting it filter out around me into the air. In response, the breeze picked up and flowed through the crowd, whipping people's hair around their faces.

After all of my failed attempts at controlling the wind, I expected the same difficulties, but with Quetzalcoatl's wind magic came a distinct sense of genius born of countless years of experience. I suddenly could move a single particle of air at a time, or, if I wanted to, I could send them all rushing like water over the land, reducing everything to dust. The breadth of his knowledge and magic was staggering, and humbling.

Calming the thrill, I whispered, "Move your arms around," and when he did, I made the wind move in the same direction.

The people watched in awe, and many cried in joy as the wind caressed across their faces.

I could have played with the air currents for days, churning up the pollen and flower petals in intricate patterns, but I was only borrowing this wonderful magic, and I needed to return it home again. I reduced the pull on Quetzalcoatl's teotl until the wind disappeared, returning the air to stillness.

"He *is* the god!" someone shouted and still more cried their agreement. Many took to their knees in supplication.

"Thank you," Quetzalcoatl whispered with a hint of breathlessness.

I answered with a smile.

"Is the queen a god too?" one of the younger priestesses asked, clamoring to the front of the crowd.

I knew the time would come when I had to finally tell everyone the truth, but I hadn't yet given any thought to actually announcing it. I looked to Quetzalcoatl, and he gave me an encouraging smile of his own. I cleared my throat before telling the priestess, "I am the goddess Mayahuel."

Her face lit with pride and excitement, and a gasp of awe passed among the crowd. "We have two gods leading us!" she shouted. "We are truly a blessed people!"

Movement off to my left drew my attention away from the crowd.

A massive group of men armed with weapons and farming implements moved down the path from the sacred precinct, headed towards us. Matlacxochitl walked at the lead, surrounded by soldiers in padded armor and carrying macuahuitl swords. I tapped Quetzalcoatl's arm to get his attention.

Matlacxochitl stopped at a distance and stared us down. "You're looking remarkably better today, Lord Topiltzin."

The crowd of priests pressed closer to us, an anxious murmur passing through them as Quetzalcoatl stepped up. "And you're looking well as usual, Lord Matlacxochitl." His gaze wandered to the armed crowd behind him. "I'm sure this is merely an oversight, but only members of the priestly orders are allowed inside these gardens."

"Much has changed since this time yesterday."

"Indeed."

Matlacxochitl looked over our crowd of priests. "There are important matters that we must discuss, Topiltzin. About the future of Tollan."

"Very well." Quetzalcoatl motioned to the ruins of the priestly retreat. "Shall we speak over here?"

Matlacxochitl nodded, but when I moved to follow them, he stopped. "With all due respect, Lady Quetzalpetlatl, I've already dealt with you as much as I care to, and we all know how your negotiations ended for the city. I will speak with Topiltzin alone."

Quetzalcoatl narrowed his eyes. "She is Tollan's queen—"

"Then we have nothing to discuss. We can instead deal with this matter through military might."

I set a hand on Quetzalcoatl's shoulder. "It's all right. I will stay here with the people and make sure they are kept safe from treachery." I cast a challenging glare at Matlacxochitl.

Matlacxochitl sneered in answer.

"You're sure?" Quetzalcoatl whispered.

"Of course."

They walked off and I remained back with Mazatzin, watching the gathered army. Still more people entered the garden behind them, filling it back to the sacred precinct.

"Amoxtli and I gathered everyone we could find who was still loyal to the god or Topiltzin," Mazatzin whispered as we watched. "We are vastly out-manned."

"That may be, but we have the gods on our side," Amoxtli noted.

I turned to look at the families who had gathered to leave with us. "Where's Cuicatl?"

He sighed. "She's decided to remain behind. I believe her exact words were, 'I'm not leaving home yet again for the sake of any good-for-nothing gods.'"

I set my hand on his shoulder. "She is a woman now, so she will make her own choices."

He nodded, but still looked ready to cry. "I know she's not *my* daughter, but still…I feel like I failed her."

I wanted to say something to comfort him, but I knew all too well what he felt, and that no words could fix it. I'd failed Ehecacone too.

Quetzalcoatl and Matlacxochitl were talking peaceably, but Quetzalcoatl was also watching the gathering crowd. Their discussion went on for several more minutes before both men returned. Matlacxochitl went to his ranks while Quetzalcoatl took his place before our crowd. He looked pained as he stood there, perhaps thinking about what to say, but eventually he found his voice.

"I want to thank each and every one of you for your loyalty and support, particularly in this most trying of times. It was good people such as yourselves that moved me to make these reforms, which makes what I must say all the more painful. In the interests of the safety of her citizens, I am stepping down as Tollan's king."

A gasp travelled through the crowd, but a blustery cheer rose behind us.

"But you're the god!" a man yelled from the crowd before us. "You could easily crush anyone who opposes you!" Those behind us were being too loud to hear the declaration over their own cheers.

Quetzalcoatl shook his head. "There has been enough unnecessary bloodshed already, and the majority of Tollan's citizens are in favor of me stepping aside. I will respect the wishes of the majority, and I will leave."

"But what about the Queen?"

"I'm stepping down as well," I said.

"And what about us?" one of the priests asked.

Quetzalcoatl nodded. "The decision is yours alone. You may choose to stay, but know that the new king requires an oath of fealty from each and every citizen, and all priests will have to renounce their worship of the Feathered Serpent."

That garnered angry shouts, but when he raised his hands for silence, they immediately fell quiet.

"The other choice is to leave Tollan, either on your own, or you may come with me and Lady Mayahuel as we attempt to find a new land to settle. It is starting over with no civil support or allies—and we'll likely have many enemies to contend with—but we will be free to live as we wish, and every man and woman will have a voice."

A discontented murmur ran through the crowd as everyone looked at their neighbor.

"You needn't make a decision this moment. Take today to discuss it with your family, and in the morning, those who wish to join us can gather here."

◻

Quetzalcoatl, Mazatzin, and Amoxtli spent the rest of the afternoon building a pyre in the remains of the priestly retreat while Mitotia and I prepared Malinalli's body for the funeral. We spoke little to each other as we cleaned her up and wrapped her in the traditional paper bandages; the process reminded me of preparing Ehecacone for his burial, complete with the dull ache that wouldn't go away. I would never get to see her again; we'd never again discuss our day or listen to each other's troubles, and I'd never have the chance to thank her for her faith in me when I needed it most.

But I also knew in my heart that my own pain and loss was nothing compared to what Mitotia must be going through. And I was the cause of it. I had no idea how to bridge this new gap between us.

But as we sat waiting for the men to finish building the pyre, I knew I couldn't maintain the silence between us forever. "I'm so sorry for your loss, Mitotia." Though even then I couldn't speak louder than a whisper.

Mitotia gave me a wan smile, but said nothing.

"You should know...I knew her a very long time, and in all of those years, I never saw her happier than when she was with you. You were everything to her, and her sacrifice...it was more for you than anyone else."

Mitotia sniffled. "I keep thinking I should hate you, for bringing us all to this juncture, but...but I'm so proud of her, giving everything she had to save us all. It's a debt I can never repay." She squeezed her eyes shut against fresh tears. "Forgive me, My Lady, but I fear it will be a while before I'm able to reconcile my feelings on this."

"I'm struggling with it myself...and whether I can ever be worthy of such a precious gift, given the choices I've made."

She opened her eyes and took a deep breath, as if she'd just set down a heavy load. "The thing about the future is that there's always new choices to make, new opportunities to either repeat our mistakes, or commit to a new path."

¤

As the sun set, everyone gathered around the funeral pyre where Mazatzin and Quetzalcoatl had set up Malinalli's body for the ceremony. In accordance with custom, she sat upright, cross-legged and wrapped from head to foot in paper bandages, over which we'd dressed her in the robes and white heron-feathered headdress of the high priestess. Mitotia tied a little brown dog to the pyre—our offering for Xolotl.

Quetzalcoatl gave a stirring speech about faith and love and sacrifice, but it couldn't keep me from dwelling on what awaited Malinalli in the afterlife. Thanks to my not having a heaven for my sacrifices, she would wander the mists of Mictlan just as my father did. Such a travesty that she'd given so much and I couldn't repay that with paradise or even eternal rest.

Once Quetzalcoatl finished his speech, he called me forward. "Would you like to say the prayer?"

I nodded then took my place where he'd stood.

"Lord of the Final Road,
Hear my prayers and accept my sacrifice.
Lend your guidance to this woman
On the treacherous road ahead.
Calm her fear in crossing the Black River,
Shield her in the cavern of arrows,
Teach her the words to sooth the savage snakes,
Bandage her feet as she summits the bladed mountain,
And stand with her when she faces the eternal mists.
She made the ultimate sacrifice for the people she loved and served,
So show her your mercy."

I slit the little dog's throat and laid its body upon Malinalli's lap. "Goodbye, my friend." I gave her bandaged hand a final squeeze before stepping away to rejoin Quetzalcoatl, Mazatzin, and Mitotia at the clay brazier.

We lit pine-pitch torches then gathered at the four corners of the pyre, lighting one side at a time: first the east side, where the sun rose, giving birth to the new day, then to the north where the sun rose to the height of its life, then the west where it slowly died on the horizon, having lived all day long, and then finally the south, where the sun made its journey into the underworld. As with the sun, so went humans, except their journey lasted many, many years rather than a single day.

The pyre burned deep into the night, and only a handful of us remained awake to watch it. A makeshift camp had sprung up in the field outside the remains of the retreat, and judging from the number of tents, no one seemed to have decided to stay behind, and in fact, as the hours passed, a small scattering of new people arrived to join our group. It was heartening to see we hadn't lost the faith of all of the people of Tollan.

I spent hours staring into the flames, thinking first about Malinalli wandering the mists of Mictlan, but then about Ehecacone. I'd promised I would come back for him, but I'd failed. When Lord Death grew tired of waiting, would he make good on his threats to torture my son? What if he already knew I wasn't coming with Quetzalcoatl? Perhaps he'd already started taking his frustration out on Ehecacone.

Someone cleared their throat behind me, and I looked over my shoulder to see Quetzalcoatl standing there, head bowed. "May I sit with you for a while, Mayahuel?"

I moved aside to make room for him on the stone rubble I was using as a bench. Sitting this close to me, I could just make out the subtle glow of his aura, like dawn's soft light squeezing past a curtain's edge, and he smelled faintly of reptiles and feathers—that same smell I'd detected in the teoyoh when I'd taken him to the priestly retreat. My orange rabbits hopped closer to him, curious, their own glow illuminating the outlines of his spectral feathered serpents curled into tight coils as if they were sleeping.

Once he was settled, I said, "I must admit, it feels weird to hear you call me that, but then it also feels strange calling you Quetzalcoatl."

"It feels the same to me, but I suppose it will get easier for us with time."

I felt a twinge of resentment; I'd hoped he would ask if he could still call me Papalotl, so I could continue calling him Little Reed, but perhaps some things just couldn't be anymore. I nodded though, accepting it.

We sat in awkward silence a moment before he said, "I know I told everyone you were leaving with us, but if you'd rather be on your own...I understand."

"No, I want to come along...if that's all right."

"Of course it's all right. The people will be glad you're coming along."

I chuckled. "From what I've heard around camp today, everyone's leaving to follow you, not me, but...they find it weird—and unfair—that we won and yet we're the ones leaving."

"That's because we didn't really win."

I gaped at him. "But I defeated Smoking Mirror—not just beat him, but sent him to Mictlan. How can you say we have lost?"

"I misspoke; *we* didn't lose anything. *I* lost it for us, a long time ago. Back during the battle for Culhuacan."

Frowning, I said, "That doesn't make sense at all."

He shifted on the stone, as if he was about to confess something embarrassing. "You already know that I offered up my own mortal life to bring you back from the dead that day, but by doing so, I was also sacrificing the success of my plans to end human sacrifice."

A ball of guilt and anger formed in my stomach. "You sacrificed humanity's future…to save me?"

"It was a spur-of-the-moment decision that I didn't think through very well because I couldn't bear the thought of losing you forever…."

"But then why didn't it just end that day?"

"Because you made your sacrifice, which meant I wouldn't have to face the consequences of my thoughtlessness just yet. Instead, I would have to live on not knowing the precise moment Heaven would collect on my debt."

I stared at the bonfire. "I don't understand…if there was no hope for success in ending human sacrifice, why didn't you just give up? Why go through with building Tollan and passing all of those laws if it was all for naught?"

Quetzalcoatl shook his head. "It wasn't all for naught, Mayahuel. While I was lying abed recovering from my wounds from the battle, I realized the true consequence of my sacrifice, but I also realized I owed my friends and followers better than to just abandon them to the growing power of darkness and fear that Smoking Mirror would bring. I couldn't hand them the safe future I'd promised, but I could show them what the future could be, and grow hope and courage in their hearts so that some day they might stand up to their oppressors and accept nothing less than a future free of fear."

"That seems to have failed too though," I said, glum. "Most of Tollan's citizens have rejected us and our reforms."

"But look how many haven't." He motioned to the tents and cooking fires spread out over the field beyond the remains of the retreat. "These men and women carry on the hope of a better future, and so long as that continues in their children and their children's children, Smoking Mirror will not ever win completely."

"That is true, but…must they really leave? This is their city, built on the blood and sweat of the faithful. It should be Matlacxochitl and his lot that is marching out tomorrow."

Quetzalcoatl looked further into the gardens, beyond the field, to where the flag stone path led to the sacred precinct. Several patrols of Matlacxochitl's men were keeping watch there, making sure we didn't attempt to sneak back into the city proper. "If our numbers were reversed, that might be feasible, but we both know that our people would just be throwing their lives away."

I laughed. "Yes, our numbers are few, but that hardly matters. I could take the city on my own—"

"Yes, but do you truly want to just be the next Smoking Mirror?"

I snapped my mouth shut, my face growing hot with embarrassment. "Maybe some day I will learn to stop feeling so bloodthirsty."

He set his hand on mine. "Don't be down on yourself, Mayahuel. Your heart is in the right place, but the easy answer is often the wrong one, for it demands little effort from us."

The silence fell between us again as we both stared into the fire, but eventually I said, "Can I ask you some questions?"

"Of course."

"I understand why you forbade Citlallotoc from pursuing me—I would have driven him crazy with my love magic, just as I did to Black Otter and Red Flint—"

"You aren't to blame for what those two did," Quetzalcoatl said. "You didn't make them feel or think anything they weren't already capable of; you just made them show their true natures for everyone to see. That's how love magic works; it intensifies what is already there. Red Flint was already paranoid, and Black Otter was an obsessive personality."

"And a murderer," I muttered. When Quetzalcoatl cast me a puzzled look, I said, "He tried to murder both his father and his brother, and he succeeded in murdering our son, because he was jealous of our marriage."

Anguish descended upon his eyes and he turned to stare at the ground.

"You can understand then why I wouldn't want to visit such chances upon Citlallotoc," I said.

He shook his head. "Citlallotoc would have been unquestioningly loyal to you to his dying breath, for that was his nature, but that wasn't my concern. There's always deadly consequences for humans engaging in physical intimacy with the gods; in your case, you consume their life force, but in my case…I would impregnate anyone I was intimate with, and giving birth to a divine being is always fatal to a human."

"Is that why you refused to consummate your marriage to Anacoana?"

He nodded. "You saw first hand what happened to Chimalma when she gave birth to my mortal incarnation. I couldn't do that to yet another woman, not even to ensure an heir to Tollan." He stared at his hands as he said, "I didn't give any thought to what my request would do to Chimalma, and it never occurred to me that it might affect you so…. I think back on what kind of a god I was before all this, and I hardly even recognize myself. Being a human being, and an everyday part of others' lives as a friend, a leader, a brother, and a father…I realized just how selfish and thoughtless I was. I had no business calling myself the benefactor of humanity when I treated their lives as expendable as any of the other gods did. Knowing people like Citlallotoc, and Mazatzin, and Malinalli…and Nimilitzli…. The hardest thing I ever had to do in my life was to to ask Nimilitzli to take on the burden of fulfilling your sacrifice to make sure Red Flint won that ball game against Obsidian Eagle."

I gaped at him. "You asked her to sacrifice herself, for me?"

"I didn't have to; when I told her you were struggling to make a fitting sacrifice, she stepped up without hesitation, much like Malinalli did today. I've benefited greatly from such sacrifices throughout my existence but I've never actually sat at someone's side while they made that ultimate sacrifice, and I…." His voice broke, but eventually he went on, "I'm humbled by the selflessness the human heart is capable of."

I hadn't realized I was crying until I felt the tears on my cheeks. "I often think our kind is unworthy of such selfless devotion."

He nodded. "That doesn't mean we can't strive to earn it going forward." He sniffled a bit but then stood up. "I should really get some sleep." He then bade me goodnight and headed back to his tent set up in the rubble of what used to be our meditation room.

I watched him go, but just before he ducked inside, I called out to him, "You know why they're capable of such selflessness, don't you? It's because they came from Ehecatl's blood, and while Ehecatl had much darkness in him, he also had a great deal of light, and you're proof of that."

He smiled stiffly, as if he might cry, but he nodded then retreated into his tent.

CHAPTER THIRTY-FOUR

After Quetzalcoatl retired, I went back to staring at the fire, but soon movement by the far right side of the pyre drew me out of my thoughts. My stomach leaped when I noticed the tall, shaggy black dog watching me.

But my concerns that it was a wolf were quickly extinguished; the firelight didn't reflect upon it, and a faint dark green glow surrounded it. Spectral dogs bounded around it, dragging its tendrils of magic behind them.

The wolf-dog jogged over to me. When it stopped, I greeted it with wariness. "Xolotl."

He inclined his head. "Mayahuel."

"I see you've come to collect my friend."

He shook his head. "No, I came for her earlier today. I saw what she did for you; that's quite a selfless gift."

"Then why are you here?"

"Lord Death wishes to see you."

My stomach clenched. "I'm sure he does."

"He was quite surprised to find that you'd sent Smoking Mirror to him instead of Quetzalcoatl."

I smiled. "Well, he was Ehecatl too at one point, so I figured he was just as good as the Feathered Serpent for payment of our agreement."

Xolotl showed off his fangs as he smiled. "While that is true, I'm afraid that the master wasn't impressed. He's already raised Smoking Mirror from the dead."

"Then he's upset that I killed his friend?"

"They are not friends, and Lord Death doesn't raise anyone from the dead for free. Both Xochiquetzal and Mextli paid a formidable sum of magic for Smoking Mirror's return. He was, however, disturbed to learn that you have the Feathered Serpent in your possession, and yet have made no efforts to bring him to Mictlan."

I laughed. "Quetzalcoatl isn't *in my possession*, but yes, I have no intention of handing him over to Lord Death. Not even for my son."

"He'll be disappointed to hear that."

"I'm sure he will be."

Xolotl sat down, looking contemplative.

"Aren't you going to go tell your master that I'm reneging on our deal? I'm sure the two of you are looking forward to making my son's afterlife miserable."

"I have no desire to harm your son, Mayahuel—"

"And yet you abandoned him to walk the road himself."

"That wasn't my choice. You have no idea what is like to be a slave to another god; I have very little will of my own and must do things I despise because I am bound to Lord Death for eternity. I feel guilty for leaving Ehecacone at my house after accepting your sacrifice, but when my master said I must, I had no choice."

"Why would he do that?"

"To lure either you or the Feathered Serpent into walking the road with your son, of course. A living god that walks the road can die a mortal death if they do not reach Mictlan in time, and that's one of Lord Death's favorite bargaining chips to play against his enemies."

"So, if you'd already taken Ehecacone to Mictlan?"

"You could have just left at any time. By making you take the road, he could exact tolls and favors from you, not only on behalf of your son, but yourself as well. And if it had been Quetzalcoatl who had walked the road with your son...Lord Death could have held him indefinitely."

"Then it was a good thing it was me who went down there rather than him."

"Indeed. And Lord Death can't trap you down there now. You needn't fear that."

"That's not my fear; what I'm afraid of is telling him that I can't give him Quetzalcoatl, and he repays that by making me watch him raise my son from the dead so he can torture him. He's already threatened it."

Xolotl nodded. "That is absolutely what he intends to do, but there is one thing you should know. He's not aware of the nature of your magic."

I narrowed my eyes at him. "What do *you* know about the nature of my magic?"

"I see everything my nahuals see, and as we both know, a human died when you confronted Smoking Mirror. So yes, I know how your magic works. I haven't, however, told my master."

"Why not?"

"Because information is the most powerful currency. If Lord Death had told you that Quetzalcoatl had withheld knowledge of your divine nature out of necessity rather than malice, would you have made that deal with him?"

"Probably not," I admitted. "That's why he wouldn't let you talk to me that day in Mictlan, isn't it? Because you might tell me something he didn't want me knowing." When he nodded, I said, "But why wouldn't you tell him about what you saw this morning?"

Xolotl looked around but then whispered, "Because Quetzalcoatl is the only god who has ever been kind to me. All of the others have always treated me worse than dirt, and my master is the worst of them. But the Feathered Serpent treats me like a thinking, feeling being, and I will do anything to help him. My being Lord Death's servant sometimes makes that difficult, but I do what I can."

"But what does that have to do with me?"

"Because the Feathered Serpent loves you, and he loves his son too, so I will help both of you when I can. That's why I helped him convince Lord Death to resurrect you, and why I was going to tell you who you really were when you died in Culhuacan."

Memories of that day washed over me. He had in fact started to tell me something.... "But I thought no one could tell me the truth—"

"When you were still alive, yes," Xolotl corrected me. "But once you were dead, the rule no longer applied. And because you had not yet crossed through the gate into the underworld, you could still reclaim your godhood; like I said, information is powerful. Unfortunately, Quetzalcoatl made his sacrifice before I could actually tell you, meaning the deal came back into force."

My mind reeled. "But...but what if Lord Death found out you told me?"

He shrugged. "He would have punished me severely. But it's hardly fair that you should face oblivion because my master hates the Feathered Serpent. Besides, he'd never actually kill me; he needs me to be his eyes here on earth."

I stared at him, guilt welling up inside me. "I'm so sorry, Xolotl, for treating you so badly. I owe you better than that."

"I would hardly consider your treatment bad, Mayahuel. If anything, appearances justified your suspicion, and I'm sorry I couldn't be more forthright with you the last time we spoke."

"I still feel horrible. Please accept my apologies."

"Very well. I accept."

I stared into the burning pyre. "So you really didn't tell Lord Death about my being able to pull magic out of other gods?"

Xolotl nodded. "If he did know, he wouldn't have sent me to bring you to Mictlan to speak with him. He would quietly go about his plans and hope you didn't think to come see him on your own."

"But surely Smoking Mirror or Mextli told him?"

"Smoking Mirror would never admit a weakness that someone might use to exploit him, and Mextli is loyal to him. And as for Xochiquetzal, she's far too desperate to gain Smoking Mirror's affections to dare say anything he might disapprove of."

"But surely Lord Death knows I'm powerful enough to have killed Smoking Mirror, and so will be on the lookout for treachery?"

Xolotl chuckled. "You do not understand Lord Death very well, Mayahuel. The rules of normal gods do not apply to death gods; he cannot be killed by anyone or anything, so he doesn't fear things the rest of us do. What concerns him is being made a fool of in the eyes of the other gods, hence his loathing of Quetzalcoatl. But he doesn't worry about you; to him, you're a minor goddess whom he fooled into agreeing to deliver the god she loves to him. It doesn't even bother him that you didn't fulfill your end of the bargain, for he will take joy in your pain when he exercises his cruel power over those dearest to you. He cannot even fathom that you can use his own magic against him."

"Quetzalcoatl is always saying everyone underestimates me," I said. I doubted Smoking Mirror would ever make that mistake again. *And if I succeed in getting Ehecacone back, Lord Death won't either, so I had better make sure I do this right.*

◻

I thought to tell Quetzalcoatl that I was leaving for Mictlan with Xolotl, but decided against it; he might try to talk me out of it, but I had to do this. Ehecacone couldn't be left to suffer down there.

I never thought I'd ever look forward to returning to the cold mistiness of Mictlan, but when Xolotl and I materialized at the doors to Lord Death's palace, I was brimming with excitement.

Xolotl changed into his limping human form. "There are a few things you should be aware of before facing the master," he whispered. "Lord Death's magic is some of the most powerful there is, but because of that power, he's incapable of leaving the underworld. That means that so long as you have any of his magic inside you, you can't leave either. You must get rid of all of it if you're to leave."

"All right." I then followed him inside.

He loped down the long hallway of articulated bones, to the curtain of brown owl feathers. He gave me a final pointed look before pulling the curtain aside for me. I thanked him with a nod then stepped into the great hall.

Lord Death sat upon his throne of jade bones, Ehecacone sitting upon his lap, seemingly asleep. He watched me as I approached the dais, a pleased smile on his skeletal face. His magic glowed light blue, like his ghostlit eyes, but the tendrils formed claws and grinning skulls.

Once Xolotl announced me, Lord Death said, "So wonderful to see you again, Mayahuel. I'd started wondering if I ever would."

"It took a bit longer than I thought it would," I said.

"Then you've brought me a gift?"

"I indeed have."

He leaned forward to look around me. "Funny, but I don't see Quetzalcoatl with you."

"My gift is your chance to renegotiate our deal."

He stared at me for a bewildered moment before bursting into screechy laughter. "My dear little thorny one, you forget to whom you're speaking!"

"I'm well aware, and that's why I'm giving you this opportunity. I know you're a god with an eye for a good bargain, so I'm making you an even better offer."

He laughed louder, clutching his sides. "I fear you've scrambled something in your head. But I confess curiosity: what is this better deal?"

"A healthy portion of any sacrifice I receive—say a full half—as tribute from this day forward. In return, you give me back my son."

He narrowed his ghost light eyes at me. "Now you just insult. No one sacrifices anything to you."

"Not true. I already have a small collection of restless souls wandering through the mists on the plain, and while it's true that not many sacrifice to me now, the power of my sacrifices is more than a hundred of Smoking Mirror's or Mextli's. You're getting an excellent deal."

"And you're asking for your son to suffer for your insolence." He squeezed Ehecacone's arm with his bony fingers.

My temper flared, but I kept my voice even as I asked, "Then you're turning down my generous offer?"

Lord Death bared his skeletal teeth. "I spit at your pathetic offer."

"Very well then." I crested the step up onto the dais and reached for Ehecacone.

"Need I remind you that you're being foolhardy?" Lord Death asked.

In answer, I set my rabbits loose on his wispy claws and skulls and yanked the magic out of him. In the brief moment he sat stock still in bewilderment as he tried to figure out what was happening to him, I snatched my son off his lap and cradled him in my arms. When Lord Death launched to his feet to stop me, I knocked him back into his throne with a blast of his own magic. He stared at me agape. "How—?"

In answer, I let his death-god magic flow into Ehecacone, sparking awake my son's own divinity. My boy's teotl—rich chocolate in color and smelling like fresh octli—burst to life and his eyes snapped open. He blinked a few times before focusing on me. The look in his eyes reminded me of the first time he had recognized me when he was an infant, and I thought my heart might break from sheer joy. "Mother!" he cried and wrapped his arms around my neck. I hugged him back, tears in my eyes.

"How in Mictlan is this even possible?" Lord Death muttered, an expression of utter befuddlement on his skeletal face.

I started backing towards the doorway. "I'm sorry, but I can't let you use my son to harm Quetzalcoatl. I meant it when I said that I would share my sacrifices with you, but now you've forced my hand, so I get my son and you get nothing."

Lord Death sprang to his feet again and fired a blast of magic at me, his teeth gritted, but I swiped it aside. His ghost lights grew brighter with surprise, then glowing blue wisps started streaming in through the obsidian window overlooking the Black Lake, coming from the misty plain where the heavenless sacrifices wandered. He was pulling extra magic from them. It would do him little good though; I could match him no matter what, but I didn't like the idea of Ehecacone possibly getting in the way of a battle.

When I reached the doorway, I set my son down and pushed him behind me. I set my hand on his, but didn't take my eyes off of Lord Death. "Can you feel my magic, darling?"

"I can," he whispered.

"Feel what I'm doing with it?"

"Yes."

"Do the same thing, but think about becoming something else—something fast. An animal of some kind."

Ehecacone turned into a very large brown rabbit. He sat upon his haunches, looking at his furry front paws with wonder.

"Now, follow the hall to the front door, and go outside. Wait for me there."

"But Mother—"

"I won't be long. I promise."

After another hesitation, he dashed off down the hall, his claws clicking on the obsidian floor.

"You're wasting your time, fool." Lord Death's ghostlit eyes glowed painfully bright. "You've cheated the wrong god." He threw his full load of magic at me.

I braced myself, unsure exactly what to expect, but I really hoped Xolotl was right about death-god magic.

The blast hit me, and I immediately knew it was intended to kill. I felt no pain though, no stripping of my own magic. My hair blew away from my face, but otherwise I remained unaffected. Lord Death gaped at me, disbelieving.

"Don't you know you can't kill a death god?" I asked.

"You're no death god!"

"No, but I've got your death-god magic, and I'm not above using it." And just to demonstrate, I swiped my hand across the room, letting loose a wave of magic that penetrated the palace walls and spread over Mictlan and out onto the misty plain beyond. Suddenly, the constant buzz that had once been a staple of the atmosphere ceased.

Lord Death's eyes visibly dimmed and he stumbled back until he fell onto his throne. "What have you done?" he whispered.

"I gave all those trapped on the plain of Mictlan their eternal rest," I answered with a smile. "Surely you don't mind? After all, you complained bitterly about how annoying their constant buzzing was, but now you don't have to listen to them anymore."

Lord Death clenched his bone-fingers in fury. "You will regret this treachery, Mayahuel."

"Perhaps, but not today." I too transformed into a rabbit and dashed off after Ehecacone. Behind me, Lord Death shouted at Xolotl to bring me back immediately.

I burst through the front doors of the palace to find my son crouched among the bone-dry reeds, watching the doorway with anxious eyes. He bounded out to meet me.

"This way!" I called, not slowing down. He leaped after me, catching up easily. Hearing the door creak open behind us, I chanced a glance over my shoulder.

Xolotl bolted out into the palace's courtyard in his wolf form, and he took off after us at full speed.

"Faster, my darling!" As we came down the road, heading back towards the plain of Mictlan, I said, "Do you see that doorway ahead? The one in the cavern wall to our left?"

"Yes!" Ehecacone panted as we ran.

"Go there, and get out to the other side. And whatever you do, don't wait for me. Climb the stairs and get out of the underworld!"

"You're coming with me, aren't you?"

"I will, but I want to make sure you make it first. Understood?"

"I guess."

"Now go!"

He took off even faster, turning up clouds of grey dust under his broad feet. I, however, slid to a stop and turned to face Xolotl as he bore down on me.

I'm sorry, Xolotl. I know you're only doing what your master ordered you to, but I've come too far to let him win.

Half a breath before he ran into me, I turned into a large wolf-dog too, so while the blow took me over, my sheer size was enough to knock him over. We tumbled across the dusty ground, our legs tangled, and after slashing our fangs at each other, we separated, both of us limping.

Except his wounds looked worse. I hadn't bitten him very much, but he was gushing golden dust and strange iridescent insects from numerous wounds. He looked down at the bugs then lapped them up with his lolling tongue, and his wounds healed. "You're not fully drained yet," he whispered as he moved towards me again, hackles raised and fangs bared. "You won't be able to leave the underworld until you rid yourself of every last drop of his magic."

I backed away, changing back into my human form. "I don't want to hurt you, Xolotl."

"We all do what we must." A growl rose in his throat. "There is no other way."

I glanced over my shoulder to see Ehecacone waiting for me on the other side of the door way, an anxious expression on his face.

"It's now, or you stay in Mictlan forever, Mayahuel." Xolotl lunged at me.

I didn't think; I just blasted everything I had left of Lord Death's magic at him. Hopefully it would shield me from his fangs.

The blast knocked him backwards and he rolled a few times before coming to a stop. Though even then, I noticed his fur moving like boiling water. He screamed as his skin split open and insects began pouring out.

"Dear gods, Xolotl!" I hurried to him. My impulse was to set a soothing hand on him, but the streaming bugs left none of his fur exposed. Only his wide, panicked eye was visible. "Oh no! What have I done to you?"

"Go," he croaked. "The master is coming."

I looked up to see Lord Death gliding down the path from the palace. He hadn't seen us yet, but he would soon if I didn't run. "I'm so sorry, Xolotl," I whispered then turned and ran. I changed back into a rabbit midstride and bounded through the doorway to the stairs out of the underworld. I slid to a stop as Ehecacone bounced up and down in front of me in excitement.

"I almost thought you weren't going to make it, Mother! I was sure he was going to get you!"

I gazed back at Xolotl. Lord Death now knelt next to his body, staring at the mess with disgust. He cast me a hot glare. I had little doubt at that moment that he hated me just as much as he hated Quetzalcoatl. "I'm not proud of what I did, but we should always remember Xolotl in our prayers, for I doubt either of us would be leaving right now if not for him." I nudged Ehecacone's bottom to get him moving and we headed up the stairs.

¤

I expected the stairs to open onto the same cenote in the desert where Xolotl had brought me out before, but to my surprise, we emerged into a cave dimly lit by a single kettle brazier. I recognized the stacks of octli jars near the ladder leading up; we were in the vision cavern below the priestly gardens in Tollan, where we stored all of the octli, and initiates made their first foray into the Divine Dream before becoming priests and priestesses. We would be back at the temporary camp in a matter of minutes.

"Change back into your human form," I told Ehecacone as I did the same myself. He managed it after a few failed tries, but he still wore his tatty rabbit costume, complete with the holes and rips he'd gained during our journey into Mictlan. He started climbing up the ladder, but I grabbed his arm. "We need to talk about a few things first."

"All right." He climbed atop the jars of octli and sat.

I took his hands in mine. "Do you remember the talk we had on the road, about Quetzalcoatl?"

He furrowed his eyebrows deep. "Oh, I remember."

I nodded. "I said a lot of things about him...things that I thought were true at the time, but I've since discovered are false. I was so very wrong about him, Ehecacone, and I made a mistake in holding a grudge against him."

"Then he didn't kill you long ago?"

"The truth is complicated, but now that I know what really happened, I don't hold him responsible. And I found out that since my first death, he had been working hard and making sacrifices to bring me back, and I'm so very grateful for that."

Ehecacone smiled. "So am I."

"I want you to have a good relationship with your father, so please, don't hold anything I said against him. Get to know him and form your own opinion about what kind of god he is."

Perking up, Ehecacone asked, "Then he's here and I can actually talk to him?"

I nodded. "Remember the other conversation we had, when you asked if the king was Quetzalcoatl?"

"He is, isn't he?" He jumped down off the jars. "I just knew it!"

"You did indeed, my darling," I said with a smile.

"Can we go see him now?" He hooted in excitement when I nodded.

"But one last thing before we go, and this is very important. No using your magic around other people."

He frowned. "But why not?"

"Because you're new to it, and it's very easy to hurt people when we don't know what we're doing. I will teach you how to properly use your magic, but until then, pretend you're still a human boy, all right?"

Once Ehecacone agreed, we both headed up the ladder and came out through a trap door in the floor of the initiation building. He skipped and ran the entire way to the camp, and it made my heart swell to see him so happy.

A few people who had known Ehecacone when he was still alive stared at him agape when we came into camp, but he hurried through the crowd, calling, "Father! Where are you? Father?"

Quetzalcoatl stepped out of his tent, a disbelieving look on his face, but his eyes widened when he saw Ehecacone running towards him. "Ehecacone?" he gasped but then scooped his son up into his arms, hugging him tight. Tears clogged his voice as he whispered, "But how can this be?"

"Mother rescued me!" When he looked at his father, he furrowed his brow, cross. "What happened to your hair? Where's all the silver?"

"I've been rejuvenated," Quetzalcoatl said with a smile. An edge of worry tainted it though when I came to stand next to them. "You really went to the underworld again?"

I nodded and Ehecacone piped up, "You should have been there! She was so brave! She brought me back to life, then showed me how to change into a rabbit, and Xolotl came after us, but then she changed into a giant wolf, just like him, and they fought, but then she threw magic at him and all these bugs came scurrying out from under his skin!" He paused to take a gasping breath. "I couldn't believe it!"

Quetzalcoatl raised an eyebrow at me. "You took Lord Death's magic?"

"He wanted something I wasn't willing to give him, and was going to hurt our son because of it, so I did the only thing I could. Are you disappointed in me?"

"Hardly. You could have told me what you were going to do though."

"I didn't want you worrying about me. We have a lot of marching to do today."

He nodded. "It would have kept me up all night." I wasn't sure what to make of the cross look on his face, though he let it slip away once he returned his attention to Ehecacone and listened to our son regale him in detail with the tale of our journey into Mictlan.

CHAPTER THIRTY-FIVE

We left Tollan without incident. Matlacxochitl's men lined the streets with weapons ready, in case anything went amiss, but our long caravan trudged out of the city without raising a fuss. As we came to the hillside where I'd first laid eyes upon the land where the Feathered Serpent's temple would be built, I stopped to look back, wondering if I'd ever see it again. The city looked much the same as I always remembered it, except perhaps the lack of greenness, but in my heart, it had changed.

Just like all the other dear things in my life.

But other changes were for the good. Every day, Ehecacone and I wandered away from the rest of the group for a few hours, and I would teach him how to use his magic and about the responsibilities that came with being a god. He was an eager learner, and I was always the proud teacher, especially as the weeks passed and his abilities grew by leaps and bounds.

Not that everything between us was perfect; as when he was still human, small things would trigger his darker side, but now that he wasn't flesh and blood anymore, the drunkenness didn't make him fall asleep. Instead he'd rant and rave at me for my mistakes or past choices then storm away into the forest. I always followed at a distance, to make sure he didn't hurt himself, or anyone else, but mostly he sat alone and wept. Some wounds would take time and patience to heal, and I intended to give him both.

Quetzalcoatl and I spoke little that first month after we left Tollan. When we did, it was about Ehecacone or logistics of the march or setting up camp. We each kept our own tents, though I used mine for escaping into the Divine Dream. Often I wished he would use the Teonanacatl to join me in there, but he never did, and I grew increasingly anxious that despite our cordial relationship, we were no longer friends as we'd once been.

My other friendships were going strong though. Mazatzin was always there with a smile and an ear, should I need it, and even Mitotia and I had grown closer since Malinalli's death. We never talked about her, nor about the conversation we'd shared before the funeral, so it caught me off guard when she asked me to bless her as my very own high priestess.

"I want to serve love, in all its varied and wondrous forms, and how better can I do that than devote my life to the goddess who gave it to us to begin with?"

Yet it felt so wrong that her personal pain was my source of power. Even a month after that fateful day in Tollan, my new powers had yet to wane as I thought they would with time. That troubling feeling only grew when Ehecacone and I found her sitting alone in the woods late one night, knelt over a burnt bone and muttering prayers of thanks not only to me, but Malinalli as well. When Ehecacone asked her about it the next morning, she admitted to taking the bone from the funeral pyre after the fire went out, so she'd have something of Malinalli to keep with her always.

"It's tradition among my people, to keep a bone of our loved ones who die in service to the gods, so we never forget the sacrifice they made for us. And so their memory lives on."

Oh how much I wished I had one too, not just from Malinalli, but my father, my mother, and from Nimilitzli. All I had now was memories, and often it felt that those weren't enough.

ロ

"When are you going to take me to Omeyocan, Mother?" Ehecacone asked when we came back to camp after a night away in the woods practicing our shapeshifting skills. He was still in his giant rabbit form, and I suspected that someday soon he would leave his human one behind completely and stay a rabbit permanently. I tried not to feel a loss at the thought, for I wanted him to choose his own self image as much as I chose mine, but I couldn't help it.

In truth I hadn't mentioned Omeyocan to him at all because I was a little anxious about going back myself. It was difficult to say how my actions in Tollan were playing among the gods who'd remained uninvolved, and a part of me worried that I might put Ehecacone in danger by taking him there.

But if I could kill another god with such little effort, I doubted anyone would dare try anything—especially Smoking Mirror or Mextli. "I suppose there's no good reason not to take you there."

"Can we go now then? Yesterday, Father told me about his house and I really want to see it."

I glanced up at the puffy clouds drifting serenely overhead in the growing dawn. "All right. I should probably check in on my own house while we're there."

"You have a house too?" When I nodded, he asked, "Can I see it too?"

"Of course. Now change back into your human form, so we can go."

"Why?"

"Because I need to hold your hand during this first trip, so you don't fall."

Ehecacone morphed into his human form—a lanky boy of thirteen who looked eerily like Night Wind had the last time I'd seen him, before Smoking Mirror's magic ate his vitality away. I wondered if he knew he'd chosen such a self-image. Even though the resemblance sent a shiver of hostility through me, I wouldn't lecture him about it. He would choose his form and I would accept it no matter what. I took his hand in mine and together we jumped into the teoyoh.

We landed at the crossroads, at the foot of the steps leading up the mountain to Quetzalcoatl's house. Ehecacone stared up into the swirling clouds with an awestruck gasp then pulled me along up the winding staircase. When we reached the top, he stood staring, his mouth hanging open as he gawked at the round building.

But disappointment replaced his awe when we walked inside. "It's empty?" he asked, looking around. Nothing had changed since the last time I'd been there. "But...he said there was a great city, and in the middle was a grand garden bigger than any found on earth. He told me he fashioned Tollan itself from it."

"He said that?" I too stared at the empty room, puzzled.

"You don't think he lied to me, do you?" Ehecacone asked with a pang of hurt.

"Your father doesn't lie. You'll just have to ask him about it when we go back."

Ehecacone's shoulders sagged. "I was so looking forward to seeing it."

I gave his hand a gentle squeeze. "I'm sure you will, someday."

We went to the window and looked out over Omeyocan, and that seemed to alleviate his disappointment. "Wow! You can see everything from up here!"

"Indeed."

"Where's your house, Mother?"

I pointed at the temple precinct below. "That's it right there."

His eyes widened. "Yours is so much more interesting! Can we go down and look at it?"

"Of course we can—" But I paused when I noticed someone sitting on the stone ring of the cistern. It was too far away to make out who it was, but I could tell the person was female. Could it be Xochiquetzal? I hadn't thought to set up any kind of magic barrier to keep the other gods out the last time I'd been here, but maybe it would be a good idea to do so, to make sure my enemies weren't snooping around my house.

Though I cringed at the thought of calling my only daughter my enemy. She had chosen Smoking Mirror over me and Quetzalcoatl, but it seemed unnecessarily harsh to ban her from my house. Still, who knew what poison Smoking Mirror was whispering in her ear these days?

I didn't tell Ehecacone any of this as we walked down the stone stairs, back to the crossroads, but I hesitated when we reached the tall, broad staircase that led up the hill to the sacred precinct.

"What's wrong, Mother?" Ehecacone asked.

I took a deep breath then said, "Someone is in my house, and I don't know who it is."

He swallowed, a worried look on his face. "There is?"

I nodded. "I saw her, from the window up there in your father's house."

"Do you think she'll try to hurt us?"

"I will protect you, so you needn't worry. I just want you to do one thing for me, all right?"

"Anything."

"Don't let go of my hand, no matter what. I don't want you to fall. Understand?"

He nodded then added his other hand to his grip of mine.

We walked cautiously up the stairs and emerged onto the precinct. With the stairs emptying near my replica of Xochicalco's calmecac, the cistern was in plain view now.

I stopped short, my heart skipping. It wasn't Xochiquetzal sitting on the stone ring.

It was Malinalli.

My feet carried me forward at a jog, but when she looked up at me, I stopped short. I waited to see recognition in her eyes, but she looked right through me as if I weren't there at all.

"Are you all right, Mother?" Ehecacone asked when I said nothing.

I nodded slowly, but to Malinalli, I said, "Hello."

She sighed then returned her attention to the cistern, staring into the water.

"Who are you talking to?" Ehecacone asked, puzzled.

"Malinalli." I gestured to her with my free hand. "Can't you see her?"

He looked right at Malinalli but shook his head. "I don't see anyone."

How could he not see her? She was just as close to him as she was to me.

A familiar voice spoke up behind me, "Others can't see into your heaven, Mayahuel." I turned to see Cihuacoatl shuffling towards us from the stairs.

Ehecacone brightened upon seeing her. "I can see *her* though, Mother."

Cihuacoatl chuckled and came to stand next to us. "Of course you can see me, Son of the Wind. We're practically family, you and I. If I hadn't taught your father the secrets of creation, he never would have taught them to your mother, and you would have never been born."

"Does that make you my grandmother?" he asked, a hint of hope in his voice.

She laughed louder. "I am everyone's grandmother, so yes."

I looked at Malinalli again, confused. "But...I don't have a heaven for my sacrifices, and that's why they were collecting in Mictlan. I was told I would need a great deal more sacrifices than I have."

"Or just one very meaningful one."

"You mean...her sacrifice...she gave me a heaven?"

Cihuacoatl nodded. "Such a powerful one; we all felt it when it happened. It's not every day that a new heaven forms unexpectedly."

Was there any end to the gifts Malinalli's friendship and love could grant me? I stifled a sob with the back of my hand as I watched her sit there gazing forlornly into the water. "So my sacrifices will come here for now on?" When Cihuacoatl nodded, I looked around expectantly. "But where are the others? The ones Lord Death was keeping in Mictlan?"

"From what Xolotl tells me, you granted them their eternal rest, along with all the other sacrifices Lord Death was holding. They've disappeared into the ether, never to be seen again. You've made it necessary for both Smoking Mirror and Mextli to start over from scratch."

I raised an eyebrow. I hadn't thought about that possibility at all. "They're probably very upset with me now, aren't they?"

"I wouldn't go seeking them to find out if I were you," Cihuacoatl said with a grin.

I turned to Malinalli again, a hollowness growing in my chest. "Why can't she see me though?"

"She's dead, and you are not. When others join your heaven, she will be able to see them. That's how it works."

"So she'll be alone here until more people offer their lives to me...or until people start sacrificing people to me?" When Cihuacoatl nodded, I said, "But I don't want lives. And...she doesn't look happy."

"Humans have always needed the company of others. They inherited that trait from their father."

Ehecacone tilted his head, thoughtful. "We were taught in calmecac that Quetzalcoatl is the father of mankind. Is that what you mean?"

She nodded, a patient smile on her face. "He created them from his blood, so they are his children, just as much as you are."

"So I have countless brothers and sisters!"

I wanted to smile at Ehecacone's newfound excitement, but I couldn't turn my mind away from Malinalli's situation. We'd always been taught as humans that sacrificing ourselves led to paradise, but now that I saw the truth...this was hardly it. I bit my lip.

"You have a question, my dear?" Cihuacoatl asked me.

I sighed, trying to find the right words. "This just...it's not fair. She gave everything she had—for me, for Quetzalcoatl, for the people of Tollan—and her reward is to spend years—maybe even bundles of years—alone here with no one to talk to? I know what that's like, and I wouldn't wish that on anyone. Least of all my best friend."

Cihuacoatl's face turned sober. "Well, you could always give her eternal rest, or you could turn her immortal."

"I don't have the power to turn humans into immortals."

"Of course you do. You're a creator goddess, the same as me, the same as Ehecatl."

"But Mextli said—"

"Mextli knows nothing about creation. He knows only how to sow war."

"But what about Smoking Mirror? He turned Coatlicue immortal."

"Because he too is a creator god, of course. He's the destructive element of the cycle. Creation often involves destroying the old to make way for the new."

I cast my gaze back to Malinalli again, indecisive.

"You should know though that doing anything other than just leaving her be has consequences for you. You will no longer be able to draw magic from the sacrifice she made, and while your heaven will remain regardless, for you it will be as if she didn't make the sacrifice at all. You're quite powerful now thanks to her, so keep that in mind."

"I don't really care about the power. She gave it to me to do one specific thing, and I did it, so it's only right to let it go now, for her."

Cihuacoatl bowed her head. "Do whatever you think best. Just be sure to hold onto her if you do; there's no ruder introduction to one's new divinity than to find yourself falling from Heaven." She patted Ehecacone on the head with a smile then she turned and headed back towards the stairs, walking leisurely.

Ehecacone watched her too, smiling, but then he turned to me. "So what are you going to do, Mother?"

"The only right thing to do," I said.

Together we walked over to Malinalli and I took hold of her arm. She looked around, confused—and a bit frightened. My magic flexed and pulsed, and with each wave, my power waned. She tried to pull away from me, but I held her firmly, making sure she didn't break free and fall through the clouds beneath us.

After what felt like an eternity, the pulsing finally ceased. And Malinalli looked up at me again. This time she saw me. "Quetzalpetlatl?"

I smiled, my insides aching with joy.

She looked at Ehecacone standing next to me, and furrowed her brow.

"Night Wind?"

Ehecacone screwed his face into a frown. "I'm not him!" He looked to me. "I don't look like him, do I?"

"Maybe a little, dear," I said.

He gasped, but then changed his features a bit, so he looked more like Little Reed had at that age. "How's this?"

I smiled. "Whatever makes you happy, my love."

"Ehecacone?" Malinalli asked with a gasp. "You're alive?"

He nodded. "And so are you!"

She looked to me, struggling for words.

I squeezed her hand. "Let's go."

"Where?"

"Home."

Chapter Thirty-Six

When we came out of the teoyoh, we were in my tent, which someone had set up in my absence. Ehecacone rushed outside ahead of me, letting in the smell of salty air and a streak of bright sunlight. The cries of strange birds filled the air, as well as the crashing of waves. Ehecacone shouted a greeting to someone and told them I was inside, but his voice quickly faded away.

A moment later, Mitotia parted the tent flap and stepped inside, holding a cup of blood for me. "My morning offering for—" But she froze when she saw Malinalli standing next to me.

Malinalli was still holding my hand from the journey, but when I nodded to her encouragingly, she finally let me go and rushed to Mitotia, practically knocking the cup from her hand when she embraced her. "My love," Malinalli whispered, burying her face in Mitotia's hair.

Mitotia gripped her tight. "But...but how?"

"One sacrifice begets another." When Malinalli looked at back at me, I said, "I realize this will be difficult to reconcile, but I promise to be there for you, to help you cope with it. You're immortal now."

Her eyes bulged. "I am?"

I nodded. "Knowing your true nature is the important part, and as for the rest...we'll figure it out as we go along."

Malinalli looked about ready to faint but she held onto Mitotia tighter. "But why?"

"To thank you for your faith in me, when I needed it most. Every one of us owes you a deep debt of gratitude, and I hope this makes a start at paying back my portion of it."

She wiped tears from her eyes. "Then everything turned out all right?"

"We had to leave Tollan, but we're all doing well," I assured her.

"And Quetzalcoatl?"

"He's alive and well, and he's leading us into the future."

"As is My Lady," Mitotia added, smiling through joyful tears. "They're doing it together, as they've always done."

It was time to find out if that was even possible anymore.

◻

I left Mitotia and Malinalli in my tent to talk and went to find Quetzalcoatl. The salty breeze was warm and many of the men were out in the surf with nets, bringing in dinner. As I walked along the sand, searching, Ehecacone appeared next to me.

"You shouldn't be using the teoyoh unless absolutely necessary, dear," I warned him. "The blood offering supply is limited." We had yet to figure out his primary means of gathering magic, and I'd been giving him all of my blood offerings, since I hadn't needed them when I had Malinalli's sacrifice to live on, but having given that up, I would have to go back to my old feeding habits; a thought I didn't relish, but for Malinalli, I would make do.

"Sorry," he murmured. "It's just so much easier than walking."

"I know. Have you seen your father yet?"

"He's out fishing with the men."

I scoured the line as we walked until I spotted Quetzalcoatl. He wore only a white loincloth, and I marveled at how much bigger his muscles had become in the last month. Sweat shone on his dark brown skin, but he smiled and laughed with the other men. The sight of him made my heart quicken.

Ehecacone and I sat in the sand and I watched Quetzalcoatl for a long time while Ehecacone built palaces and temples in the hot sand. Eventually boring of the game, he knocked down everything then sat next to me again. "Mother?"

"Yes."

"Why doesn't Father have magic, like us?"

"He does, but he can't use it anymore."

"Why not?"

I sighed. "Because in my ignorance and shortsightedness, I let Smoking Mirror trick me into trapping him inside a mortal body."

Ehecacone gasped. "Can he die forever now?"

"No, he's still immortal."

"Why would you say it's your fault?"

I sighed. "I'm the reason your father is trapped in his human body. In my ignorance, I bound him to flesh, and I don't know if it's possible to ever reverse that."

"Oh." He sighed too, but wiggled his nose like a rabbit. "I'm sure he still loves you, Mother."

"I'm hoping he does."

"Maybe you should ask him about it."

"I'm going to, as soon as he's done fishing."

"Good!" Ehecacone took hold of my hand and smiled.

After a while, the men dragged their nets in and Quetzalcoatl came ashore. When he saw us and waved, Ehecacone waved back. When he reached us, he ruffled our son's tassel of black hair. "You wouldn't believe all of the fish we caught!"

"I'm glad I don't eat anymore, because I always hated fish," Ehecacone said, and Quetzalcoatl laughed.

His smile became formal when he turned to me. "You two were gone for quite a while."

"We were?" I asked, puzzled.

"About a week."

My face heated with guilt. "I'm sorry. I didn't know we were gone that long."

"Mother took me to Omeyocan," Ehecacone added.

Quetzalcoatl raised an eyebrow. "Oh you did?"

"I'm sorry," I said. "If I'd known we'd be gone that long, I would have told you where we were going."

"I got to see the inside of your house, Father," Ehecacone went on. "It looked nothing like how you described it."

Quetzalcoatl chuckled. "It does look very different to me than to anyone else."

"And I got to see Mother's house too. It looks like a sacred precinct."

"I fashioned it after Xochicalco," I said.

With a smile, Quetzalcoatl said, "I'd very much like to see it someday."

Guilt—for him being incapable of going there now, or possibly ever again—halted my tongue, but Ehecacone was more than willing to fill the silence. "And Mother has a heaven of her own, and she brought Malinalli back from the dead!"

Quetzalcoatl blinked at me. "You did?"

I shrugged. "I couldn't just leave her there. The place was empty, and since I don't approve of human sacrifice in my worship, it's my intention that it will remain so for a very long time to come. She gave all of us so much…it seemed cruel to condemn her to an eternity alone. I wouldn't even have a heaven if not for her." Embarrassment lit my cheeks as I asked, "Should I have left her there?"

"That's hardly my call," he said. "I'm sure Mitotia is happy to see her again."

"She is."

Mazatzin came down from the camp, holding Quetzalcoatl's high priest robe over his arm. He bowed when he reached us then he helped Quetzalcoatl shrug himself into his robe. "Will you be doing a service tonight, My Lord? It's been several weeks since the last one, and the people are anxious to hear you speak again."

"I will." Quetzalcoatl tied his robe shut. "Let us discuss it over lunch."

Swallowing my anxiety, I said, "Can we talk for a moment, My Lord? In private?"

Quetzalcoatl cast me a questioning glance but nodded. To Mazatzin, he said, "We'll discuss it when I get back. My Lady and I are going to walk down the beach a ways, so can you see to it that we're not disturbed?"

"I'll make sure everyone knows to give you privacy, My Lord." Mazatzin gave me a smile and a bow before turning to Ehecacone. "Perhaps you could help me catch some butterflies for this afternoon's prayers?"

"You bet!" Ehecacone gave me an encouraging smile then he hurried up the embankment, back into camp. Mazatzin followed.

Quetzalcoatl and I headed south along the sand, keeping an arm's length between us as we walked. I didn't want to barge into the topic right away, so I started off with something else. "Are we staying here through the winter?"

He nodded. "It will be warm here, and there's plenty to eat, though I'm sure by spring we'll all be tired of fish." He chuckled.

"Sometimes I miss eating. I have such good memories of food and meals with friends and family."

"You're welcome to eat at the meals with everyone at any time."

"I know, but I would be wasting the food. We don't have an unlimited supply anymore."

"True, but you're still welcome to sit with us."

"I think I will start doing that. Thank you."

With the sounds of the camp now distant, we fell into awkward silence. Eventually though, Quetzalcoatl said, "Ehecacone is progressing very nicely with his magic. You've been a most excellent teacher."

"Thank you."

"I'm sorry that I haven't been much help with any of it—"

"You've been teaching him a great deal," I countered

"It's just...he's very interested in the physical aspects of being a god, and that's not something I can help him with."

"The novelty of physical magic will wear off, but he'll always need to know more about what it means to be a god, and you're very good at teaching him that. You're still teaching me a great deal."

He smiled. "Yes, I can help him with that." He sighed then added, "I must admit, I never thought something as simple as being a parent could be so overwhelming. I don't know how humans have more than one child at a time!"

I folded my hands behind my back. "Speaking of children, I wanted to ask you something, about our other child."

He furrowed his brow. "Our other child?"

"Well, children, to be more precise. I'm talking about Xochiquetzal and Xochipilli."

Quetzalcoatl stopped, a look of utter puzzlement on his face. "I don't understand."

"When I met Xochiquetzal, she said you were her father—that you made her from a flower on the plant that grew from my bones."

"I made her?"

My cheeks flushed as I said, "She claimed you...released your essence on one of my flowers and she grew from that."

At first his face was unchanged, but then a slow creep of realization changed it. "Oh my. Well, I suppose it's possible...."

I raised an eyebrow.

Lowering his voice, he said, "After you...died...I thought your essence might still be inside the plant, so I...bonded with it, hoping to find you inside. Instead, I found only disappointment."

Chuckling, I said, "I'd say you found more than that."

His face darkened with embarrassment.

"You should know that Xochiquetzal thinks that you abandoned her."

"I didn't even know about her." Quetzalcoatl went to the water's edge and stared out onto the horizon. "You said children?"

"Well, there's also Xochipilli, but he and Xochiquetzal aren't exactly separate beings. Like Ehecatl's darkness and light, they are separate aspects of a single god, but those aspects manifest as different gods depending upon which one is in control."

"Smoking Mirror and I used to do that, when we were still Ehecatl." He sighed, looking run-down. "Are you disgusted with me?"

"Of course not. Though if we're to have any more children, I do ask that you don't spring them on me as a surprise."

I meant it as a quip, hoping to lighten the mood, but it had the opposite effect. He covered his face with both hands and groaned. "I owe you an apology, Mayahuel. I should have been more careful, and I should have foreseen what would happen when I possessed your human body in Culhuacan."

"I don't need any apologies. I was surprised to find out about Xochiquetzal and Xochipilli, and Xochiquetzal doesn't like me any more than she likes you, but as for Ehecacone...I have no regrets, only gratefulness. Thank you for our son."

Tears shone in his eyes. "I'm grateful for him too." He looked back up towards camp, as if expecting to see Ehecacone running down the beach to us. When he turned back to me, he said, "About Malinalli...I'm sorry if I sounded like I was questioning your decision. I do understand your reasons; I think if I had the chance...I would bring Citlallotoc back too. If only because there's so much I wish I could tell him now...so much I would not only thank him for, but also apologize for."

"I too wish I would have gotten the chance to say goodbye to him," I admitted.

"How did he die, exactly?"

"Mextli poisoned him."

He clenched his fist. "Then he's down in Mictlan with the rest of Mextli's sacrifices, giving that feathered menace more power."

"Actually...I sent both Mextli's and Smoking Mirror's sacrifices to their eternal rest when I confronted Lord Death for Ehecacone."

Quetzalcoatl stared at me with a mixture of fear and awe. "Well, that's one way to make sure Smoking Mirror doesn't come back looking for revenge right away."

I hadn't even thought of that possibility. Now I was more grateful than ever that I'd wiped out their sacrifices.

"What about Anacoana? How did she die?"

"Yaretzi slit her throat when she tried to murder you."

He blinked. "Anacoana tried to murder me?"

"She was under the influence of a heavy love potion, courtesy of our daughter, so she certainly wasn't in her sanest mind. But ironically, if she'd finished you, you wouldn't be trapped now as you are." I frowned; Itzpapalotl's suspicious rescue made frustrating sense now. I shook my head.

"I'm sorry I left you to deal with such a mess on your own," he said, guilt and sadness invading his voice. "I didn't think I would linger in the inbetween as long as I did."

"I'm pretty sure that Smoking Mirror was plying you with medicines to keep your mortal body hanging on long enough to bring his plans to fruition."

We stood in long silence again, but I knew if I waited much longer, I might let the fear win and I'd just stay exactly where I was, never moving forward. Whatever his answer, I had to know the truth. "The reason I wanted to talk to you...."

"Yes?"

"It's about our future."

"What about it troubles you?"

"I'm not necessarily troubled, but...." I stepped closer to him, and with a deep breath, I said, "I know it might be too much to hope for, given what I did, but...is it at all possible that our relationship can be what it once was?"

A glimmer of hope came to his eyes. "Do you mean like when we were married?"

"I nodded. "Or maybe even more than just husband and wife...for political purposes?"

"You mean lovers?"

"Yes?" I said, daring to let the hope grow.

In answer, he bridged the gap between us and kissed me. My teotl felt as if it would burst out everywhere, but once we separated again, I could barely stand. "I'd hoped you would ask me that," he whispered, leaning his head against mine. "And I must admit that I started worrying that you hadn't yet."

"I'm sorry, Little Reed, for everything—"

"It's the past, and let's not speak of it again." His next kiss brought the desire dancing joyously in my belly. When we separated again, he whispered, "I so missed you calling me Little Reed, Papalotl."

"And I will always be your precious Butterfly," I promised then kissed him again.

He pulled his robe off and took my hand. "Over here," and we retreated to the shade beside an outcrop of red lava rocks, where we were unlikely to be seen from a distance. He laid the robe on the sand for us, and I stretched out on it, leaving space for him to join me.

But when he made to untie his loincloth, I grabbed his hand. "That's my job," the desire purred. I pulled the knot loose slowly, watching the joy and anticipation play across his face. I marveled at how clear and open his gaze was; none of the usual drunken haze, but also none of the indifference I'd seen in Mextli's eyes. I saw only love and devotion of the kind I'd craved my entire life; the kind that mirrored my own feelings for him.

Little Reed couldn't undress me, but I played to the illusion by making my dress melt away under his hands, much like he'd done that first time we were intimate in the Divine Dream, when he'd promised that someday we would be together in the real world. It had taken far longer than either of us had thought, but that day was finally here. "Now?" I whispered, digging my fingernails into his nape with desperation.

He smiled. "Now."

Unlike our desperate coupling in our meditation room back in Tollan, he eased himself into me with infinite patience. There was no reason to hurry and we both took our time, testing our bodies against each other, figuring out what worked and what didn't. Unlike with human men, I couldn't automatically read Little Reed's desires and preferences, but I preferred it this way. It had never lasted so long in the real world, so I'd never known the joys of the slow, steady build outside the Divine Dream. Until now. And I never again wanted it to be any other way.

But that was all just foreplay; the real pleasure came after the climax, when the world melted away into blinding white light, and our tendrils of magic coiled around each other, his white feathered serpents swimming in a joyous, intimate dance with my vibrant orange rabbits. As the flow between us began, his consciousness mingled with mine and we held no more secrets.

I saw his meeting in Mictlan with Lord Death and the sure odds that one of us would end up back there—never to return—but the chance at redemption, for us to fall in love all over again and find the future together that Smoking Mirror had ended for us so many years ago, it was all worth the risk.

But because I had to be reborn as a human being, he made the decision to bear himself into the human world as well, so we could be equals and bring changes to humanity together. It meant sacrificing his ability to use his own magic until his trapped divine essence finally devoured its fleshy prison, but it was the only way to bring about the reforms the world needed.

Without his magic to defend himself against Smoking Mirror, everything would fail before it could even start, but it was Xolotl who pointed out the workaround. *Entrust Mayahuel with the ability to release your divinity for brief moments, in exchange for a sacrifice. Your mortal body will be at its most vulnerable during those moments, for your consciousness cannot be in two places at once, but if love is as strong as you claim, then it will keep you safe and ensure your plan's success.*

And in those early years, love indeed protected him, whether it was me shielding him with my own body against an assassin's knife, or Mazatzin standing in defense of his unconscious body while Chichimecs ambushed our camp in Teotihuacan, or Citlallotoc carrying him nearly dead from the limestone quarry after Red Flint's men had slit his throat.

But it was also love that prompted him to sacrifice everything he'd worked for in order to bring me back from the brink of death. From that day forward, he was destined to fail in his reforms, and I felt all of his pain and guilt in knowing there was nothing he could do to stop it.

But he never turned from the path; we built Tollan and made our reforms, and we tried to show everyone that love was more powerful than fear. Yes, we'd failed in Tollan, but our journey was far from over. We'd shown humanity that things didn't have to be as they always had been; we'd given them hope, and that was something as precious as love itself.

As in Tamoachan so long ago, awash in each other's memories and thoughts and emotions, we became one again: one consciousness, one body, one destiny. I wanted it to last forever.

Eventually though, reality brought us back to ourselves. The magic I'd used to bind him to flesh exerted itself and I felt him slipping away from me again. I tried to counter it, hoping since it was my own magic, I could control it or even take it back and free him, but no matter what I did, it continued pulling him away from me.

Our bodies re-solidified and the dull ache of guilt and loss filled the new emptiness left by his departure.

When I opened my eyes, I found him crying as I held him. The sight crushed me. "Little Reed...."

"Thank you," he whispered.

I blinked through my own tears, confused. "For what?"

"For helping me feel like a god again."

◻

That evening, Little Reed, Ehecacone, and I gathered around the massive central bonfire set up on the beach. Someone had made a set of crude reed thrones for me and Little Reed to sit upon, and Mitotia had even found wild bone flowers to decorate mine with. The familiar sweet scent mixed with the briny smell of the ocean was oddly comforting.

There were too many people to fit everyone around the fire at once, so the meal went in shifts, giving every person the chance to sit and eat with us. It reminded me of the communal meals in the priesthood in Xochicalco, before my taking the mantle of queen had kept me from participating anymore.

Once the final meal shift completed, the night had fallen into the late hours, but everyone remained on the beach, waiting to hear Little Reed speak. Once he rose to his feet, everyone piled in closer to the fire, standing to make sure everyone had a spot within the firelight.

"I know I usually do the services, but tonight, Lady Mayahuel will share wisdom with us." Little Reed gestured to me to stand.

The crowd turned their attention upon me as I stepped up to the fire. "I'm sure everyone is tired after a long, hard day, and the many that came before as we left Tollan, so I will make this speech short. Lord Topiltzin-Quetzalcoatl and I thank each and every one of you for your contribution and hard work, and for your continued faith in our leadership. Many of you no doubt still feel the keen pain of having to leave Tollan, but know this: Tollan has not left you! Tollan is not buildings or gardens or even laws: it is the notion that everyone gets back what they give, and that goes most especially for the gods. So long as we all continue living by this principle, Tollan will continue to flourish, in the hearts and minds of each and every one of you, and there will come a day when it is the philosophy of self-sacrifice rather than fear that will rule the hearts of mankind, and Tollan will return to the people once again. As will her king, and her queen!"

A cheer rose over the beach, and many prayers were said and dances performed. In the celebrating crowd, I spotted Malinalli and Mitotia dancing together with eyes only for each other, and Ehecacone bounded about as a large rabbit, beating his paws on a drum slung over his neck with a jaguar hide strap and regaling everyone with all the songs I'd taught him as a boy.

The festivities finally wrapped up near the midnight hour, but as the crowd dispersed back to their tents, Little Reed and I went out onto the empty beach with Mazatzin, and like before, he bound us together in marriage. We didn't bother with the usual religious rituals; I doubted many of the gods would bless our marriage, nor did we need their approval. It was enough that we had each other. I retired to Little Reed's tent with him, to celebrate our renewed partnership, then I lay at his side while he slept, thinking of the future ahead, surrounded by my husband, my son, and all of those friends dearest to me.

For the first time in countless bundles of years, my heart was finally content.

◻

In the morning, as we sat around the fire eating breakfast, a group of men and women came up the beach from the south of camp carrying baskets of food—maize, beans, and dried deer meat. They bowed as they approached and Little Reed rose to greet them.

"Our king sent us to welcome you," the big warrior leading the group told us. Red designs decorated his body, and his head was shaved and his earlobes hung low with heavy wooden spools. "Our shaman had a vision that you were coming, and that you'd lead us out of the misery that has claimed our village." As the others with him set the baskets down in the sand before us, he went on, "We bring you gifts and ask that you come back to our village and listen to our king and consider his plea."

Little Reed smiled. "We'd be honored to do what we can to help your people." He then held out his hand to help me up. "Won't we, my love?"

"Absolutely," I agreed, and squeezed his hand in mine.

◻   ◻   ◻

LIST OF CHARACTERS

Ahexotl - (deceased) former high priest of Quetzalcoatl in Xochicalco

Amoxtli - son of Ihuitimal, brother to Black Otter, cousin to Quetzalpetlatl and Topiltzin

Anacoana - daughter of King Flame Tongue of Xico, former concubine of Black Otter, Topiltzin's legitimate wife

Black Otter - son of Ihuitimal, former husband of Quetzalpetlatl, high priest of Smoking Mirror, father of Cuicatl and Night Wind

Blood Wolf - Justice of the Peace under Quetzalpetlatl

Chimalma - (deceased) wife of Mixcoatl, mother of Quetzalpetlatl and Topiltzin

Cihuacoatl (Snake Woman) – very old creator goddess

Citlallotoc - Topiltzin's best friend, former Justice of the Peace, contender for Tollan's throne

Coatlicue (Snake Skirt) - mother of Mextli, former human turned immortal

Coyolxauhqui - (deceased) sorceress sister of Mextli

Cuicatl - daughter of Black Otter and Jade Flower

Ehecacone (Yamehecatl) - son of Quetzalcoatl and Mayahuel

Flame Tongue - King of Xico, father of Anacoana

Huemac - younger brother to Citlallotoc, King of Acolman

Ihuitimal - (deceased) brother of Mixcoatl, King of Culhuacan, father of Black Otter and Amoxtli

Itzpapalotl (the Obsidian Butterfly) - minor goddess, ally of Smoking Mirror

Jade Flower - (deceased) Quetzalpetlatl's half-sister, wife of Black Otter, mother of Cuicatl and Night Wind

Jade Skirt (Chalchiuhtlicue) - Goddess of Rivers, Streams, and the Seas.

Lord Death (Mictlantecuhtli) – God of Death, Lord of Mictlan

Malinalli - high priestess of Quetzalcoatl, Mayahuel/Quetzalpetlatl's best friend

Mayahuel/Quetzalpetlatl (Papalotl) - Goddess of the Maguey, mother of Ehecacone, Xochiquetzal, and Xochipilli, and former high priestess of Quetzalcoatl, Empress of the Tolteca and wife to Topiltzin

Matlacxochitl - governor of Chimalhuacan, younger brother of Blood Wolf, contender for Tollan's throne

Mazatzin - high priest of Quetzalcoatl, brother of Red Flint

Mextli (Huitzilopochtli) - god of war, leader of the Mexica, brother to Smoking Mirror

Mitotia - fire priestess of Quetzalcoatl

Mixcoatl - (Deceased) former king of Culhuacan, father of Quetzalpetlatl

Mixcoatl (the Cloud Serpent) - god of the hunt, husband of Coatlicue

Mozauhqui - son of the king of Tepanec

Night Wind - son of Black Otter and Jade Flower, possessed by the Smoking Mirror

Nimilitzli - (deceased) foster mother to Quetzalpetlatl and Topiltzin, former high priestess of Quetzalcoatl in Xochicalco

Nanahuatzin (Tonatiuh) - the leper god, the sun god

Nochuatl - (deceased) brother of Ihuitimal and Mixcoatl

Ozomatli - (deceased) high priest of the Smoking Mirror

Patli - guard in Tollan

Quetzalcoatl (the Feathered Serpent) - god of civilization, father of mankind. Also known as Ehecatl, god of the wind.

Red Hawk - son of the chief of the Mexica

Red Flint - (deceased) King of Xochicalco

Tezcatlipoca (the Smoking Mirror) - Chichimec god of war and sorcerers, god of the night

Timaltzin - Justice of the Peace under Matlacxochitl

Tlaloc - god of rain

Topiltzin (Little Reed) - son of Quetzalcoatl, Emperor of the Tolteca

Tzitzimime (Monsters Descending from Above) - celestial monsters

Tzitzimitl (the Earth Monster) - grandmother to Mayahuel

Xihuitl - high priest of Mayahuel

Xipe Totec (The Flayed Lord) - god of the harvest

Xochipilli (Flower Prince) - god of music and dance, brother of

Xochiquetzal, son of Quetzalcoatl and Mayahuel

Xochiquetzal (Precious Flower) - love goddess, sister of Xochipilli, daughter of Quetzalcoatl and Mayahuel

Xochitl - high priestess of Mayahuel

Xolotl (the Black Dog) - servant god to Mictlantecuhtli and the guide of the dead

Yaretzi - high priestess of the Smoking Mirror

Acknowledgments

My many thanks go out to the members of my writer's group, Written in Blood: Keyan Bowes, Genevieve Williams, Douglas Cohen, Christopher M. Cevasco, and Aliette de Bodard. They keep me honest not only on good story, but on the tough issues as well.

A big thank you goes to my tireless editor Dario Ciriello, who stuck with me through this whole trilogy, from the very start way back at the first terrible draft nine years ago, all the way to this book you just read.

As always, I couldn't have done any of this without the love and support of my husband Jeff, and the encouragement and understanding of my kids Dana and Gaaron.

And lastly, a huge thank you to my fans, whose enthusiasm for this story and its characters kept me going when things got tough and I wondered if I would ever finish.

FURTHER READING

Richard Blanton, Stephen A. Kowalewski, Gary Feinman, and Jill Appel, *Ancient Mesoamerica: A Comparison of Change in Three Regions*, Cambridge University Press, 1981.

Burr Cartwright Brundage, *The Phoenix of the Western World: Quetzalcoatl and the Sky Religion*, University of Oklahoma Press, 1981.

David Carrasco, *Quetzalcoatl and the Irony of Empire: Myths and Prophecies in the Aztec Tradition*, University Press of Colorado, 2001.

Sophie Coe, *America's First Cuisines*, University of Texas Press, 1994.

Nigel Davies, *The Toltecs Until the Fall of Tula*, University of Oklahoma Press, 1977.

Richard A. Diehl, *Tula: The Toltec Capital of Ancient Mexico*, Thames and Hudson, 1983.

William Gates, *An Aztec Herbal: The Classic Codex of 1552*, Dover Publications, Inc, 2000.

Rich Holmer, *The Aztec Book of Destiny*, BookSurge, LLC, 2005.

Miguel León-Portilla, *Aztec Thought and Culture*, University of Oklahoma Press, 1963.

Roberta H. Markman and Peter T Markman, *The Flayed God: The Mythology of Mesoamerica*, Harper San Francisco, 1992.

Mary Miller and Karl Taube, *An Illustrated Dictionary of the Gods and Symbols of Ancient Mexico and the Maya*, Thames and Hudson, 1993.

H. B. Nicholson, *Topiltzin Quetzalcoatl: The Once and Future Lord of the Toltecs*, University Press of Colorado, 2001.

Guilhem Olivier, *Mockeries and Metamorphoses of an Aztec God: Tezcatlipoca, "Lord of the Smoking Mirror"*, University Press of Colorado, 2003.

John M. D. Pohl, *Aztec, Mixtec and Zapotec Armies*, Osprey Publishing,

1991.

John Pohl, PhD and Adam Hook, *Aztec Warrior, A.D. 1325-1521*, Osprey Military, 2001.

Fray Bernardino de Sahagún, *The Florentine Codex: The General History of the Things of New Spain*, translated by Arthur J. O. Anderson and Charles E. Dibble, The School of American Research and The University of Utah, 1975.

Jacques Soustelle, *Daily Life of the Aztecs*, Dover Publications, Inc., 2002.

ABOUT THE AUTHOR

T. L. Morganfield lives in Colorado with her husband and children. She's an alumna of the Clarion West Workshop and she graduated from Metropolitan State University with dual degrees in English and History. She reads and writes way too much about Aztec history and mythology, but it keeps her muse happy, which makes for a happy writer, so she has no plans of changing her ways.

You can join her mailing list at www.tlmorganfield.com to receive updates on her latest work.

www.ingramcontent.com/pod-product-compliance
Lightning Source LLC
Chambersburg PA
CBHW070910260626
47162CB00007B/2622